David Clement-Davies is a writer and travel journalist who has journeyed to many strange and wonderful places. His adventures in the great deserts have provided inspiration for *The Alchemists of Barbal*. David is fascinated by history, and the myths and stories surrounding ancient sites. But, like the alchemists of the past – and present – he has a passion for science too, and the perspective it brings to the world.

David lives in London and is the author of the acclaimed *Fire Bringer* and *The Sight*.

THE ALCHEMISTS OF

BARBAL

DAVID CLEMENT-DAVIES

MACMILLAN CHILDREN'S BOOKS

First published 2005 by Macmillan Children's Books

This edition published 2006 by Macmillan Children's Books
a division of Macmillan Publishers Limited
20 New Wharf Road, London N1 9RR
Basingstoke and Oxford
www.panmacmillan.com

Associated companies throughout the world

ISBN-13: 978-0330-41008-3
ISBN-10: 0-330-41008-3

A CIP catalogue record for this book is available from
the British Library.

Typeset by Intype Libra Ltd
Printed and bound in Great Britain by Mackays of Chatham plc, Kent

For Francesca

Contents

Stardust	1
The Temple	16
Silas Root	28
The Last Wordmaster	47
Banishment	72
Yaharlars	94
Soothsaying	110
A Strange History	134
The Elusive Camel	158
Demigods	172
A Makina of Time	189
The Tears of Zorastar	211
Beneath the Temple	228
Nimrod	245
Mardak the Dark	265
The Ticking of the Sun	288
Seven Gods	305
Epilogue	334
A Guide to Naming	339

STARDUST

'Look, boy, a storm comes,' whispered the Dunetrader guide gravely, peering into the burning desert sands.

The figure was leaning on a wooden staff as he pointed into the sunlight and lifted the edge of his turban to protect his mouth and nose. The two thin columns of dirt and dust that had risen like flames on the edge of the horizon were still far off, but the air was already filled with tiny coloured specks that sparkled and glittered brilliantly.

'It looks like gold, Ashtar,' said the wondering boy next to him. His name was Kerbogah.

'Then perhaps the Lord Alchemist has succeeded at last, Kerbogah,' said the Dunetrader cheerfully, 'in making all things gold.'

Ashtar rolled the word 'Alchemist' about his tongue like an almost sacred thing. The Alchemists were mysterious figures to the Mahara Dunetraders, especially to wide-eyed children like Kerbogah. They were the ones who sat above the secrets, communing secretly with the Gods and ruling in the sacred city of Barbal and the Seven Lands beyond it, where the Mahara Dunetraders lived and traded. Many believed that without the Alchemists' holy work the Sun God Zorastar would not rise or the rivers keep flowing, the winds blow or the Moon Goddess wash the skies with her heavenly light.

The Alchemists' oath was not only to rule wisely, but to bring new inventions to the people, and to change the nature of things, for like the wind that taught the shifting sands the law every single day, the Alchemists believed that change is the very law of magic and of life.

This truth was upheld in the Alcemoth, the sacred oath of Alchemy. It said that since the great God Lol, who dwelt in his tent at the centre of the universe, had thought of the world and, in his eternal mind, brought order out of the sea of chaos to make all things, the truest law of existence has been change.

Each one of the Alchemists in the Seven Lands lived in a tower, along with their priest apprentices, and each had their own title too. In Barbal City they were called the Lord Alchemists, and had spent centuries studying the heavens from their open-ceilinged Observing Room. Here they combined Alchemy with predicting the future by astrologizing from the stars, for Barbal was also known as the City of Soothsaying.

'We must keep our mouths properly covered, Kerbogah,' grunted Ashtar, in the desert. 'When the storm passes we'll all have to be in good voice too. If our songs are to move the sands again.'

'But how long till it hits us, Ashtar?' asked Kerbogah nervously.

'Nightfall, Kerbogah,' answered Ashtar. 'It'll be a bad one this time too, by the looks of it.'

Kerbogah gulped.

 2

'We'll need all the aloe soup we can cook up, that's for sure, Kerbogah. The whole caravan must shelter in the great tent tonight and perhaps for suns to come too.'

'Keep still now, Relak,' said Kerbogah suddenly. 'This is serious.'

Kerbogah was talking to the little brown desert mouse that had just pushed his snout from the folds of his robes. It was Kerbogah's pet, for the boy loved animals dearly.

He and Ashtar turned together to survey their encampment in the coming storm. Among the sparse palm trees surrounding the scrubby little oasis, other frightened boys were already starting to bind the camels' legs with slender leather cords. Everywhere stooping figures were busily at work securing the flimsy tents too. Ashtar was reassured by the activity and he suddenly noticed his own camel standing beneath a palm tree, its great leathery lips sucking mournfully at a little hole in the ground to get to the precious water beneath.

'Aspis,' he muttered darkly. 'The Destroyer. Lord of the Underworld. Aspis himself rides his camel through the shifting deserts, and in his wake come chaos and destruction.'

Ashtar looked strangely pleased at the Destroyer's approach.

Beyond the stone kitchens and makeshift latrines stood a huge white tent, much bigger then the ones around it. Men were pulling the guy tethers taut, and forcing pegs deeper into the sand to secure it.

'Are you frightened, Kerbogah?' asked Ashtar suddenly. 'Sandspirits are said to come during such storms. Old women believe some-thing of their Chi lives on in the winds.'

The Mahara Dunetraders called the lifeforce 'Chi' and believed it lived in everything. In the rocks and in the flowers, in the air and the very sunlight. It was the force that Lol had first bestowed on everything at the dawn of time and creation.

3

Kerbogah shivered, for his mother Selera had often told him horrible stories of Sandspirits, phantoms almost as terrifying to children as Aspis, the Uncrowned King of Night. But Kerbogah shook his head.

'Good lad,' cried Ashtar, slapping him warmly on the back. 'For as the Dunetraders believe, the only true sin is cowardice.'

In fact, Kerbogah was frightened, but he was also too proud to admit it, and at least he felt safer standing next to Ashtar, a renowned Dunetrader guide.

'But go now, Kerbogah,' said Ashtar. 'Tell the other children to make sure our water bellies are filled to the brim before the wells choke with sand. Take them inside with Relak and your friend Farjay and we'll use them as pillows too. At least we'll all sleep a deal better.'

Kerbogah nodded and Ashtar knelt down beside his staff to pick up a coil of rope that was lying in the sand.

'Take this, too, Kerbogah. Rope's a God-gift in a sand-storm.'

Kerbogah slung it over his shoulder, but before he could go, Ashtar reached inside his robe too. The Dunetrader plucked something from his pocket and flicked it through the air with his thumb. It spun as it flew and the boy caught it in his fist. When he looked at it in his palm his face lit up.

'A Groot,' he cried delightedly, 'a solid golden Groot.'

'Don't get too attached to it,' said Ashtar. 'Though it's real gold, Kerbogah, you'll find that goes as quickly as it comes, and there are far more important things in life. But you can change it for something really nice in the Sacred City. A new dagger perhaps.'

Kerbogah turned in the direction he thought Barbal City lay, but pain and worry transfixed his bright young face.

'What's wrong, Kerbogah?' asked the guide kindly. 'It's your brother Kalman, isn't it?'

'Yes, Ashtar. How do you think we'll ever find him?'

Ashtar put his hand on Kerbogah's shoulder. He had only recently been hired to lead the caravan across the Mahara Desert – and as fast as he could, for Kerbogah's elder brother Kalman had gone missing in Barbal the last time these Dunetraders had gone trading there. Many children were disappearing, or so it was rumoured. Almost as soon as they had arrived, though, all Dunetraders had been ordered from the Sacred City again; they frequently were by the authorities, who needed their trade but feared them too. So they had been forced to abandon Barbal – and Kalman too, and now the ban had been lifted, they were returning to search for him again.

Kerbogah had not been with them at the time, for then he had been too young to travel so far across the deserts from their winter camp, but he never stopped asking about Kalman, whom he missed dearly.

'We'll find him, Kerbogah,' said Ashtar softly. 'Don't you worry.'

Kerbogah seemed a little reassured, but as he and Relak turned towards the oasis he caught sight of something in the corner of his eye that made him jump.

'Camel's blood!' he cried. 'Look, Ashtar.'

Among the seemingly endless dunes a group of camels had appeared in the distance. High on their strange humped backs were figures dressed much like Ashtar and the boy. They had been moving through the sands all morning, but now the turbaned train had stopped, for the dune they were approaching was high and difficult to pass.

'Another caravan,' said Ashtar.

'You think they come to fight us, Ashtar?' asked Kerbogah. 'Should I warn the camp?'

Ashtar had put his hand to a dagger at his belt, but as they stood there he relaxed his grip and shook his head.

'No. But they go to Barbal City, by the look of it. To trade.'

'Why are they travelling, though? They can't have seen the dust pillars yet. They can't know about the storm.'

It was true. Behind the dunes this caravan could not see the advancing sand pillars. But they suddenly yanked down the ends of their turbans and Ashtar and Kerbogah knew exactly what was about to happen.

The strange, haunting sound began with a low hum that silenced even their bellowing camels. At first their voices were pitched differently, but in no time at all those strong throats began to quiver together and out of their mouths came their Dunetrader chant. It was a song that both the onlookers knew as well as their prayers.

> *Born of desert, work of clay,*
> *Sing the songs that make our way.*
> *Camel riders, tribe of tunes,*
> *Chant the path and clear the dunes.*
> *Sacred City, leagues away,*
> *Draw us down the path you lay.*

As the Dunetrader voices broke across the sands the chant turned from a song back into a powerful, resonating hum that seemed to shake the ground and sky. At first nothing happened but suddenly the sand itself started to move. The Dunetraders' ancient song was moving the Mahara Desert, as it had done for centuries heaped on centuries, like the voice of some mighty prophet parting the waves.

'They're in good voice, aren't they?' cried Kerbogah admiringly. The boy loved to see the Dunetraders use the magic Sandsong. He ached to do it himself, but his voice had not yet broken, and only when that happened would the strange power of the Sandsong come.

 6

'But, Ashtar,' he added, 'shouldn't we try to warn them of the storm?'

The guide shook his head again.

'It's too dangerous with the wars, Kerbogah. They may be hostile indeed and try to steal the tribute we carry.'

Kerbogah's eyes flickered at the mention of the tribute.

'My friend Farjay says there is talk, Ashtar. That our Sandsong will fade because of the tribute we must pay to Mardak.'

There was a touch of fear in Kerbogah's voice as he spoke the infamous name of Mardak the Dark. Mardak was the High Priest of Barbal, who lived in one of the two wings of the city's great temple, her ancient Ziggurat. There Mardak was said to practise black arts and to pursue fearful rituals, to summon demons and to talk to the dead.

That very year though Mardak had sent out a decree that any Dunetrader wishing to barter in Barbal must pay him a tribute of a whole bushel of Stardust, one of the Dunetraders' most prized and magical possessions.

'Mardak has spies everywhere now,' said Kerbogah excitedly, 'or so Farjay says. They often try to infiltrate the caravans to make sure the Stardust tribute is being collected.'

For a moment Ashtar seemed almost reluctant to speak.

'And what else does Farjay say?'

'He says Mardak even spies on Ogog, the Lord Alchemist,' answered Kerbogah, 'that he hates Ogog with all his heart and wants to overthrow him.'

Suddenly there was something veiled in Ashtar's eyes.

'Hate is a strong word, Kerbogah,' he said quietly. 'But such rivalry has existed for an age between the Alchemists and their High Priests. Since the time of the Great Schism in fact, the time when there was an ancient rift in the two wings of the holy Ziggurat. Ogog is the Lord Alchemist now, who resides in the Halls of the Sinking Sun.'

7

'I know it. Trying to make gold with holy Alchemy,' said Kerbogah, nodding and rubbing his Groot fondly, 'and watching the skies from his Observing Room. While Mardak the Dark lives in the Halls of the Rising Sun, praying and prophesying from his Incanting Room. But the Lord Alchemist tried to remove Mardak and so he bears Ogog a grudge.'

'It's more than a grudge,' said the guide, smiling at the boy's simplicity. 'Although they try to rule the city side by side, there is great contention between them. Both have the right, by ancient custom, to enact laws. This tribute of Stardust is Mardak's latest law and Zolos, the Captain Lord of the Barbalissaries, enforces it for him. With an iron hand too.'

Kerbogah shivered. Barbalissaries were soldiers who maintained order in Barbal and guarded against unauthorized entry into the Ziggurat. Zolos was their leader and a cruel and merciless warrior. He was also known to hate the Dunetraders, for he had interests in the markets of Barbal, her great bazaars, and their trade competed with his own. But Captain Zolos had another reason for his emnity. He had once been a Dunetrader himself, until he had been expelled from his caravan in return for trying to sell Stardust for golden Groots.

'What does Mardak want all the Stardust for, though, Ashtar?' asked Kerbogah, scratching his head.

Ashtar's finger was stroking his dagger.

'They say Mardak is making something inside the holy temple and he needs Stardust to complete it.'

'You know, Ashtar,' whispered Kerbogah suddenly, 'I've never even seen it work. Stardust, I mean. Old Imlay says I'm still too young.'

Kerbogah was staring hopefully at Ashtar's belt, for there, next to the curved Dunetrader dagger, hung a little cloth bag, bound with string. The tribute.

 8

Ashtar looked back at Kerbogah and he flinched. The boy had always thought his eyes extraordinary, even a little frightening, for they were a strange blue-green, tinged with yellow. They had a way of staring straight into you and as Kerbogah gazed back now he thought the little twinkle of light in them looked like the moon. But Ashtar put his hand to the bag of Stardust.

'Would you like to, then?' he said.

'You don't mean it!' cried Kerbogah delightedly. 'Wait till I tell Farjay.'

'It can't hurt, Kerbogah,' said Ashtar, his eyes dancing mischievously. 'But we'd better look before the wind really gets up. Now, take off your turban and lay it flat on the ground.'

As Kerbogah did so, Ashtar began to unwind his own turban too, revealing a wild mop of sandy hair and a long, hooked nose. When he was finished there was so much cloth in his hand it looked like a small tent. Ashtar threw it over the staff he had been leaning on and, using Kerbogah's turban to make a kind of rough groundsheet, they both crouched down in the temporary darkness.

'Now then, Kerbogah,' said Ashtar, holding up the little bag, 'behold and be amazed.'

The guide cast the contents of the pouch onto Kerbogah's turban. It glittered like gold dust as it fell but, as it landed, the boy leant forward excitedly. Instead of the turban where the Stardust had just been sprinkled there suddenly seemed to be a sheen of blackness before them. They were now looking into a dark pool.

Among this blackness, though, specks of Stardust were actually glowing like tiny dots of twinkling light. As they grew stronger and stronger Kerbogah felt his head beginning to spin. It seemed that he was suddenly looking into a vast night sky. Here and there some of the specks of Stardust seemed actually to be moving, swirling like little whirlpools on the floor.

They looked like stars, for Stardust's nature was to reflect the heavens. It was why the Dunetraders so prized the stuff. The Dunetraders navigated by the stars but used Stardust to cross the desert when clouds covered the skies. With the stars and the art of calculation and sacred geometry, Dunetraders could always tell where they were, and where they were going too.

'Can you tell me some of the stars' names, then, Kerbogah?' asked Ashtar as they crouched there, looking at the tribute. 'For naming is the first magic.'

Kerbogah shook his head. He was rather bad at lessons and learning his star maps.

'Look at the shape of that group,' said Ashtar suddenly. 'That's called the Hippopotamus, a mighty creature with enormous teeth, that lives along the banks of the sacred river in the distant land of Khem. My friend Ramset calls them the Indestructible Ones. Many Gods come in the shape of animals, and so the Alchemists in the Seven Lands all have pets.'

'Hear that, Relak?' said Kerbogah, addressing his little mouse. 'Just like you, Relak. In Barbal the Lord Alchemists keep chameleons. Now keep still.'

'Chameleons, and peacocks too,' said Ashtar. 'But as for the stars, although they may look like the shape of animals, it's their appearance and disappearance in the skies that really matters for navigating, with the help of some careful Dunetrader calculations of course.'

Kerbogah nodded uncertainly.

'There,' said Ashtar, pointing again. 'One of the Seven Wandering Stars, which never stay still in the heavens and which the Alchemists predicted even before they pinpointed them in the dark desert night.'

Kerbogah's head was beginning to spin.

'The stars tease a Dunetrader out of thought, Kerbogah,' sighed Ashtar dreamily, 'for they are at the heart of the art of astrologizing.'

'Perhaps Mardak is using Stardust to watch the heavens, then,' whispered Kerbogah, 'in the darkness of the Ziggurat. They say he loves dreams and prophecies and astrologizing.'

'Perhaps he is,' said Ashtar quietly, although he seemed suddenly distracted. 'For they say too he is waiting for some great happening.'

Kerbogah was mesmerized by the glittering brilliance before him but quite suddenly the lights vanished and the pool of blackness disappeared. Kerbogah blinked as he realized that Ashtar had already started to scoop the Stardust back into its pouch. The guide stood up again and, throwing his turban aside, bathing them in bright, windy sunlight once more, bounced the bag a couple of times on his fist.

'Not at all bad,' he said. 'But that's always the trouble with Stardust. When you use it in the air, you lose a little more each time.'

'What is Stardust made of, Ashtar?' asked Kerbogah.

Before the guide could answer him though they heard another voice behind them.

'Don't lose it before we reach Barbal, will you, Ashtar, my friend? Or I'll have to pay out another mountain in Groots to get into the city.'

The Dunetrader who had stepped up beside them had a strong and handsome face, grey-black hair and a dagger at his belt too. It was Kerbogah's father, Karleg, and he led the caravan.

'Though I'd pay anything to get my son back,' added Karleg warmly.

'Of course, Karleg,' said Ashtar.

'The tents are being secured,' Karleg went on. 'When do you think the storm hits?'

'Nightfall, Father,' said Kerbogah immediately.

'All this damned sand,' grunted Karleg. 'I'm already so sick of it. It'll be grit in the aloe soup, and cracked lips for our breakfasts. The food will taste of sand for suns and suns too, once the sandstorm passes.'

'When we reach Barbal again the caravan will feast to their hearts' content, Karleg,' said Ashtar, 'Remember that little tavern on the edge of the city's Great Square – Bolor's place?'

'How could I forget it? The finest roasted meats I've ever tasted. Not to mention Bolor's famous pomegranate pies. Even the Wordmasters visit Bolor's.'

The mention of Wordmasters was as thrilling to Kerbogah as any food, or even the magical Stardust. They were Warrior Priests who served the Lord Alchemist Ogog directly, guarding his secrets and his person, and fighting with their voices and their hands alone.

In Barbal the fifty-strong bodyguard lived below the Ziggurat in a huge chamber called the Room of Changes, where they guarded the most secret of all the Alchemists' holy possessions. Here was an ancient clay tablet bearing the Seven Commandments themselves, the oldest laws of Barbal, believed to have been sent down from the Gods and burnt there by a firebolt from heaven. With that was Barbal's most sacred book, the Book of Destinies, inscribed not only with the earliest secrets of living Alchemy, but with many of the stories of the Gods and men.

Only the Lord Alchemist was allowed to enter the Room of Changes and open the Book of Destinies. Meanwhile, on joining the Order of the Wordmasters, each disciple swore to defend him and his secrets with his life. For this they practised something called the Chi Dance, a special kind of fighting, without weapons, and a form of prayer too.

The Wordmasters of Barbal also had mysterious powers and some said the gift of holy divination. Their deepest art though was to make new words of power which were summoned forth during a secret Word Rite, when they would ask the Gods to reveal the true names of things.

Wordmasters believed that only once you name a thing do you begin to have power over it, and so know its real nature. Because of this they had another sacred duty. They were sent forth by the Alchemists to distribute new words of power to the people, words that the Lord Alchemists considered would help the people to learn and grow. These were marked on clay tablets and copies were also kept in the Room of Changes. Icons, they were called.

Karleg's words now shook his son from his thoughts.

'I fear unhappier things than food await us in Barbal, Kerbogah,' he said, 'even if we do find your brother. And first we must navigate the desert and avoid the wars. There are raiding parties everywhere. We must hurry, now they let us into the city again. We should be watchful too when we get there. Captain Zolos hates the Dunetraders and there are darker and darker rumours about Mardak.'

'What rumours, Father?' asked Kerbogah, proud to be discussing such important matters with the men.

'This thing he designs in the temple, for a start, Kerbogah,' answered Karleg. 'Some say it's a terrible makina. A machine. A weapon that Mardak wants to use to become the Lord Alchemist himself. Others say that he even seeks Mazgol to aid his fight. One of the ancient Turnstones.'

'The Turnstones!' cried Kerbogah. 'Oh, tell me about the Turnstsones, Father.'

'Gol and Mazgol,' whispered Ashtar gravely, 'the Stones of Deep Power – the black and the white. Mazgol the Mighty, whose power is Night. Gol the Magnificent. The Lightbearer.'

'Fabled to have been given to the Alchemists by Lol and Enlis themselves,' said Karleg, ruffling his son's hair. 'Before they were lost long, long ago.'

'But I thought the Turnstones were just a story, Father,' said Kerbogah.

Ashtar suddenly looked sternly at the boy.

'They're no story, Kerbogah, and there's a prophecy about them. Inscribed in the Book of Destinies.'

'A prophecy?' said Kerbogah excitedly.

All the boys in the camp loved listening to stories of prophesying in Barbal.

'Ogog has long tried to suppress it, for he does not hold with dreams or prophecies any more. It was prophesied in the Book of Destinies that the Turnstones will return. Though none knows when.'

'Is that what Mardak is waiting for then?' asked Kerbogah.

'Perhaps,' answered Ashtar quietly. He paused and looked strangely at the boy. 'But others say Mardak seeks something far greater, even than the Turnstones. That they themselves would only be a tool in his lifelong search.'

'But it would be fearful indeed if the black Turnstone Mazgol fell into his hands,' said Karleg coldly.

'Why, Father?' asked Kerbogah, squeezing his desert mouse tighter to him and making him squeak.

Ashtar's piercing eyes ranged the desert but he had fallen silent and brooding.

'Because then it is said that evil shall cover the whole world,' said Karleg darkly. 'For Mazgol's coming could open the doorway to the Underworld itself and unleash the ancient demons again. Perhaps even Aspis the Destroyer himself.'

'Camel's blood!' Kerbogah exclaimed.

Still Ashtar was silent but Kerbogah was shaking and Relak felt it and started to squeak. In the distance the storm seemed to be getting worse.

 14

'Fear not, my boy,' said Karleg. 'The black Turnstone's whereabouts is safe. As is the white's. Their secret is hidden deep within the Book of Destinies and the Wordmasters guard that with their lives. Mazgol cannot come again.'

They were all silent but Kerbogah was looking hard into the swirling distance again, out towards the distant city of Barbal. The boy was wondering even more fearfully what had become of his brother Kalman.

THE TEMPLE

'**U**p, scum,' grunted a soldier in the darkness. 'I need three of you to go into the passages again.'

The soldier was dressed in a heavy leather breastplate and studded helmet. It was the uniform of the feared Barbalissaries and around him there was a painful groaning as several gaunt, weary figures raised themselves and struggled forward. About them came a clicking and the rattle of chains. Somewhere a door creaked and slammed.

'I can't go on,' said a frightened little voice. A child's voice.

'You must,' whispered another. 'Just keep marching, Rathanor. It's our only hope.'

'No, please. I must rest.'

The boy next to him took his arm and helped him forwards. Or rather helped him in his work, for although the children's bleeding feet were pressing against the wooden slats that moved below them, the children themselves stayed almost exactly where they were, walking on the spot.

'They'll change us over soon, Rathanor, don't give up heart.'

'I don't care. I want to die.'

'Don't ever say that, Rathanor. As the Dunetraders cross the desert we say that above all a man must never give up hope.'

'Dunetraders,' said Rathanor wonderingly. 'Are you really a Dunetrader, Kalman?'

Kalman smiled back weakly. He looked a bit like Kerbogah, only he had sandy hair and a little mole on his right cheek. At his throat was a necklace in the shape of a newborn camel, which Karleg had given him for his eleventh birthday.

'I'm a camp boy like my brother, Rathanor,' answered Kalman proudly, 'but when I mount my own steed I'll be a true Mahara Dunetrader. Then I'll travel the trade routes and see all the wonders of the wide world.'

Rathanor seemed to walk faster, suddenly heartened by this talk.

'The wide world,' he whispered longingly. 'Even Ederyl?'

Kalman looked a little doubtful at this. The hidden valleys of Ederyl were famous throughout the deserts around Barbal City. They were inhabited by the tribe of Childars and one of the most beautiful places on earth, it was said. Yet few had ever seen them, for only the Wordmasters, carrying their Wordboxes, were allowed to enter, and perhaps the occasional intrepid stranger. Equally, it was forbidden for any Childar to ever leave. It was one of the Childars' greatest sins.

'Perhaps not Ederyl,' muttered Kalman.

'Well, it doesn't matter,' said Rathanor cheerlessly. 'I'll never see anything now. All I'll see is the dark.'

'Hush,' said Kalman, 'we must think of a way to escape, or at least get a message to my father. Then we'll show you the true secrets of the desert.'

'No, Kalman,' said Rathanor sadly. 'It is not for me.

You've your parents to go home to and your brother. Well, I've nothing at all. My mother and father both died when I was born. Died of the sweating sickness.'

'Then you're an orphan?' said Kalman. 'Like Kerbogah's friend, Farjay.'

'So it's better I don't complain and learn to serve the Alchemists dutifully.' Rathanor nodded.

'The Alchemists!' snorted Kalman angrily, thinking of his parents and missing them and his brother with all his heart. 'Before I came to Barbal, all Kerbogah and I thought of was the Alchemists. But now I never want to hear of them again. I want the open sands and a full waterskin. The sun on my face and the clear, cloudless skies.'

'The sun,' said Rathanor mournfully in the dark. 'I wonder where the sun is now.'

Kalman didn't even hear Rathanor. The boy had just felt a heavy hand on his shoulder.

'Come,' grunted a voice. 'They need another child in the temple.'

As Kalman was dragged away, the sun did not shine, not even outside the ancient Ziggurat, for night had fallen and beyond the boys' labours a gigantic silver moon already hovered over the sacred square of Barbal City and the fires that flickered below the city's ancient mudbrick walls. They were called the Eternal Flames, for Barbalonians believed that the twenty-four fires burning in their golden bowls around the square were kept alight with the power of magic and holy prayer alone — just as the great wooden waterwheel that turned and creaked now, cranking up gigantic golden buckets that tipped into a stone watercourse sloping along the edge of the city wall, had always worked by the magic of the Lord Alchemists. The huge wheel was one of the Alchemists' greatest inventions, the first of the Seven Wonders of the World.

 18

In the centre of Barbal Square was a great, flat, golden plate, too, and from the middle of the disc, at an angle, rose a golden metal arm. Incised into Barbal's ancient sundial, in a perfect arc round the bottom half of the metal plate, were these twelve golden symbols:

♈ ♉ ♊ ♋ ♌ ♍

♎ ♏ ♐ ♑ ♒ ♓

Just along the edge of one of the city walls stood a mudbrick temple that climbed like a mountain, rising in three tiers, towards the mysterious heavens. It was the Ziggurat. On the far side, the Ziggurat was approached by three ramps, two rising on either side of the central stairway to an enormous wooden doorway, with a snake scored into its middle. It was an awe-inspiring sight, although it most instilled a sense of fear and oppression, like a shadow falling over the whole city.

The glittering stars shone down through one of the windows of the holy Ziggurat and down a passageway came two soldiers, dragging Kalman between them. They stopped for a moment as they reached a doorway to their right. Through the door they were assailed by a great blast of heat and flame.

The craftsmen inside were blowing glass.

On the Barbalissaries went, down the passage towards another chamber at its far end, from which came an eerie blue light. Inside, a row of men were seated on wooden benches in a wide room. On poles all around it were little glass globes, giving off the weird blue glow that suffused the whole place. Amazingly there was no flame to the lights, nor kindling either, yet they flickered away quite on their own, spreading their strange blueness everywhere. The chamber lay in the

Halls of the Rising Sun, the home of Mardak the Dark himself, for this was the Incanting Room.

The seated men were priest apprentices who were moving little rows of coloured wooden beads around on strings, as they listened to a man in flowing black robes who stood declaiming before them. He held a wooden staff in his hand with carved snakes weaving around it, which seemed for a moment to move in the strange light and wrap themselves around his fist.

Suddenly he strode up to a fire burning on a plinth before him and cast a powder into the flame, which blazed for an instant and died. As the light flared and faded, his skin was washed with rich shadows and his darting, watchful eyes and thick, sensual lips carried an especially menacing look.

'Now,' he cried, 'let the new apprentice step forward and proclaim the Alcemoth.'

A young man rose and advanced.

'Alumar. Today you enter the sacred Order. You have chosen to join the Halls of the Rising Sun, not the halls of that fool Ogog. To serve and learn from a true Alchemist, the High Priest, Mardak the Dark.'

Alumar nodded nervously, but an old man rose to his feet next to him.

'What is it, Hammurar?' asked the speaker irritably.

'Forgive me, Captain Zolos,' answered the priest apprentice, dipping his head slightly, 'but should it not be the High Priest himself who invests a new apprentice?'

Some of the other priest apprentices began to mutter in agreement.

'Indeed, Hammurar,' answered Zolos coldly. 'You know the laws of Barbal well. But Mardak the Dark is away from the city with graver work. Work that takes time and care, but work that shall change things forever, I assure you. He has left me in charge in his absence.'

'But why is it that a soldier holds the staff? The holy Caduceus,' said the old man disapprovingly. 'Even if he is a Captain Lord of the Barbalissaries.'

'Sit down, Hammurar,' snapped Zolos. 'I too have taken the oath now and Mardak has entrusted me with leading your prayers while he works in secret.'

Some of the apprentices around the room looked most disapproving, for a soldier in the Order of Alchemists was virtually unheard of, but Zolos ignored them.

'So then,' he cried, turning again to the young apprentice, 'all in the Ziggurat must swear the sacred oath. But as they do so they must be certain too. For it is death to break it, or to try to leave the Order, just as it is death for a mere commoner to enter the temple.'

The lad raised his head and nodded glumly. He clutched his worry beads tightly and started to recite the sacred Alcemoth.

'*I swear by the Gods to follow the truth,*' he said loudly, '*and to keep myself and my mind pure. To abstain from following any law but the law of change, which is the law of magic and of life. I shall turn my art to the transformation of all, to invention, to discovery and to revelation, and to unearthing the great secrets that are hidden in the stars and within the very mud and clay of the Seven Lands. As above, so below.*'

For a moment the apprentice seemed to falter, but then he remembered the oath.

'*Through magic, study and invention I shall pass these secrets on to the people, but only when they are ready for their coming. And I shall never knowingly do any wrong or harm. In the name of Lol and Enlis and the greatest law — change.*'

'Very good,' whispered Zolos, as Alumar finished the Alcemoth. 'Now let us return to our experiments. By the ancient staff, and all the secret forces that work in the wide world, may my words enlighten you. May Lol and Enlis hear my prayers.'

Zolos's arm was trembling, for he was not used to the rite and he was trying to impress the priest apprentices. The soldier stepped further forward and spoke even more loudly now, appealing to the listeners around him.

'For too long,' he cried, 'that fool Ogog has been obsessed by things of this world. For too long he has been interested in mere gold and has put reason and number magic at the heart of Alchemy. He ties to suppress astrologizing too and the sacred prophecies.'

The priest apprentices began to grumble angrily and Zolos smiled, for he could see he was winning them over.

'But as servants of the High Priest Mardak and as Alchemists of the immortal spirit, we serve the Gods truly and seek the real prize. The Turnstones and the secrets of the soul and of the holy Balm. So again we shall blend. You Hammurar, you may come forth.'

Hammurar rose again and hobbled over towards him nervously, while Zolos walked up to a table where there sat a little stone bowl, a pestle and a number of carefully measured mounds of powder. All the watchers were on the edges of their seats in the Incanting Room. Hammurar picked up some of the yellow powder and dropped it in the bowl, adding river water to it. He took a pinch of something that looked at first like sand but which glittered strangely as he popped it in the mix. Hammurar began a chant now. His voice was old and cracked but it grew stronger and stronger.

'By the eternal and immortal Gods,' the old man mumbled, 'hear our prayers and lead us to revelation.'

'Drink, Hammurar,' ordered Zolos. 'And show us the power of faith.'

Hammurar drank from the bowl. The light from the globes seemed to swell in the Incanting Room and

Hammurar's eyes grew fixed and glassy in the strange blue glow. Suddenly he threw back his head.

'Zorastar,' he cried ecstatically, raising his withered hands to the ceiling as if he would draw down the heavens themselves, 'YAW ROUY NO, ZORASTAR, RAF YREV YDAERLA ERA OUY, ZORASTAR, SIHT EES OUY FI.'

The watchers were transfixed as Hammurar invoked the name of Barbal's God of Sun and Fire, Zorastar. But, as for the rest of it, this was no language any of them had ever heard before, not even in Barbal.

'Hammurar is speaking in tongues,' cried Zolos delightedly, as he watched the ageing apprentice. 'The power is descending again from heaven like a firebolt and entering the mix. Bring me our supplicant. Quickly.'

At his command two soldiers emerged from an alcove, dragging Kalman between them. They thrust him roughly into the seat next to Zolos. Kerbogah's brother looked terrified and exhausted and his teeth were chattering violently. Zolos took the crucible from Hammurar, who himself was led away by the soldiers, for his eyes had grown misty and he no longer seemed to know where he was.

Zolos stepped up to Kerbogah's brother.

'Now, my young friend,' he hissed softly, smiling in a way that chilled the watchers to their bones. 'You are thirsty with your ceaseless labours, so drink and refresh yourself.'

The apprentices strained forward as Kalman took the bowl nervously and drank. The watchers waited, but seeming to take advantage of the distraction, Zolos walked over to a window of the Ziggurat and looked down on Barbal Square. He spied two figures hurrying across it but he had no thought for them, for Zolos was looking towards a soldier waiting on horseback in the shadows. He smiled to himself, for the plan was carefully laid. Zolos waved his hand, a secret signal long pre-arranged between them, and turned once more to the Incanting Room.

Kalman had just drained the cup and put it back down. Zolos smiled as he drew closer but suddenly he stopped.

'Now then,' he whispered, 'let us truly test the mix.'

From inside the folds of his robe the soldier pulled something out and Kalman gasped as he saw what it was – a huge, gold-handled knife.

Down in Barbal Square the two characters Zolos had seen from the Ziggurat crept passed the Sundial and those Symbols through the dark. They had no thought for what went on in the temple, they just wished that those fires on the pilasters did not throw so much light on their dangerous crime. One of the men, his back bent and rounded into a painful hump, carried a rough hemp sack over his shoulder and inside it something that was struggling frantically to get out. It was about the size of a small child.

'I wish this one would keep still,' he grunted.

'Keep your blasted voice down,' snapped the other angrily. 'If the Barbalissaries hear us and find out what we're about, they'll have our entrails on the end of their golden spears.'

Suddenly the two thieves heard the clatter of horses' hooves at the edge of the square behind them.

'Barbalissaries,' hissed the hunchback. 'Hide.'

Down they ducked and soon, all around the square, were soldiers on horseback, dressed in leather helmets and breastplates. As they galloped passed, they were led by the soldier who had taken Zolos's signal.

'Sergeant Akadeem,' whispered the hunchback, recognizing him immediately from their hiding place. 'They're making for the Ziggurat. Something's afoot.'

'Mardak's star is rising,' said the other grimly. 'He's hand

24

in glove with Zolos now. Ogog had better look to the Wordmasters this night.'

'The Wordmasters,' said the hunchback. 'They say they are all together again for a great feast in the Room of Changes. To celebrate the coming Solstice. But why does Mardak hate them and Ogog so?'

'The Great Schism comes to a head,' answered the other. 'The ancient battle between the Lord Alchemists and their High Priests. And Mardak thinks Ogog has finally gone mad.'

'Mad?' said the hunchback. 'Why mad?'

'Because not only does Ogog suppress prophecies and beliefs, and spend his days in calculations, but he wants to abolish magic from the Seven Lands completely.'

The hunchback's eyes opened wider. 'Abolish magic!'

'Lord Alchemist Ogog may be, but an Alchemist who has come to believe there is no real magic in the world. Some say he evens scorns prophecy and astrologizing. Ogog believes we must use reason to understand the real world.'

'Reason!' snorted the hunchback scornfully. 'How can reason reveal the true secrets of the heavens? The mind and messages of the Gods? It's sacrilege. At least Mardak has sworn never to let prayer and magic fade from the Seven Lands, so he will never let the Gods die.'

'Mardak may uphold magic,' said the other, 'but they say too that his heart is rotten. You know what they did to his bride. That's really why Mardak hates them all. If Mardak gets control he will return Barbal to the ancient ways of darkness and fear and human sacrifice. Not for a thousand suns has that been seen in Barbal City.'

His accomplice looked up fearfully at the Moon Goddess above them. His beard was knotted into ringlets, like a beaded curtain. The two villains crept on and found themselves now in the shadow of a plinth topped by a strange stone statue. The statue's features were obscured by the night but its sinister shadow fell on them in the moonlight, as tall as a man, with horrible clawed hands and wings folded on its great stone back. The hunchback shuddered as he looked up at it.

'I hate that thing,' he whispered. 'Let's get a move on. It's almost time to light our fires. Then we can work our own magic and make some Groots into the bargain, especially with all the visitors that will be in Barbal for the coming Solstice.'

Even as he said it, both men saw something suddenly above them, high in the twinkling night. It flashed like a shooting star over Barbal, out of the vastness of the heavens and plunged through the darkness in a trail of livid flame. It was coming straight towards them.

'Look out,' cried the first man, for the burning fireball was getting closer.

He hurled his accomplice to the ground, squashing the sack between them, which resulted in a terrible noise from within the mysterious bundle. He was just in time, for the shooting star hit the ground right at the base of the statue. There was a thunderous crash and a blaze of light, as earth and paving were hurled into the sky, showering the square and the cowering villains in rubble. Below the statue now was a great burning crater and at its charred bottom lay a stone. It was perfectly black, but shining strangely too.

'What is it?' whispered the hunchback, looking up fearfully.

His companion was silent, but only momentarily. He shuddered as he spoke, wiping dust and grit from his eyes.

'It can't be. I think . . . I think it's a Turnstone.'

'What?'

They were both looking intently at the ugly black rock, smoking in the crater, and they felt a strange tingling in their bodies.

'But it's impossible,' said the hunchback. 'The prophecy.'

'Look at the colour of it,' whispered the other. 'Mazgol the Mighty, whose power is night.'

For a while they both stood staring down at the thing, with open mouths.

'Come on then,' said the hunchback suddenly, with a greedy glint in his eye. 'If it's really Mazgol it must be worth a small fortune in gold. We can sell it in the bazaar.'

'No,' said the other fearfully, clasping his accomplice's arm. 'If it's Mazgol, then the stone is pure evil. In its wake the doorway to the Underworld opens and through the doorway shall come . . .'

Suddenly the hunchback stepped back. His face was looking up in terror. Above the crater the weird statue had just moved its stone head. Both men screamed and cowered back in horror, as the stone being turned and looked straight at them. Barbal's giant statue was glaring down with ghastly, glowing, orange eyes. Then it opened its stone wings and with a screech rose like a giant bat from the plinth, high into the night air.

'A demon,' quavered the hunchback. 'An ancient demon come back to life.'

The demon lifted higher into the skies and swooped towards the thieves. The men screamed again and huddled together, for a sickening feeling of hopelessness had just engulfed them, but the creature was not making for them at all. It was making for the rock glowing at the bottom of the crater.

The demon snatched it up in its stony talons, from among the still burning flames and with another horrible cry, half of pain and half of triumph, it rose high into the endless night sky, and flapped off into the waiting darkness. As it did so the demon's wing-beats stirred the dust in Barbal Square and another wind seemed to arise, as if from nowhere.

SILAS ROOT

'Oh blast it!'

An angry young Childar leant on his hoe under the spreading apple tree and, sighing deeply, turned to look out at the timeless scene before him: blossoming apricot and walnut trees and the Childars' colourful wooden homes, daubed in pigments scratched from the earth. It was a scene that had not changed for as long as anyone in the beautiful, hidden valleys of Ederyl could remember, and Silas Root was thoroughly sick of it.

Silas was getting hot too with all his labours and his hand strayed to his neck and touched the little birthmark just below the line of his collar. The tiny pink thing, with two winding lines of freckles running down the centre, looked as if it had been tattooed there in red pigment. Silas was rather proud of the strange mark, although the other children always teased him about it.

He turned in his pale damask smock and beige cotton trousers, and peered around the temple yard that he was in the

28

process of weeding. It was where the male Childars went to worship, to make sacrifices of goats to the Gods and to bury their dead. Silas's hazel eyes fell now on one of the little wooden memorials. It was to his own dear father, Timon, who had died of the sweating sickness last season, and it had been put there by his mother Alara.

We fought like wild jackals hard and long
But sometimes, now, I wonder where you've gone

Silas Root felt a lump in his throat, but he choked back the sad feeling and his quick gaze fell on another memorial. Silas loved words, which was exactly why he was having to till the temple yard under the great tree in the middle of Ederyl. It was his punishment for behaving so badly at the last Wordfeast, when the Wordmasters had come to Ederyl from Barbal City with a new Wordbox.

It was always a thrilling time, for then new words would circulate among the simple tribe and strange new ideas would begin to find a currency in the valleys. The season before, the word of power handed down by the Lord Alchemist Ogog had been 'Incarnation', which everyone had talked about for suns on end. But at the most recent Wordfeast there had been a special excitement in the air, possibly because of all the dark rumours that had started to circulate about Barbal City.

Silas had drunk far too much bellberry liquor for someone his size, stolen an ember from one of the fires and crept into the darkness of the tent where they were keeping the Wordbox. But he had dropped the ember before he had a chance to open it and nearly sent them all up in flames. It might have gone harder for Silas Root if the Elders hadn't taken into account his years and his father's recent passing. To keep Silas out of further mischief they had set him to weed the entire temple yard of Ederyl, all on his own, while they thought about his real punishment.

Silas was feeling very hard done by, but he went on scratching at the ground with his hoe as the leaves rustled overhead. At this rate it would take someone his size twenty moons at least to finish weeding, Silas thought bitterly, and he'd never have a chance to do anything important in life, like visit Barbal City.

Like most young Childars, Silas Root craved wonders and magic and longed to be an Alchemist himself. He had heard strange rumours recently, though, that Ogog wanted to abolish magic and it worried Silas deeply. Magic wasn't really a thing that visited Ederyl, except perhaps when the Wordmasters made their rare appearances, or when the Childars sat round their fires at festival and the men and women danced and the drums beat like thunder. Then the younger Childars began to see magical spirits moving around in the flames.

At the fire festivals the Elders would tell the children stories of how Ederyl had been created by the Gods and how the Childars had been fashioned in their own holy image, like little clay pots. It was after Lol had slumbered for seven whole suns, they said, and dreamt the whole world and everything in it into being. Silas adored sitting there, listening to stories by the sparking fires. In fact, he adored fire and was often playing with it, much to the fury of his Lesson Masters and the Elders.

Silas thought now of the lesson house and the strange square map on the wall, scored in fire charcoal onto an animal skin. He loved standing alone, when the younger Childars had gone home, poring over the great map. 'The Mappa Mysticum Mundorum' it said at the top, and it showed the four corners of the world laid out flat like a picture-book, and, at each corner, one of the four pillars that held up the skies.

Since Childars never travelled beyond Ederyl – for that was a deadly sin – they had little use for or understanding of maps. But Silas loved to study the thing nonetheless. On it were Ederyl's beautiful valleys, painted in green, and ringing them the deserts that lay beyond the high mountains, where the Dunetraders lived. In the centre was Barbal City, above lay the Depthless Sea, and beyond that the strange lands of Khem and of Heleras, the land of Centaurs, of Barbarag and of Jesladom and Moorcaria – other worlds of wonder and deep mystery. Around the edges of the map there was a great forest, the Forest of Clay Animals it was called, and a region called the Chasm of Dreamless Night. To the side, in a kind of circle and disconnected from the rest, lay a country called Pengalis.

Perhaps most fascinating, though, was the list at the bottom of the Mappa Mysticum of all the Alchemists in the Seven Lands. In Barbal it was the Lord Alchemist who ruled, alongside his High Priest. In Khem, also known as the Land of the Black Soil, it was the Mystifier. In the land of Heleras the Alchemist was called the Philosophon, while in Barbarag he was known as the Tellweaver, a very dangerous magician. There was only one Alchemist between the regions of Jesladom and Moorcaria, the Histogron, who was also called the Hooded Master, and for Pengalis, strangely, there was no listing at all, except these words: 'All Records Sealed'.

'Oh, I wish something really exciting would happen,' said Silas to himself, thinking of all the strange worlds waiting out there. But then Silas found himself thinking of something else too, something his favourite Lesson Master, Sultan Ash, used to say to him when he caught him gazing dreamily out of the window in the lesson house.

'Don't be bored, Silas Root. Adventure can turn up in the most unlikely places if you really look for it, even in your own garden.'

Sultan Ash wasn't of the Childar tribe himself but he had been bold enough to infiltrate Ederyl's valleys long ago and, because of his knowledge, been accepted. He was only an occasional supply teacher in Ederyl now, and had the habit of turning up when he was least expected but most needed. Sultan was the only foreigner allowed in the valleys and he always came in the most extraordinary clothes: turbans like the fabled Dunetraders and capes and robes with purple stripes, and all manner of finery.

Silas Root suddenly had another idea as he thought of Sultan Ash.

'I know!' he whispered, dreaming of Barbal and far-off adventures too. 'The Alcemoth!'

Silas knew perfectly well that it was forbidden to recite the Alcemoth out loud but Sultan had once shown him it and Silas, with his keen memory for words, had learnt it by heart. Silas stood up straight.

'I swear by the Gods to follow the truth,' he whispered, looking about a little guiltily, 'and to keep myself and my mind . . .'

Almost exactly as he said the mysterious words Silas's hoe jolted on the earth and broke in two. It had hit something very real. Silas pushed a hand through his locks of curly black hair and bent down to see what it was.

'Ouch!' he cried, jumping back.

Silas had just been stung by a wild netlar flower. There was a flash of green in the undergrowth too and Silas saw a tail slither away around the bowl of the tree, amongst a crop of little white and red bloodroot flowers. Silas clutched his red and throbbing hand, but he was a bold Childar and certainly not afraid of grass snakes, and he knew that wherever wild netlars grew there were bound to be some shaman leaves to counteract the sting.

Silas bent down again and began to tug at the ground.

With a little effort he pulled away the clod of earth below the broken hoe. Silas stepped back. There was a stone lying in front of him, largish, smooth and perfectly white. A stone as white as snow. Silas shivered. Magic was tickling the back of his neck.

The stone didn't seem that big, and it felt warm and chalky to the touch as Silas picked it up. Shrugging to himself, Silas slipped it into his smock pocket. But as he did so he gasped. *Whoosh*. The stone passed straight through the cloth and landed on his toe. Silas was flabbergasted. He stooped again to grab the stone, but when he popped it into his smock a second time he was amazed that the white stone stayed exactly where it was. Silas scratched his head.

'Silas? There you are, Silas.'

Silas jumped and swung round.

'Who's there?'

A Childar girl was standing behind him. She was tall, with a wash of freckles about her delicate nose, in a kind, open face, surrounded by thick, reddish brown hair. They were friends in the lesson house, but Silas was cross that she had crept up on him like this.

'What are you doing here, Rarza?' he grunted irritably. 'You know girls aren't allowed in the temple yard.'

'I know,' said Rarza Stormheart, although there was nothing guilty in her look and her green eyes twinkled. 'I thought you might be lonely, though, Silas. Are you all right? What have you done to your hand?'

'Nothing, Rarza. It's only wild netlars.'

Rarza was looking at Silas in that kind, almost pitying way that so irritated him. He disliked the way she was always saying how sorry she was for him about his father, too. Silas scowled and suddenly wondered unkindly if Rarza had been spying on him, but with that he noticed something in the corner of his eye. Even in the sunlight a bonfire was beginning to flicker on one of the hills, sending up a little plume of smoke.

'Look, Rarza,' cried Silas.

It wasn't just any bonfire, it was one of the beacon fires of Ederyl. They were only lit in times of the greatest danger.

'I know, Silas,' said Rarza excitedly. 'An Elder spotted a foreigner in the valleys this morning. Near the Council House.'

'A foreigner?' said Silas. There was little more frightening or exotic to a Childar than a foreigner. 'But it's sacrilege.'

'Punishable by death,' said Rarza cheerfully. 'Ouch!'

Rarza was rubbing her head now and Silas couldn't help but laugh. In the tree above, which the breeze had just stirred, a little crabbing apple had fallen on Rarza.

'Don't be unkind, Silas,' said Rarza reproachfully.

Silas shrugged.

'Sorry. I wonder what this foreigner wants. And how far he's come.'

Rarza looked oddly at Silas. She had been thinking of speaking to him for some time, because Silas was the only person she would have trusted the idea with.

'Silas,' she said. 'You know, I've often wondered what Barbal is like and what it would be like to run away. To go to the Sacred City, I mean.'

Silas almost laughed again, not because he hadn't often had the idea himself, but because a girl was suggesting such sacrilege.

'Don't be stupid, Rarza. It's a sin to leave the valleys. Especially for a girl.'

Rarza scowled. She knew Silas dreamt of Barbal too, and all its magic, but Rarza had a much more serious reason for wanting to leave Ederyl.

'Well, you're always saying nothing ever happens in Ederyl, Silas Root.'

'Except that I think something has just happened, Rarza,' said Silas.

'The foreigner?'

'No, Rarza. Look.'

Silas dipped into his smock and pulled out the stone. Rarza was still angry with Silas and she looked studiously unimpressed.

'What's that?'

'I think it's something very special.'

'Special? It's just a stone.'

'Yes. But just now it fell straight through my pocket.'

Rarza raised an eyebrow. She knew Silas was always making up stories and she thought it was largely because of his father.

'It's just a hole in your smock, Silas.'

'No it isn't,' said Silas, annoyed that Rarza didn't believe him. 'There isn't a hole – and watch.'

Silas popped the stone back but once more it stayed just where it was.

'Well, there you are,' said Rarza, with that horribly pitying expression.

'Oh, you're just a girl,' said Silas crossly. 'What would a girl know about magic anyway?'

'Silas. How could you say—'

'Go home, then. Don't you have to help your parents or something?'

Rarza glared at her friend. She was always having to help her parents, and at most inconvenient times. But Rarza was very proud and, rather than saying anything, she turned and stomped away.

Silas sighed, but after a while he started feeling hungry, so he lodged the bits of hoe under a nearby bellberry bush and set off cheerfully down the hill. Silas found himself taking a short cut home, through the little walnut spring where the Childars often went to pick wild thrushthroat mushrooms.

The spring had an odd effect on everyone. When the sunlight streamed through the trees and made them glow an incandescent golden green, it was a wondrous spot. But when clouds crossed the sky and a darkness settled it became a very threatening place indeed.

Now, as Silas Root walked along, the shimmering trees suddenly went dark and, high above, Silas felt a shadow reach across the sky. The leaves around his feet stirred too and Silas was seized with a cold fear that made his legs feel like stone and bolted him to the spot. Silas wanted to cry out but as he opened his mouth he found his voice was choked completely. The shadow passed as suddenly as it had come, though, and the walnut trees glowed once more beneath a clear and cloudless sky.

Silas was about to go on when the sharp crack of a breaking branch behind him swung him round to face the trees on his right. He tried to peer into the shadows but they were too dense to see anything at all.

'Who's there?' called Silas angrily, feeling really frightened now.

Silas was answered by a sound he had never heard before, nor ever wanted to again. It was like the cry of a bird, only far off and misshapen. It had anger in it and spite and a cold, primeval malevolence that filled Silas Root with a horrible sense of hopelessness. It was a piercing, screeching cry that clawed at his mind, and the thought suddenly swam into Silas's terrified brain that, whatever it was in the skies, it was hunting him.

But with that something else happened. In his smock-pocket the stone he had found had started to feel warm, a warmth that gave Silas an odd kind of courage.

Silas was wondering what the stone was and what he

should do now when suddenly there was the rustle of shaking leaves behind him. Before he could even turn, a hand was clamped fast about him. He felt an arm lock around his chest and as Silas looked down he saw that the forearm that held him was very dark and, close to the wrist, bore a strange weaving mark in the shape of a serpent.

'The foreigner,' thought Silas fearfully.

With that, the Childar was lifted clean off his feet as the foreigner went hurtling down the path. To Silas's horror he realized that they were going downhill towards the Grave Grove beyond. The Grove was the only place in Ederyl where the Childars weren't allowed to venture, for there were dark tales about the wood. Before them lay a wall of ancient trees, looming ahead of them like some nameless dread.

'Stop it!' Silas cried furiously, flailing his arms wildly. 'Who the demon are you?'

The foreigner gave no answer.

'No,' cried Silas Root angrily, 'we mustn't go in there. That's the Grave—'

Before they reached the trees, though, the stranger stopped suddenly, and put Silas down. He grabbed him by the scruff of his neck.

'Get off me,' snarled Silas.

'By the Seven Stars, be quiet,' said the man urgently, as he peered behind them.

His face was strong and dark-skinned, with bold, flashing eyes ringed with black circles, and a scar across his cheek. He had a prominent chin and his hair was extraordinary, shaved completely on his bald head, except for a knotted bolt of hair at the back, like the tail of a pony. He was dressed in a white robe and he had two jewels round his throat, one in the shape of a circular eye on a little cross of metal, and the other like a green beetle.

Silas could hardly understand the man's odd accent, yet

there was something about it that calmed him. He was furious at what was happening to him, but this voice spoke not of anger or fear, but of strength, and the thought of that cry suddenly made Silas Root want to trust this stranger, to trust anyone.

'What the demon do you want? Why are—'

'Hush, it's still searching,' whispered the stranger, looking back. 'It swooped as you entered the spring. I think it hunts you. Why should that be, boy?'

'What . . . what is it?'

The stranger's dark-rimmed eyes flickered at Silas.

'The Pazgog,' he hissed, relaxing his grip. 'The demon servant of Aspis the Destroyer.'

Silas Root went pale. 'The Destroyer!'

'Though now I believe it serves the Black Magician Mardak.'

Although Silas had no inkling of what a winged demon or a Pazgog really was, he had heard its horrifying cry and felt its shadow too.

'When it came,' he whispered, 'I couldn't speak.'

The day was turning out to be very strange indeed, but almost as extraordinary, and nearly as fearful, was standing here on the edge of the Grave Grove, in front of a clearly desperate foreigner. Around them it was growing darker and a moon was rising in the heavens of Ederyl.

'But who are you?' asked Silas nervously.

'In my lands they name me Ramset,' answered the stranger, lifting himself to his full height in his white robes. Those black circles round his eyes made him look like a giant cat.

'I'm a Warrior Priest and a Scribe of Khem, the Land of the Black Soil,' said Ramset proudly. 'There the doorway has been opened, the doorway that hides the passage into the

Underworld itself. With it my land has been struck with seven terrible plagues. A storm comes to us all.'

Silas could hardly believe his ears. He was fascinated by the idea of a scribe, for he had heard that in Khem they were like Barbal's Wordmasters, bodyguards to the Alchemists.

'And who are you, boy?' asked Ramset.

'Silas. Silas Root.'

Night was coming now and the shadows were growing among the trees. Silas looked up and in the rising breeze he heard a weird moaning. It was coming from the tree on his right, which the wind was sighing through.

'What are you doing in Ederyl, though?' asked Silas. 'It's sacrilege for foreigners to enter our hidden valleys.'

'I know it, Silas Root,' said the Scribe, 'but I came to find a word.'

'A word?' said Silas in surprise, thinking immediately of the Wordbox he himself had tried to open.

'Yes, boy. A word of very great power. There are rumours of it leaving Barbal. It was sent here by mistake. A word so revolutionary that the Mystifier, the Alchemist of Khem, believes it has the power to turn everything upside down. Even unseat the Alchemists themselves, perhaps. So the Mystifier wants it suppressed. He sent me to find it.'

Silas was about to ask Ramset what the word was when suddenly he felt it again. The feeling of horror and hopelessness was far worse than it had been before. Far closer. It nearly knocked them both backwards.

Just then a shape rose right above them in the skies, silhouetted in front of the lustrous moon. The creature's gigantic wings were open wide above it and as Silas saw the Pazgog hanging there like a monstrous kite, its great talons hanging below it and slowly flapping its wings, his heart nearly stood still.

'By the Seven Stars,' hissed Ramset. 'Run! Run for your life!'

High above, the horrible demon began to wheel in the skies, turning on its back and sweeping in a great arc as it circled above them.

'Quick, boy. Over there.'

Ramset started to run straight towards the Grave Grove. Silas didn't need to be told twice. They jumped behind a tree just in time. The terrible demon had just landed. It screeched again and its cry quivered like pain across the air. Silas crouched low and very slowly edged around the side of the tree to have a look at it. The Pazgog was standing a way off, half a walnut tree tall, its head crowned with a kind of raised claw that jutted out along the line of the demon's vicious beak. It was looking about like a wild animal, scenting the air.

Silas ducked back again in terror.

'What can we do, Ramset?' he whispered desperately.

Even the Warrior Priest looked frightened now. They heard a shuffling again and Silas peered round the tree a second time. The Pazgog's great leathery wings were lifted back and up above its head, flapping gently as though shielding it from the moonlight. Its beak was enormous, and it had livid orange eyes that glowed like burning coals.

Silas was sickened to his very soul and he thought that if this demon was a servant, what must its master Mardak be like – or even worse, Aspis, the Lord of the Underworld? In the air the Pazgog had soared free but on the ground its movements were harsh and jerky, highlighting the angularity of its horrible body. It had looked black in the skies, too, but on the ground its pitted skin seemed more of a very dark grey and, as one taloned leg lumbered after the other, it seemed as though it was made of stone.

Silas dived back behind the tree again, but his foot dislodged a rock that rolled out into the open with a thud.

 40

The Pazgog swung its head straight towards them. In a single hungry hop it had covered half the distance to the tree. Ramset looked round frantically as he felt its approach, raising his hands in some kind of motion of defence, but he seemed to realize that they were both trapped. Suddenly they felt the air churning. The Pazgog had landed right on the other side of the tree.

'Shield your eyes,' hissed Ramset. 'By the Seven Stars, don't ever look at it.'

'My eyes?' cried Silas, glaring at the Scribe. 'Why?'

'Because it is a creature of darkness. If it sees inside you, it will steal your very soul, boy. Turn you into a Grasht.'

'A Grasht?'

'The dead ones, who walk without breath or feeling. The army of the dark. They rise around Barbal.'

Ramset swung his head away, clutching the jewels at his throat, and Silas dropped his gaze to the ground. Yet in the moonlight he could see the Pazgog's shadow in the grass. A wing-tip was stretching towards them and a sickening smell was coming from the creature too: the smell of rotting flesh. Silas and Ramset seemed frozen, as the ghastly shadow hopped even closer and lifted its beak to strike.

Silas knew that he should not look at it but he couldn't help lifting his head and, as his gaze caught the light in the creature's eyes, images flashed into his mind of dark and loathsome shapes. Half-formed things in the night, and animals and beings that seemed to change shape but yet be part of one terrible form; to be part of the Pazgog itself.

But suddenly the warmth of the stone came again in Silas's smock. Without knowing why, Silas reached into his pocket and seized it in his fist, thrusting out his arm angrily towards the Pazgog. As Silas opened his palm he gasped. The plain white stone had become almost translucent and from its very centre a light was beginning to glow and with it came that wonderful feeling of hope.

Ramset, his eyes closed, didn't see any of this, but again the Pazgog shrieked, as the light seemed to grow, swirling outwards from the centre. It flashed like a star and blazed with a brilliantly pure whiteness that lit up the whole wood. The stone burst like lightning, illuminating the earth and trees and sky, shining steadily, as if boring into the darkness itself. The Pazgog let out a horrible cry, as if wounded, and Silas felt a gust of air again. The demon was retreating.

The brilliant light grew stronger still, seeming to push the creature back, and as the Scribe and the Childar crouched below the wonderful light, Silas saw that the Pazgog's skin had become transparent and that underneath he could see ribs of bone and a mire of tangled veins. Higher and higher climbed the ghastly Pazgog, out of sight, as his eerie cries grew fainter on the trembling air.

Silas was shaking like a leaf and in his hand the light dwindled and died. He was holding nothing but a plain lump of rock again. Silas was truly astounded, but knowing so little of this stranger, he suddenly didn't want to trust him with his secret, so he popped the magic stone safely back in his pocket.

'That was close,' he sighed. 'It's gone, Ramset.'

Slowly the Scribe opened one eye and peered about in surprise.

'Thank the heavens,' he said, standing up. 'It can't have seen us. The Pazgog never gives up once it knows its prey. But quickly. It may return.'

'We should go down to the council house,' said Silas, 'and warn the Elders.'

'No,' said Ramset, 'it's not safe for me in Ederyl. Your Elders are searching for me everywhere. I need somewhere to hide for a while.'

Silas was shaking badly but he knew Ramset was right and

if the Elders discovered that the intruder had broken their commandments it would go gravely for him. Nothing as exciting had ever happened to Silas Root before. It might be a sin to help the foreigner but he was suddenly determined not to let this chance slip.

'I know, Ramset,' he said. 'Our lesson house. Lessons don't start again for ages and it stands alone on the hill. I'll hide you in there, if you like. I can bring you food and drink and in the meanwhile you can tell me what's happening. What you want with this word.'

Ramset looked down warmly at the boy.

'You're brave,' he said. 'Very well then, young Childar, I'll trust you. Lead the way.'

Silas beamed. He was greatly relieved to leave the Grave Grove behind them as he led Ramset off through the dark, and it wasn't long before they were mounting the hill towards the lesson house. As they went they passed by a simple home set back in an orchard. From inside came angry shouts, and a girl's voice raised indignantly, before Rarza Stormheart's mother cut her short.

'I told you you're not going anywhere else today. And what were you doing nosing about the temple yard anyway? Now get to bed immediately.'

A man's voice rose gruffly in the darkness too.

'Always breaking our rules, you ungrateful brat. And showing no respect to yer father neither. Can't you grow up and face reality, Rarza? You ought to be ashamed of yourself. Now fetch me some more liquor, quick.'

Silas suddenly felt rather sorry for Rarza, although he had teased her about her parents, but he couldn't think about such silly things now. The voices dwindled in the night and near-by Silas and Ramset saw a beacon fire. Silas went and pulled out a burning branch, so that they could see the way better

43

and felt the flames hot against his face as he held up the lovely torch.

'These plagues in Khem, Ramset,' he whispered as they walked on through the dark. 'What are they?'

The Warrior Priest almost blanched.

'It is terrible, Silas Root,' he answered. 'Frogs, locusts, fire, blood, snakes and darkness. Oh yes, and the death of first-born children. Seven. The Mystifier, the Alchemist of Khem, blames himself, for it has always been his sacred task to protect the doorway to the Underworld, from whence they and the Pazgog came. I believe other forces are at work now.'

'Other forces?' said Silas, feeling very uncomfortable again.

'Yes. I must find some knowledge to help protect my people,' whispered Ramset, 'and the ruler of my beloved Khem. Blessed be the mighty Faron's name. World without end. Ammon.'

Silas knew something of the land of Khem and the great Faron who ruled alongside Khem's Alchemist, the Mystifier. But he had never thought he would meet someone from the Land of Black Soil, certainly not in Ederyl, and it made him feel very special indeed.

'There, Ramset.'

They had reached the plain wooden building which acted as the Childars' lesson house, but before they drew closer, Silas stopped.

'Wait here, Ramset,' he whispered. 'I'll see if anyone's around.'

The door was locked, but Silas Root picked up a little pot, flowering with verdigris plants and underneath was a wooden key. Silas felt strangely grown up as he turned the lock and opened the door.

The main room of the lesson house was empty, although

the floor was still covered in the little woven mats where the Childars sat to listen attentively to their lessons. There on the wall was the Mappa Mysticum Mundorum and the board on which the Lesson Masters, including Sultan Ash, would write things with a piece of fire charcoal. Below it, on the table where the Lesson Masters sat, Silas noticed a heavy camel-leather book.

Silas had often seen Sultan Ash carrying it around with him but had never got so close to it before. Now he saw it had letters down the spine. His lips mouthed the words as he tried to decipher them.

AN UNOFFICIAL HISTORY OF THE SECRET AND TROUBLED ORDER OF ALCHEMISTS
(Including a new version of the Alcemoth)
Read it. They banned it in seven realms.

Silas wondered how on earth it had got there as he opened the cover. At first there was a page imprinted with the words 'The First Spell', followed by two lines of weird symbols:

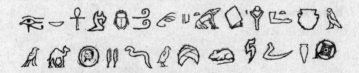

Silas turned over another page and saw this:

THE TRUE STORY OF METALS

In Barbal the Alchemists have discovered several hard substances which they have begun to name metals. Seven in fact. Gold is the most highly prized, of course, especially in the Street of the Groot Changers.

45

Silas turned over another page. The hide pages were thick and felt lovely to touch as he went on reading.

> *Hermet is the Messenger of the Gods, who comes suddenly and in the strangest guises.*

Silas shook his head and looked deep inside the pages of the History, but now he blinked stupidly at what he saw.

> *Chaos Theory, which suggests everything is interconnected, even by the faintest fluttering of a butterfly's wing, is all very well when theorizing about the Stars, or the nature of matter, but especially useless when crossing the desert.*

Now utterly confused, Silas closed the strange book. But as he turned it over he saw that on the back, in glittering golden markings, were twelve symbols, ordered in a circle. Silas put down the History and opened the door of the lesson house again.

'Come on, Ramset,' he called, 'it's all clear.'

But as Silas Root stepped outside he felt a breeze blowing from the mountains and something hard and gritty on the air. It was sand.

THE LAST
WORDMASTER

Ashtar the Dunetrader guide had been right about the storm. It had hit the encampment that same night, bending the palm trees almost double. The two sand columns had merged into one, a great swirling vortex of red mischief. It broke around them in a tidal wave of hot sand and noise that seemed to carry the fury of some haunted demon with it.

The whole caravan had taken shelter in the Great Tent. The Dunetrader men were grouped cross-legged in a circle around the fire in the middle of the tent now, while the boys sat together in a corner and the women began to make another supper. The Dunetraders sat propped up on swollen pig bellies that served as water bottles, covered with brightly coloured carpeting, patterned with strange and mysterious weaves.

Their dark eyes seemed to grow in size in the firelight and, although the flap of the tent had been well sealed with woven saddlebags and stones, the air was heavy with glittering sand. Someone started to cough and Kerbogah's father, Karleg, got up and strode towards the fire.

'It rages,' he said in a strong, calm voice. Karleg was well used to soothing his caravan when the windstorms struck. He looked over to Ashtar and the guide nodded approvingly.

'But we must wait and listen,' said Karleg, 'for nothing can fight the desert now, or the anger of the Gods.'

Some of the men grunted, while a beautiful woman stirring the pot broke some cactus leaves in half and then took out a strangely shaped stone bowl and a kind of flat stone hammer. Kerbogah got up and sat on the ground next to her, for it was his mother, Selera. Next to Kerbogah another boy sat down too, Kerbogah's best friend Farjay. He was playing with a little leather sling that he often use to hurl stones at desert lizards.

Selera laid the bowl carefully on the ground and popped the cactus inside it. Then with the hammer-like object she began to ground the stems down, releasing the strange green gel inside: aloe.

Kerbogah leant over.

'What's that, Mother?' he whispered, looking at her cooking tools and stroking Relak, who was nestling comfortably in his robe.

'The first tool of Alchemy, Kerbogah,' answered Selera. 'It's called a mortar and that's a pestle, although the Alchemists name it a crucible. Names, you see, are very important to their work.'

'Names, Selera?' said Farjay. 'Why names?'

Selera smiled kindly at Kerbogah's friend, for as an orphan she often felt sorry for the lad and always tried to make him feel part of their family.

'Just try to imagine things without names, Farjay,' she answered softly, 'or the names you already have for them.

 48

What would you call them and how would you start to explore them to find out what they really are?'

'Explore them?' whispered Kerbogah. 'What do you mean, explore them, Mother?'

'To examine their essence and their truth. You'd have to put something of yourself into them, wouldn't you? Something of your own knowledge and spirit and dreams to try and see what they are. Well, so do all the Alchemists. In the Ziggurat they believe it's a very holy thing. That only when you name a thing do you have power over it.'

Selera held up the bowl and scraped the sticky green liquid that had oozed from the crushed cactus into the soup, and started to season the mix with rock salt. Kerbogah licked his finger and let some salt stick to it, then started to feed Relak, who was soon nibbling away happily. The Dunetrader men watched Selera cheerlessly. Although the women only prepared the aloe soup when the storms came, to protect their voices, the Dunetraders were heartily sick of it.

The aloe began to bubble and pop over the dung fire, and each of the Dunetraders took out the rough wooden bowl in his pack again, and the spoon that was even dearer to a Dunetrader than a sword, and filed up to take his turn.

'Come,' said Karleg as the caravan ate. 'We are a people of song and need to be entertained. Read to us, Imlay. From one of the Rubaiyats.'

The Dunetraders looked expectantly towards an old man who was sitting nearer to the fire than the rest. His face was well lived in and one eye was closed up with a heavy scar. He sported a long white beard that reached to his waist and he was clearly used to being listened to with great respect.

'Tonight we should be making sacrifices or praying, Ashtar,' said Imlay sternly, 'to appease Aspis and these wild spirits of chaos. But if you all insist.'

As the others settled themselves, Imlay put down his bowl

and lifted a huge leather book fastened with a silver buckle onto his knees. One of the elders lit a pipe that began to send up wisps of cool apple smoke as it bubbled happily through the water bowl in front of him, and the others lay back on the water bellies to listen.

There were few greater pleasures for the Mahara Dunetraders than to sit together in their tents, safe from a terrible windstorm, and share a meal or a pipe, listening to the ancient enchantments of the Rubaiyats. Imlay's gnarled finger scanned the page as he started to recite to the desert travellers in a deeply hypnotic voice.

> *For in and out, above, about, below,*
> *It's nothing but a magic shadow-show*
> *Played in a box whose candle is the sun,*
> *Round which we phantom figures come and go.*

Imlay's chant climbed louder and louder as the verses went on and the powerful storm howled outside, raising thoughts in the listeners of great journeys and distant lands, of friends long gone and friends yet to come.

Farjay was entranced as he sat next to Kerbogah and toyed with his catapult, for he loved poetry and as the desert storm raged and shook the Dunetraders' tent, the verses went on still, for the Rubaiyats had been woven out of the wisdom of the ages. Some of the other lads had started to doze in the dusty firelight when Imlay closed his book again.

'Now,' cried another voice loudly, as soon as he did so. 'Which of you philistines wants a real poem?'

'Real poem?' said Imlay, raising an eyebrow.

A thin, tall, waxen-faced Dunetrader got to his feet. He swayed back, though, as he stood there and he was clearly drunk. In his hand he was holding a sack of wine and a leather beaker.

'Khayarumi's off again,' chuckled someone next to him. 'I'd rather watch some Dancing Derwishers. But very well then. Give us a song of the Alchemists.'

'Alchemists be damned!' cried the poet scornfully, tottering sideways and almost falling over. 'What use are Alchemists? It's not the Alchemists and their stupid prayers or inventions that change the world, but artists like me. Feeling and art, that's what truly counts in life.'

'Hush, Khayarumi,' said Imlay immediately. 'It's sacrilege to speak so.'

'That's better than the Alchemists' magic, is it, Khayarumi?' said another Dunetrader.

'There is no magic,' snapped the poet, and Imlay bit his lip. 'As Ogog now says. No magic anyway but poetry and love. Keep your Alchemists and your Seven Wonders of the world. Keep your inventions and your mounds of gold. As long as I've a glass in my hand and a poem on my lips, as long as I can sleep in the arms of the one I love.'

Khayarumi lifted his beaker high and almost sang to one of the women in the tent, a beautiful girl named Frannemar.

'Her lovely lips like crimson petals on a rose
Are all life's answer, till the tempest blows.'

Frannemar dropped her pretty eyes and smiled.

'Aaaach, stop your blessed poetry, Khayarumi,' growled Imlay, a little jealously, for he was far too old for love and he thought the Rubaiyats the only poetry anyone should be allowed to listen to.

'No,' the poet answered defiantly, taking a deep swig of rose wine from the beaker and dribbling it right down his chin. 'Alchemists love their secrets all right, but I'll tell you life's real secret. The Alchemists may have invented a Ziggurat, or even a giant Waterwheel and a Sundial. But none of them at all has worked out how to change things into gold.'

'Haven't they?' whispered Kerbogah by the fire.

'No. And why not? Because they're really all a pack of fakes,' said the poet. 'Ogog. Mardak the Dark. The Priest Apprentices. All of them, with their dark rituals and their silly secrets.'

Kerbogah and Farjay looked deeply shocked and Khayarumi's voice had grown so harsh that the tent seemed suddenly duller to the boys sitting cross-legged about him. Under the weight of his words everything had taken on a leaden reality and the walls of the tent seemed to crowd inwards on them.

'I don't need an Alchemist to solve the true secrets,' mumbled Khayarumi, sinking cross-legged to the ground suddenly and staring at the floor as he drank again. 'Or to see the whole universe in a single grain of sand. Well, a grain of Stardust at least. Except one secret, perhaps,' the poet added mournfully. 'The secret that none of us can solve in the end and none of us ever escapes. Death.'

Khayarumi was so drunk by now that as he lifted the beaker to his lips the blood-red wine spilt onto the carpet.

'Death,' he mumbled bitterly. 'It swallows us all in the end. Like this blasted sandstorm. And then what? Nothing. All gone. So what's the point of anything at all?'

The beaker slipped and fell to the floor, but Khayarumi didn't even notice it. The Dunetrader poet had fallen sound asleep and soon he was snoring loudly. Outside the wind screeched furiously and the boys bunched even closer together.

'A story, tell us a story,' cried one of the Dunetraders. 'Khayarumi's asleep.'

'What story?' came another voice.

'"The Fall",' suggested a third. '"The Fall of the Tower of Barbal".'

A large, smiling Dunetrader stepped into the middle of the circle as the others sat up to listen.

'Very well. It was after Tulon, the first Lord Alchemist,

had been given the stones of power and had ordered that an enormous tower be constructed in the desert to climb as high as the Seven Heavens themselves.'

The Dunetraders smiled approvingly.

'For a long while, you see, Tulon had dreamt of asking Lol himself for the very secrets of the universe. He had already made a sacrilegious pact with some of the lesser Gods to share their powers though and help him build the tower to the Gods.'

Kerbogah shifted himself to get more comfortable.

'But Lol and his consort Enlis discovered his plan,' cried the Dunetrader, 'and they grew angry that man should want the secrets of heaven. So Lol hurled the other Gods from the skies and sent them to dwell in the hidden places of the earth, among the rocks and stones and metals that littered the land.'

Farjay put his hand in his pocket and pulled out the pebble he had saved for his slingshot.

'Then Lol and Enlis came down to earth in pillars of fire and Lol snatched back the holy Turnstones. They destroyed the blasphemous tower, bringing it tumbling down.'

'The Fall,' whispered Kerbogah, looking at Farjay.

'And made all the peoples of the world and the tribes in it speak in different tongues, so they could no longer understand each other. There was darkness and confusion as the peoples spread across the face of the earth.'

Even Imlay was smiling as he nodded to himself at the familiar tale.

'But Enlis's tender heart grew sorry for the frightened humans and so from the tower's ruins she allowed Barbal City to rise, and the Ziggurat too; a mighty tower itself, but not so mighty that it should be an affront to heaven. The Goddess also prophesied that the Turnstones should come again to man, and showing them to Tulon, made the Waterwheel move by their magic. There. That is the story of the Fall.'

There was loud applause in the Dunetrader tent but Selera turned to the children.

'Come, Kerbogah,' she said softly. 'Come over here and sleep now. And you too, Farjay.'

'No, Mother,' pleaded Kerbogah. 'Relak and I want to listen. How else will I learn to be a man and move the desert?'

'Move the desert?' said Farjay, snapping his catapult. 'At our age, Kerbogah, you might as well try to move a mountain. Our voices haven't broken.'

The grown-ups chuckled but Kerbogah refused to budge and Karleg smiled at his son.

'Have faith, my boy,' he whispered. 'Your time will come, Kerbogah. But, Ashtar, would you do some Sandwork and tell us how far Barbal is?'

The boys didn't look at all pleased at this suggestion. Sandwork, or number magic as it was also called, was the main way of calculating for the Mahara Dunetraders and the boys' least favourite thing in the world. From under one of the waterskins though Ashtar had drawn a square board, scored with lines to make columns, and was holding up a little bag filled with pebbles. He scooped up some desert sand from the floor of their tent and sprinkled it lightly over his board.

'Sandwork,' whispered another Dunetrader, as Ashtar opened the bag and pulled out a pebble. 'They say the High Priest so loves prayers and incantations and so hates Sandwork that he longs to ban its use in the streets of Barbal completely. Ban it on pain of Alchemical Torture. Can such a thing be true?'

'Who knows?' said a third. 'But Ogog will never let him. The Lord Alchemist has put Sandwork at the very heart of his rule.'

'Yes. And Mardak hates Ogog for it—'

'Let me see now,' interrupted Ashtar. 'Ten leagues to the last well, then five to the white dunes. No, that's not right.'

Ashtar worked away, placing pebbles from the bag on the board. He was adding and subtracting stones as he calculated. It was soon clear, even to Kerbogah and Farjay, what the dusting of sand was for. If Ashtar made a mistake, at least he could see the path of his sums by the marks the stones left in the layer of sand. His knowledge of Stardust and his skill in Sandwork were two of the reasons Ashtar was such a famous and accomplished guide in the desert.

'There,' cried Ashtar at last, rubbing his hands and smiling with satisfaction. 'By my reckoning still twelve Barbalonian leagues.'

The others nodded and Selera looked most anxious, for she was wondering when she would see her son Kalman again. She clasped Kerbogah's hand warmly but Karleg suddenly turned his head towards the flap of the tent.

'Hush, what's that?'

Imlay had heard it too.

'Could it be spies?' he whispered. 'They say they are everywhere now.'

'Or an ambush,' said another Dunetrader, putting his hand to his dagger. 'Perhaps that caravan wants our Stardust and they've doubled back in the storm.'

'Camel's blood!' breathed Kerbogah to Farjay.

'It's nothing, Karleg,' said Ashtar after a while. 'Just the voice of the windstorm.'

'No, Ashtar. There.'

Deep within the moaning belly of the wind, they had began to hear it, faintly at first; a single human voice, somewhere outside. A voice that was crying for help.

'A Sandspirit?' said Farjay nervously, clasping his slingshot even tighter.

Karleg had already sprung towards the flap of the tent, though, and Ashtar was too slow to hold him.

'Stop, Karleg,' he cried. 'This storm's a killer—'

'No, Ashtar. Hospitality. It's the first law of the desert.'

Karleg kicked a saddlebag aside and as he slipped outside, the wind and sand came funnelling straight in, upturning the empty cooking pot and billowing the desert through the once still air. The Dunetraders swung away their heads and clamped the end of their turbans across their mouths to protect their magical throats, as Ashtar sprang towards the doorway too. He stopped suddenly and turned towards Kerbogah.

'That rope, boy. Where is it?'

Kerbogah had been guarding it and he reached down and, with a proud grin, threw the rope to the guide. Ashtar tied one end tightly round his middle and, handing the other end to one of the larger Dunetraders, turned to address the caravan.

'Seal it tight after me,' he ordered, 'and after you've made some more soup, pray to Lol and Enlis above for us both.'

The boys shuddered as Ashtar vanished into the storm too. He felt its scouring anger immediately, raking at his skin and blinding his eyes, even through his veil. The noise was furious, like a wave-broken shore, and he was almost turned by it, like a child's wooden spinning top. But Ashtar managed to keep his footing and press forward through the fierce storm, feeling a little more certain as he sensed the rope unwinding steadily behind him in the shattering wind.

'Keep close, Karleg,' he cried frantically, 'for Lol's sake!'

Ashtar's cry was swallowed by the screeching sand, and he gagged and spat as he tasted it, searching deep into his throat. Every now and then he would pull down a corner of his turban to see where he was going, but immediately the sand-storm blinded him again.

'Karleg? Where the demon are you, Karleg?'

Ashtar felt him before he even saw him. Beyond the tent, towards the spot where the dune had been, Ashtar bumped straight into Karleg and nearly knocked him over. The two friends crouched down, turning their heads away to try to keep out the wind and sand, as their ears nearly burst with the noise.

'I think it came from over here, Ashtar,' cried Karleg faintly.

'We must get back. We won't last much longer in this.'

'Wait, Ashtar. Look.'

Ashtar strained to look, holding up a hand before his eyes, the skin stinging like a million heated pins and needles. All around him now he fancied he could see shapes forming in the swirling sand, only to disappear again as soon as they had appeared.

'There's nothing, Karleg. Only Sandspirits.'

'No, Ashtar, there.'

Ashtar could just see it now. It emerged from the maelstrom, becoming real as it approached among the whisping phantasms. A single figure was staggering straight towards them. More and more solid he became as he drew nearer. They knew for certain it was no spirit, as the stranger, exhausted and stumbling, collapsed into their arms. As he fell against them though, he knocked against Ashtar's belt.

'No, Ashtar,' cried Karleg.

The little bag of Stardust had dropped to the ground and the string binding it had come loose. In an instant the storm caught the magical powder and, with little flashing sparks, the Stardust vanished into the swirling air.

'The tribute,' whispered Karleg helplessly, as Ashtar struggled to lift the stranger.

'Never mind that now, Karleg. We must get him inside.'

'If we can even find our way back, Ashtar.'

Ashtar had already closed his hand around their lifeline and started to haul all three of them back through the sand sea to safety. At the other end the Dunetraders had begun to pull too. The tent was closed again and the terrible noise shut out.

Inside they threw the stranger face down by the fire, as Ashtar and Karleg collapsed in a fit of coughing and spluttering, and, bit-by-bit, the heavy air settled. Kerbogah was on his feet, furiously relieved that his father was safe.

The other Dunetraders all began to crowd in to look at the stranger, and Selera and another woman were already at his side. Selera turned him over gently and began to clear the sand from his mouth and eyes with her skirts. His hair was so thick with sand that it looked like a matted carpet and his cheeks and lips were scratched and bleeding.

'Who the demon is he?' spat Karleg, raising himself on his elbows next to Ashtar and coughing to clear his throat. 'One of Mardak's damned spies?'

Selera was dusting down the stranger's clothes as old Imlay hobbled up to investigate too. He had put the book aside and tied his beard in a knot to keep it clean.

'See there,' he said. 'He wears the saffron robes.'

Only now, as Selera cleared away the yellow sand from his body, did they begin to make out the colour of the robing beneath: a deep, rich ochre, bound with a black silken waistband, from which hung a long cleft stick.

'He's a Wordmaster,' whispered Imlay.

The Dunetraders were all observing the stranger with sudden awe. Many drew back nervously, for although they respected these strange figures, they knew too of their Wordpower, which, when it descended, or so it was said in Barbal Bazaar, could enchant and control and bend wills to their holy bidding.

'His horse,' said Karleg. 'It must have dropped in the storm.'

'It'll be bad for us if he dies,' said Imlay with a scowl. 'We'd do better to turn our backs on Barbal and bury our cargo in the sand. Ogog might blame us.'

'Quickly,' cried Karleg. 'Get him some water.'

 58

There was a hasty scrabbling and soon they were dousing the stranger's head, not caring as they wasted the drops in the greedy sand around him. A strong, proud face emerged and his lips began to move as he tasted the precious draught, but the Wordmaster didn't open his eyes.

'Leave him to sleep a while,' said Ashtar. 'He must have drunk a skinful of sand out there and he'll need his strength. Wait till it settles in his stomach and then slowly try to clear his throat, but don't let him drink too much. It's his only chance.'

The Dunetraders were all steeped in the Sandlaw, and knew better than to argue with a guide like Ashtar, but suddenly the Wordmaster began to speak.

'Not natural,' he groaned.

Karleg sprang forward. He bent low over the stranger, straining to hear him, but the Wordmaster's eyes were still shut and his fevered face was drenched in sweat.

'What, my friend? What's not natural?'

'This storm. Unnatural. Evil comes. Chaos. Nothing but chaos and despair. Barbal in danger.'

Ashtar drew closer too and there was something strange in his eyes.

'Mardak the Dark,' whispered the Wordmaster. 'The prophecy.'

Beside the fire Kerbogah and Farjay sat up. The strange Wordmaster was tossing his head violently now, left and right, as he gripped Karleg's arm and talked of a prophecy. Karleg almost cried out, but suddenly the Wordmaster opened his eyes. They were a rich yellow, like his robes, but glazed and lost.

'Captain Zolos and Mardak. They've broken the Seven Commandments. Opened the Book of Destinies itself.'

'But it's sacrilege,' said Imlay, looking around the Dunetraders. 'Only a Lord Alchemist may enter the Room of

Changes to consult the Book of Destinies. The oldest book in the world.'

'There they read the prophecy. The prophecy Ogog thought to suppress. The prophecy that speaks of the return of the Turnstones. And a demon. The Pazgog.'

The Wordmaster hissed the name and it seemed to suck the air of dust and smoke and sand. The brave Dunetraders had shrunk back, as the walls of their tent shook furiously in the storm.

'The Pazgog brings death and destruction,' whispered the Wordmaster, 'and sucks out the soul to leave the Grasht. An army of the dead. Until . . . until *he* comes. The Destroyer.'

Selera reached out and clutched her son's hand but suddenly the wind dropped and a strange silence settled around them all. Karleg noticed that Imlay had begun to shake furiously and his face had gone as white as his beard. The Wordmaster gave a terrible shudder.

'My Chi,' he gasped. 'It is fading, failing . . . no time.'

'No,' said Imlay, splashing his face with water. 'You must try to tell us more.'

The Wordmaster forced himself up on his elbows and seemed to revive a little.

'Mazgol the Mighty has returned from the heavens. The black Turnstone,' he gasped, 'and with it the Doorway to the Underworld opens. Through it the Pazgog's spirit came to animate the statue. None may defeat the Pazgog and it serves Mardak now.'

Ashtar got to his feet and for a moment seemed to turn away.

'But the Wordmasters,' said Karleg, crouching forward. 'They protect the Book of Destinies and all its secrets. How can this be?'

'Gone,' whispered the stranger bitterly, 'all gone. The sacred bodyguard has been murdered.'

The Dunetraders gasped.

'Stone cold they lie, in the Room of Changes,' said the Wordmaster sadly. 'Mardak told Captain Zolos to prepare a feast for the Solstice festival. Of wines and meat and poison too. Meanwhile Zolos's men stormed the Halls of the Sinking Sun. Ogog himself is a prisoner in Mardak's dungeons, while the Wordmasters have gone. I was delayed and travelling to the feast when I learnt the news. I am the last.'

The wind was hammering the walls of the great tent again.

'The last?' said Imlay in disbelief. 'It can't be. Why has Mardak done this?'

'Revenge,' whispered the Wordmaster, 'and Ogog's fear of magic and prophecy and love of reason and Sandwork. Mardak seeks to make himself the Lord Alchemist. To return Barbal to the ancient ways. Of fear and blood and human sacrifice.'

Kerbogah had begun to tremble by the fire.

'So each sun the Pazgog waits once more in the square, restored to stone,' said the Wordmaster angrily. 'But by night it comes alive again and swoops over the city to carry off the souls of any who oppose Mardak's will. Its look alone can draw their spirits from them and leave them as the walking dead. While Zolos's Barbalissaries roam the outskirts of the city collecting its victims to swell the ranks of their own. Some, though, the Pazgog feeds on too. It eats their flesh.'

Kerbogah was looking in amazement at Farjay. Barbal had suddenly become a terrible place indeed.

'But there is something else.'

'Go on, man,' said Karleg.

'This makina Mardak makes in the Ziggurat,' said the Wordmaster. 'It is something of unspeakable power.'

In Kerbogah's robes Relak began to squeak and wriggle, for the boy was squeezing him too hard.

'But there is hope. As there is always hope in the darkness. The prophecy talks too of one who shall help to free us all. Free us with his sacrifice. One who has been marked from birth. He shall bring the second Turnstone. He shall be the Lightbearer.'

Ashtar strained forward. His eyes were fixed intently on the Wordmaster.

'Where?' he asked.

'The Wordmasters have always known that secret. We have always spoken of a hidden land, a land of innocence and purity. There Gol must come. To fight Mazgol. It is the only hope. Otherwise we are all doomed.'

'Calm yourself,' said Karleg, reaching for some more water to bathe the Wordmaster's head. 'Try to tell us more slowly.'

The stranger had slumped back, though. His eyes had closed again and he was beginning to babble. Kerbogah was literally shaking with excitement.

'Did you hear that, Farjay?' he whispered. 'A prophecy. Then Barbal really is the City of Soothsaying.'

But Kerbogah was suddenly jolted. The Wordmaster had opened his eyes again and was staring straight at him across the tent, with those piercing yellow orbs.

'You, lad. Come here.'

'Me?' gulped Kerbogah, as the adults eyes turned towards him.

'Yes, you, child. Draw closer.'

Kerbogah got up very nervously and walked slowly towards the Wordmaster.

'Why, sir?' he stammered, clutching Relak to his heart.

With great effort the Wordmaster drew himself up on his elbows again.

'Your Chi,' he whispered, grasping Kerbogah's hand. 'It is

strong. I feel it. As I heard it in your voice. You have courage and you are young.'

The Wordmaster put his hand to that stick at his belt and slowly got to his feet too. It took enormous effort and he was horribly shaky as he stood there, but he took the cleft stick in his trembling hands and, laying his palms flat, he balanced it between his thumbs.

'Ogog did not like us to use our power of Divination,' the Wordmaster whispered faintly, 'but it is time again. To see. Though the very effort may kill me.'

The Wordmaster began to mumble and Kerbogah was amazed to see that the stick started to move.

'All is Chi,' he whispered. 'All attraction. All repulsion.'

'Divination,' said Imlay. 'He's divining.'

The stick quivered and at first it pointed straight at a waterskin near Kerbogah's father. The Wordmaster pulled it away irritably and, closing his grave eyes again, grasped the stick with even greater determination. His arms shook as he did so and very slowly he swung left and then right.

Kerbogah was watching carefully but no matter how hard he looked he could not decide whether the stick was turning him, or he was turning the stick. First the Wordmaster turned towards Ashtar and the stick pointed straight at his head. For a moment the Wordmaster opened his strange eyes and they seemed startled, but he closed them again. Then, following the stick once more, he swung straight back towards Kerbogah.

'I see things,' he cried, 'about you, boy, and about events that will touch you all. The flying demon. War. A terrible sacrifice in the Sacred Square. The Wheel. If the Great Waterwheel stops, the temple itself shall be rent in twain.'

The Dunetraders looked up in amazement.

'I see the world turned upside down. I see the Alchemists, the Alchemists themselves . . .'

The stick and the Wordmaster's arms began to shake so violently that his whole body seemed to vibrate. The stick was still pointing at Kerbogah though.

'Mardak the Dark,' he muttered. 'The light of reason shall be . . . He is . . . No. Even I cannot . . .'

Suddenly the divining stick snapped clean in two and, with a groan, the Wordmaster slumped to the ground. He looked more drained than ever.

'What did you see?' demanded Kerbogah.

As the Wordmaster lifted his head and looked around, at first Kerbogah thought he seemed terrified of something in the tent, but with great effort he recovered himself and his face settled again as he looked into Kerbogah's eyes.

'Listen carefully,' he whispered, clutching Kerbogah's wrist again. 'You will meet this Marked One.'

'Me?'

'Your destinies are bound together. You must get to him before Mardak does, if you can. Tell him that his greatest defence is taught by the Alcemoth itself. The search for truth.'

It wasn't only Karleg and Selera who were staring at their son in astonishment. But Farjay's look was suddenly mixed with jealousy too.

'His defence? But who is he?'

'May the truth be a blazing light in the darkness that leads him to peace once more,' said the Wordmaster tenderly. 'But, like love, the truth is a hard thing. To encompass it he must seek what every soul seeks in the journey.'

'What's that?'

'To hold man we build cities with four square walls. To hold water we make crucibles and pots of earthen clay. To hold fire we make circles of stone. But the Chi Dance of the living soul that fills the free air, what can really hold that?'

 64

The Wordmaster bent forward and drew a plain circle with his finger in the sandy floor at the edge of a carpet.

'The soul seeks only be whole. So tell him he must keep to the centre. The Golden Mean.'

The Wordmaster's eyes were closing again and he nearly slumped forward.

'But warn him too. Warn him that he will be betrayed, and by one very close to him. He shall know the tree by its fruit.'

Ashtar's eyes were flickering and Kerbogah was both amazed and terrified.

'But know this too, boy. If the Darkness comes to Barbal, the light shall never be far behind. And it shall appear in . . .'

They did not hear what the Wordmaster had to say for he slumped back completely onto the floor. Kerbogah felt like running away, if there hadn't been such a terrible storm outside.

'Where, man?' said Karleg. 'Where will it appear? Ask him again, Ashtar. Make him tell us.'

Ashtar looked down again at the Wordmaster and there was a ghastly pause that made the Dunetrader boys shiver.

'I can't,' said Ashtar simply. 'He's dead, Karleg. Dead.'

Zorastar the Sun God was high over the desert as the Dunetraders buried the last of the Wordmasters, easily enough in the still sand. There was nothing to mark his grave but the sash that had bound his robe, held in place with a single wooden tent peg. Imlay read another verse from one of the Rubaiyats, about man always returning to the clay from which he comes, as the boys struck the tents and with the women began to load the cargo onto the animals.

Ashtar looked about them solemnly. The sandstorm had died completely but the toll had indeed been high. The wells' throats had all been stopped and sand had got in everywhere.

65

Five camels too had perished and they lay now, covered in sand like little dunes themselves. But more importantly for the Dunetraders, just as Karleg had predicted, all around them the landscape had been altered completely by the strange windstorm. Where before there had simply been one line of dunes, now the hills of sand seemed to stretch for leagues, blocking out the view to the horizon.

'We must be getting on, Ashtar,' said Karleg, as the turbaned traders began to mount their groaning camels. 'And by the sounds of it we need to hurry.'

'Father,' said Kerbogah, who had been thinking of it all night and morning, 'this Marked One. The Wordmaster said that I had to get to him. To help him and protect him from Mardak the Dark.'

Karleg's eyes darkened.

'But we don't know who or where he is, Kerbogah,' said his father softly, smiling at his son. 'Or even if his divination is true. Besides, we have a greater search. For your brother, Kalman. Although I don't know how we shall enter Barbal now our Stardust has gone.'

Ashtar looked grave and he raised his voice to address the others.

'Come, Mahara Dunetraders,' he cried, 'our journey is to Barbal and now we need our own magic. The oldest magic in the world. Dunetrader magic.'

As one, the mounted riders swung their heads to where, somewhere not so far beyond, lay the great walled city of sacred Barbal and the fearful Ziggurat of the Alchemist.

'Sing us a path, men,' cried Ashtar.

The Mahara Dunetraders all raised their hands and yanked down their turbans to expose their mouths. As they began to sing Karleg looked nervously at Ashtar, for at first nothing happened, but then the desert started to move before their strong, proud voices.

 66

'Hutt, hutt!' cried Ashtar, striking his camel which, with a loud grunt, lurched forward down the path of song. The caravan was moving once more, singing its way through the deserts, a thin column of camels and riders winding into the distance towards the Sacred City. Shapes that, as the Mahara Dunetraders got further and further away, seemed to blend into one, before being finally lost all together in the vast immensity of shifting sand.

But as the mysterious Mahara Dunetraders disappeared, and the sun burned high in the heavens, a camel slowed its pace, then, with another tethered behind it on a long leash, it dropped further and further behind, and at last, turning away secretly from the troubled caravan, the rider set his course by the sun overhead. It was none other than the Dunetraders' guide, Ashtar.

Ashtar was not completely unregarded in the desert, for four other men had suddenly come riding out of the heat haze towards the dusty oasis. They were dressed in strange, brightly coloured clothes, quite inappropriate for desert travel, and they carried saddlebags over their shoulders as they rode their camels awkwardly. Their nervous eyes ranged about and suddenly one of them mopped his brow and grunted angrily.

'Jeslas, it's hot!' he cried. 'I can't put up with this much longer. And I'm sick of this endless travelling. That storm nearly finished us off and I wouldn't call these camels exactly comfortable.'

'Then you shouldn't have joined Special Ops, should you?' said the figure riding next to him. He seemed, from the way he spoke at least, to be their leader.

'What, Mandrax? And spend my whole life rattling along through the infernal Underworld to work instead?' said the man. 'Nine to five-thirty, sun in sun out, and in search of nothing in life but a bigger and bigger Groot account. What's the point of that?'

67

'So you thought you'd go adventuring?' said the leader, Mandrax, with very little sympathy. 'Well, I bet you never expected to end up in a place like this.'

'That's just what my father said to me when I was born,' muttered the character at the end of the row of camels. He had a long face and heavy mournful eyes. He was sweating terribly and his name was Habulan. 'Not that I had any real choice about it, did I? Being born, I mean. But where are we really, Mandrax?'

Mandrax's eyes flickered immediately.

'Perhaps I'll reveal that when we reach the Sacred City, Habulan. But for now I'll tell you we are in a place no one has been before. Ever.'

The others looked at each other nervously.

'But come,' said Mandrax, 'let's rest here in the shade a while.'

Mandrax slipped from his camel and the others dismounted too, but Habulan suddenly noticed that Mandrax was holding a round clay object in his hand that was covered in symbols.

'What's that?'

'One of their tablets. I picked it up at that caravanserai. I've just been translating it.'

'What does it say?'

The leader held it up and began to read carefully.

'First basic principles of Barbalonian calculation. One: Divide and rule. Two: All things are rarely equal. Three: Add to the sum of knowledge. Four: Go forth and multiply.'

Habulan started to laugh.

'Wherever we are, they're primitives, Mandrax', he said scornfully.

'Silence, Habulan,' snapped Mandrax immediately. 'We'll have no more ignorant talk like that. You have to start somewhere. Show some respect at least.'

 68

'That storm,' said another of the strange party. 'Do you think it really is Chaos Theory at work?'

'Chaos Theory,' said Habulan thoughtfully, 'developed by some of our most eccentric Sandworkers. Which claims that everything is interconnected, so that even the very smallest events, the flapping of a bird's wings say, or a stone dropped in a pond, can affect things far, far away. Even in other worlds.'

'Other worlds,' whispered another of the party, whose name was Tellor. 'I wish we could contact home.'

'Impossible,' said Mandrax immediately. 'The transfer is too unstable, Tellor. It might take us back before we've even got to Nimrod.'

'He's in this city?' asked Tellor.

'I believe so. There were only two points of entry. Where experiments have been taking place. Barbal City and that caravanserai.'

'This High Priest,' said Habulan, 'Mardak the Dark. Why was he experimenting?'

'He's designing a makina,' whispered Mandrax. 'Probably the only thing in the whole universe that could have brought Nimrod or us lot all the way back here. The Entropoth.'

'The Entropoth,' cried the last of the men in amazement. 'But the Entropoth is mere speculation. It can't be real.'

Mandrax was already rummaging in his saddlebags and he suddenly pulled out a strange glass object. It consisted of two small glass balls, one perched on top of the other, inside a wooden frame, and in the bottom globe was sand. He turned it on its end and put it down on the duneside in front of them, then stood with his hands on his hips.

'There, Deemar.'

'But that's just an old hourglass,' said Deemar, looking at the sand already running from the top globe into the bottom.

'I know,' said Mandrax, 'and they've started to use them

all around Barbal now. It will take precisely one Barbalonian hour for the sand to fall though completely. Simple Sandwork really. You just measure your hole and go on pouring sand through for an hour, then, hey presto, you know how much sand you need.'

'But how do they know how long an hour is yet?' said Tellor. 'Without a watch.'

'They use a sundial, of course,' answered the leader, 'but this ordinary-looking thing is also the blueprint for the Entropoth, ten times the size and far more sophisticated.'

'Sophisticated?' said Deemar, looking extremely doubtful.

'The Entropoth would tell the time more precisely than anything has ever done before in Barbal. For every one of the twelve symbols that the hand of the Sun touches on the Sundial in the square, exactly sixty grains would fall from one chamber into the other. Hourglasses were Ogog's idea initially.'

'Their Lord Alchemist?'

'Yes, if those men we talked to in the caravanserai have their facts right. In his search for how the world really works, Ogog has become very fond of Geometry and Sandwork, of inventions and makinas. But it was Mardak the Dark who saw that they might be turned to more spititual purposes. And a more unusual makina entirely.'

The others looked decidedly disapproving.

'That's why that fool Nimrod was interested in it,' said Tellor.

'Yes, Tellor. The Entropoth, you see, doesn't just tell the time or use ordinary sand. It uses Stardust. SIP.'

Their eyes were sparkling.

'Thus it is much more than an hourglass,' said Mandrax. 'It can show you things, and far more than just the stars.'

'Show you things?' said Habulan.

'Mysteries and great secrets,' whispered the leader,

'harnessed from heaven. Some claim it can unlock the very secrets of the universe itself.'

The men all looked up.

'So we must get to Nimrod as soon as we can. Who knows what damage his presence here has done already.'

Mandrax looked down at the little hourglass. The blueprint for the Entropoth.

'But come. We'd better get a move on. The sands of time are running out.'

'What secrets can the Entropoth reveal though, Mandrax?' said Habulan, as they mounted again.

'Mardak the Dark is ambitious,' answered Mandrax gravely. 'Very ambitious indeed. He searches for the fabled Turnstones and other agents of wonder. But the High Priest of Barbal, in his battle with the Lord Alchemist, really seeks the final Alchemical Proof.'

'The Final Proof?' said Habulan in amazement.

'That's right, Habulan,' said Mandrax calmly, as their camels stood licking their lips in the great Mahara Desert. 'The Final Alchemical Proof for the existence of the Creator.'

BANISHMENT

In little Ederyl the Sun God was falling fast over the lesson house as Silas Root crept in secret up the hill to find his new friend. He was carrying a basket full of food secured from the local rest house and he looked about him nervously as he went. He was still feeling drowsy and a little shaky too. Silas had fallen asleep that afternoon, while his mother Alara was cleaning their home and he had had a very strange dream. Silas was walking in the desert under a heavy yellow sun and ahead of him had stood a great tent of pure white, the entrance flapping gently in the breeze. Silas Root had suddenly heard a voice from within.

'Enter,' it had whispered.

Even in sleep Silas seemed aware of some distant story that he had heard of a tent at the very centre of the universe and, lifting the flap, he had stepped inside. But as Silas had looked around the tent there had been no one there.

'But I do exist, you know,' the voice had said gently, and

 72

it had been outside the tent and all around him too. 'You just have to look for me in the right place.'

It was five suns since Silas had found the strange white stone and felt the presence of the demon. Since he had met Ramset too. Every day he had gone out in secret to take Ramset food. Much of the commotion in the valleys had died down for, although the Childar Elders had searched everywhere, they had seen nothing more of the intruder.

But on the hills the beacon fires of Ederyl were still lit, for they had all felt the Pazgog's coming and other rumours had begun to circulate of dark doings, fed by the sand blowing in over the mountains from a terrible storm in the desert. The Childars and the Elders were very nervous.

Silas had begun to grow afraid too that someone would find out that he had helped a foreigner, and the only person he had confided in about Ramset and the Pazgog was Rarza Stormheart. Of course, Rarza had accused Silas of telling stories again, so Silas had told her to meet him that same night up at the lesson house.

'Ramset?' whispered Silas, as he pushed open the lesson house door again. 'Are you here, Ramset?'

Silas had told the foreigner not to go outside in the daylight, but the lesson room was empty and Silas put down the basket irritably.

'Ramset?'

As Silas walked towards a door at the back of the lesson house he suddenly felt that warm feeling in his smock pocket. His stone was glowing gently again. The door opened on the room where the young Childars would use a special wheel to make pots and jugs out of river clay. There was no one in the little room, just the throwing wheel and the shelves lined with any number of awkwardly shaped creations. Some were plain and ordinary, others more imaginative, with little shapes and faces worked into them.

Silas was about to turn round again when he blinked. For an instant Silas fancied the last pot on the shelf had just winked at him. The pot was a plain-looking thing, although the side was defined by a little wizened face, with thick lips and a sharply pointed nose. Silas shook his head and he was about to walk away, when suddenly those lips most definitely moved.

'Well then, Silas Root,' came a small, chirping voice, 'are you ready yet?'

Silas stepped back in utter astonishment.

'What the demon . . . ?' he stammered.

The pot looked back at him and winked again.

'What's the matter?' it said cheerfully. 'Don't you believe in magic? Didn't you see what happened with that stone of yours?'

Silas's mouth opened and shut like a fish. How on earth did a pot know about his stone? For that matter, how on earth could a pot be talking?

'Yes,' Silas answered. 'Of course I believe in magic.'

'Then you can't be surprised by a talking pot, can you, Silas Root? Around Barbal, anyway, nothing is quite as it seems.'

'Isn't it?' said Silas.

'Oh no, Silas Root. But who's the potter and who the pot?' squeaked the face cheerfully, clearly delighted by Silas's amazement. 'That's what we all want to know, really. Even if the answer can be most elusive. Although, if you really think about it, it's all a question of design.'

The pot grinned mysteriously at Silas from its shelf.

'But never mind that now. You'll need your wits about you soon enough.'

Silas was just thinking he had lost his wits completely.

'Why?' he asked. 'Who are you?'

The stone was getting warmer and warmer in his smock and the pot grinned cheekily.

'You might as well ask where I am,' it answered. 'That's a far better question, and I always find questions so much more valuable than answers, don't you? I mean, if you ask the wrong question, how will you ever find the right answer, fool?'

It was just the sort of thing Sultan Ash had been so fond of saying to the Childars in the lesson house, especially on exam days. But Silas almost wanted to pick it up and smash it for being so rude.

'If you must know, though,' said the pot merrily, 'I'm a gatekeeper and one day you'll understand just how important they are. As important as keys. As important as knowledge itself, perhaps. But for now you may call me Hermet, though some call me Hermes and others Mercurius.'

'Hermet?' cried Silas, suddenly remembering the History. 'Hermet the Messenger?'

'I said so, didn't I?' said the pot a little indignantly. 'I thought you might need a friend. So I've come to warn you.'

'Warn me?'

'About Mardak the Dark. The High Priest hunts you. And I'm here to give you some good advice about Barbal. You're going there, aren't you?'

'No,' answered Silas. 'Childars aren't allowed beyond the borders. The Elders say so.'

'Oh, I think you are,' said the pot. 'The call to adventure has come, Silas Root. So I've come to tell you there is real trouble in Barbal City. Zolos, Captain Lord of the Barbalissaries, has murdered the Wordmasters under Mardak's orders and taken Ogog prisoner. Mardak the Dark builds a magic hourglass, the Entropoth, while he seeks the ultimate proof for the existence of the Creator.'

Silas's mouth was hanging open again.

'He's looking for God?' said Silas in disbelief.

'Exactly. And Zolos uses the Pazgog to steal souls to make an army of Grasht too, when it isn't hunting you. While at the Great Solstice,' said the Pot gravely, 'Mardak will sacrifice Ogog and enthrone himself as the new Lord Alchemist.'

Silas's heart was beating furiously. The Solstices were always worshipped as holy days in Ederyl too.

'The Solstice?' said Silas. 'But that's in seven suns' time.'

'Quite, Silas Root. At precisely midday it's curtains for Ogog, if you don't hurry.'

'Are you a God?' asked Silas.

'Are you?' said the pot.

Silas looked taken aback.

'But, Mardak,' he whispered, 'you said he hunts me. Why?'

'He wants your stone. Like Stardust, Mardak needs its magic Chi to build the Entropoth. And it has very powerful magic indeed. Though there are other interesting ingredients to the Entropoth.'

Silas put his hand to his smock pocket and he was just about to ask about the stone when the pot piped up again.

'You'll have to go to Barbal if you want to learn the great secret too.'

'Great secret?'

'For an age now, they say, there has been some great mystery about Barbal City,' whispered the pot, rolling its strange clay eyes lugubriously and winking at Silas again, 'which the Lord Alchemists have been trying to keep at all costs. After all, they love their secrets, do Alchemists. Some secret about the magic Chi that turns the Waterwheel.'

Silas stepped even closer to the pot.

'Mardak the Dark,' he whispered. 'What does he look like, Hermet?'

As soon as he asked it, the pot's eyes seemed to bore into Silas Root's soul.

'That I don't know. That none know. Mardak always had a fear of being known and in the Ziggurat he wears a golden mask, to keep his face secret from his enemies. The Mask of Tulon. They say his features are hideous, though. His face was badly burnt in one of his experiments and a horrible scar distorts Mardak's mouth. It happened when he was trying a Resurrection.'

'Resurrection?' said Silas.

'That art that the Mystifier of Khem studies above all things,' said the pot, 'using Alchemy to bring things back from the dead.'

Silas was shaking with excitement now, wondering who Mardak had tried to bring back from the dead.

'Reliable information. There's no more valuable commodity, even in Barbal Bazaar. That's what youngsters really need in life, don't you think?' said the pot merrily. 'Not to be crammed full with your Elders' silly rules and beliefs, which, after all, change all the time, but valuable information. Especially about how things really work.'

Silas nodded stupidly, wondering how things really did work, especially this talking pot. The pot's remark about parents suddenly made Silas think of how Rarza Stormheart's mother and father were always scolding her and it made him cross for his friend.

'Well,' said the pot suddenly, 'I am a messenger, so is there anything else you want to ask me?'

There was lots Silas wanted to ask the strange messenger, especially where he had really come from, but another thought popped into his head.

'Ogog,' he said suddenly. 'Is it true that he no longer believes in Magic. Is that why Mardak the Dark so hates him?'

'Something like that,' answered the pot. 'Although Ogog

does believe in a kind of magic. He believes in Sandwork for a start. And that's very powerful magic, if you really understand numbers. Number Magic.'

'Is it?' said Silas.

'Oh yes. Mardak on the other hand upholds the power of dreams and holy prayers to gather the secrets of the heavens. Sacrifice too and the black arts. How they both hope to rule in Barbal is a bit of a paradox.'

Silas tilted his head at the new word.

'Something that seems contradictory,' explained the pot. 'And I really have no time for someone who doesn't understand the nature of a paradox, let alone the Great Paradox itself. But perhaps it'll help you learn about a very deep mystery indeed. Language, and why it is just as magical as Sandwork.'

'Please,' said Silas, 'will you stop talking in riddles?'

'Suit yourself,' said the pot, 'and I'd better be off anyway, for you have important things to do. Don't worry, I'm here to help in the search.'

'Search?'

'For the Final Alchemical Proof, of course. Of where you and I come from. And Silas, don't trust anyone. I will return.'

'Stop,' cried Silas. 'Wait.'

The pot had stopped talking though and no matter what Silas asked it would say nothing more. Silas's mind was in a whirl and he was furious that the Messenger had gone, for there was so much more he wanted to know. What his stone really was for a start. But as he looked at the dull clay vessel Silas began to wonder if he had been dreaming and at last he stuck out his tongue at the useless thing and went back into the lesson room to look for Ramset.

As soon as he came in the door opened and there stood Rarza Stormheart, in the coming twilight. Silas wanted to tell her what had just happened but the Childar girl was looking sceptically around the lesson room as she stepped inside.

'Well, Silas,' she said, putting her hands to her hips, 'where is he, then? This famous scribe of yours. This Warrior Priest.'

'I don't know,' answered Silas, blushing. 'Ramset's gone.'

'Oh come on, Silas,' said Rarza a little angrily. 'Stop telling lies. I know you're bored sometimes and sad about your father . . .'

'I'm not telling lies,' snapped Silas indignantly, 'and will you stop talking about my father? Ramset did come to Ederyl from Khem looking for a special Word. My stone did fall through my pocket and drive away a demon and just now a magic pot . . .'

'Magic,' said Rarza rather scornfully. 'Why are you always going on about magic? I think you should face up to real life sometimes.'

Silas was furious and he would have told his friend about Hermet but suddenly something happened that shut them both up. They heard a cry, an angry, hungry, evil cry that Silas knew only too well and in the coming darkness Rarza felt it too. That sickening fear all around them.

'The demon,' hissed Silas. 'Quick, Rarza, under the table.'

Rarza hardly needed to be persuaded as Silas dived under the lesson-room table, for the shadow of flapping wings was falling through the windows of the lesson house. As Silas knelt on all fours, though, Rarza Stormheart looked at her friend in utter astonishment. All around Silas Root a strange white light was spilling out through his smock pocket.

'What the . . . ?'

'I told you, Rarza,' said Silas angrily. 'It's my stone. It happened the last time that Pazgog thing came. Mardak the Dark wants it.'

'Mardak?' whispered Rarza nervously. 'What's going on, Silas?'

'I don't quite know yet,' answered Silas, 'but I've got to get to Barbal.'

'Barbal? But you said yourself we can't . . .'

'I've got to, Rarza,' insisted Silas. 'Somehow. Otherwise Mardak will sacrifice Ogog at the Great Solstice, in just seven suns' time. Terrible things are happening in the Sacred City.'

'What things?' asked the girl nervously.

When Silas had finished telling her about the Pazgog and the Underworld and Mardak and the Entropoth, Rarza was shaking uncontrollably, and wondering how on earth her friend knew all this. But suddenly there was a crash and the lesson house door flew open again. The children peered at one another in terror.

'Mardak,' whispered Silas.

But Silas had recognized the thick foreign accent.

'Silas. Where are you, Silas?'

The shadow of the Pazgog had passed again and under the table the light in the stone had just faded. Silas popped it back into his smock pocket.

'Ramset, we're down here.'

Quickly the huge, dark-skinned foreigner with his black-rimmed eyes was kneeling beside them too. Rarza felt like an utter fool and looked very guiltily at Silas for having doubted him.

'Who's this?' asked Ramset warily.

'My friend Rarza. It's all right. We can trust her.'

Rarza smiled awkwardly at the foreigner.

'The demon, Silas,' whispered the Scribe. 'I was outside when it came again. Then I saw a strange light in here.'

'But what were you doing, Ramset?' whispered Silas, still not wanting to reveal much about his stone. 'I told you to stay . . .'

'Praying,' answered Ramset. 'Praying to the great Sun God, Rahr. I was doing the Chi Dance.'

'You mean Zorastar,' corrected Rarza politely under the table, wondering what a Chi Dance was.

Ramset smiled darkly at the Childars.

'In the land I come from we worship the sun as Rahr. Or sometimes Ammon–Rahr, blessed be his name,' said Ramset. 'And, if you are really interested in mastering Alchemy, first you must learn a very basic piece of magic, crucial in the art of changing one thing into another. You must learn to translate.'

'What is the Chi Dance?' asked Rarza.

'It was given to the Wordmasters by the Gods themselves at the dawn of the desert,' answered the Warrior Priest proudly. 'A secret form of fighting, and prayer too, to keep off Sandspirits, but without swords or spears or daggers. And the way not only for Wordmasters and Scribes to defend the Alchemists, but their own Chi Shield too. Perhaps I'll teach it to you one sun.'

'Chi Shield?' said Rarza, none the wiser.

Ramset lifted his hand and held it up to Rarza's cheek.

'Can you feel anything?' he asked.

He hadn't actually touched Rarza's face and she shook her head.

'It takes sensitivity,' said the Scribe, moving his hand closer but still not touching Rarza's cheek. 'There.'

'It feels warm,' said Rarza suddenly.

'Exactly. Chi. It's in everything, children. And we've all a Chi Shield around us to protect us from the forces of darkness. Guard that at all costs.'

Silas thought of his stone and its strange heat.

'But what is Chi?' asked Silas.

'None know, Silas,' answered Ramset. 'But the Mystifier, the Alchemist of Khem, believes that it is pure spirit.'

The fear inside them was dwindling and it was clear that the Pazgog had gone. They climbed up from under the table, when suddenly they heard another sound outside and Ramset started. His hands came up in front of his face immediately and, pirouetting on one leg, he span round.

'Elders,' he hissed. 'Can they have found out I'm hiding here?'

Ramset looked suspiciously at Rarza, and they all stepped backwards as they heard a pair of heavy, booted feet stomping up the lesson-house steps. Ramset seemed ready to fight, weapons or no, but as the handle turned and the door swung open, the Childars saw the most astonishing thing they had seen all day. It wasn't an Elder at all. There, before them, was a Mahara Dunetrader.

'Ashtar,' he cried, dropping his hands.

Ashtar looked back at him with those smiling blue-green eyes.

'Well, well. It's been a long time, Ramset, since we travelled together with the Dunetraders and I tried to teach you Barbalonian and a little of Barbal's ways.'

'But what are you doing here, Ashtar?'

'I might ask you the same thing, my friend,' said the turbaned guide. 'It's strange to see you in a forbidden land like Ederyl.'

'The Mystifier, the Alchemist of Khem. He has long been spying on the lands around Barbal,' said Ramset guiltily.

Ashtar's eyes twinkled just as they had done in the desert.

'Spying, Ramset? How?'

'Astral journeying. In his sleep the Mystifier sends out his spirit in the shape of animals to spy on the wide world. The hawk, the scarab beetle, the dreadful hippopotamus. But in Barbal it was a chameleon. So he heard of a word of great power, Ashtar. One that suddenly appeared in the Sacred

City. He tracked it here and then visited me in a dream to order me to fetch it.'

'Well, there's no time for that now, Ramset. I've come to get you all away.'

'Us all?' whispered Silas, looking at Rarza in bewilderment.

'Of course, Silas Root.'

'But who are you?' said Silas. 'And how do you know my . . .'

Ashtar pulled at his turban. In a single sweep the cloth fell from his head and mouth. It looked like a snake uncoiling. Silas and Rarza nearly leapt backwards in surprise.

Before them was no longer an Elder or a Mahara Dunetrader at all, but their very own Lesson Master, Sultan Ash. Sultan Ash's eagle-like eyes seemed to take in everything over the beak of his hooked nose, and they looked at the young friends now with an expression that might have been amusement or disapproval. You could never quite tell with the Lesson Master.

'Sultan,' cried Silas wonderingly.

'Sultan?' grunted Ramset.

'Hello, Silas Root,' said the Lesson Master warmly, striding further into the lesson room. 'Good evening, Rarza Stormheart.'

Ramset was shaking his head in utter bewilderment.

'You are changed, Ashtar,' he growled, 'since I last saw you with the Mahara Dunetraders.'

'And all is change,' said the Lesson Master cheerfully, in a deep, rich voice that was ripe with humour. 'But there's work to be done. *Hurry, hurry — never worry — time is moving in a flurry.*'

Silas and Rarza both felt the thrill that they always did when in the presence of the Lesson Master.

'And we must certainly hurry if we are to use that

Turnstone you found weeding the temple yard, Silas Root,' said Sultan Ash, 'if the light I just saw coming from the lesson house when the Pazgog came is anything to go by.'

'A Turnstone,' cried Ramset, rounding on Silas in astonishment. Silas was just as amazed.

'That's right. Give it to me, Silas.'

Silas was wondering how on earth Sultan Ash knew that he had found a stone in the temple yard but he pulled it from his smock and gave it to the Lesson Master. Rarza Stormheart went bright red.

'Behold,' cried Sultan Ash, holding it up before them. 'For centuries the Alchemists waited for the Two to return. And this is one of the stones of true power. One of the ancient Turnstones themselves. Gol the Magnificent.'

Rarza's eyes were filled with wonder, but Silas felt a little sick.

'The Pazgog,' Ramset whispered, marvelling too at the fabled stone. 'That's what drove the demon away? The Lightbearer?'

Silas blushed, since he had kept it hidden from Ramset. But he nodded at the Warrior Priest.

'It lit up the whole wood,' Silas whispered, 'and frightened off the Pazgog. When I found it I'd just recited the first line of the Alcemoth and it dropped straight through my pocket.'

'Ah yes, and like the most advanced Sandwork,' said Sultan Ash, 'the Turnstones are most elusive. They're always trying to get away. So be careful of it, Silas. Gol has very great power. And now Mardak the Dark wants it for himself.'

'But what can Gol do?' asked Silas, almost frightened to touch it again.

'Drive out the darkness for a start,' answered Sultan. 'But different things too. You will see soon enough. But beware,

 84

Silas Root. The stones of deep power will call to each other too, the black to the white.'

Silas's hands were suddenly hot and clammy.

'Yet that may teach you something of what any hero must confront in his journey. Something that will tell you much of Alchemy too. Especially in Khem, the land of the Two Kingdoms. The Upper and Lower Realms.'

'What?' asked Silas, wondering nervously why Sultan was suddenly talking about heroes.

'Dualism, Silas. The points between which all things travel. Day and night. Dark and light. Good and bad. Opposites.'

Sultan paused and for a moment seemed reluctant to give the stone back to Silas, but he quickly handed it over to him.

'Now then. You're ready, aren't you?' he said. 'We must hurry across the desert to sacred Barbal, if we are to free Ogog and stop this sacrifice.'

'Me? But why me?' said Silas.

'You found the Lightbearer, didn't you? Or perhaps I should say, the Lightbearer found you. Consequently you must bear it.'

Sultan's eyes flickered mysteriously again and Silas trembled. All his life he had wanted to travel to Barbal, but this was far more than he had ever bargained for.

'I can't. The Elders say I've got to weed the temple yard.'

'Oh, that nonsense can wait,' said Sultan, smiling indulgently. 'Besides, do you enjoy it?'

'Don't be silly. Of course I don't.'

'Well, if something's wrong just change it,' said Sultan, putting his hand on Silas's shoulder and beaming at the others. 'Simple. Besides, you haven't really got a choice.'

'What do you mean?' said Silas. 'Of course I've got a choice. It's my life, isn't it?'

'I'm terribly sorry, Silas Root,' answered Sultan quietly,

although the bizarre Lesson Master was smiling again and he didn't seem a bit sorry. 'Before I came up here I went to the council house. The Elders have gathered this very evening to open the Wordbox formally and examine that word you so impudently tried to look at at the Wordfeast.'

'The Word?' said Ramset immediately. 'What is it?'

'I don't know, Ramset. That the Elders wouldn't tell me. But they were debating something else too. You, Silas Root. In their wisdom, they have finally decided on how to punish you for breaking their commandments and setting fire to their tent. Banishment from Ederyl.'

Silas swayed backwards and Rarza looked at her friend in horror. It was as if Silas had suddenly been struck or the very ground beneath his feet in the lesson house were moving. He was banished from his lovely home. Cast out of Ederyl. Silas wondered what on earth his mother Alara would say.

'But if Mardak and the Pazgog hunt the Turnstone, Ashtar,' said Ramset suddenly, 'then why go to Barbal? Won't we be walking straight into the lion's den?'

Something flickered in Sultan's strange eyes.

'I'm afraid so, Ramset. But according to Chaos Theory nowhere is safe any more and the High Priest will hardly expect you to bring him the Lightbearer, will he now, Silas? Hide in plain sight, eh?'

Silas felt his heart stir. It was strangely exhilarating, the thought of Barbal and a magic hourglass, of what the pot had said about the sacrifice and the Underworld. In that instant he was decided.

'All right,' he cried, 'I'll come. What else can I do?'

Sultan seemed very pleased. Almost relieved.

'Good lad. I knew you wouldn't let me down.'

'But, Ashtar, who are you really?' asked Ramset, looking strangely at the Lesson Master. 'I mean, I know you as the guide Ashtar, but these Childars . . .'

Sultan held up his hand.

'Let's just say, Ramset, that I'm on special commission from the Hooded Master. The leader of the entire Order of Alchemists in the Seven Lands.'

Sultan raised that golden eyebrow and grinned again, mysteriously.

'By ancient custom the Hooded Master is not allowed to intervene directly in the affairs of the Alchemists in the different lands, but he always keeps a hand in. I've spent many years travelling under his sanction. I've seen much and made many useful friends, and learnt above all the value of a change of clothes. All along I have been working on a very secret mission.'

'Mission?' said Rarza.

'To end the Great Schism once and for all, Rarza,' said Sultan portentously. 'To heal the ancient rift between dreams, prayers and prophecies and the great arts of Sandwork, of reason, calculation and observation. Fed by the doubts that sometimes flourish about the existence of a Creator. The answers lie somewhere inside the Ziggurat.'

Silas took a tight hold of Gol, the stone, and Rarza was thrilled that their very own Lesson Master was in fact some kind of secret agent.

'Now we should be going,' he said.

'But the Wordbox,' insisted Ramset. 'If it's in the council house, as you say, I couldn't go there openly but you . . .'

'There is no time,' said Sultan immediately. 'Besides, Ramset, there will be a copy below the Ziggurat, in the Room of Changes. All the icons are there. It's imperative we reach Barbal before the Great Solstice.'

'When Mardak plans to sacrifice Ogog and enthrone himself,' said Silas, 'in just seven suns' time.'

'I see you know much already, young man,' said Sultan, smiling approvingly. 'I wonder who you've been talking to, but it helps us a great deal. But this is rather more serious than a mere sacrifice, Silas, messy as that might be. At the Great Solstice Mardak the Dark's shall be a double enthronement.'

'Double?' whispered Rarza.

'If my hunch is right, Rarza, Mardak will use the blood sacrifice to call forth Aspis himself from the Underworld.'

Silas and Rarza looked as if they wanted to turn and run.

'Aspis?' said Ramset.

'In his search for the Creator,' cried Sultan, 'Mardak the Dark not only builds an Entropoth but plans to bring forth the Creator's opposite. The Destroyer. He plans to crown the Lord of the Underworld himself. The Uncrowned King of Night.'

The darkness seemed to thicken around them and Rarza suddenly felt faint. Sultan eyed Silas with amusement but he addressed Rarza.

'Now then, Rarza, what about you? You're coming to help your friend, aren't you, my dear?'

'Me?' cried Rarza, perking up immediately. 'Oh, yes please. If Silas is banished, then so am I.'

'But she can't,' said Silas. 'She's just a girl and it's against all our commandments, and a sin.'

Rarza glared at Silas and he dropped his eyes.

'Don't be so old-fashioned, Silas,' said the Lesson Master sternly. 'We'll all ride hard over the hills to the edge of Ederyl and the Mahara Desert. I've calculated enough water and provisions to get us safely to the Elusive Camel, before we reach Barbal.'

The Childars shivered with excitement. They had heard many mysterious rumours of the Camel. It was a caravanserai, a kind of rest house, perhaps the most famous of any. It lay somewhere in the Mahara Desert, near Barbal City, victualling the Dunetraders' caravans and others who came to seek work and passage through the sands.

'Come then,' said Sultan. 'Our mounts await.'

Sultan turned but he stopped suddenly and his eyes ranged the room. They fell on the book on the table, the one Silas had looked at when he had first sneaked into the lesson house. The History.

'Fetch me that, would you, Rarza, my dear?'

Rarza collected it.

'I'm not leaving this behind,' said Sultan, taking it fondly. 'My History contains knowledge and information of very great value indeed.'

Rarza was looking keenly at the book but Silas was staring at the Mappa Mysticum behind them.

'Barbal,' he whispered, 'I can hardly believe we're really going to Barbal.'

They all stood there, regarding the picture of the known world.

'Sultan,' said Rarza suddenly, 'I've always wondered. Why is Pengalis all on its own like that? In a circle.'

The Lesson Master's eyes flickered.

'Because, Rarza,' he answered, 'Pengalis doesn't exist yet.'

'Doesn't exist? Then why's it there?'

'Because the Mappa Mysticum Mundorum is a truly mystical map. "Pengalis" means everything that hasn't been discovered, named or even thought of yet. But come. It's time we got going.'

Sultan swept round and opened the door to the lesson house. Rarza gasped delightedly as they stepped into the moonlight. In the middle of little Ederyl, two camels stood there, chewing on their great leathery lips. They were piled high with bulging waterskins and packs loaded with wood for a desert crossing. Blankets too were heaped on their humped backs and the Childars wondered what they were for in the heat. Sultan went over and began to pull out some new clothes: robes, and long rope belts.

'You'll need to disguise yourselves,' he said. 'Especially a Childar girl. We mustn't draw attention to ourselves as we travel. It's enough with the Pazgog on our heels.'

As they changed, and Rarza and Silas looked at each other, they both burst out laughing. They looked liked little wizards.

'Silas,' said Sultan. 'You can ride behind me on my camel. Ramset can take Rarza.'

Sultan went over to one of the camels and whispered something in its ear. Almost immediately the strange creature grunted and sank to its knees.

'Now, try to hold on,' said Sultan Ash, when at last they were all mounted. 'And no sloth, eh, children? That's a sin too, according to the Seven Commandments anyway, the commandments Mardak has broken.'

'But, Sultan?' said Silas, trying to keep his balance behind him on the strange animal and wondering what all the Commandments were. 'How did you know? To come back to Ederyl, I mean?'

Sultan chuckled.

'You want that solution, eh? Well, the Alchemists are very interested in all sorts of solutions and balms, Silas, just as they are in changing one thing into another. Trust me, there will be plenty of time for an answer, though,' he cried, kicking their camel on.

As Ramset's camel came after him and the Scribe's bolt of hair swung in the wind the two Childars found themselves bouncing along in the direction of the council house. The beacon fires of Ederyl were still burning brightly on the hills as the little party moved off through the valleys. Sultan kept up a steady pace and soon they were climbing the slopes of Ederyl's great hills.

They travelled all night and near dawn Sultan slowed his

camel as they saw a fire burning before them. It was the last of the beacon fires of Ederyl. They were nearing the borders of the little land. Sultan felt Silas tense up behind him and came to a halt as the flames blazed in the Childar night.

'You love fire, Silas, don't you?' he cried.

'What's wrong with that?' said Silas a little defensively, but he grinned as he remembered the tent and what he had done at the Elders' feast when he had tried to open the Wordbox.

'Nothing at all. Fire can show you many marvellous things and aspiring apprentices like you need to discover not only the nature of fire, Silas, but of the Four.'

'The Four?' said Silas, feeling very pleased that his Lesson Master had just called him an aspiring apprentice.

'Fire and Earth, Air and Water. Although fire of course is the very greatest catalyst.'

'Catalyst?'

'A word of great power too. Like so many names.'

'Names?'

'In Khem the Mystifier teaches that only by naming may you have power over a thing, remember. And it is after Khem that the work of the Order really takes its name: Al-Khem-Y.'

'Oh,' said Silas, looking towards Ramset but not really seeing at all. The flames were sending long red shadows dancing over their taut faces.

'And in the distant land of Jesladom,' said Sultan cheerfully, 'the word "Khemia" gives its name to something that will really set the lions among the peacocks, one sun: Khemistry. The very beginnings of science and the scientific method.'

'What does "Catalyst" mean, though?' asked Silas, wondering what 'Science' meant too.

'It's something that makes other things happen,' laughed Sultan, kicking their camel on again. 'Like me.'

They climbed higher and higher and the light began to soften towards morning when Sultan stopped the camels again and pointed. Below them in the valley five figures were moving towards the council house on horseback. They were only vague shapes in the shadows, but clearly in a very great hurry.

'Others are on the move,' said Sultan, 'and not Childars by the look of them. What business can they have in peaceful little Ederyl?'

'Mardak?' whispered Silas fearfully.

Higher still they went, and Silas and Rarza sensed that they were close to the borders of their land. As the light suddenly came they all looked back over the hidden valleys. To Silas and Rarza, peaceful Ederyl seemed like one great, glorious garden.

They journeyed on, winding along a rough path towards the mountain top. The trees around them had become sparse and spiky, with few leaves, and the earth too was becoming sandy. It was in marked contrast to the lovely vision they had just beheld and Ramset kept shaking his head.

'What is it, Ramset?' called Sultan.

'When I came through these parts, Ashtar, there was much more vegetation. And listen.'

The Childars dropped their hoods and lifted their heads but could hear nothing at all.

'Silence,' whispered Rarza, behind the Scribe.

'That's just the problem, child. The birds and the animals seem to have fled in fear.'

Sultan nodded in the eerie stillness.

'The storm must have done it, Ramset, but it's as if the desert is spreading beneath the Pazgog's wings.' Sultan's whispering voice seemed to fill the spaces. 'And chaos with it. The Destroyer awakes.'

Even as he said it they crested the summit and came to the

top of Ederyl's last mountain. What lay beyond made Rarza Stormheart gasp in amazement. Below them lay the open desert. Beyond a single scraggy bush, twisted and gnarled by the wind and clinging to a rock, there was nothing at all, just a winding drop of barren cliffs and then, as far as the naked eye could see, nothing but sand and grit and the distant line of dunes or hazy mountains, shimmering far away in the blue-grey mist of morning. It was the great Mahara Desert.

'Come,' cried Sultan Ash. 'The desert awaits.'

Ramset seemed most reluctant to move.

'It is no longer safe for man nor beast out there, Ashtar,' said the Scribe, clutching one of the strange jewels at his throat as though they might protect him from the vastness of it all. 'With the Dunetrader wars. And the Pazgog.'

'But we must cross it, Ramset,' said Sultan quietly, 'for beyond that inferno, and the creatures that inhabit it, lies ancient Barbal.'

Silas shuddered and thought of the stories he had heard from his parents of Sandspirits. But Rarza found herself thinking of the mythical creatures she had heard about in the stories learnt on her mother's knee, especially in the distant land of Heleras, the land of Centaurs. Like Winged Packonies and One-eyed Giants, like the Anthropophagons, who fed on human flesh, and the Solopods, men who walked on one gigantic foot.

'But don't be too frightened,' said Sultan Ash. 'Remember, I'm a Dunetrader guide also, and a master of Sandlaw.'

YAHARLARS

A half moon was rising as Karleg, old Imlay and the poet Khayarumi led their camels before the winding Dunetrader caravan. Karleg was furious with their guide for abandoning them so mysteriously after the Wordmasters' fearful news. Karleg would never have suspected Ashtar of such open cowardice or desertion. Since the accident in the storm the caravan didn't have any Stardust either to pay Mardak's tribute with and Karleg had been wondering all the while how they would even enter Barbal to find his elder son.

The Dunetraders were near their destination, though, passing a great stone quarry, littered with boulders, where ancient workmen had long laboured to hew rocks for the building of the Sacred City. In the moonlight Kerbogah blinked as he rode next to his best friend Farjay. He had seen little sparks of blue on the ground. At first he thought they were stones but he suddenly realized they were moving in the sand. They were beetles.

As they passed beyond the quarry they suddenly caught

sight of Barbal. The city's huge mudbrick walls reared before them and seemed to dwarf the dusty, moonlit plain. Even from here they could see a great line of people and camels snaking towards one of Barbal's four huge arched gates.

'Bravo, Karleg!' cried Imlay, pulling his turban from his mouth. 'We've made it, man, and without that blasted traitor. Unlike those poor fools caught in the storm.'

The sun after leaving the oasis they had come on the Dunetraders that Ashtar and his son had spotted riding into the storm. They had all been dead. Choked by sand. Despite the wars and the growing hatred among the caravans, Karleg couldn't help but feel sorry for them.

Kerbogah and Farjay were trembling at the sight of Barbal, and Kerbogah thought of what the Wordmaster had told him in the tent. He'd been brooding on who this Marked One was and how on earth he would warn him. He wanted to find an answer in the City of Soothsaying.

But now Kerbogah was suddenly filled with thoughts of a far closer search: finding his brother, Kalman.

It was what lay to the side of the city, though, rising from one of the walls, which astounded the boys.

'See there,' cried Imlay. 'The holy Ziggurat.'

'Look, Relak,' said Kerbogah, lifting himself on his camel and holding up his little mouse to show him the mighty temple. Right around the gigantic walls stood armed Barbalissaries.

As they rode on, the Dunetrader caravan suddenly came into the shadow of three wooden towers that distracted them from even the awesome Ziggurat. They were topped with a terrible sight: piles of bones and skeletons, above which desert vultures cawed and wheeled in the free air, swooping to pick at the bits of flesh left on these once living, breathing bodies or knocking and rattling against the drying bones.

'Camel's blood, Relak!' whispered Kerbogah, dizzy and

sick at the sight. 'Remember what the Wordmaster said of Mardak and the ancient ways. It's human sacrifice.'

The desert mouse twitched its nose but Karleg was gazing at the towers with a melancholy eye.

'Not sacrifice, Kerbogah,' he said. 'Not this anyway. Barbalonians leave their dead beyond the city to be cleaned by the sun and wind, before their souls, purified by the air and heat, will be taken again into Lol's bosom. They're called the Towers of Silence.'

As the camel train paused below the towers a strange sound came to their ears. And a group of people came hurrying through the sands in the moonlight. They were dressed plainly and the women among them were making the most horrible wailing.

'The Pazgog!' cried one, as they passed. 'Flee for your lives. It steals our men. Turns them into Grasht to serve Zolos and the Barbalissaries. Or feeds on human flesh.'

They all looked up fearfully into the night. Clouds were racing against the glittering stars above the Towers of Silence and a vulture screeched in the night sky.

'We'd better not be out in the open, Karleg,' said Imlay.

'We must hurry to the city.'

'You won't get in yet,' cried a man in the frightened party. 'Zolos has imposed a curfew from dusk till dawn. For the Barbalonians' own safety, he claims. To keep them in their beds while the Pazgog hunts for his army of soulless ones, among the villagers and common folk.'

'But those people . . .' said Karleg, looking out towards Barbal and the lines of camel trains snaking towards it.

'I know,' said the man. 'They won't be allowed into the bazaar until morning, but they'd rather take their chance with that thing than miss the Solstice, or Mardak's enthronement. Well, good luck to them. And to you too. Barbal has become an evil place now Ogog is imprisoned and the light of reason and Sandwork is extinguished forever from the Sacred City.'

'Then we will halt the train,' announced Karleg, as the frightened travellers moved on, 'and watch the skies until dawn draws closer.'

The Dunetraders began to dismount and establish their watch and soon fires were burning brightly near the Towers of Silence. Farjay had picked up a stone to place in his sling, ready for an attack and he and Kerbogah stood quietly near Karleg and Selera, watching the reassuring flames and wondering about all they'd heard. But after a while Kerbogah left Farjay poking at the fire and found himself wandering away. Kerbogah was suddenly more excited than frightened. He wanted to get a better look at Barbal and the Ziggurat beyond.

As Kerbogah and Relak walked together into the shadows, away from the train, they heard a strange sound in the night. A kind of low moaning. Kerbogah saw a little light ahead in the darkness. It was coming from another fire, burning on its own. As Kerbogah drew closer he saw a figure seated on a log, looking into the flames. Kerbogah suddenly started.

'It can't be, Relak.'

Kerbogah was sure that he knew the shape of that face.

'Kalman,' he called, trembling as he drew closer. 'Is it you, Kalman?'

The boy said nothing but Relak was making a strange, nervous squeaking.

'Kalman. It's me. Kerbogah. Your brother.'

As Kerbogah got even nearer he stopped and sighed sadly. It wasn't his brother at all. The lad, maybe thirteen years old, looked a bit like Kalman but he had long, unkempt hair and ragged, dirty clothes, not like a Dunetrader at all. Kerbogah drew closer still, wondering what on earth he was doing out here in the desert, and as he did so his boot scuffed a rock.

The stranger turned immediately. To Kerbogah's amazement he saw that the boy's eyes were clamped tight shut and that he seemed to be sniffing the air like an animal. His face was drawn and gaunt and so white it looked like chalk in the firelight. A strange feeling washed through Kerbogah, a terrible sadness.

'Relak. Something's wrong.'

Suddenly the boy stood up and walked straight towards them. His eyes were still shut and as he smelt the air, he lifted his hand towards Kerbogah, as though pleading for something. But although he began mouthing at Kerbogah, his lips moving, no words came out.

'Who are you?' whispered Kerbogah fearfully as the stranger sniffed again.

The boy opened his eyes and a cold horror seized Kerbogah's heart.

'No, Relak!'

The orbs in the boy's eyes were perfectly dead and black. No pupils gazed out to give them character, no light to give them life and intelligence. Still he went on sniffing.

Kerbogah began backing away and as the thing came even closer those black stone eyes changed colour. An orange glow flickered in the centre of them and a terrible feeling of hopelessness washed through Kerbogah's soul. All around him, he began to see shapes about the stranger's head. They swirled in little tornadoes, like formless birds that rose and flapped above him, ghastly beings that Kerbogah had no names for, looming before his eyes.

'Help!' cried Kerbogah as they swooped, waving his arms frantically to ward off the horrid creatures, but striking nothing but thin air. 'Help me!'

Kerbogah felt as though he was choking and as the demons attacked him it was as if he was being sucked down-

 98

wards through the sand, sucked into some kingdom of ghastly, eternal night.

'Lol!' he cried desperately. 'Help me, Lol!'

As the prayer came, something soothing touched Kerbogah's heart, a kind of warmth within him, and then the shapes were gone. The boy was still before him, though, his eyes once more as black as jet. He let out a terrible cry of rage and hate and lunged for Kerbogah's throat.

His hands clutched at Kerbogah's neck, cold and clammy, holding him in such a strangling grip as he sniffed again that Kerbogah knew he was lost. Relak was squeaking terribly now and, as those black orbs bore into him once more, Kerbogah felt that same hopelessness. But with it came something else, a kind of pity for the creature, for Kerbogah suddenly felt a ghastly loneliness too, and he knew that it was the loneliness of this child. As he struggled he became aware of another shape and he could breath again and the grip about his throat was broken. The boy's head had been pulled backwards.

'Father!' cried Kerbogah, as Karleg's arm locked around the boy and his hand tugged back his head. He was dimly aware that Farjay was there too, holding his sling, and Imlay and Khayarumi. Kerbogah saw the flash of his father's dagger and remembered the terrible pity he had felt for the boy.

'No, Father, don't. He . . .'

Karleg hesitated but the boy pulled an arm free and reached up to grab Karleg's knife. As he twisted the dagger it cut deep into the Dunetrader's arm. Karleg swore and wrenched it free again and in an instant he had passed the blade across the creature's throat.

The skin parted but Kerbogah was horrified to see that, unlike Karleg's wound, there was no blood. Those terrible eyes closed though and the boy slumped to the ground. He was dead.

'Father,' whispered Kerbogah in horror. 'You killed him, Father.'

They were all staring down at the strange, bloodless corpse.

'No, Kerbogah,' said Karleg, shaking his sadly, 'not in truth. For he was dead already and would have killed you, my son. But it's a blessed release.'

'Release? But who was he?' asked Kerbogah nervously. 'I thought at first it was . . .'

Another vulture screeched and lifted into the air from the Towers of Silence.

'One of the Pazgog's poor victims,' answered Imlay, stepping forwards gravely. 'He was a Grasht, Kerbogah.'

Kerbogah went as cold as ice and touched his throat.

'A Grasht?'

'Yes, Kerbogah.'

'When I first saw him, his eyes were closed. And it was as though he was sniffing the air to see.'

'The Grasht are the children of the demon Pazgog and so use their senses to know the world. And your father did well. For there is nothing more terrible than to walk the earth without a soul.'

'Without a soul?' whispered Farjay, trembling between them.

Kerbogah was shaking too but he felt another wave of pity for the lad lying at their feet.

'I saw such dreadful things through his eyes,' whispered Kerbogah. 'Demons and Sandspirits that tried to attack me. I felt – I felt such terrible loneliness. Relak felt it too.'

'Because the Grasht have no feelings any more,' said Imlay softly, putting his hand on Kerbogah's shoulder. 'No hope or pain or love. They are like empty vessels, although the Pazgog's Chi still animates them. But if spirits were there too, they were trying to get through your own Chi Shield and make you like themselves. You have glimpsed down into the Underworld, Kerbogah. The doorway opens all around us.'

Kerbogah shuddered and hugged Relak closer, as Farjay clutched his sling.

'Come, Kerbogah,' said Karleg softly, wrapping a cloth about his wounded arm. 'The dawn approaches. It's time to find a way into the city. We shall take the Grasht and lay his body on the Towers of Silence. Perhaps that shall clean his soul.'

The Dunetraders were putting out their fires when they returned and, after they had climbed a tower with the poor child, they were soon mounted again. Karleg led them on towards the city and, as they came through the shadows, the walls of Barbal towered above them. They were approaching the line of travellers waiting to enter. Swords were everywhere and the men kept looking up at the skies.

'The Pazgog,' whispered Kerbogah.

'If it comes, Kerbogah,' said Farjay, snapping his slingshot, 'I'll show it. I'm not turning into one of those things.'

Karleg jumped down from his camel, wrapping his turban tightly about his face.

'Wait here,' he ordered. 'We can't enter anyway without the Tribute, but I'm going to try and talk to the guards.'

Karleg hurried off on foot. By the time he returned Selera had dismounted from the group of Dunetrader women travelling behind the caravan and she was standing by her son and Farjay.

'The city gates are still barred,' Karleg announced, 'but I think I can get a few of us in anyway.'

'How, Father?' whispered Kerbogah. 'Without any Stardust?'

'Groots, Kerbogah,' answered Karleg. 'Men change little, my son, and bribery still works in Barbal. We'll have to put on different clothes, of course, but even a Dunetrader can't be distinguished from ordinary travellers, unless he sings the Sandsong.'

Karleg suddenly turned to his wife.

'Selera, take the caravan back to that quarry and wait for us in safety. But for now I must hunt for Kalman.'

'Find him, Karleg,' said Selera hotly, clutching his hand. 'Promise me, husband.'

'I will, my love. Have faith. We'll be back before Sunset this evening. Imlay and Khayarumi, come with me.'

The old man and the poet nodded but Kerbogah and Farjay stepped up smartly too.

'And what do you think you are doing, Kerbogah?' said Selera immediately, glaring at the children.

'Going to help look for my brother, of course. Me, Relak and Farjay.'

'You're doing no such thing. You'll stay with the women.'

'But, Mother, please. I know all the sorts of things Kalman likes and, besides, there's so much Farjay and I want to see and learn in Barbal.'

'You'll do as you are—'

'Father,' implored Kerbogah.

Karleg looked doubtfully at his son but he smiled too as he remembered himself at Kerbogah's age and how excited he had been at his first visit to the Sacred City.

'All right, Kerbogah.'

'Hooray! We're going too, Relak.'

Kerbogah was hopping up and down delightedly.

'But, husband . . .'

'He must learn to grow and be a man, Selera. And you too, Farjay. Their voices have almost broken, Selera. But, boys, you must stay close and keep your eyes peeled. In Barbal you will see sights you are unlikely to forget in a very long time to come.'

As they were getting ready, though, they saw others coming towards them, moving in the direction of Barbal. This time they were all men, dressed in bright orange with shaven heads and walking in a line. They were chanting strangely.

'Who are they, Father?' said Kerbogah.

Farjay was grinning and starting to giggle.

'Yaharlars,' answered Karleg. 'Very holy men, Kerbogah, who seek enlightenment wandering the desert wastes. They say they see the Gods in everything.'

As they drew closer it wasn't just their robes that distinguished the Yaharlars, for their faces looked nothing like the Dunetraders. They had taut, yellowish-brown skin and high foreheads, while their eyes seemed drawn in slits over their cheeks, a little like the wild cats that sometimes wandered into the Dunetrader tents.

'They're soul workers, Kerbogah,' said old Imlay. 'The Yaharlars hold that it is really the inner life that truly counts and that all of us must work on our own spirits if man is to change and grow. They must be on their way for the Solstice too.'

As they approached Imlay clasped his hands flat together and raised them to his forehead in greeting. One of the Yaharlars nodded softly to him and smiled. Kerbogah and Farjay copied Imlay's strange greeting and as they did so Kerbogah felt an oddly pleasant feeling move through his whole body. But suddenly the wandering Yaharlars drew into a circle and knelt down. They reached into their robes and, pulling out clenched fists, thrust them towards the centre of the circle and began to chant again.

'Aaaaaaaa-om.'

'Look, Farjay,' whispered Kerbogah, 'look what's coming from their hands.'

It was coloured like sand, some orange like their robes,

but other colours too: fire-red and charcoal-black, waterskin-blue and Wordmaster-yellow.

'Aaaaaaa-om.'

The circle of Yaharlars were moving their arms together, round and about, pouring sand as they worked, chanting and lost in deep concentration. Karbogah and Farjay were transfixed by these strange, bald men and they both noticed an odd scent on the air.

'It isn't sand at all,' said Farjay suddenly.

'It isn't?'

'Spices,' whispered Karleg, drawing closer to the boys, 'they're using spices. You'll see more in the great bazaar. That yellow stuff, for instance, it's called saffron, rare and highly prized in the temple and used too to dye the Wordmaster's robes.'

'And turmeric,' whispered Khayarumi, scenting the delicious odour, 'and capsicum. Oh, I can't wait for Bolor's place.'

'Barbalonians use them in cooking too,' explained Karleg, 'to spice things up and cover the flavour of rotting meat.'

'Pepper's my favourite,' said Khayarumi wistfully. 'I'll never forget that time I made a stew of peppered peacock.'

'You did what?' said Imlay, swinging round and glaring in horror at the poet. 'But it's sacrilege, man. Peacocks have always been sacred birds in Barbal. The Lord Alchemists once used them to sacrifice to the Sun God, and tell the future.'

The poet grinned.

'How can a bird tell the future?' asked Farjay.

'Sacrifice,' answered Imlay. 'If the entrails were clean the weather would be fair; if covered in green slime or black bile the crops would fail.'

'Yuck,' said Kerbogah.

'Quite right, my boy,' said Imlay with a smile. 'So at last they turned to more advanced forms of soothsaying, like searching the night skies for the Gods' great plan and using the twelve symbols on the Sundial in the square. The Zodiac.'

At this talk of soothsaying, Kerbogah thought of the prophecy again, but the Yaharlars suddenly stopped their chant and drew back their hands. They had painted something quite beautiful on the ground in the different-coloured spices. The main part of it was a simple circle but bisecting the centre were two distinct lines weaving up and down, like two snakes spiralling in and out of each other, so intricately that the boys couldn't decide if there was just one line there or two.

'Contemplating this helps us drive back demons and strengthen our Chi Shields,' said a Yaharlar softly, as they finished their sand painting, 'against the spirits of chaos that threaten us all. It's called the Yaharl. The magic circle. As we chant, it helps us to look within, too, for do not all true secrets lie within? To really know the outer world you must master the secret of inward looking too.'

'The holy Yaharl,' said Imlay, stroking his beard reverently. 'The Yaharlars wander the Seven Lands drawing that symbol everywhere.'

'Your cities and ziggurats come and go like mere fragments in the desert,' said the Yaharlar mournfully. 'But in the end who really conquers more than six feet of sand? Freedom lies with the God within. Perhaps only there lies enlightenment.'

Farjay smirked, since wandering the world drawing this symbol seemed a very pointless thing to do, but Kerbogah was thinking of the prophecy again and of one coming to free them all. He suddenly wondered what the God within meant, but he thought the Yaharlar's deep chestnut eyes were grave and rather wonderful.

'Is it not beautiful?' said the Yaharlar softly. 'It represents the Wheel.'

'The Waterwheel?' said Farjay, dying to see it for himself. 'The First of the Seven Wonders of the World?'

The Yaharlar's soft eyes were amused and kindly.

'No, no. The wheel of being,' he answered. 'The invisible and eternal circle and the course of all true Alchemical transformation. The wheel of death, but of rebirth and life too, from which we Yaharlars ultimately seek to free ourselves and return to the Great Being. The Enlightened One first drew this, to help him body forth the floating world, as the Gods themselves dreamt the world into being.'

'The Enlightened One?' said Kerbogah. 'Is he an Alchemist, sir?'

Again the Yaharlar smiled, a smile that seemed to hold some impossible mystery in it.

'Not of the Order, and his spirit has long since left us.'

The Yaharlar looked up. Farjay thought he was peering at the Towers of Silence, but his eyes seemed to be ranging elsewhere. Up towards the gigantic starlit canopy above them. The heavens.

'Like the Alchemists,' whispered the Yaharlar in the scented night, 'the Enlightened One's search was surely for transformation. He soon learnt to say the One Word silently, that resonates through everything. He was a master of Sandwork too. He could count the smallest grains of sand in your hand, to the untold combinations that make up eternity. He could count the number of ants that stream across the marble floors of heaven.'

Suddenly the Yaharlar stood up and his companions followed.

'But now we must be on our way once more.'

'May we give you something for your picture, holy one?' said Karleg. 'Some Groots perhaps?'

The Yaharlar smiled again and raised a graceful hand.

'No, no, my son. What use have we for golden Groots?

We are not of this corruptible world and never shall be. All we seek is purity and enlightenment. Meanwhile we go to beg in the city of men. But some fresh water perhaps, to clean our voices.'

Karleg willingly gave the holy man a waterskin and in their line the Yaharlars continued towards Barbal, drinking and chanting as they went.

'Aaaaaaaaaaaaa-om.'

The little party was ready now and there were tears of worry in Selera's eyes as she watched them set off together. The jam in the line was even worse closer to the city and it took them an age to arrive at one of the gates. They could already feel morning on the air but the Barbalissaries on guard were still holding up the travellers, clammering to be let in. Kerbogah and Farjay could hardly breathe with excitement as they overheard two of the guards talking.

'It's not dawn yet,' said one. 'Should we open up?'

'There'll be a riot if we don't,' answered the other. 'They know that when the Pazgog returns there'll be more chance to hide. And Zorastar is close. But keep your eyes peeled for Dunetraders. They'll not pass without the tribute.'

The soldier's eyes flickered but he nodded and hammered on the doors. They all heard the sound of a huge metal bolt being drawn back and the great central gates of Barbal City swung open before them. The throng pressed forward but as Karleg and the others got closer and closer Relak started squeaking and one of the soldiers pointed at Kerbogah.

'Hey you there, boy. Stop.'

Kerbogah froze but Karleg stepped in front of his son. He looked at one of the guards who had been talking and quickly pulled the turban down to show his face.

'It all right, Nelador,' cried the guard immediately, recognizing the man who had payed him so well, 'I know this lot. Just ordinary travellers. Let them pass.'

With a sigh Karleg's little party was waved through and the Dunetraders suddenly found themselves passing along a narrow, cobbled alleyway lined with tiny windows that looked in on low and dingy houses. They were entering Barbal City.

Along the edges of the walls were open watercourses, just as there had been in Ederyl. In Ederyl, though, they had naturally all been built on slopes, carrying water straight down from mountain springs to the Childars' homes, but here they ran perfectly flat, yet the water seemed to be gurgling along magically. Khayarumi dangled his hand in the lovely water and Kerbogah and Farjay looked around in amazement.

'Hey, don't push,' cried Kerbogah furiously, as someone barged him from behind. Everybody trying to get into Barbal, and seek protection in the narrow alleyways, pushed and shoved, and every now and then someone would pull out a sword or a knife and a struggle would break out.

One sight immediately made Kerbogah and Farjay fearful too. The urchins that threaded the alley in the darkness had a haunted look, as though something was chasing them through the streets. Kerbogah was watching one little beggar crouching in a doorway when he suddenly blinked in astonishment. He couldn't be sure through the heads of the passing throng but he was almost certain that a hand had suddenly reached out and pulled the child backwards into the shadows. Kerbogah looked around.

'Come on, Relak,' he whispered. 'You must help me find Kalman.'

Further on the little party of Dunetraders came to a row of grimy homes where the doorways were daubed with red pigment. They were marked with one or other of four weird symbols:

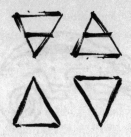

Kerbogah and Farjay shuddered as they realized what they were painted in. It was blood.

'What do those mean?' asked Farjay fearfully.

Kerbogah shook his head, but a toothless old crone shuffling next to him lifted a gauzy black shawl and leered at the children with a face as ancient as the walls.

'The Pazgog,' she hissed. 'Each night it flaps overhead, waiting to steal souls. The Sign of Four keeps out the angel of death.'

Kerbogah shivered and the hag reached out a gnarled hand and stroked his hair tenderly.

'Get off,' cried Kerbogah, and Relak gave an indignant squeak.

'You have nothing to fear if your heart is loyal and true,' crowed the old women. 'Mardak cares for us all like his own children, if we show loyalty to the ancient ways. The High Priest had a dream telling him that if the Barbalonian's doorways were marked in pig's blood, then the angel will always pass safely overhead.'

They hurried away and Kerbogah was wondering about his brother when he noticed now that they were no longer on the flat, for the alley had begun to climb. It rose steadily and then levelled out again and at last it opened.

They had come finally into the Great Square of Barbal City.

SOOTHSAYING

All around the edges of Barbal's Great Square the Eternal Flames were burning in golden bowls supported on twenty-four white marble pilasters. The sacred fires, scented with incense, sent up little swirls of bluish smoke that curled into the fading moonlight and mingled like a mist that made all in the square look strange and other-wordly.

'Wow,' said Farjay.

Kerbogah and Farjay looked about wonderingly in the dancing firelight. The whole city was on a natural hill so that the square itself was raised and they were almost level with the tops of the city walls. They could see clear out into the land beyond and Kerbogah fancied he could make out his own caravan.

'Look, Relak, it's Mother.'

Selera was making safely for the stone quarry with the rest of the Dunetraders. Light was coming quickly and suddenly they knew that the Sun God Zorastar was lifting across the plain. With that, though, there was a terrible scream.

'Relak!' whispered Kerbogah in the half light. 'What is it?'

The mouse seemed to have gone mad, for it was trying to jump out of Kerbogah's robes.

'There!' cried someone from the mêlée, pushing into the square.

A great winged shape was hanging high over Barbal, flapping its gigantic wings.

'The Pazgog!' exclaimed Imlay.

The demon swooped, straight towards the square and, as one, the crowd ducked. The Pazgog, tired of its night's hunting and fearful of the eye of the Sun God, sailed down in the direction of a free-standing plinth, larger than the pillars that supported the fire bowls. Everyone shrunk back in terror.

It settled on top of it like some monstrous toad and flapped its great grey wings. Several women wailed or screamed as they saw what it was holding in its claws. As its huge form squatted there, the demon's beak jabbed forwards and pecked at one of the Yaharlars. The demon was feeding on his stomach, and his orange robes had turned blood-red.

Suddenly, though, the first rays of morning lifted over the horizon. As full sunlight struck the creature, it let go of its horrid prey and once more the demon was turned to stone. The Pazgog stood lifeless again, a giant statue in the square, blood dripping from its stony beak, as a pair of Barbalissaries ran forward to remove the poor Yaharlar. The Pazgog's sightless eyes gazed down like some ancient God over Barbal, its giant stony wings still open on its back.

The sunlight was coming fast now, sending splinters of light down to pierce the gloom and as it lifted the veil of darkness over Barbal, the Dunetrader children blinked in utter astonishment. In front of them, on the far side of the square, stood the Great Waterwheel of Barbal City: the first of the Seven Wonders of the World.

'It's amazing,' whispered Farjay.

'One of the Alchemists' greatest inventions, Farjay,' said Kerbogah. 'It's moving by magic.'

The contraption was gigantic and around the base of the huge wooden O was a pool at the edge of which several beautiful green and blue birds were strutting about. They had magnificent shimmering bodies, with the most exotic feathers, and some of them had little plumes on their heads. As the enormous Waterwheel turned and creaked, quite on its own, golden buckets on its outer rim dipped into the pool and lifted up water. At the top of their arc they hit a pole which tipped the buckets, so the contents fell into a deep watercourse that sloped down along the edge of the city wall.

'There, Khayarumi,' cried Imlay. 'If any could doubt the Alchemists' magic, see how the great Wheel turns all on its own, to carry water round the city.'

'Magic!' snorted the poet Khayarumi. 'It can't be.'

As the buckets struck the post a kind of strange clicking sound came from it, which filled the entire square. But Khayarumi was admiring the birds.

'Sacred peacocks,' he said. 'I shall compose them an ode myself. I'll never forget the taste.'

'Hush, Khayarumi,' snapped Imlay.

'Look there, Kerbogah.'

Karleg was pointing to the very centre of Barbal Square and they all had to turn away their eyes for a moment, for the rising sun had just caught the Sundial's huge golden disc and made it flash like fire.

'Gold, Relak,' whispered Kerbogah to his mouse, who had calmed down again. 'The Alchemists love gold.'

The Sundial was very beautiful, but as they drew even closer the children were fascinated by the twelve symbols arcing around its base.

'The Zodiac,' said Imlay, 'which gives its names to the

 112

constellations of the stars. Some believe they are the crests of the first twelve Alchemists.'

Imlay had noticed that Farjay had begun to drift away, and he suddenly caught him by the collar.

'Not that way, boy. In Barbal you must move to the right around the Sundial. To go to the left is very unlucky. They say that something sinister awaits all who go to the left.'

The children thought this very strange but they were delighted by the Wheel and the Sundial and the peacocks, which had just fanned out their tails as if welcoming in the morning. They swept out behind them like gigantic fans, and were beaded with huge gold–black circles splashed with colour like golden eyes. Strangely, the soldiers and most of the watching Barbalonians immediately averted their gaze.

'More superstitious nonsense,' muttered Khayarumi. 'They think it's an evil omen, looking a peacock in the "eye".'

The sacred peacocks seemed greatly pleased with the effect though, for there was something rather nervous and fearful about the wonderful birds. As Farjay and Kerbogah drew closer a Barbalissary raised his golden-topped spear.

'Get back,' he grunted.

'Why, sir?' asked Kerbogah.

'You know why,' answered the soldier. 'Someone is stealing them. Sacrilege spreads throughout the city. If Mardak catches the thieves there'll be the demon to pay.'

Kerbogah and Farjay turned away. It was only now that they noticed a tall stone building, lined with pillars and defined by a great arched doorway. The arch was covered in a mosaic depicting a menagerie of exotic animals, with a growling lion right in the centre, but it was the door itself that held the gaze of any onlooker. Its two sides were studded with great black bolts and it was also made of pure gold.

As they watched there was another commotion behind

113

them and suddenly the crowd of Barbalonians parted like a sea. Kerbogah and Farjay could feel a wave of fear move through the crowd and they heard a loud cracking sound. Barbalissaries were marching towards them, holding whips in their hands.

It was what the soldiers were herding towards the building that sickened their hearts, though. The men being driven along like animals were dressed simply, like the party on the outskirts of Barbal, and all had their eyes closed as they shuffled forwards, row after row of them, sniffing at the scented air.

'Grasht,' whispered Kerbogah, feeling the same nameless dread he had felt at the sight of the child. The grown-ups could feel it too now and they all began to back away. They were both repulsed and strangely attracted; for as they passed it was as if something was touching them from these haunted walkers. Like a cold flame, or a wind.

The sightless Grasht moved like dead things, straight towards the golden doorway and in Kerbogah's robes Relak began to tremble furiously.

'A good night's collection,' a Barbalissary grunted as he passed the boys. 'Zolos will be delighted. The demon was hungry last night.'

'And Zolos won't even have to give them a single Groot in payment,' laughed another, 'now he has a slave army.'

But Farjay was also shaking. One of the Grasht suddenly turned its head straight towards him and was sniffing. But before it could open its eyes a woman in the crowd lunged for him and grabbed his hand.

'Mezuman!' she cried bitterly. 'Not you, my husband.'

Mezuman seemed not to feel her touch at all. He stopped scenting and kept walking with closed eyes as she clawed desperately at his arm.

'I told you to stay indoors, Mezuman. Mardak's symbols would have protected you.'

'Out of the way,' grunted the Barbalissary, grabbing the woman roughly and thrusting her aside. 'None may touch the Grasht.'

'But please, sir, he means no harm. Give him back to me.'

The soldier's lips turned up cruelly and he laughed.

'Give him back to you? You might as well light a votive fire below the statue and pray to Aspis himself. Can't you see he is no longer your husband?'

'Oh, Mezuman! My beloved Mezuman!'

'He's a Grasht,' said the soldier harshly. 'The soulless ones. Servants of the Underworld. And now they enter Barbal Barracks to be equipped and trained properly by the bravest Barbalissaries. To swell Zolos's soulless horde.'

The golden doorway swung open and the train of soldiers and Grasht began to pass inside. The Barbalonians watched the terrifying spectacle, but were too petrified to do anything to stop it. The door to the barracks slammed fast again with a great boom, and now they saw not wonder but horror as they gazed at the city's barracks. Mezuman's wife was left in the square. She had thrown herself at the foot of the Pazgog, which looked down pitilessly from its plinth, as she sobbed her heart out.

'But why, Father?' whispered Kerbogah angrily. 'What do they want with such an army?'

'For the coming fight,' said a voice beside them. 'The Captain Lord thinks of little but war now. Zolos is turning all of the inventions in the Ziggurat to his purposes too and he wants blood all right.'

It was an old Barbalonian with a beard as white as Imlay's. His back was stooped and he looked tired and very sad.

'Especially Dunetrader blood.'

Karleg looked nervously to Imlay, who pulled his turban even tighter about his face.

'Come on,' said Karleg. 'Let's keep moving.'

They had come to the other side of the square and suddenly they entered a wide avenue, filled with stalls and jostling people. Everyone was laughing and shouting as they streamed down the cobbles.

'Barbal Bazaar,' said Khayarumi delightedly. 'Music to my ears.'

Kerbogah and Farjay found this anything but music. The din was horrible and everybody seemed to be speaking at the same time. Among the Barbalonians they suddenly realized that many of these people were jabbering away in different tongues and set up such an infernal racket that Kerbogah wanted to block his ears.

'How can anyone understand a thing they're saying, Relak?' he whispered to his mouse.

Little alleys ran left and right off Barbal's main market street and they were stuffed with goods, though each seemed to contain just one kind of merchandise: copper pots or clay bowls, woven rugs or long, coloured turbans.

'It's a crazy place, Relak,' muttered Kerbogah, 'and I wish you'd keep still. Oh, how are we ever going to find Kalman in this?'

In the swelling morning men were laying out bowls made of cedar and pine, dogwood and ebony, piled with the most amazing foods Kerbogah and Farjay had ever seen. There were bulging watermelons and glistening mangoes, luscious eggplants and crunchy collywobble flowers, plump pomegranates and striped star fruit. There were dried flowers and herbs and more thrushthroat mushrooms than Kerbogah or Farjay had ever seen in their short lives. Piles of purple bellberries jostled with bundles of bloodroot, too, and great mounds of spices. Karleg walked up to a basket of fine orange-yellow dust and scooped some up in his palm.

'More saffron,' he said. 'Barbalonians use it not only for spicing up their rice dishes, but to dye the Wordmaster's robes. Here, Kerbogah, take some.'

He handed his son a handful of the stuff and Kerbogah rubbed it in his palm.

'Dyeing is an art as ancient as perfume making, Kerbogah.'

'Not any more,' said the stallholder. 'They're all dead now. Murdered by Zolos and Mardak.'

Karleg's eyes flickered.

'Tell me, man,' he whispered. 'We're looking for a boy. About twelve years old. Sandy hair, with a mole on his right cheek.'

'What's it to me?'

'Have you seen him? There's a Groot in it.'

The stallholder shook his head irritably.

'Don't be foolish. How could I remember who passes through Barbal? Especially children. They're all over the place. Now, are you going to buy anything?'

'No,' answered Karleg.

'Then leave me be. I've enough work on my hands. Prices in Barbal are going through the roof with the Solstice and the damned Dunetrader wars in the desert.'

'Relak!'

Farjay and Imlay turned. Kerbogah had put the saffron in his pocket and was looking about desperately for Relak. The mouse had just slipped from his robes and Kerbogah was already growing frantic.

'He's gone,' cried Kerbogah bitterly. 'Relak's gone too. We'll never find him again in this.'

'There, Kerbogah,' said Farjay, pointing to one of the

117

stalls. The mouse was sitting right on top of a pile of pome-granates, testing the air with his whiskered nose.

Kerbogah scooped him up again and they left the stall and came to the entrance to an alleyway on the edge of the square. All along one side of the wall sat old men, cross-legged on the ground. Some were talking loudly as the ordinary Barbalonians crowded round them to listen.

'The Street of Fables,' said Khayarumi eagerly.

'But what are they selling?' asked Farjay, for he could see no stalls or merchandise.

'Stories, Farjay,' answered the poet. 'Barbalonian story-tellers spin yarns here as rich and complex and beautiful as the weave on our Dunetrader carpets. Especially ones with hidden meanings. Parables.'

The voice of one of the storytellers came drifting to their ears.

'In the beginning were the words and the words were the Gods' names . . .'

Beyond the Street of Fables, they came to another corner and a street thick with smoke and incense where, in the dirt, great circles and spirals were drawn in the ground.

'The Street of Soothsayers,' cried Imlay excitedly. 'The very heart of Barbal City. The source of vision and prophecy.'

'Now this is more like it, Farjay,' said Kerbogah, nudging his friend. 'We can find out about this prophecy and the Marked One.'

Everywhere Barbalonians were throwing bones and coins across the earth, while others had stopped one or other of the passers-by, staring intently at their palms, nodding sagely and stroking their beards.

On one side of the street a man held up a pig's liver and was muttering strange charms over it as its blood dripped into a stone crucible, while another was about to cut the throat of a goat that was sending up a terrible, agonized bleating. Next to the goat an old man sat cross-legged in the dust against a brick wall with four clay containers in front of him. A little fire was burning in one of the bowls and next to it was a crucible with nothing in it at all. By that was another bowl heaped with what looked like soil and a bowl with water in it too.

'Behold,' said the soothsayer, as several Barbalonians stopped to watch him, 'the Four. With these we may Alchemize the future.'

The soothsayer sprinkled some of the earth into the water, which swirled and fizzed wildly.

'Now let me see,' he said, with a very holy expression.

'He must be astrologizing, Kebogah,' said Farjay excitedly.

'He's soothsaying,' grunted a stocky Barbalonian near Farjay, who was looking on sceptically at the soothsayer. 'There is a distinction, boy. Astrologizing is done with the stars above, and the Zodiac, for the Alchemists say we are all affected by those when we are born. That portents from heaven herald the arrival of great ones too. But soothsayers use all sorts of techniques to cheat honest folk of their hard earned Groots.'

'Cheat?' said Kerbogah.

'This place is full of charlatans,' grunted the man, 'in search of nothing but golden Groots.'

Kerbogah didn't want to hear this for he couldn't stop thinking about the prophecy now and he had wanted to ask the soothsayers if the Marked One was already in Barbal. He looked rather disappointed.

'Then they can't really tell the future?' he whispered.

'Not like this,' answered the man. 'It's stuff and nonsense. As far as I'm concerned, all astrologizing ever proved is that there's one born every minute. And what future do you mean anyway, boy? Doesn't the same miserable fate await us all in the end? Whether you pretend to see it in the stars or chaila leaves, or wherever. Bones, bones beneath the Ziggurat. Like all the Alchemists.'

Kerbogah looked up at the giant Ziggurat and shivered, but he remembered what Khayarumi had said about death in the tent.

'Or perhaps you mean our souls,' said the man mournfully. 'Will they fly up to the heavens or descend into the Underworld and be swallowed by Aspis, or be doomed eternally to the river of blood that flows through the Underworld? Will the Pazgog steal them, or will we all be resurrected after the Last Judgement?'

Kerbogah and Farjay were suddenly looking very unhappy indeed.

'But you don't need tricks to tell the future,' said the man. 'What you really need is this.'

He suddenly tapped his head.

'What do you mean, sir?' asked Farjay.

'Imagination, boy. And vision. And like the great Ogog himself, my years of contemplation in Barbal have given me many strange and wonderful visions. I see cities swarm like locusts and huge towers of glass and metal rise into the heavens. I see metal birds flying through the skies. Vision's what really counts.'

'But, sir,' whispered Kerbogah, 'I was told a prophecy in the desert. It said that One would come and that the temple would be rent in twain.'

Behind Kerbogah the soothsayer overheard and he scowled immediately.

'That old legend, that's just fanciful nonsense. I've much better prophecies.'

'Oh,' said Kerbogah, but then his eyes narrowed with a thought. 'My brother,' he cried. 'Could you use your power to tell me anything of my brother's fate?'

'Of course,' answered the man immediately.

 120

'Come on, Kerbogah,' urged Karleg suddenly, behind the children. 'We must keep searching.'

They went on but at the end of the Street of Soothsayers a group of Barbalonians were gathered near a wall, pointing and whispering excitedly. They were discussing these strange symbols, daubed in blood on the brick, like the Sign of Four:

$$E = MC^2$$

'Now what on earth's that?' asked Farjay. 'Does it keep off the Pazgog too?'

Karleg shook his head but a tall and very intelligent-looking Barbalonian had overheard the question.

'It appeared suddenly on the wall,' he said thickly, 'and no one knows what it means. Perhaps the Gods are already speaking to us in signs.'

Another man suddenly sprang out from the shadows. His clothes were rather tatty and he wore broken hemp sandals. The Barbalonian clearly hadn't eaten in a long while, but his eyes were as bright as glass.

'I'll show you a real portent,' he cried, 'for a golden Groot.'

He dipped into his pocket and pulled out a little numbered cube which he thrust towards Kerbogah.

'There, roll it along the ground, lad, and watch closely what happens.'

The strange man looked rather too dangerous to disobey. Kerbogah pushed Relak back into his robes and bent down to roll the die through the dirt. Each time the cube landed on a number, the man told him to turn it to its opposite side.

121

Kerbogah suddenly realized what the busker was getting at, because every time Kerbogah added the numbers on the opposite sides of the die together, six and one, four and three, two and five, they added up to the very same total: seven.

'There,' whispered the busker. 'Magical seven. Sandwork and Number Magic are far more mysterious than you can even imagine. In fact, than anyone can even dream of yet.'

'Hush,' growled a passer-by. 'If the Barbalissaries hear you they'll throw you in Mardak's darkest dungeons. Or wake the Pazgog again to punish us all. You know Sandwork has been banned in the streets on pain of Alchemical Torture.'

The busker simply shrugged.

'Tell me, boy,' he said. 'How many times have you come across the number seven on your way to Barbal? The Seven Lands, the Seven Commandments, the Seven Wonders of the World, not to mention the Seven Heavens.'

'Lots,' Kerbogah had to confess.

'Seven's everywhere. And you can't believe it's all just a coincidence,' whispered the busker, suddenly looking up at the giant Ziggurat. 'That anything is really a coincidence.'

'What do you mean, sir?'

'I think there is a hidden pattern all around us, that we can only discover by looking both within and without.'

'Pattern?' said Kerbogah, thinking of the Yaharlars.

'Of course. Which we can only see using Number Magic. Just as with the twelve signs of the Zodiac, Barbalonians have divided up the year into twelve precise parts, called months, to pay homage to the crests of the Lord Alchemists, so with magical seven the Lord Alchemist has just invented the seven days too. Which make up a week.'

'A week,' said Kerbogah, rolling the word around his tongue and looking rather impressed now. 'Has he really?'

'Number Magic is what we should all be interested in,' insisted the mathematical busker, looking about him defiantly. 'And reason. To order the world and see how it really works. As Ogog says. Not the smoke that hovers over the sacred square, nor those foolish Elixirs and balms they cook up in the Halls of the Rising Sun. Certainly not a return to human sacrifice. That's Mardak the Dark's kind of magic and it must stop.'

'Yes,' whispered Kerbogah, 'I suppose it must.'

'But there isn't a chance now Ogog is gone.'

'Come on, Kerbogah,' said Karleg suddenly. 'This talk is too dangerous.'

Karleg had led them away again by the time the man turned to look for his reward. The busker looked disconsolately after them, but just then he felt a heavy hand on his shoulder. A Barbalissary's hand.

'You, scum. Zolos wants to see you. Now.'

The boys hadn't seen this and as they turned into another alley it was Khayarumi's eyes that lit up hungrily. The scent of roasting meat curdled the steamy air. It was coming from a doorway further down the alley, the door to a tavern.

'Bolor's place!' cried Khayarumi. 'At last! I'm starving.'

'I wanted to search some more first, Khayarumi,' said Karleg, 'but now we're here I suppose we should have breakfast.'

Karleg led them inside and as soon as they entered the little tavern, filled with tables and hungry Barbalonians, their ears were assaulted by singing and raucous laughter. Everywhere people were drinking and eating and talking furiously.

'I love Bolor's place,' said Khayarumi delightedly. 'When they're not bowing to Zorastar or trying to tell their blessed futures, Barbalonians are great sensualists and pleasure seekers, very partial to the Seven Deadly Temptations.'

'The opposite of the Seven Commandments, children,'

explained Imlay, looking at Khayarumi sternly, for the poet was beaming as they heard a shout in the tavern.

'Hey, Mishtar, one collywobble soup with a sprinkling of cardamom and paprika, and two Bolor Specials. And look lively about it.'

'And, Bolor,' called another of the drinkers to the man who had just cried out, 'three cups of sweet chaila.'

A bald little man scurried about, serving food and tea and beer and taking orders. It was Bolor, the tavern keeper. In a dimly lit room to the left a cook scowled wearily and wiped his brow on his sleeve, as Karleg led them towards a table by a shuttered window. There was a strange candlestick in the middle of it, with two arms and spiked holders for candles, but a little, sculpted lizard in the middle. Karleg left them at the table and went over to speak to Bolor.

Kerbogah had settled Relak but now he noticed the drinkers at the neighbouring table. One was a splendid old man with an enormous beard like a gigantic bird's nest and kind, though wary, eyes.

A young man was sitting next to him with a thin, pale face and a blank expression, almost like the Grasht, and his arms hugged tightly around him. His eyes were closed and he was rocking back and forth gently and Kerbogah thought he looked quite mad. But suddenly the bearded man knocked over a cup filled with little wooden sticks, which went scattering over the floor towards the children. Kerbogah leant down to pick them up, but before he could even touch one, that strange young man had darted his head forward like a snake, his eyes wide open.

'Forty-eight,' he whispered.

Kerbogah sat back in surprise.

'What do you mean, forty-eight?'

The young man didn't answer. He sat further back, as

124

though frightened or hurt, clutching his arms about him, and started to rock again, and moan slightly.

'What's wrong with you?' said Kerbogah, but his bearded companion put his hand gently on his friend's head to calm him and smiled at Kerbogah.

'Don't talk to him, young man, he doesn't really like it. He doesn't see things as ordinary Barbalonians do. But if you're to be kind enough to collect our toothpicks I suggest you count them.'

Kerbogah shrugged, wondering how a toothpick worked, and why anyone would want to pick their teeth out anyway. But as he did so and counted them under his breath, Kerbogah was astounded.

'But it's impossible!'

When the toothpicks were back in their cup, although the young man had certainly not had enough time to count them himself, they added up to exactly forty-eight, just as he'd said.

'But how?'

'He can see numbers,' answered the man, and he shrugged. 'Just like that.'

Kerbogah suddenly thought of what the busker had said about seeing a pattern. The bearded Barbalonian got up and led his friend away. Kerbogah was quivering with excitement at this extraordinary bit of Number Magic, but Farjay looked extremely unhappy.

'All this Sandwork, Kerbogah. It hurts my head.'

'I know, Farjay. And mine, and Relak's. But it's better than the Pazgog, I suppose. That'll hurt your soul.'

Farjay nodded but Karleg had just returned.

'Any word, Father?' asked Kerbogah as Karleg sat down at the table too.

'Bolor knows nothing about missing children,' whispered Karleg gravely. 'Except that many have vanished in the city. I've ordered us all some food. The Special's finished, but they've still some pomegranate pie. It cost an extra Groot, but I think we've earned it.'

Khayarumi was rubbing his hands and soon a great tin platter of pie arrived and with it an earthenware jug of chestnut beer, as the smells from the kitchen took on the delicious temper of baking pomegranates, in lightly clarified camel butter. Farjay seemed more interested in the cook, though, for he had never seen a man before with such an ugly hunchback.

They ate greedily and Kerbogah fed Relak on his hand. They were truly stuffed when a reveller stepped into the middle of the room and placed a little wicker basket on the ground. He whipped off the lid and then held up a flute and began to blow. Farjay gasped as the music folded about them but Relak was squeaking horribly. A hooded cobra had just risen from the basket, and it was dancing and lapping its spindly, forked tongue in the tavern air.

'Hush, Relak.'

'A snake charmer,' whispered Imlay.

'Ah yes,' said Karleg. 'The snake is holy in many Barbalonian homes, boys, because of the ancient Story of Gilgamar and the snake that crept into his garden.'

'What story?' asked Farjay with his mouth full, as Kerbogah tried to calm his mouse again.

'Tell us, Imlay,' said Karleg, picking up a beaker of beer. 'It will help the meal settle.'

'It's quite a classic,' said Imlay, cleaning his plate with his finger. 'Gilgamar was a great Barbalonian hero, you see, part God and part man.'

'Part God?' asked Farjay.

'Gilgamar was a Demigod. One of the Gods who live on earth and so are mortal.'

Farjay's eyes twinkled as he took another bite of pie.

'After a great flood Gilgamar stole a beautiful flower under

126

the Depthless Sea that would bestow eternal life on all mortals,' said Imlay, 'but Lol and Enlis, jealous even of a Demigod like Gilgamar, sent down the magical snake Ouroborus.'

'Hush, Relak. It's all right.'

'It slithered into Gilgamar's garden as he slept, testing the air with its tongue and stole the plant again and ate it and shed its skin, and so took back the secret of Resurrection.'

Khayarumi was nodding happily.

'Belief in the power of the snake is why two serpents are carved on the Caduceus too,' said the poet, 'the staff of power the High Priests wield in the Incanting Room, where for so long they have tried to create the Balm of Eternal Life.'

'Do you think we'll see a Demigod in Barbal?' whispered Farjay excitedly.

'Of course not, Farjay,' answered Khayarumi, smiling at the lad. 'Like Sandspirits, it's just a story. Though beautifully poetic.'

The others looked taken aback but Khayarumi just smiled at them smugly.

'But Sandspirits aren't just a story, Khayarumi,' said Kerbogah. 'When that Grasht attacked me, I saw them myself.'

Khayarumi fell silent and thoughtful for a while.

'Ah, yes,' he said at last. 'But we see many things in the mind's eye do we not, Kerbogah, especially children and poets? Because children really are poets. But you need not always fear stories of snakes or Sandspirits. As a boy they always filled me with horror too, but my favourite teachers would tell me better stories. They'd show me how to translate what the best stories are really telling us. Even though stories change too over time.'

Imlay seemed to want to argue with the poet, as he had done in the Great Tent but Karleg put a hand on his arm.

127

He could see that what the poet was saying was calming the children.

'What do you mean, translate?' whispered Farjay, straining to understand.

'By listening very carefully to what the ancient stories are really trying to get at, Farjay,' answered Khayarumi. 'No matter what land they come from, perhaps we can see what connects them all. Then discover what universal truths lie behind the words of poets and dreamers, of visionaries and madmen. Here,' he added, tapping his head, 'inside the mind of men.'

Khayarumi seemed to be growing very animated and Farjay was entranced, but Kerbogah was still sure what he had seen of the Sandspirits was more than a story.

'For instance, Farjay, in the Land of the Black Soil, the priest apprentices of Khem tell the story of Creation. They say that in the heavens it was Ammon-Rahr, Lord God of the Sunlight, who married Murd, Goddess of the Earth. Their blessed union first brought forth the crops themselves and all the plants of all the world.'

'So what?' said Farjay.

'Some are foolish enough to believe that it is a real thing,' answered the poet, taking a deep draught of beer. 'But others know that it is only a way of sensing the truth of something far older and deeper. Some deeper reality, before you have the true words for it. For doesn't every common gardener know that nothing will grow from the land without the sunlight, and that a marriage between the sun and the earth takes place every single day?'

Kerbogah felt a strange shiver down his spine, as if someone was watching him.

'Just as holy Inspiru, Khem's great God of Creation and Truth, first made mortals by dreaming the great dream of being,' cried the poet, 'as he climbed onto the mound of

Creation. Then he breathed life and magic into the very clay of the world, to animate the creatures of the earth and air and sea. And gave, in a dream, the first of all holy words to man. A word which itself means to breathe life into something.'

'What word?' asked Kerbogah wonderingly.

'Inspiration. The living breath of the Gods.'

The boys were delighted and wanted to ask more, but suddenly there was a commotion by the doorway. A soldier had stepped into the tavern. He looked about the guests as Bolor himself shuffled over to him. The tavern keeper seemed very nervous indeed as he approached the Barbalissary.

'Can I help?' he asked, dropping his eyes. 'Some apple wine perhaps.'

The hunchback had appeared from the kitchen too and was looking nervously at Bolor and the soldier. There was something almost guilty in his eyes.

'No,' grunted the Barbalissary. 'Now I'm seeking Dunetraders.'

Karleg started and Kerbogah and Farjay gripped the edge of the table.

'Dunetraders?' said Bolor.

'Spies have returned and there are grave rumours in the desert.'

'Rumours?'

'Of many Dunetrader caravans crossing the sands towards Barbal. They come as we speak. Zolos has ordered all Dunetraders from the city once more. On pain of death. But a party has entered Barbal secretly. One of the guards at the Great Gate was talking about it in his sleep.'

At the table Karleg clutched his dagger.

'But the tribute?' said Bolor, smoothing his bald head.

'Mardak no longer needs Stardust,' said the soldier. 'He's quite enough already. And Zolos has no love for the

Dunetraders. If the rumours are true nor should any loyal Barbalonian. So keep an eye out.'

The soldier turned and was about to leave when he stopped and spoke again.

'And be careful, all of you, tonight. If you value your souls, that is. Zolos has ordered a new guard to look for them. Tonight the barracks are opened and Grasht walk the streets of Barbal. The Dunetraders better beware, now *they* are on the scent. A Grasht can sniff out anything.'

'But how do you know what a Dunetrader smells like?' asked one of the revellers.

'Aloe soup,' answered the Barbalissary. 'Dunetraders reek of it.'

The soldier smiled coldly and strode from the tavern as Imlay leant forward.

'Banned from the city again, Karleg. This is bad.'

'And the Grasht,' shivered Farjay, vowing never to eat aloe again. 'They'll be sniffing us out.'

'Something is happening,' whispered Khayarumi, 'among the caravans. Why are they moving towards Barbal?'

'Father,' said Kerbogah, 'if we have to leave already, then what about Kalman?'

'We must ignore the order,' said Karleg gravely, 'until we have found out more about your brother, at least. We must continue searching the streets.'

'But the Grasht, Karleg,' said Imlay, 'and the curfew. You told Selera you would be back by sunset too.'

'I can't help it,' said Karleg angrily. 'If we leave Barbal now we shall never get back into the city. So we shall rent a room in this tavern and bide our time in the shadows until all the fuss dies down.'

The Sun God Zorastar was sinking over the Ziggurat and the walls of Barbal City and in the Street of Soothsayers, largely empty now, four oddly dressed characters were peering at the wall, inscribed with those strange symbols, 'E=MC².'

'Hell's teeth,' whispered Mandrax, as they looked on. 'Nimrod must have given it to them. This is bad.'

'Bad?' said the mournful Habulan.

'Of course. This High Priest couldn't start the Entropoth without an understanding of the Great Equation,' said Mandrax, shaking his head as he looked at the symbols.

'But maybe Nimrod hasn't told them what it means yet,' said Tellor. 'Look at the way they've written it. Downwards. Besides, even if he has told them, how could they really understand it?'

'Let's hope you're right, Tellor,' sighed Mandrax gravely.

'Why are you making such a fuss about it, Mandrax?' asked Habulan. 'Aren't we all sworn to the Alcemoth? *Through magic, study and invention we shall pass the secrets on to the people.* And that's just what Nimrod seems to have done.'

'*But only when they are ready for their coming,*' snapped Mandrax. 'That's what the Oath says. Do you really think Barbalonians are ready for this, Habulan? It could change everything, but far too fast for them to cope with. Let's hope Nimrod hasn't done anything stupid and started throwing words about irresponsibly too.'

Mandrax was suddenly looking at Tellor, who was shuffling his feet. He felt the leader's gaze fall on him and turned away.

'What is it, Tellor?'

'Boss,' he said bitterly. 'I think I've done something rather stupid.'

Mandrax stepped closer and pushed his face into Tellor's.

'What now, Tellor?'

'In the caravanserai. When we first appeared. I was bored and trying to work something out and I . . . well, I wrote it down too. The Great Equation, I mean. But I dropped the paper.'

Mandrax's eyes narrowed angrily.

'Just the equation, Tellor?'

'No, boss, that's just the point. On the back, I wrote it out properly.'

Mandrax grunted and shook his head.

'I'm sorry, Mandrax,' said Tellor. 'I was just doodling.'

'And if it gets into Mardak's hands, with what consequences God alone knows . . .'

'But it was back there. I think it's safe.'

'Let's hope so.'

'Where do you think Nimrod is now?' asked Tellor guiltily.

'I don't know,' answered Mandrax, looking up at the Ziggurat suddenly. 'We must find out somehow. And soon.'

'Boss,' said the last of the men. 'You said you'd tell us where we really are when we got to the city.'

Mandrax looked rather furtive.

'All in good time,' he whispered. 'All in good time.'

'It's a pity we can't contact home, though.'

'Nonsense,' snapped Mandrax. 'What we do is unstable enough. You know the transfer here will run out soon enough anyway and if we tried to contact home it could be even sooner. Before we get Nimrod safely away and try to clean up all this blasted mess.'

'How long have we got, boss?'

'Five days now. Five days left until the Solstice, at any rate.'

'But if we contacted home at least we could order up a reality check, or a forecast.'

'A forecast? How often do those bungling weather diviners ever get it right?' scoffed Mandrax. 'I don't need a diviner to help me predict what's coming to Barbal. I can see that with nothing more than my eyes. You saw those Dunetrader caravans in the desert, for a start? They were on the move.'

The man's gaze had left the companions and was casting out towards the desert.

'What can you see though, Mandrax?' asked Tellor.

Mandrax smiled grimly, his spying eyes glittering in the hazy twilight.

'War, of course.'

'The Dunetraders?'

'Yes. Whatever happens, there will soon be much blood around the sacred city.'

A STRANGE HISTORY

Silas and Rarza looked out bleakly across the endless Mahara Desert. They were riding together now, for Sultan and Ramset were up ahead, and their hoods were up.

'Silas,' whispered Rarza wearily, as she felt a bead of sweat running down her forehead. 'What do you think it will be like in Barbal?'

Silas was just as hot and thirsty. After two days his cracked lips were starting to hurt horribly.

'I don't know, Rarza. But it will be worth the journey to see the city.'

'I suppose so. If we ever make it.'

'And think of it, Rarza,' said Silas, looking all about him under the burning eye of the Sun God, 'we're travelling, Rarza. No Childar has ever done that before.'

'But it frightens me. To have broken the Elders' Commandments, I mean. Can we ever go back? And the desert. It's so . . . so cruel. Hardly a sprig of green and it's so hot. I miss lying in the grass, or by the stream. I dreamt about it all last night.'

'Me too, Rarza,' said Silas, feeling closer to his friend. But Silas fell silent too, for he had dreamt about other things too the night before. About Mardak and his strange stone. He had been holding Gol in his hand, but it had suddenly begun to turn black.

'Silas,' said Rarza suddenly. 'Our mission. Do you think Sultan has a plan? I mean, there are only four of us. And so many in Barbal. Zolos and the Barbalissaries, the Grasht and the Pazgog and . . . *him.*'

Silas was quiet for a while as their camel laboured on in the terrible heat. The odds didn't seem very good at all.

'I'm sure he has,' he answered unconvincingly, trying to cheer them both up. 'Sultan knows everything. And besides, I've always got Gol.'

They laboured on and camped at sunset. As they all climbed down Silas noticed that Sultan's book had dropped out of his bag into the sand. He picked it up and gave it back to the Lesson Master.

'Thank you,' said Sultan, patting the thing like an old friend. 'We mustn't ever lose this. It will tell us many useful and unusual things about the ancient Order of Alchemy. Things that the Alchemists would never admit even to themselves because . . .'

Sultan Ash suddenly looked hard at the three of them, and for a moment the Lesson Master seemed to be wondering if they would understand what he was about to tell them.

'Because half the time, much as people always pretend to, no one actually knows what is really happening in the Seven Lands at all. Especially with the Uncertainty Principle, which Sandworkers developed from Chaos Theory.'

'Uncertainty Principle?' said Rarza, looking out uncertainly on all that sand. Chaos Theory was bad enough, but an

Uncertainty Principle – this was almost too much for any normal Childar to cope with.

'It states, Rarza Stormheart, that we can't be absolutely certain of anything at all in life. Because we always affect the very things we are looking at or studying at the time. So things are very rarely quite as they seem, especially around Barbal.'

'Oh,' said Silas, not understanding a word Sultan was saying either, but recalling that this was exactly what the pot had said in the lesson house.

'And while books can be wonderful things, the problem is always getting to the good bits.'

Sultan suddenly turned over the History. On the back were those twelve beautiful golden symbols.

'Except for these, of course.'

'They're lovely,' whispered Rarza. 'What are they?'

'The Zodiac, Rarza,' answered Sultan. 'They give my History a very special quality indeed. If you offer up the right prayer and hold your hand on the symbols, the book should open at a really meaningful page.'

'Could I have a go?' asked Rarza immediately.

'All in good time,' answered Sultan, smiling at the Childars. 'Things must find their right time.'

But Sultan suddenly cursed.

'Blast! This is bad,' he grunted, putting the History back in his bag.

Sultan had noticed one of the waterskins. In the heat it had split at the bottom and its precious contents had leaked away. But now Silas was more interested in Ramset, who had walked out into the sands towards the setting sun.

The Scribe suddenly raised his leg and balanced on one foot. He held himself quite motionless for a while and then began to move swiftly, chopping at the air with his hands, or punching at the space and turning so gracefully that all his movements seemed to blend into a kind of dance. It was the Chi Dance he had practised each night since they had left Ederyl. At last the Warrior Priest turned and bowed his head to the gigantic sun, as Sultan examined the other skins and Silas and Rarza walked over.

'Ramset,' said Silas cheerfully. 'You said you'd show me.'

'Try then, Childar,' whispered the Scribe. 'Try standing on one leg and kicking. Move in a circle. To the right first.'

'Why a circle?'

'The spirit is always at the centre of the circle, Silas. And it is sometimes as important to look behind as it is to look ahead. But to the right and left too.'

Silas tried it but as soon as he did so he fell flat on his back in the sand.

'Don't worry, Silas,' laughed Ramset as they helped him up again. 'It takes practice and balance. And you must let the Chi in you move your arms and legs, rather than you moving it. Let your spirit guide you. Always.'

Ramset went over to the camels and began to unload branches and kindling to light a fire, for as the Sun God plunged in the skies and the light vanished in almost an instant, as it does in the desert, the air was quickly growing cold. Sultan had already explained to Silas and Rarza that with no clouds in the heavens to cover them, the desert nights were always colder than a winter night in Ederyl. It was why they had all been so glad of the blankets.

First Ramset made a rough circle in the sand for the branches and then began to rub two twigs together to spark the kindling. As he did so, the Warrior Priest's dark eyes wandered the heavens, twinkling like lights above them. Silas and Rarza had never seen such wonderful, gigantic skies, not even in Ederyl, and it had woken a feeling of utter awe and amazement in the Childars as they crossed the great desert, like entering some forgotten temple.

137

Ramset seemed to be searching for something among the beautiful dots of light and at last he sighed deeply, as if he had suddenly been reassured by what he saw up there. Rarza felt strangely drawn to him. It was good to travel with a Warrior Priest.

The woodchips Ramset was using had been stored by the leaking waterskin, though, and were too wet to give flame. At last the Scribe threw them down irritably.

'Here, Ramset,' said Sultan, immediately reaching into his bag and pulling out a large wooden box with a rough edge on one side. Inside were what looked like long sticks with rounded, bright yellow ends. Sultan grazed the end of one against the edge of the box and Silas and Rarza leapt backwards in astonishment. The stick blazed with a marvellous little yellow flame which Sultan touched to the kindling.

'But they're magic,' cried Silas, marvelling at the fire that had started to catch already. 'What are they?'

'Tapers, Silas, although in Jesladom they know them as Lucifers. After their own Lord of the Underworld. And they're not magic at all, just a special mix of powders that flame when rubbed together.'

Silas looked a little abashed, but Sultan gave him one and he popped the Lucifer proudly under his robe, next to Gol. Sultan's expression had softened.

'In a way there's magic in them, though,' he whispered more kindly. 'I mustn't be an old fool and forget that thing which will change ideas about everything one day. The test of us all in the end. Time. But that's the trouble with adults, I suppose, we always forget what it's like to see a Lucifer, or a sacred peacock, for the very first time.'

The fire was beginning to blaze now in the desert night and as they all sat round it to warm themselves Silas found himself staring deeply into the flames. So often Silas had lost himself in firelight in Ederyl and now as he looked he felt suddenly safe and warm again, as though he was connected once more to something ancient and eternal.

'Let's eat now and then rest,' said Sultan. 'We'll get moving at first light. I've miscalculated though, I'm afraid. Our water is already running badly low, especially with that leaking skin. We may have to travel by night soon to avoid the heat. How are you all feeling?'

'I'm scared,' said Rarza truthfully.

'You must have courage, Rarza,' said Sultan, 'and something too that may truly move mountains, as the Dunetraders move the deserts with their songs: faith.'

'Faith in the living Gods?' said Ramset, holding the eye necklace around his throat. Sultan looked closely at the Warrior Priest and his eyes shimmered and danced.

'Faith in each other too, Ramset,' he answered quietly. 'For Dunetraders have a saying as they cross the deserts, especially now the wars return between the caravans. Have faith in the Gods, by all means, but tether your camels carefully at night.'

Ramset smiled.

'So I want you to swear loyalty to each other,' added the Lesson Master suddenly.

Sultan's eyes moved around the fire and Ramset and Silas both nodded.

'Rarza?' said Sultan. 'What about you, my dear?'

Rarza had a crabbing apple in her hand from the provisions and she was biting into it as the others stared at her and waited for her word.

'Mmm,' mumbled Rarza, crunching on the luscious fruit. 'Oh yes. I swear too.'

'Then you must never betray each other,' said Sultan sternly.

The Childars seemed embarrassed and for a while they all ate on in silence.

139

'Sultan, you said you'd tell us how you really knew about me and Gol,' said Silas, at last. 'Was that by magic?'

Sultan shook his head.

'There is a prophecy, Silas, that says the Turnstones would reappear together.'

Rarza looked up immediately.

'A prophecy?'

'Written down long ago in the Book of Destinies. I learnt in the desert that Mazgol had returned at last to Barbal, so I knew Gol must be at hand too. It was from a dying Wordmaster that I realized it would be in Ederyl. In a land of innocence and purity.'

Rarza almost wished she was back at home with her parents, although the thought quickly faded.

'So I left the caravan and as soon as I arrived in Ederyl I felt the presence of the Pazgog, and guessed that the stone had been found already. Knowing that your punishment for trying to open the Wordbox was to till the temple yard, Silas, a sacred place full of stones and rocks, I concluded that my best pupil had found it. That was pure logos.'

'Logos?' said Silas.

'A Heleran word actually. Logic. Logic and the eternal light of reason. Then I really saw a light. In the lesson house, when you were under the table.'

Silas and Rarza marvelled that anyone could know of things he had never actually seen with his own eyes. Logos sounded like a kind of magic too.

'You can do it too, Silas,' said the Lesson Master. 'You've a mind which is very powerful. Use it, Silas Root.'

Rarza looked proudly at her friend.

'And the Wordbox,' said Silas, smiling at the compliment. 'It has something to do with all this too, doesn't it?'

'So it seems,' answered Sultan, looking at Ramset. 'And I've learnt in life, especially studying Chaos Theory and the

Uncertainty Principle, to look for connections where at first I thought there might not be any at all. But then, life itself is the strangest of detective stories.'

Sultan got up and it was clear it was time to sleep. They all lay down and huddled beneath their blankets in the sand and the cold desert night, as the fire flickered away under the vaulting heavens.

As the others' eyes drooped, though, Rarza stirred. She had half an eye open and seemed to be waiting for something. When she was quite sure the others were fast asleep, she got up quietly and crept like a thief straight towards the dozing form of Sultan Ash. For a moment Rarza stood looking down at the strange secret agent and then, very carefully, reached past his head into his bag and pulled out the History.

A loose piece of parchment fluttered out from the back of it and Rarza picked it up. It was covered in writing.

AN INFORMAL TREATISE ON CHANGE AND ALCHEMICAL LEARNING
by
SULTAN ASH

Contrary to many opinions and beliefs, the debate on schooling still rages among the Alchemists. Some stick religiously to the tired old idea that knowledge is just a gradual, rather unmagical process and a matter of collecting things. Ogog, for instance. Others, especially among the mystic Sufis of Moorcaria, believe in a very mysterious process that cannot simply be explained by the passage of time, or the accumulation of facts, facts, facts or indeed, words, words, words.

141

This has perhaps explained sudden moments of spontaneous revelation that cannot be attributed merely to individual pupils swallowing everything they are told by their parents. After all, like teachers, how do we know that Elders really know the truth of it? Since this actually suggests that the Gods, or certainly their messenger Hermet, are always about, and that many children may in fact know far more about the universe, the heavens know how, than their elders and betters, it is crucial that full sway be given to something much debated among the Alchemists, namely inspiration and the eternal power of imagination.

Since no one is ever sure what strange thing they might learn on their road, emphasis too should be placed (a) on travel, (b) on being nice to foreigners, (c) on making people think for themselves. It also confirms Sultan Ash's first famous rule of thumb, namely that any teacher's lessons worth their rock salt should always be fun.

'What are you doing, Rarza?'

Rarza jumped. Silas was sitting up in his blanket and rubbing his eyes.

'I couldn't sleep, Silas,' answered Rarza guiltily, but grinning too. 'I wanted to read.'

Silas yawned, got up and came over to Rarza.

'The History. Let's look together, Rarza.'

The Childars sat down side by side near the fire and Rarza

suddenly thought how nice it was to be with her friend in the desert. She had always wanted to sit next to Silas Root in the lesson house. She suddenly didn't miss Ederyl at all and she looked fondly at Silas.

'Stop gawking at me, Rarza,' whispered Silas. 'Open it up.'

Rarza opened the book where they saw these words:

> Poems, writing, life and fighting,
> Not as clear as holy lightning.

'Turn the page,' said Silas.

> Twinkle, twinkle, little star,
> How I wonder what you are,
> Up above the world so high
> Like some gemstone in the sky

'This is silly,' said Silas. 'Keep going.'

As Rarza thumbed on they found there was lots inside that seemed either half mad or equally silly.

'Rarza,' said Silas suddenly. 'What Sultan said about the Zodiac and putting your hand on them, then offering up a prayer. Let's try it.'

Rarza felt rather foolish but as soon as she put her hands on the signs and whispered a prayer to Zorastar she felt a warmth in her own hands and when she opened the strange book, both children sat bolt upright.

THE TRUE STORY OF
MARDAK THE DARK

Mardak the Dark was always the most promising apprentice and he rose through the ranks like a shooting star. But it was his belief in prayer, prophecy and dreams that set him at odds with the Lord Alchemist and saw him at last installed as the High Priest of Barbal.

'Now this is more like it, Rarza,' whispered Silas.

They fought over the true nature and purpose of Alchemy and, believing only in Sandwork and Reason, Ogog sought a way to depose him. This opportunity arose when it was discovered that Mardak the Dark was about to break the Alcemoth. Mardak had fallen in love with a beautiful Barbalonian girl named Tapputi, legendary for her loveliness, who worked in the Street of the Perfume Makers.

'But what happened?' asked Rarza, as they reached the bottom of the page.

'Turn over, Rarza,' said Silas excitedly.

Barbalonian priests often visited the street to learn the ancient secrets of distillation, using flame to change the nature of unnamed liquids and to trap magical essences. But Mardak would go there to meet Tapputi through the maze of passageways that lie beneath the city. It is believed that Tapputi had an interest in Alchemy - sacrilege for a woman - and that she begged Mardak to reveal some of the holy secrets of the sacred Ziggurat.

At first Mardak refused because of the Alcemoth, but Tapputi so enchanted him with her own extremely powerful charms that, being a sensualist, Mardak finally gave way, in return for her promise of marriage. The ceremony was about to take place one moonlit night in the bazaar when they were discovered by Wordmasters and, though they could not touch one as powerful as the High Priest, Tapputi was banished into the deserts to die at the hands of the Sun God Zorastar.

'Mardak,' whispered Rarza. 'They murdered his bride. Think of that. How he must have loved her.'

Rarza's eyes were almost moist in the firelight and her gaze suddenly made Silas uncomfortable.

'So Mardak murdered the Wordmasters too,' Silas grunted, scuffing the sand, 'and broke the Seven Commandments. Now he'll summon Aspis from the Underworld. The Destroyer.'

'Unless we can stop him, Silas, and free Ogog. But how? It's death to enter the Ziggurat.'

Rarza's eyes flickered.

'Silas,' she whispered, looking very small and sad. 'I don't want to die.'

Silas looked strangely at his friend. He felt rather awkward but, very gently, Silas reached out and took Rarza's hand.

'Don't worry, Rarza, nobody's going to die. We'll think about the Ziggurat when we get there. I promise. I've my stone to protect us. And Sultan said we should have hope and faith.'

Silas suddenly pulled his hand away, though, and they fell

silent again, both peering gloomily into the firelight. Silas looked very troubled.

'My father, Rarza,' he said cheerlessly as he saw her look. 'I wish he wasn't . . . I wish he was here, Rarza. Perhaps he'd know what to do.'

'Timon and Alara always loved you.' Rarza nodded rather sadly. 'But my parents . . . They're always fighting and shouting and telling me off. It's why I always wanted to run away.'

'And now you're here,' said Silas, looking at Rarza proudly, 'to stop Mardak's evil.'

'Evil?' said a voice behind them.

They both jumped. Sultan was yawning loudly but smiling too as he stood there.

'Evil's a strong word, Silas Root,' he said, rubbing his eyes sleepily. 'Perhaps Mardak is just overambitious. I'm glad you're using the magic History, though.'

Silas and Rarza were embarrassed to be sitting so close and Silas moved away a little as Sultan crouched down beside them and rubbed his hands in front of the fire.

'What do you mean, overambitious?' asked Silas. 'After all that Mardak's done. You've come to punish him, haven't you?'

'Punish Mardak? I've come to end the Schism, Silas, and to free Ogog, yes,' answered the Lesson Master quietly. 'But Mardak is the High Priest, remember, and very brilliant too. He has many sincere followers in the Ziggurat. Although he always sought an apprentice worthy of his own mind and talents.'

Silas looked grimly into the flames.

'You fear him, Silas,' said Sultan, warming his hands, 'but Mardak argues that it is fear that really keeps us in chains. A fear of life and of sin that holds us back. Mardak would abolish fear and sin, and think anything he can. He would know all things. Even the answer to the greatest secret. The true nature of the Creator.'

Nearby Ramset moaned and rolled over in his sleep and Silas and Rarza looked up at the myriad stars.

'But he's broken the Seven Commandments, Sultan,' said Rarza, 'sent down by the Gods themselves from heaven. And now he turns Barbal back to the ancient ways. To darkness and blood sacrifice.'

'Ah yes, Rarza, but throughout the Seven Lands you'll find that Gods are very fond of sacrifices. And that their sacrifice is man's sacrifice too. As for the Commandments, Mardak says they only keep us in ignorance and servitude. He was never one for the rules. Like you two, I think.'

'What do you mean?' asked Rarza and she remembered her own father again, shouting at her for not obeying orders.

'For years the Alchemists and the Wordmasters inscribed "Thou Shalt Not" above the Ziggurat with their rules and their Seven Commandments,' answered Sultan quietly, picking up a stick and stirring the fire. 'With their control of the Wordboxes too. But Mardak the Dark thought to inscribe another commandment in letters as tall as a spire. "Thou Shalt".'

Sultan's eyes were shining in the desert night, as a little flame caught at the end of the stick. Silas and Rarza were startled, for it was almost as if Sultan seemed to admire the Black Magician.

'But after she went,' said Sultan. 'Tapputi. Mardak grew obsessed with death and so with the greatest secret of Alchemy.'

'Resurrection,' said Silas.

'Yes, Silas. And perhaps rightly so, for with all our struggles to understand, all our loves and hopes and fears, are they not meaningless in the face of death?'

The fire sparked and spat an ember into the sand and the Childars looked rather frightened again.

'After all, as Mardak argued, why should we be afraid of any laws or rules, if we know that we are going to die anyway? Unless of course we really must pay for our crimes in another place, and for all eternity. So, following the teaching of the Alcemoth, Mardak wanted to look beyond the Seals and see the truth.'

'The truth?' said Silas, remembering the oath.

'The Alchemists believe that while there are Gods around us all the time, the truth and the visible nature of the Creator is always hidden from us, veiled from us behind seven seals, that we must first open to gain true knowledge. When Mardak summons Aspis from the Underworld he will open the Seventh Seal.'

'The Pazgog comes from the Underworld,' said Silas nervously, wondering what the Seventh Seal was. 'And Ramset's plagues too. It must be a terrible place.'

'Perhaps, Silas. Yet the Alchemists and the High Priests are searchers, and some say the power of true Alchemy must draw on all the secret forces of the universe to really see the truth. Darkness as well as light. As above, so below. As it says in the Alcemoth.'

'Below?' whispered Silas. 'Down in the Underworld?'

'Which some also call the realm of dreams and intuition.'

'The Doorway lies in Khem,' said Rarza, looking at Ramset under his blanket, sleeping peacefully beside them.

'In a manner of speaking, Rarza,' said Sultan, 'although many believe that it isn't a physical doorway. In Heleras, the Land of Centaurs, followers of the great Goddess Psyche teach that the Lower Kingdom dwells inside us all.'

'Inside us?' whispered Rarza in horror.

'Oh yes, Rarza,' said the Lesson Master, raising his eyebrow. 'Many try to keep the Doorway closed on it, just as they try and suppress their fears and hopes and feelings. Yet others believe that we must never do that, for inside us lurks such power and wonder and insight that it could transform everything.'

The children both shivered. The desert and the fire, the sand and the stars suddenly seemed gigantic.

Ramset moaned and turned over once more and Silas wondered what he was dreaming about.

'But the Underworld is evil,' said Rarza. 'Like Mardak.'

'Is it, now?' said Sultan softly. 'And are you sure what you really are yourself? What angels and demons you have inside you? So be careful how you judge things, Rarza, for you may find them judging you in return.'

'Sultan,' said Silas suddenly. 'You've met Mardak the Dark?'

Something flickered behind Sultan's blue-green eyes, but he nodded.

'Oh yes, Silas. We go back a very long way.'

'But all that's happening,' said Rarza. 'It seems so muddled.'

'It's Chaos Theory,' said Silas matter-of-factly, trying to impress their Lesson Master.

Sultan smiled at him and dropped his stick into the flames.

'The important thing about Chaos Theory, Silas Root, the really logical thing about it, isn't the chaos at all.'

'It isn't?' the Childars said at once.

'Of course not' said the Lesson Master. 'The really important thing about Chaos Theory is seeing the pattern. Inside what appears to be chaos. Like seeing the true pattern of the stars in a sandstorm with Stardust.'

Ramset suddenly cried out in his sleep.

'Agh! Stop it. Don't.'

Ramset was lashing and kicking in the sand and Sultan jumped up and started shaking him.

'Ramset! Wake up, Ramset!'

The Scribe clutched at Sultan's arms.

'Ramset, let go. You're just having a dream, that's all.'

Ramset relaxed a little and opened his strange eyes. Sultan was smiling down kindly at him.

'Are you all right, my friend?'

'Yes, yes I think so. Thank you, Ashtar.'

'We must all learn to let go of things,' said Sultan, looking at Silas and Rarza. '*Take hold tightly, let go lightly*. What were you dreaming of, Ramset?'

'First the Mystifier was trying to visit me,' answered Ramset, sitting up and stroking the symbol on his arm, 'and then I dreamt of snakes.'

'Snakes?' said Sultan, turning to Silas. 'Now that's very interesting. In Barbal the snake is worshipped because of the story of the hero Gilgamar and the serpent Ouroboros.'

'In the Land of the Black Soil,' said Ramset, stretching himself and trying to shake the dream off, 'the snake has an even greater significance. Each night Rahr the Sun God descends into the darkness of the Underworld, just as the Faron visits the realm of sleep in his dreams, and rows his golden barque along the terrible river. There he must pass through exactly twelve gates.'

'Twelve,' said Sultan thoughtfully. 'A very sacred number. Like seven.'

'And there the Faron must avoid the demon serpent,' said Ramset. 'The serpent that lurks in the shadows waiting to swallow souls.'

'What serpent?' asked Silas.

'Aspis, Lord of the Underworld,' said Ramset. 'The Destroyer's form is a terrible snake.'

Silas looked at Rarza and gulped hard.

'It's why the double crown of Khem bears a golden serpent too. In the world above, the snake crowns the Faron, but below it deprives Aspis, the Uncrowned King of Night, of his powers.'

'Aspis,' murmured Sultan. 'Why don't you tell us his story, Ramset? None of us is sleepy now.'

The Warrior Priest sat up properly in the sand.

'Very well, Ashtar. I will tell you the story of what happened when the great Sun God Rahr grew weary of ruling over man and the earth and retired to the heavens once more.'

Ramset's strong, dark features were glowing and Silas and Rarza felt comforted.

'Rahr's son Ossir and his beautiful consort Isor came to rule over the world of men and so, under the Gods' kingship, great plenty came to the Land of the Black Soil,' began Ramset. 'But Ossir's brother Aspis grew jealous in the night and slew Ossir horribly and so death was born into the world. But Isor was a Goddess, and had the power to bring Ossir back to life again. To resurrect him.'

The Childars looked up hopefully and thought of Mardak and Tapputi.

'But only long enough so that they could conceive a son together,' continued Ramset, 'a beautiful God child named Hos. His mother Isor reared their beloved son in secret to avenge her husband and with Hekka Magic she protected him from the familiars of Aspis, the desert dwellers, poisonous snakes and venomous scorpions, and diseases too that snatch away souls in the night. The Seven Plagues.'

'Hekka Magic?' asked Silas. 'What kind of magic?'

'She gained power over the emissaries of Aspis by learning their names. For in the beginning is the word and naming is the first power. Yet you must know the true name.'

Rarza was wondering how a word could have a beginning.

'So Hos learnt to handle the desert creatures,' said Ramset

151

softly, 'as if they were his closest friends. He would hold snakes in his heavenly hand and scorpions would run along his arms and he learnt too the secrets of poison. So Hos grew and was ready at last to avenge his father in heaven.'

'What happened, Ramset?' asked Silas, thinking of his father, Timon, and wondering where he had gone.

'In the great desert they fought for dominion, Hos and the terrible Aspis,' answered Ramset, 'and Hos slew the Lord God of Chaos and sent him to dwell in the Underworld. Where he lurks still, coiled in the shadows, waiting to take back what he believes is his by right. From whence, if the Pazgog is any sign, he shall soon return himself.'

'At the Great Solstice?' whispered Silas.

Ramset nodded.

'But what happened to Hos?' asked Rarza, who loved the sound of this brave Godchild. He filled her with hope.

'The Lord God Hos had conquered for the time being and taken his revenge, Rarza. But in their battle Aspis had plucked out one of his eyes. His mother prayed to the Goddess of Wisdom though, the Moon Goddess, and as the moon waxed and grew full, she healed the eye of Hos. So for evermore the symbol of the eye is the symbol for the watching moon.'

Ramset held up one of the two little medallions round his throat and the eye glittered in the firelight.

'And for those with true wisdom in the Land of the Black Soil. For you may only attain wisdom if you really look closely at things.'

'Now let's sleep,' said Sultan suddenly.

'And no more bad dreams, Ramset,' whispered Rarza, liking their friend more and more.

'At least he *was* dreaming, Rarza,' said Sultan. 'That's better than going to a place where there are no dreams. Good or bad. The Chasm of Dreamless Night.'

 152

Rarza and Silas were exhausted with their lesson and the story, and Sultan put the book back in the bag and they went to lie down under their blankets. In no time at all Rarza and Silas had fallen sound asleep and Silas began to dream that he was doing a Chi Dance in the desert, in a great circle, but that he fell over and landed against a flat doorway in the sand which began to open before him. It seemed only an instant, though, before Sultan broke into his visions.

'Stir yourselves, the stars are going out.'

'Oh, bother it,' said Silas, opening his eyes to see Sultan stretching by the fire. It had died and was smouldering faintly, but in the sky the Sun God was mounting again. It was already hot, and Ramset stood there on one leg again, chopping at the air.

'Sunrise,' mumbled Rarza painfully as she got up too and stretched. 'So soon.'

'And what if I told you the sun doesn't rise, Rarza?' said Sultan cheerfully, looking up at the fiery orb. 'Well, not exactly anyway.'

Silas and Rarza were too drowsy to worry about Sultan's strange remarks. They mounted the camels again and talked little, for now it was just too hot. Even the camels seemed to be wilting as they rode on and Silas noticed that Sultan started to look grave. During their occasional stops he began to ration their water too.

'The skins are already running desperately low,' he said that afternoon. 'We must find the caravanserai soon, but I'm no longer sure of the path.'

'Path?' said Silas, looking about helplessly at all that sand.

'I find my way by the sun, and certain permanent features, but the storm has changed the Mahara Desert greatly.'

Silas wiped the sweat from his brow.

'I wonder how the poor camels manage,' said Rarza,

looking sadly at her mount. 'They haven't drunk a thing since they left Ederyl.'

'Ah,' said Sultan. 'Camels are very special beasts, Rarza. They were designed for the desert. Even by it.'

On they rode, and towards twilight Sultan raised his hand and pointed. A single palm stood in the desert.

'Water!' he cried. 'If there's a tree, there must be water.'

It was only one drooping palm tree, scorched by the sun, and at its bottom a shallow pool in the sand. But it was what lay around the edges of the oasis that terrified Silas and Rarza. There were four bodies. The Dunetraders were all dead. Two lay face down in the sand, while the other two had fallen on their backs, their sightless eyes gazing up at the heavens.

'They must have been attacked as they lay down to drink,' said Sultan, as they climbed down.

Silas was too thirsty by now to let even the presence of the dead hold him back from water. He was already stooping beneath the palm tree, dipping his hands in the dirty pool at its base, when Ramset gave a furious shout.

'By the Seven Stars, *don't*, Silas!'

Silas had his hands cupped to his lips but the Scribe sprang forward and knocked them open, spilling the muddy brown water into the sand.

'Hey. What are you . . . ?'

'The Dunetraders,' snapped the Warrior Priest. 'Look at them, Silas. There are no wounds.'

Ramset was peering closely at the edges of the pool and as he did so he suddenly noticed something and crouched down to pick it up. As he rose he had a little blue bottle in his hand and he sniffed it.

'Poison,' he whispered, pulling his nose away at the smell. 'Just as I thought. The water has been poisoned. This is bad news for the desert dwellers.'

'Was it another caravan that did it?' asked Silas, stepping back. 'In the wars?'

Ramset looked up at Sultan and shook his head.

'That's just the point. I believe they only make this kind of tinted blue glass in Barbal.'

Sultan and Ramset managed to drag the wretched Dunetraders a little away from the palm and Ramset mumbled some words over the bodies, before they walked back to Silas and Rarza.

'Well,' said Ramset, 'if we can't drink we will join them quickly enough anyway.'

Sultan was already scouring the sand though. He walked up to a little dip in the ground nearby where the sand was darker and, dropping to his knees, began scrabbling with his hands. But after a while he gave up.

'It's no good. Any fresh water is too deep.'

Rarza had just noticed that Silas was clutching his hand to his chest.

'Silas, what is it?'

'Gol, Rarza,' whispered Silas. 'It's getting warm again and whenever that happens . . .'

Silas pulled out Gol. The stone was glowing brightly as Silas held it out. Rarza's eyes were on stalks. Suddenly, where Sultan had been digging away, there was a little spurt of water. A spring had bubbled up.

'Hooray!' cried Rarza. 'Good old Silas!'

'The Turnstone,' said Sultan delightedly. 'Gol's Chi has drawn water from the earth. Quick, Ramset, your waterskin.'

Ramset collected enough of the water to fill it half full – and just in time, for Gol had stopped glowing again and suddenly the little spring stopped flourishing. The water was desperately bitter and brackish, but at least it slaked their thirsts.

They camped once more and lit another fire. A breeze had

started to blow and far out beyond the ring of fire they heard a gentle moaning across the desert. Rarza shifted closer to Silas as they looked on those breathless Dunetraders, but as they sat there Sultan suddenly reached into his pocket.

'Silas, you'll want this back.'

'Gol,' cried Silas as he held it up. 'But how . . . ?'

'It slipped from your pocket. I told you it would try to get away.'

'Gol and Mazgol,' whispered Silas, looking rather shame-faced as he took the Lightbearer and put it safely back in his smock. 'Where do the Turnstones really come from?'

'Where does anything really come from, Silas?' answered Sultan thoughtfully. 'Childar Elders say that everything was created when mighty Lol slumbered for Seven Suns, and dreamt the great dream of being.'

Sultan's nose twitched.

'But Elders say a lot of things, don't they? They tell the story of the Fall of the Tower of Barbal too. When the Gods created man. But is it just a story? And if the Gods created us, who created the Gods? An even bigger God perhaps. And what is the very first substance? Not even the Alchemists know that yet, for it takes time to read the truth of things.'

'Read?' said Silas.

'When you look at a chair you think of it as nothing but a chair, don't you?' said the Lesson Master. 'But if you looked deeper at it, and took away the word "chair", what would you see then? Perhaps other worlds, Silas Root. For in the land of Heleras their Alchemist, the Philosophon, believes that everything is made up of smaller and smaller things, which we can't even see.'

Ramset suddenly leant forward and picked something up in his hand. It was a little beetle with blue-green skin that scurried across his palm.

'Your jewel, Ramset,' said Rarza. 'It's just like your jewel.'

'The holy scarab beetle,' said the Warrior Priest. 'They're very determined little creatures, Rarza, so in Khem they symbolize Resurrection and eternal life.'

'But as for the Turnstones,' Sultan went on, 'studying the nature of heavenly matter like Stardust, the Alchemists learnt that some stones were inert, which means their magic Chi was not strong enough to make things react, but that two in particular have very special properties.'

Silas was silent and brooding and the little party, so small and fragile in the desert, again sat gazing up at the endless stars.

'But now we should sleep again,' said Sultan. 'Tomorrow, if we rise before sun-up, we can get a good way before Zorastar grows too angry. With so little water we will rest again in the middle of the day, but we must find the Camel before death or the Pazgog find us.'

They rose well before the Sun God, camping again in the shade of their own camels when Zorastar reached his anvil, its hottest point, and going on well past sundown. They made steady enough progess but Silas and Rarza could see that Sultan was now frantically worried. On they went, feeling as if the Fire God and a million demons were chasing them and not until their waterskins were bone dry did they begin to grow really terrified.

'I'm so thirsty,' gasped Rarza bitterly.

'Yes, Rarza. We must find the Camel soon and I pray it's close,' said Sultan gravely. 'It's our only hope now.'

THE ELUSIVE CAMEL

The going was hard and the stars had long peeped out in the desert dark when Sultan Ash cried out again. 'Look there, children!'

Silas and Rarza expected to see some dwelling on the horizon, or another little oasis, but they saw nothing but the endless sands.

'What?' drawled Silas wearily. He was riding behind Sultan again.

'See, Silas. In the sand.'

A gigantic moon was rising and suddenly Silas saw it. A tiny flash of light in the desert. As Silas and Rarza's eyes grew accustomed to the changing shadows they saw another flash and then another. Tiny flickering flecks of light sparking on the ground, one after the other, like little dots of golden fire, forming a path through the dunes straight ahead of them.

'Stardust,' cried Ramset, 'it's Stardust.'

'Dunetraders have been this way,' said Sultan excitedly. 'They'll be making for the Elusive Camel too. We're saved.'

Silas thought the flickering trail looked wonderful and beneath his robe Gol had begun to glow once more. Almost instinctively the Dunetrader camels began to follow the trail, but as they went Rarza was shaking her head.

'Sultan, I know they use it to navigate the skies by, but what is Stardust really?'

'Let me tell them, Ashtar,' said Ramset on his camel.

'Very well, Ramset. It's fitting for a Scribe and a Warrior Priest.'

'Stardust is sand,' sang the Warrior Priest. 'But no common or garden sand. It is sand that has been touched by the voices of the Mahara Dunetraders. Voices which carry a magic Chi older and more powerful than any in Barbal can understand.'

Ramset's voice suddenly climbed like lovely music around them.

'For how has man struggled out of the darkness of ignorance and fear, out of the desert of nothingness and unknowing, except with the faith of his hopes and dreams and the power of his very deepest beliefs? Over the ages, the Mahara Dunetraders, struggling to forge a path of song, living, trading and dying, used their voices alone to move the great Mahara Desert. They used the power of Song.'

Silas felt a strange churning in his stomach and he remembered how the terrible Pazgog had stopped his throat.

'But it was a Lord Alchemist who sent his Wordmasters out to follow the caravans, and discovered that where their voices had moved the sand, something very remarkable had happened.'

Ramset was looking down at their camels' feet with shimmering eyes.

'Traces of special sand had been left. The Chi of the Dunetraders' songs, summoned by their longings and feelings, had touched the Chi in the sand itself and transformed it. The power of song and inspiration, the very power of the spirit, had entered into matter itself. Matter now had life. It was never very much, but each time Dunetraders moved the desert, just a little more was made each time.'

The Childars' eyes had opened as wide as whirlpools and Silas suddenly thought of that pot again. Matter with life in it. It was everywhere.

'The Dunetraders had been watching the heavens to navigate the deserts,' the Scribe went on, 'as the Lord Alchemists had been using the stars to try to see the future. Perhaps that's why their songs made Stardust reflect their very thoughts and memories as they watched the pattern of the skies. So you see, children, what we follow now is a Songtrail.'

Ramset fell silent and Sultan smiled delightedly.

'Well done, Ramset,' he cried. 'You'd have pleased even Khayarumi. And it's hard to please a poet. Especially one that's always going on about seeing the universe in a grain of sand.'

Sultan lifted his head and began to chant himself as the Stardust led them on through the cold desert night towards safety. A chant that soon warmed their frightened hearts.

> *Born of desert, work of clay,*
> *Sing the songs that make our way.*
> *Camel riders, tribe of tunes,*
> *Chant the path and clear the dunes.*

Silas Root's head was spinning up into the beautiful night sky as he tried to understand, reeling like a drunken Dunetrader. He wanted to lie down suddenly in the desert among the glittering Stardust and let it all engulf him, as he wondered and dreamt about all he had learnt and the lands and secrets that lay ahead of him.

They rode through the night, comforted and guided by

the Songtrail and, although the next day the Stardust vanished in the sunlight, Sultan seemed to know where he was again. He kept them going all day, though, for they were still in terrible danger, and it was close to sunset when Gol began to glow again.

They suddenly saw it. At first it was a tiny dot on the horizon, like a large rock, but it grew more and more discernible as their camels came closer. Rarza could hardly believe her eyes. There stood the Elusive Camel in the middle of the Mahara Desert, like a delightful mirage, flanked by some scrubby palm trees. It was like a little white hamlet, surrounded by a square stone wall and entered through a high stone gate. There were men wandering about a well and a few tatty cooking stalls here and there. Around them piles of camel dung steamed in the evening, filling the desert air with a thick, musty scent.

'Come,' cried Sultan, jumping down. 'We could all use a drink.'

Sultan strode towards the gate, leading his camel now and tethering it against a wall. To one side was a stack of wooden cages filled with different kinds of birds and strange and exotic lizards, dogs and cats, and bizarre desert creatures that Silas and Rarza could give no names to at all. They all looked in a pitiful condition and from the sides of the cages hung vicious metal hooks and spiked tools, rope cords and long, black leather whips.

But it was a large wooden box, with a finely slatted top, that most fascinated the Childars.

'Snakes,' whispered Rarza.

The box was indeed filled to the brim with snakes, curling and twisting about each other. Some were patterned like desert rocks and others were very brightly coloured.

'There must be animal slavers about,' said Ramset. 'They'll profit in Barbal Bazaar. In the Street of Slavers.'

'How far is it?' asked Rarza hoarsely. 'To the Sacred City?'

'Haven't you been counting, Rarza? Only three suns now,' answered Sultan. 'But tonight we rest here. In safety.'

Sultan strode through the gate into a wide courtyard, where there was a pile of weapons and a high wooden double door spilling light and noise outside.

'No weapons are allowed in the Camel,' he said. 'And not a word, mind, of who we are and where we travel. With the wars we can trust no one.' He paused. 'And Mardak the Dark is always watching.'

Ramset was looking back through the gate.

'What is it, my friend?' asked Sultan.

'There,' said the Scribe. 'A horse.'

A large black horse was now tethered near the well they had passed earlier.

'Wait here,' said Sultan, 'while I investigate.'

The Lesson Master was gone a long time and the three of them were desperately thirsty by the time he returned.

'This is bad,' said Sultan as he strode back. 'It's a Barbalissary. And there are others on the way by the looks of it. Let's get inside.'

Sultan bent down and pulled off his boots.

'Take off your shoes too,' he ordered. 'Sulphurius is rather proud of his carpet.'

'Sulphurius?' said Silas.

'He runs the Camel, Silas. And knows much of worth. He was a priest apprentice once too.'

'But I thought it was death to leave the Order.'

'So it is. Sulphurius was banished before he had had a chance to take the Alcemoth. Now he runs the Camel for his sins.'

'Banished? Why?'

Sultan smiled.

'For getting blind drunk.'

Sultan pushed on through the door of the Camel. Laughter and noise engulfed the Childars as soon as they entered the caravanserai. A great carpeted hall was suddenly before them, thick with smoke, but as Silas and Rarza peeped from their dusty hoods, all they really glimpsed were huge arms and dark faces glowering at them. There were revellers everywhere. On one side of the room was a group of turbaned Dunetraders – if you could still call them Dunetraders, for although they had left their Songtrail in the sands, it was a long time since they had traded in Barbal, or anywhere else for that matter. They looked very desperate indeed.

The carpet beneath them felt strange and scratchy against their feet, but it was a beautiful thing, woven with more colours than the Childars had ever seen before. Ranged all around the smoky caravanserai were water pipes and among them great glass vessels too, with spouts protruding from their ends in alcoves right around the room. Some were empty but many others were filled with red and white liquids, while still more were boiling away on little coal fires.

'Come on then,' cried one of the men, springing to his feet. 'Someone dance for us. Whirl for us till dawn.'

The man clapped his hands smartly and almost at his command music struck up. Three men stepped into the middle of the caravanserai and behind them a gaunt young Dunetrader began to wail, his voice following the crazy whine of a simple wooden fiddle, as the men twirled round with flying skirts.

'Spin like the spinning stars,' cried the wailer delightedly, jigging up and down, 'and let their madness shine in us like light.'

Silas and Rarza felt their heads growing dizzier and dizzier. Ramset seemed especially enchanted, for his black-rimmed eyes were glittering brilliantly and he had begun to tap his foot in time to the frantic rhythms. The Warrior

Priest's look became so concentrated it was as if he were drunk himself and Silas saw a tear running down his cheek.

'Music,' Ramset whispered, wiping it away as he noticed Silas staring at him. 'Sometimes I wonder if it is not the only real truth.'

'Real truth, Ramset?' said Silas, thinking of the Alcemoth.

'They're Dancing Derwishers, Silas. In Heleras such a show would earn them a true throne of honour,' sniffed the Scribe. 'For music heals. Just as aloe soup cures the Dunetraders' voices in the desert, music and song calm the demons in man and keep them at bay. It has a truly magical power.'

Ramset had begun to tap his foot.

'The Sufis would love such a spectacle,' he cried. 'Sufis are great mystics and magicians, from the strange and enchanted lands of Moorcaria. They believe that all is one, but that to see its pattern you need to bring on visions. By dancing.'

The dancing had just finished though and the Lesson Master pushed on ahead through the throng, but as the others followed, Silas and Rarza overheard two of the travellers talking together.

'You know the Dunetraders are turning their voices towards Barbal at last,' whispered one. 'They say many caravans are crossing the desert.'

'Not this lot,' grunted the other, looking around scornfully. 'But why?'

'The power of their voices fails.'

'And now Mazgol has come and the God of Chaos awaits, Mardak will raise Aspis himself at the Solstice. The Destroyer. Then nothing can stop him.'

'But hope comes also,' said his companion sternly. 'The Book of Destinies promised that with Mazgol comes the Lightbearer also. It has been prophesied. The White Turnstone shall come to our aid. Gol the Magnificent. The light of the world.'

Rarza touched Silas's arm but something very grave suddenly stirred inside him, a yawning feeling in the very pit of his stomach. He moved his hand to Gol beneath his robe. Silas wondered if he would have to fight the Destroyer himself and what 'The light of the world' might mean.

Sultan and Ramset had gone on ahead, though, and they hurried over to the end of the chamber after them. Behind a long stone counter, a peculiar little man was struggling to serve the guests. He had a jolly, if henpecked face, with very ruddy cheeks and eyes that kept darting about constantly, as if he expected to be ambushed at any moment. His hair fell about his shoulders in a great tangle of curly grey. As soon as he saw Sultan he rushed straight over to the end of the bar.

'Ashtar!' he whispered, in an excitable, high-pitched voice, his face pouring with sweat. 'Thank heavens you're here at last, Ashtar. I expected you sooner. But you look terrible.'

'Thank you, Sulphurius,' said Sultan, raising an eyebrow and laughing.

'What can I get you, Ashtar?'

'Four glasses of fresh rosewater, man,' answered Sultan, slapping a Groot on the counter.

Sulphurius picked up a huge glass jug and the Childars licked their lips as he poured out four beakers of clear, clean water. They all drank and held them out for more.

'Childars, if I'm not mistaken,' said Sulphurius as he filled them again. 'And a Warrior Priest of Khem. We're honoured indeed in the Camel.'

'It's been a hard crossing,' said Sultan. 'It feels strange in the caravanserai tonight.'

The funny little man's eyes darkened.

'Last night the Servant came over again. We all felt its shadow and the camels nearly bolted. As well as snatching souls it is searching for something, Ashtar. Some think Gol itself.' Rarza looked nervously at Silas. 'But thank the Gods it passed safely overhead. Back to its master.'

'Then you're right to impose your rule about weapons and shoes, Sulphurius,' Sultan said simply. 'For the Pazgog dares not attack where any are gathered together in peace.'

'Peace!' snorted Sulphurius. 'The desert wars are touching everyone now, Ashtar. And what hope of peace is there if Aspis really rises from the Underworld? Chaos shall cover everything when the Destroyer returns.'

'I know it, Sulphurius, but at least we've reached a safe harbour for a while. But tell us more of what is happening in Barbal.'

'There are terrible rumours, Ashtar,' whispered Sulphurius, 'of vanishing children, of murder, and in the bazaar Groot prices are already getting out of control. The Barbalissaries are stretched to keep order. The Pazgog roams the city and the Barbalonians protect themselves with talismans.'

Silas and Rarza suddenly blinked. A little glowing light had just gone darting past Sulphurius's head in the gloom, as if a fleck of Stardust had taken to the air. The children saw another and another and suddenly there were yellow lights all about the man's head, crowning his silvery hair. Silas's jaw dropped open but Sulphurius grabbed a cloth and waved it angrily past his nose.

'Blast it, how did those get out?

'What are they?' asked Silas.

'Fireflies. They've the strangest Chi, lad, and some of the priest apprentices used to study their nature in Barbal. I prefer to look to the great things in the Gods' universe myself, but there may be a value in studying the smallest, so I keep a few behind the counter, as part of my collection. Not as impressive as what they hold in the Ziggurat, but not at all bad.'

Silas and Rarza drew closer. They had both been dreaming about all the wonderful things they would see if they ever got inside the Ziggurat, but this collection sounded very exciting too.

'Did you really go into the Ziggurat, Sulphurius?' whispered Rarza, looking in awe at the funny little man. 'When you were an apprentice, I mean?'

'Of course, my dear, if only into the Halls of the Sinking Sun, not Mardak's wing. I was too green to see any more and spent rather too much time on my fermentations.'

'What's it like, though. Inside the Ziggurat?'

'Like nothing on this earth, my dear, though I'm not really supposed to talk about it. If the Barbalissaries or one of Mardak's boys heard me, there'd be the Underworld to pay.'

'Sulphurius,' interupted Sultan. 'Are there any beds for us tonight?'

'Well, I've nothing much left,' answered Sulphurius, looking about the crowded room. 'They all come for the Solstice. But as it's you, Ashtar, you can have that room by the gate, where you stayed last time. I'll send someone to make up the beds. Finest camel hair, with fleas for free.'

Sulphurius winked.

'We'll need food,' said Sultan, 'and plenty to drink for the rest of the crossing. What other news? I hope you've been keeping your ear to the ground as I always taught you.'

Sulphurius glanced rather scornfully about the caravanserai.

'Many are looking for work or adventure as usual, Ashtar. But I keep them happy and talkative, feeding their stomachs and their dreams. I made up another fine brew the other sun.'

Sulphurius looked proudly towards one of the clear glass vats in the corner, which had no fire beneath it. From the

167

ruddy veins in his cheeks it was plain he was very fond of tasting the vintage wines he so loved to ferment.

'Well, it certainly has a powerful effect on this lot,' said Sultan, as somebody started shouting behind them. 'But Sulphurius, those cages outside. There are animal slavers around?'

Sulphurius nodded towards the corner where a group of revellers were toasting each other loudly. He spat scornfully onto the floor behind the counter.

'The scum have been living it up for moons now. For a long time they were collecting ordinary animals for Zolos, especially snakes. But now they've turned to a richer seam – Demigods.'

Ramset stepped forward.

'Demigods? By the Seven Stars, it's sacrilege.'

'And strictly forbidden to trade in them across the borders of the Seven Lands,' said Sulphurius. 'But then things have changed with Mardak's ambitions. Now everyone seems to be breaking the rules.'

Sultan Ash's eyes narrowed but both Silas and Rarza desperately wanted to see what a Demigod looked like.

'What kind of Demigods, Sulphurius?' asked Ramset.

'Centaurs, sir. From the land of Heleras.'

The Warrior Priest whistled.

'No wonder they're getting drunk, then,' he cried, looking almost admiringly at the slavers. 'For Centaurs are a vicious breed, capable of much darkness and savagery.'

Ramset's black-rimmed eyes seemed to revolve in his head.

'They claim they even captured Chiron,' said Sulphurius.

'Chiron!' gasped Ramset.

'Who's Chiron?' asked Rarza.

'No ordinary Centaur, Rarza,' answered the Scribe, 'for, although Centaurs are mad, Chiron is of a different temper.

 168

His wisdom and earth magic are famed throughout Heleras, for he is a great musician and healer. They say his pipes, which he plays to summon in every new dawn, were made for him by the God Panos himself.'

Sultan didn't seem to want to talk about the trade in Centaurs, though.

'Anything else, Sulphurius?' he asked instead.

'I heard yesterday that somebody is stealing sacred peacocks from Barbal Square. Another sacrilege.'

'And another little riddle that needs a solution in Barbal,' said Sultan. 'Is that all?'

Sulphurius suddenly put down the cloth in his hands and leant right over the bar.

'As a matter of fact, it ain't. There's something rather extraordinary.'

Sulphurius dipped behind the bar and when he popped up he placed a scroll on the counter. Ramset stepped up immediately and smoothed it out flat.

'I've seen many like it in Khem,' he said. 'There we use papyrus leaves to make our scrolls, but this is different.'

'Yes, Ramset,' said the Lesson Master, rubbing a corner between his fingers. 'It's not made of papyrus but wood pulp. It's called "Paper".'

Sultan was looking down carefully at the scroll and his eyes suddenly lit up.

'But this is very advanced indeed.'

The scroll had symbols marked on it: '$E=MC^2$'.

'What's that?' asked Rarza, behind them.

'I believe it's called an equation, Rarza,' answered Sultan. 'We'd need an expert to translate it, though. Like the celebrated Al-Jibara.'

'Who's Al-Jibara, Sultan?' asked Silas, drawing closer.

'A very famous Moorcarian, from far across the Depthless

Sea. A master of the most advanced Sandwork studied there, very deep Number Magic indeed.'

Rarza noticed that Sultan had turned over the piece of paper and for a moment he fancied something else was marked there, but Sultan suddenly scrunched it up and put it in his pocket. Rarza wondered why his eyes were dancing so strangely.

'I know of Al-Jibara, Ashtar' said Ramset. 'He's spent his life seeking the true Equation for magic.'

'And who better to find it. Moorcarians are all wonderful Number Magicians, Ramset,' said Sultan, nodding to himself. 'And experts too in sacred geometry.'

Sulphurius looked suddenly flushed and very happy.

'And it is written,' he cried, 'above the entrance to the Great and Noble Academy in the Land of Heleras, the land of Centaurs, "Let None Enter Here Who Does Not Know Geometry". Ah, it is so good to talk Alchemy again, Ashtar.'

The ex-apprentice swung round to the Lesson Master.

'But Al-Jibara is no longer far away across the Depthless Sea,' he whispered. 'He's in Barbal too. In the temple. Mardak sent for him specifically. I believe it has something to do with the design for the Entropoth and Mardak's search for the Final Proof.'

'A Moorcarian,' whispered Ramset, 'and Centaurs from Heleras. Barbal grows busy indeed.'

Sultan's eyes twinkled.

'That Equation, Sulphurius,' he said. 'You bought it in Barbal?'

'Oh no, Ashtar,' answered Sulphurius. 'That's just the point. It was left here, only a few suns ago, by four weird strangers who suddenly appeared in the caravanserai. I'd gone into the back trying some Alchemy with Stardust, camel dung and lemon juice and when I came back to the bar, there they were, just sitting at the table. Four of them. They were dressed in the strangest fashion and they had thick foreign accents. They kept asking questions about Barbal.'

'Mardak's spies?' asked Ramset.

'These were spies all right,' answered Sulphurius, 'but not Mardak's. They're on their way to Barbal to rescue one of their own. Nimrod, I think he's called. Mardak keeps him a prisoner in the temple.'

'Their own?' said Ramset, for Sultan had grown oddly quiet. 'But who are they?'

Sulphurius suddenly looked extraordinarily furtive.

'It was only on their last night when they had had far too much wine to drink that I managed to find out where they are from. Their leader was talking. Mandrax.'

'Where?' whispered Ramset.

What Sulphurius said next made Silas and Rarza look up in absolute amazement. Because what he said was quite impossible.

'Where?' said the barman. 'Pengalis.'

DEMIGODS

'I can't stand it any more, Imlay,' whispered Karleg in Bolor's tavern.

The Dunetraders had all been sleeping in a little room upstairs, at the cost of only a few Groots, but they had come down for some supper and to stretch their legs. They felt like prisoners, though, and it had been a fearful time. Whenever they had gone downstairs to eat, the talk in the tavern had been full of the Grasht and the hunt for Dunetraders.

'I know, Karleg,' whispered Imlay. 'It's driving me mad too. It's not good for a Dunetrader to be cooped up like this.'

'Perhaps we should venture outside,' said Khayarumi. 'You heard what that man said last night. So close to the Solstice, and with the city so full, they can't hold the curfew any more. They're even trading in the streets openly at night, for the Pazgog is off again, searching for something in the desert.'

'But the Grasht,' said Imlay. 'They are still sniffing out Dunetraders.'

 172

Karleg was thoughtful for a while.

'Well,' he whispered at last, 'sleeping here and eating their food we smell like Barbalonians anyway. If we keep concealed I'm willing to take the chance. We must find Kalman.'

Kerbogah nodded, for he was sick of the tavern and Relak had kept trying to escape. Besides, last night he had dreamt he had seen his brother, calling desperately for help.

'I'm glad we're out of there, Farjay,' sighed Kerbogah, as they stepped outside. 'Relak hated it.'

Khayarumi was looking back mournfully at the tavern.

'We didn't even get to try the Special,' whispered the poet.

But Farjay was staring in amazement at the streets of Barbal. In the night it was as if the Eternal Flames had been multiplied a thousandfold, for there were torches everywhere, burning and flickering in the dark. The alleys were quite as full as in the day, except that the effect of the dark and the flames turned Barbal into a wild and lurid place.

Barbalissaries were moving about and every now and then in the crowd a group of Barbalonians would draw aside fearfully as a figure, his eyes closed, swept through the crowd, scenting the air.

'Grasht,' whispered Imlay.

They bustled along, trying to avoid being trampled underfoot, and Kerbogah and Farjay were soon entranced again by all the new names and sights and smells that once more greeted them in the night-time bazaar. They passed a street lit with torches where they saw that almost all the stall-holders were women, and the air was so thick with the scent of flowers and plants coming from the strange transparent bottles they could hardly breathe.

'The Street of the Perfume Makers,' said Khayarumi dreamily, looking quite as longingly at one of the stallholders as he had at Frannemar in the tent. Again the poet's head was filled with thoughts of love. Imlay stopped and picked up a little glass bottle with a cork stopper. He uncorked it and took a sniff.

'An essence,' he whispered with pleasure, drawing deeply on the odour.

Karleg smiled as they looked about the fabulous street.

'The oldest street in the Sacred City,' he said. 'And perhaps the very first art of real Alchemy, the art of perfume making. It's how Barbalonians first began mixing things and capturing essences.'

As they wandered on, though, the streets were also much dirtier than anything the boys were used to in the desert and, while many stallholders looked content and well fed, there were plenty of Barbalonians who seemed poor and wretched. Especially those hobbling past on wooden crutches or sitting in the dust and filth with their hands held out hopefully to the passers-by. Furious arguments kept breaking out too among the Barbalonian bargain hunters about the prices in the market which, from the complaints of most of the shoppers, were rapidly on the rise.

'The wars,' said Karleg. 'It's really pushing up the Groot price.'

Everyone seemed intent on attracting the inhabitants to their own stalls too and an air of barely suppressed violence hovered about the bazaar. But they suddenly came to the opening of a street that almost topped all the rest.

Right along each mudbrick wall were burning tapers and it was as though those animals on the square's mosaic had come to life. Although Kerbogah and Farjay had no names for them, suddenly they saw lions and leopards, black bears and huge golden wildcats, among cages filled with flightless birds and jars stuffed with lizards and scorpions and any number of horrible creepy-crawlies. The wild animals were all growling and snarling and straining at the heavy chains that held them to the walls.

'Relak, will you calm down?' whispered Kerbogah, for he could feel the little mouse getting more and more agitated.

At a table nearby a man had lined up any number of glass jars filled with a yellowish-white substance. Suddenly he bent down and from a sack that was moving on the ground drew a live snake. The creature curled and twisted in his hand, but the man was holding it behind its head so it could not bite him. He picked up a beaker and then squeazed the snake's little head. As its mouth opened with a hiss, to reveal a pink, fleshy throat and pearl white teeth, the man hooked its fangs over the edge of the beaker and little jets of liquid squirted out.

'What's he doing, Father?' asked Kerbogah.

'Milking it,' whispered Karleg. 'For its poison.'

'There,' cried the man, turning to a companion and thrusting the snake back in the bag. 'The phials are ready. You're to take them up to the temple straight away and give them to Zolos.'

This interested Karleg, but a furious commotion was now coming from the other end of the street, from a crowd of Barbalonians milling around a raised wooden dais, surrounded by candles and backed by a heavy cloth curtain. By that stood a very tall, lighted wax candle, almost the size of a man, with a dagger stuck in the side.

'A Barbalonian auction,' grunted Imlay, as they drew closer. 'When the candle burns down to the dagger the bidding will stop.'

The onlookers were bidding for a little black bear on the dais. As one ended with the shout of 'Ten golden Groots', the shivering creature was hauled back down the steps on a chain with an angry bellow, and given to its new master. As they wandered over to the foot of the dais Kerbogah saw a brute of

175

a man with a nose ring glittering brilliantly in the candlelight. In his hand was a thick black whip.

'Now then,' he cried. 'Roll up, roll up and see a sight to set wonder racing through your hearts. Not for an age has a Heleran been sold in Barbal Bazaar – and not just any Heleran.'

'How could they treat animals like this?' said Kerbogah angrily. 'Don't look, Relak.'

The crowd began to mutter excitedly but Kerbogah and Farjay were immediately captivated with this talk of Helerans. The slaver raised his whip hand, at which two of his companions strode to the curtain and began to raise it. There was an animal behind it. Four fine black legs appeared in the shadows, stamping furiously, and then a shining black silken body and a great swishing tail. It was a horse. Before the cloth was lifted further, though, the giant slaver raised his arm again to silence the chatter.

'My masters,' he cried. 'A whole sack of golden Groots ain't enough for this prize. I roped and tamed her myself in the deserts, for your delight and wonderment. These creatures are the most dangerous of all the tricksy Helerans.'

From the way the horse was straining behind the cloth it was very clear it was anything but tame. Kerbogah wondered why the brute was saying a horse could be so dangerous, when the auctioneer suddenly cracked his whip violently. His minions flung the cloth upwards.

For an instant Kerbogah thought someone was riding the horse's back. A beautiful woman was sitting there, with piercing, clear blue eyes and long, flowing golden brown hair tumbling down her slender shoulders. She was bare, apart from a binding around her breast and a golden bow and quiver of sticks strung across her shoulders. Next to them hung an instrument made of a row of wooden tubes. She blinked painfully, and her hands were bound behind her by a rope that another slaver was holding taut.

Kerbogah and Farjay suddenly gasped in utter astonishment though, an astonishment so great it drove all thoughts of Alchemists or Ziggurats, prophecies or even Kerbogah's brother Kalman, clean from their minds. This wasn't a rider at all: the beautiful woman rose out of the horse's body itself. Her waist was just where the horse's neck should have been, and around her middle, skin and bone suddenly became horsehair and mane. The rider was part of the horse, or the horse a part of the rider. Kerbogah had never seen anything so miraculous.

'See,' cried the slaver, smiling at her cruelly. 'One of the mythical creatures of Heleras. A Centaur of the wild plains. A living Demigod.'

'A Demigod,' cried Farjay delightedly. 'Then they *do* exist.'

The poet Khayarumi looked flabbergasted after all he had said about stories, but of all the onlookers it was old Imlay who was the most shaken by the vision of the Centaur. He was staring in horror at the extraordinary creature and trembling violently as he stroked his beard.

'The black arts,' he mumbled. 'She is one of the ancient spirits. The Doorway yawns.'

'Nonsense, Imlay,' snapped Karleg, seeing that Imlay was frightening Kerbogah and Farjay. 'Try to use your eyes, man. She's just a Centaur.'

'But how on earth did she get here?' asked Khayarumi.

'The Solstice,' muttered Imlay fearfully. 'It always heralds great wonders and portents.'

'Perhaps she has fled Heleras,' said Karleg. 'It has long been said that under the Philosophon's rule the mortals of Helaras are beginning to abandon their belief in the Gods, even as Ogog loses his belief in magic.'

177

'Which would be no good thing for a Demigod,' admitted Khayarumi, 'for any poet knows that when you no longer believe in a thing it suddenly won't exist any more, will it?'

The crowd's excitement was bubbling up like a cauldron and now it threatened to spill over entirely. One of the Barbalonians thrust up his hand.

'Ten Groots. Yellow gold.'

'This is bad,' muttered a Barbalonian in the crowd. 'It's sacrilege.'

'Eleven Groots of red gold,' shouted another, pushing to the front.

'Thirteen Groots of white gold,' came a third.

'Very generous, your honours,' said the slaver fawningly from the dais, 'but twelve Groots is hardly very generous. You insult your own intelligence, if I may suggest, no matter what colour they are. It cost me three of my men to even rope this beast. She moves like the wind, although she is far more malleable than her filthy mate, Chiron.'

As soon as the slaver mentioned Chiron, the wonderful Centaur went wild. She reared on her hindquarters and glared at the slaver with such a mixture of anger and longing and defiance that for a moment the brute dropped his eyes shamefully.

'Chiron,' whispered Karleg. 'This must be none other than his beloved consort Chiral.'

'But Centaurs,' said Farjay suddenly, who had just recalled one of his lessons. 'I thought they were male. Boys, I mean.'

'The herd are all male,' said Karleg, smiling down at Farjay and patting his head. 'But how on earth do you think they got there in the first place, Farjay? Chiron and Chiral mated. If anything happens to her, then the Centaurs of Heleras certainly have no future.'

Kerbogah was shaking his head, as though frightened to trust the evidence of his own eyes and Relak was making the strangest sound. But suddenly the slaver lashed out at her with his whip. Its tongue caught Chiral in the middle of her sleek back and again the Centaur kicked out with her hind hooves and shook out her golden-brown locks furiously.

'You dare risk the wrath of heaven,' she cried in the majestic voice she used so often to summon her herd.

'She speaks our tongue, Father,' said Kerbogah in surprise.

Although the Centaur's accent was strange, it sang too in the candlelight, like lovely music.

'Centaurs speak all tongues, Kerbogah,' said Karleg, 'for they are pure instinct and it's the heart and intuition that guides their understanding. Besides, they're Demigods.'

The slaver was laughing at her on the dais.

'Frisky tonight, eh, Chiral? But it shows your mettle, don't it, folks? Think how one such as this could pull a plough for you. Or perhaps serve as a sacrifice. A Demigod, now that would please the hunger of Zoraster.'

This was too much for Chiral.

'If you would dare untie me,' she snarled, 'I'd repay such sacrilege and show you all just how dangerous a Demigod can be. With the help of my magic bow.'

'Well, she's very highly strung,' said Khayarumi wryly. 'Even for a centaur.'

'Untie you, Chiral?' the slaver laughed again. 'Then I might have to put a spear though your flanks, like yer filthy mate. Dropped 'im in the desert like a snake, with that other one. A lot of work, I admit, just for a scraping of Centaur's hoof. Though Mardak paid well enough.'

Chiral's pure blue eyes blazed but Kerbogah noticed that

tears had begun to roll down her cheeks. The boy's heart went out to her.

'A great pity that we had to slay him, I admit,' said the slaver, grinning horribly, 'but at least it's put up your Groot price. Made you more exclusive.'

'Twenty-four Groots,' shouted someone else.

'There you are,' said the slaver.

Chiral glared at the slaver with such hatred and scorn that for a moment the boys thought her look alone might have knocked him over.

'And why do you treat me so?' cried the Demigod proudly. 'You bind me and keep me in the dark for more suns than I can remember. You kill my mate and my brother and cut off his hooves and now you sell a Demigod at auction like a slave.'

'Father,' whispered Kerbogah suddenly. 'We must help her, Father.'

'We can't, Kerbogah,' snapped Karleg. 'We can't afford to draw attention to ourselves now Dunetraders are banned from the city and the Grasht are—'

'Please do something, Father.'

Karleg shook his head but his son was glaring so furiously at him that Karleg relented.

'Oh, very well. Thirty Groots, then.'

As Chiral heard Karleg's voice her look was cold, but the Dunetrader tilted his head and smiled apologetically. Some understanding seemed to pass between Karleg and the strange creature.

'Thirty-five,' came another shout.

'Forty,' countered Karleg, after consulting Imlay and the poet to see how many Groots they had between them. 'And seven Minae. Payment on the nose.'

'Now there's a decent price,' said the slaver, grinning hugely. He was looking at the candle which had almost reached the dagger.

 180

'That's what you always need in Barbalonian negotiations, Kerbogah,' whispered Karleg, winking at his son. 'Leverage. And in Barbal they'd sell their own mothers for less.'

'But do I 'ear even more?' cried the slaver.

Karleg's face fell.

'Fifty Groots.'

The cry had come not from Karleg but from a figure standing on the edge of the crowd. His features were different from the others, not so dark, and his hair was cut short and there was no beard on his face. Karleg was looking really worried now.

'I don't have enough Groots, Kerbogah,' he said help-lessly.

'Please, Father.'

'Fifty-one, then,' cried Karleg. 'I'll have to sell my dagger.'

'Fifty-five Groots flat, and that's my final offer.'

'Yours,' cried the slaver, pointing to the candle which had just reached the dagger. The Barbalonian auction was over and the man who had just won the bidding walked straight towards the wonderful creature.

'And worth every Mina,' he cried delightedly. 'They'll want to see her at the Academy all right.'

The Centaur turned her head coldly and glared at him.

'It proves my theory, you see,' said the man loudly, nudg-ing one of the buyers in the ribs. 'Oh, it's marvellous. How they have laughed at me in Heleras for my theories.'

'Theories?' muttered Kerbogah. 'What is he talking about?'

The Heleran was walking slowly round the dais, studying his purchase carefully, examining her flanks and the woman that rose from the back of the horse.

'So one thing comes out of another,' he said, nodding to himself like a sage. 'Evolutia. The change of all forms. Just as our Heleran Gods are always changing shape. I had the idea lying in an ass's milk bath one boring Monday morning. "Eureka," I cried. And now here's the proof. A creature that is half God and half animal. The Philosophon, the Alchemist of Heleras, must hear of my theory of Evolutia immediately.'

Chiral had begun to stamp again and, laughing maniacally at her, the Slaver turned and lashed out with his whip. Kerbogah hardly understood himself why he did it. He could see he had little chance against these brutes, yet the sight of this strange roped creature being whipped and, almost worse, laughed at, raised such a wild fury in the boy that he couldn't control himself any longer. He had just seen something hanging from Farjay's belt too. It was the little slingshot.

'Camel's blood!' cried Kerbogah, pushing Relak deep into his robes, seizing the slingshot and picking up a stone.

'Don't, Kerbogah,' shouted Karleg.

Too late. Kerbogah whirled it round three times and released it straight at the slaver. Even in the shadows his aim was true. It hit the giant slaver smack in the middle of his forehead and knocked him to the ground. Kerbogah was wondering what else he could do when he remembered the dagger in the side of the candle. He lunged forward and pulled it from the wax, then jumped up the steps, charging onto the dais.

'No, Kerbogah!' cried Karleg furiously.

'What the demon!' hissed the slaver as he staggered to his feet again, a little pearl of blood marking his forehead. The onlookers began to whisper and point, but Kerbogah had reached the Centaur. In an instant he had cut the rope that held her hands. Chiral reared triumphantly and as her hooves crashed to the ground next to Kerbogah, he trembled, for the top of his head hardly came up to her waist. Farjay was hopping up and down with pure delight.

'Good for you, Kerbogah.'

'Stop her!' came a shout.

The Centaur moved like wildfire. With one powerful arm Chiral lifted the bow over her head and had strung an arrow with her teeth. She loosed it and before it even hit the auctioneer's throat, strung another and then another, so fast that Kerbogah could hardly see the arrows whizzing past his nose – though he could certainly feel them. In no more than the blinking of an eye three slavers lay dead around the dais and the crowd shrank back in terror.

'But how on earth?' whispered Kerbogah, at her side.

'The Arrows of Desire,' said the Demigod, smiling down sweetly. 'They move almost as fast as the thoughts of love themselves, but these always find their mark.'

Kerbogah nodded stupidly.

'Chiral gives you her thanks,' said the Centaur, stamping her front hooves. 'But who, or what, are you?'

Kerbogah was struck dumb by her severity and beauty. He couldn't speak at all.

'Whatever you are, you are courageous for one so small,' said Chiral, 'and courage is a quality that the Gods reward. As courageous as my beloved mate, Chiron. When Chiron and I ran free and wild through the long grasses and began the dance of being . . .'

Chiral bowed her head sadly.

'But it does not matter any more. Nothing matters any more. He and my brother are dead and my heart is broken like a misspent arrow. For there is no truth without love. It is the greatest magic in all the heavens.'

Kerbogah flushed.

'Yet since you helped me I owe you a debt, my friend,' said the Centaur. 'May the Gods grant me the blessing to pay you back one sun.'

Chiral suddenly lifted the strange pipes from her shoulder.

'Here,' she said, 'take these.'

'What are they, Chiral?'

'Chiron's pipes,' answered the Centaur sadly, wiping away another tear. 'He has no need of them now. Blow on them if you are ever in real need.'

Chirral had little time to say any more, for more slavers were running towards the dais. Some were shouldering through the crowd and from the other end of the alley six of them came running straight at her.

'My blessings to you,' cried Chiral, 'but now I must fly.'

Chiral put her magic bow and arrows back over her shoulder, and the Centaur suddenly turned. Kerbogah saw her sleek black haunches brace to spring, and in a single bound she leapt clean over the heads of the ducking crowd. She landed with a heavy clattering of hooves and galloped away down the Street of Slavers as the wild animals all around her snarled bitterly, straining and chafing at their chains. The Demigod had vanished into the night.

In a daze Kerbogah walked towards the dead auctioneer. He felt no pity for the brute, or far less than he had felt for the Grasht. The slaver's blood was oozing in a great red pool all around him and the crowd were in a panic. Suddenly Kerbogah felt a hand tugging him down off the platform. Karleg had grabbed his son's collar.

'Now you've really done it,' growled Karleg, although his anger was mixed with pride too. 'Come on, let's get out of here quick.'

'Go on like that, Kerbogah,' said Khayarumi, patting him on the back, 'and you'll soon be singing the Sandsong yourself.'

A Barbalonian overheard the remark and cried out to the crowd, 'Dunetraders. Dunetraders are still in the city.'

It must have been the Groot reward that set up such a terrible hue and cry around them, but it was joined by something far more worrying. The sight of armed Barbalissaries, their golden spears waving like corn above the heads of the crowd, running straight towards them. Karleg swung round but to his horror he saw more soldiers coming down the end of the street.

'Split up,' he bellowed. 'We'll meet back at Bolor's in the morning. It's our only hope.'

The little party darted left and right in the shadows and Kerbogah found himself ducking past a Barbalissary. He just avoided his grasp but gasped too as he looked back. His father had been grabbed by two guards.

Kerbogah's head was in a whirl but he kept running as another soldier spotted him. Soon he was out of the Street of Slavers and running for dear life. Barbal Bazaar passed in a whirl as he ducked right and left and right, down one alley after the other. He knocked into a stall and sent the contents flying as angry merchants hurled abuse at him. He tripped three times and barged into an old beggar who cursed him with all his might. He turned one corner and felt the breath of fear and loneliness even before he saw the two Grasht coming towards him. He ducked down another alleyway but as he looked back he was horrified to see that the Grasht had turned after him and were sniffing the air.

'Come on, Relak!'

Kerbogah stopped again. He could see a group of Barbalissaries at the end of the alley. Kerbogah had a sense of fear and sadness all around him and as the Grasht drew closer he jumped back into a doorway, and pressed himself into the dark. The Grasht were coming closer and closer and Kerbogah was consumed with horror and revulsion.

'We're lost, Relak,' he whispered bitterly. 'They can smell us.'

Kerbogah suddenly had an idea though.

'Quick, Relak!'

185

Kerbogah dipped into his pocket and pulled out the handful of saffron his father had given him. He smelt the spice immediately and now he was smearing it all over his hands and face. Just in time too, for the Grasht had stopped right in front of him. They both turned for a moment, with closed eyes, and lifted their noses as they looked straight at Kerbogah. But they did not open their terrible eyes and, changing their minds as they caught the smell of saffron rather than Dunetrader, they wandered on.

'That was close, Relak,' whispered Kerbogah, as he slipped off in the other direction, thinking that he should now go directly to Bolor's place.

At last he stopped again by a fountain, panting frantically, and looked around, wondering now what had become of his father and Farjay and the others.

'Oh, Relak,' he said, pulling his pet mouse from his robe, 'whatever shall we do? They've got Father and I'm not sure I can find Bolor's again in the dark.'

Kerbogah recovered his breath and started to walk again. He no longer felt he was being followed and now nobody in the busy city paid him any attention at all. The moon was high above the balconies and rooftops of Barbal and Kerbogah guessed it must be very late, but as he turned in the direction he thought Bolor's place must be he realized that he was lost.

Kerbogah stopped again. He had come to the end of the street where it forked and he turned left. The alley was much smaller and dingier than the last, with low-hanging wooden balconies that protruded into the street, and a few tapers casting gloomy shadows everywhere. There were beggars sitting all about and as Kerbogah wandered along, one sinister-looking ruffian got up and began to follow him.

'Relak,' whispered Kerbogah, stroking his mouse, 'I wish we had never come to Barbal.'

Kerbogah was sweating badly and he suddenly remembered the looks on the children's faces he had seen when he had arrived, and all the rumours that haunted Barbal. He shivered and, seeing a little side alley, ducked down it. He found himself in a tiny, crumbling courtyard, rich with shadows. There was no exit, though, and again Kerbogah turned round. The boy stopped in horror. A huge Barbalissary was standing right behind him, staring at him coldly.

'Well, well,' the soldier whispered. 'We've run our quarry to ground at last. No matter how you try to disguise yourself.'

The soldier was smiling at Kerbogah's frightened face, smeared Wordmaster-yellow with saffron and dirt and sweat. Kerbogah would have made a run for it but there were four more Barbalissaries around the man and the exit was blocked.

'What do you want with me?' he asked angrily.

'How about murder?' said the soldier, smiling coldly. 'The murder of innocent animal slavers.'

'I didn't murder anyone,' said Kerbogah indignantly, thinking that the slaver was hardly innocent. 'I only threw a stone.'

'Then what about being a Dunetrader?' said a Barbalissary next to him. 'That's enough for Zolos. We've mopped the rest of you up already.'

'My father,' said Kerbogah. 'And my friends. What have you done with them?'

'Kicked them out of the city, of course. Without a Groot left to their names. And they're lucky, boy. If Mardak was back in Barbal he'd probably have slit their throats or fed them to the Pazgog.'

Kerbogah scowled, but at least he felt a sigh of relief that they were safe.

'Very well,' said Kerbogah, in a very grown-up voice. 'I

187

am a Dunetrader, it's true, so you can throw me out of Barbal too.'

But the Barbalissary who had spoken first grinned evilly.

'Oh no, boy,' he whispered, stepping forward, 'we've other plans for you.'

A MAKINA OF TIME

In the Elusive Camel Silas and Rarza where both looking as if they had just seen a ghost. The smoke curled in the dusty air and made them all look as shadowy as Sandspirits.

'But on the Mappa Mysticum,' whispered Rarza, 'you said Pengalis doesn't even exist. That it lies in the future. Then how can they be Pengalisian spies? Isn't that . . . ?'

'Impossible,' said Sultan Ash, smiling thoughtfully. 'Except of course for one of the founding principles of arcane Alchemy, mentioned specifically in the Book of Destinies. That *nothing* is impossible.'

His voice had risen and one of the Dunetraders turned to gaze at the strange party. There was a longing and a sadness in his once-handsome face.

'I mean the Gods created all there is, didn't they, when they dreamt the world into being? Just because you can't explain a thing yet, doesn't mean it can't happen. Whatever do they teach Childars nowadays?'

Silas shivered and once again in his pocket the Lightbearer was beginning to grow warm and glow.

'Then it's very deep magic,' said Silas, looking at Rarza.

'Is it now?' said Sultan, who suddenly seemed a little irritated with his pupil. 'Or is magic just a name for what we don't know or understand yet? If forces from the future are among us, I think they're starting to affect everything, though. Things are beginning to turn up where they shouldn't be at all. Like that Equation.'

'And the word,' gasped Ramset suddenly. 'Perhaps the word is from Pengalis too.'

Sultan looked secretive but rather than talk of the word he turned to the the little publican.

'Tell us more, Sulphurius,' he whispered.

'After they visited the Camel I started asking around,' said Sulphurius. 'It all began, I believe, when Mardak was experimenting on Stardust. A Pengalisian appeared in Barbal Bazaar, as if by magic, and started trading words in return for information, or misinformation. Caused a real stink. Mardak took him prisoner. Now these others come to rescue him.'

'But how could Pengalisians really be here among us?' asked Rarza.

'Tell me, Rarza Stormheart,' asked Sultan, 'what has obsessed the Alchemists in the ancient Ziggurat since its great mudbricks were laid? And man, too, in the desert, in his way?'

'The Gods,' answered Rarza.

'Of course the Gods,' said Sultan rather coldly. 'But beyond the Gods.'

Rarza shrugged.

'Come on. Think of numbers and the Wheel. But think above all of the Sundial in the great square of Barbal.'

Rarza thought this was rather unfair since she'd never even been to Barbal. She shrugged.

'*Time*,' cried Sultan Ash, hushing his voice again as some of the revellers looked round.

'That's where it all starts really,' he whispered, 'and stops probably too. Finding out how to tell the time properly, whether you read it from the sun on the Sundial in the square, or from the shadows in the desert. But Mardak's makina, the Entropoth. It is partly a makina of time. A time machine. And these Pengalisians are time travellers.'

Rarza almost fell backwards, but Sulphurius was nodding his funny little head.

'But what is time?' whispered the Lesson Master almost to himself, 'and what time is it?'

'What are you talking about now?' asked Silas irritably. He couldn't understand why Sultan was talking about time as a thing at all. Time wasn't a thing, it was just the order in which things happened.

'I mean, (a) is time linear, Silas? Does time run in a straight line, like one of Barbal's four walls, and if so when will it end and when did it start? Or (b) . . .'

A rather mystical look crept into the Lesson Master's blue-green eyes.

'Is time more like the ancient Waterwheel of Barbal? A great big circle. Come to that, is the world itself really a great big circle?'

'The world's flat,' said Rarza. 'It shows that on the Mappa Mysticum.'

'Is it now, Rarza?' said the Lesson Master. 'Well, if you'd ever sailed across the Depthless Sea, you might think differently. On the horizon the sea seems to curve like a droplet from a Dunetrader's waterskin, and many mariners, navigating with astrolabes and compasses, which work by a magic Chi, believe that if you sailed on and on you might return to the very point at which you set sail. The true passage.'

'But you'd just fall off,' said Silas flatly.

'Unless some magic Chi was holding you in place,' said the Lesson Master. 'Have you ever wondered why an apple falls on your head? But it is hard to conceive, indeed. Like time being circular.'

Silas scratched his head and remembered Rarza in the temple yard.

'And if time *is* circular, why shouldn't things come back from the future, like Pengalisians? Especially when you start playing around with Stardust. Their presence confirms Mardak must be well on the way to completing the fabled Entropoth.'

'But how?' said Rarza, refusing to accept all this so lightly. 'How does the Entropoth work? What's it really for?'

Sultan smiled again and nodded.

'While the Entropoth tells the time, it also draws on the powers of nature around us. Both here, in the Upper Kingdom, and below, in the Underworld. As above, so below. For that they needed something supernatural to make it work.'

'What?' asked Silas.

'The Turnstones, for a start,' answered the Lesson Master. 'The Chi held inside the Turnstones alone can truly make an Entropoth work. They are placed in grooves at its bottom and when they glow and Stardust begins to run through, secrets are revealed.'

'Secrets?'

'Firstly secrets of both past and future,' whispered Sultan. 'For with Mazgol it will reveal things of a dark and mysterious past. But with Gol of a bright and brilliant future. It is said, too, to be affected by thoughts and prayers themselves. Yet there was always an intrinsic paradox even in the idea of the Entropoth.'

'Paradox?' said Silas, remembering the pot's strange words about some great paradox.

'The paradox of time. You see the idea of a time machine is all very well, especially in a city of soothsaying, but the Lord Alchemists, once they had had such an idea, realized that they did not know enough yet to actually make one. That they needed more knowledge from the very future they sought to look at.'

'Oh,' said Silas.

'Technically impossible, you see,' said Sultan, 'except for what was written in the Book of Destinies.'

'That nothing is impossible,' said Rarza excitedly.

'Exactly, Rarza. Somehow the future would have to come back to the present, though. Now how could that be? The second problem that the Alchemists faced was how to make the glass strong enough to contain the power of the Entropoth. Eventually the Lord Alchemists abandoned the idea altogether. Indeed, made it a sacrilege to even talk of one. But one man alone pursued the quest.'

'Mardak the Dark.'

'Just so, Silas. Mardak believed that the Entropoth alone provided a key to the Ultimate Alchemical proof. The living proof of the existence of the Creator. And Mardak's initial experiments with Stardust must have brought these Pengalisians back from the future, with words and equations that are starting to change everything in the present.'

'But how did his experiments bring them back?'

'I don't know, Silas. But, Ramset, take everyone over to that table right away and we'll eat. Don't draw attention to yourself. Hurry up, will you? We'll talk more when we've eaten.'

Silas and Rarza were starving, so they followed the Warrior Priest happily enough to the table, in the corner of the caravanserai, their heads buzzing with thoughts of this

193 ⚔

time machine and travellers from the future. But suddenly the door to the Camel burst open. A swirl of sand came with it and five fearsome characters were framed in the doorway. They wore swords at their belts and their eyes sparkled angrily. They were heavily clad in leather breastplates and pointed leather helmets and two of them carried long wooden spears with golden tops.

The Barbalissaries' leader bristled with violence and he was built like a brick water trough.

'Silas. Rarza. Don't say a thing,' hissed Ramset, as some of the Dunetraders sprang up. Rarza and Silas slunk back into the shadows and pulled up their hoods again as Sulphurius bustled forward from the counter and Sultan too retreated into the shadows. Sulphurius bowed deeply.

'You're welcome, captain. But I'm afraid you can't bring weapons . . .'

'Sergeant, not captain,' grunted the soldier through the smoke. 'Sergeant Mekmam. And be silent.'

The sergeant turned to one of his soldiers.

'Lieutenant.'

The lieutenant pulled out a roll of brown hide and unfurled it, pinning it up with a little dagger that he stuck in the wall.

'Good,' cried Mekmam. 'Zolos's orders are posted. Now we must be on our way. The Solstice draws closer and closer. Then you shall all see. When Mardak crowns the Uncrowned King of Night.'

Mekmam laughed and turned away. The door was slammed after the Barbalissaries. As soon as the soldiers left, the room burst into an uproar of nervous chatter, which at least masked the activity of the little party huddled together in the corner. The Dunetraders were crowding around the poster as Sultan came over to their table.

Sulphurius had just arrived too, with a jug of beer and a

great platter of food. The steaming mutton ribs had been griddled over an open fire and they were burnt and crunchy on the outside and looked delicious.

They all sat down to eat and the beer looked so good that Silas and Rarza could have gone swimming in it. The dusty travellers were about to dive in when Sulphurius placed a metal bowl in the centre of the table and poured water into it from a jug. But rather than drinking, Sultan plunged his hands beneath the liquid and began to rub them brusquely.

'Cleanliness,' he said. 'It's closest to the Gods.'

'Just as the Chi Dance battles spirits and cleans the soul,' agreed Ramset approvingly. 'If I wasn't so hungry I'd be insisting we all washed our feet too.'

Silas thought of how his mother Alara always insisted that he couldn't eat, or even go to bed, until he washed behind his ears. But he put out his hands like the others and as his finger came close to the bowl he suddenly felt a sharp sting and thought he saw a little blue flash.

'Ouch!' cried Silas, pulling back his hand. 'That hurt.'

'A Chi jolt,' said Sultan, smiling to himself. 'When I was your age and we felt those, Silas, we used to say the Gods had stung us. In the stories they say Lol himself first gave life to man with a spark of Chi like that.'

Silas lifted his finger but there was no pain any more and no mark of any kind and he wondered how on earth it had happened.

The cool beer was so delicious that soon Silas and Rarza were glugging away like horses. The ribs too tasted absolutely scrumptious – underneath their charcoal surface. Ramset was eating happily, throwing the bones over his shoulder and Sulphurius came back to clear the plates.

'Your room's ready, Ashtar.'

Sultan got up suddenly and walked over to the wall where the Barbalissary had pinned up the poster. The guests in the caravanserai had all returned to their drinks and conversations and he pulled out the dagger and took it down. Walking back to the table, he laid it out flat. It had these symbols on it, the same symbols that Silas had seen in the History under the heading 'The First Spell', though all jumbled up like this:

'It's the earliest Barbalonian script,' explained Sultan, as they crowded round the table to look, 'far older than the script in my History. It was invented in Barbal as a kind of special language that all the Alchemists use, most often to protect their knowledge, but to pass it on too, at least to members of the Order in the Seven Lands. It helps them sit above the secrets.'

'I've seen something similar used among our Scribes,' said Ramset. 'Is it not wonderful?'

'Wonderful?' said Silas sullenly, bemused by the strange symbols. 'Why wonderful?'

'Is not the clay disc mightier than the golden spear, Silas Root?' answered the Warrior Priest gravely. 'For the knowledge and wisdom of one man's life is lost when his Chi has gone, but with the art of inscribing he may hand down truths to other seekers. Truths that build and build, a Ziggurat of ideas that shall change everything in the end. It is Scribes who are the unacknowledged legislators of the world.'

Sultan raised his eyebrow at the Warrior Priest.

'But may not Scribes hand on something else too, Ramset? Lies and mistakes?'

Ramset looked rather offended.

'I don't know why Zolos bothers putting these up at all, though,' said Sultan. 'Not one in a bushel of Barbalonians could read it, let alone these drunks.'

'But what does it say?' asked Silas, staring at the poster.

Ramset shook his head and Sultan seemed about to answer when he suddenly turned to Silas.

'No. Let's try a little science, Silas. An experiment. Gol is a Turnstone, remember.'

Sulphurius started so violently it was as if he had been touched by a Chi jolt himself, and he stared in astonishment at Silas Root.

'Gol?' he gasped, beginning to sweat again. 'Oh heavens. You can't mean he's got . . .'

'Hush, Sulphurius, keep your voice down,' whispered Sultan sharply. 'But yes. That's why we're here. The Pazgog has been hunting it, as you suspected. I'd bet you'd like that in your collection.'

'Then it's coming true,' said Sulphurius. 'The prophecy. You know what it says, Ashtar. That the stones will appear together and the temple shall be rent in twain.'

'I hope not,' said Sultan calmly. 'We have come to end the Schism, after all. But, Silas, use Gol to change the symbols.'

Sulphurius jumped up.

'Not here,' he exclaimed. 'They'll see you and you can't trust anyone these days. Come with me. I've a room in the back.'

Sulphurius drew them over to the side of the Camel where he pulled back a curtain and led them into another room. In the middle of it was an open fire, inside a stone circle, and above it a triangular-shaped metal stand that was supporting a huge glass vat over the open flames, like the ones in the bar, though much bigger. Silas and Rarza's eyes boggled. It was the most wonderful place they had ever been.

All around the room on trestle tables were any number of powders and stones and spices. It seemed for a moment that the contents of Barbal Bazaar had been spirited inside the Camel. There was a strange smell around them too, so strong and acrid that it was as if a hundred Lucifers had been lit all at once. Inside the glass vat was a viscous liquid, the colour of saffron, that popped and bubbled over the heat. The room too was lit with an eerie blue glow, from glass balls that stood on wooden poles all about.

'May I see it?' said Sulphurius, once he had closed the curtain. 'May I hold it?'

Silas reached inside his robes and pulled out Gol. The shaking apprentice took the Turnstone wonderingly in his eager hands.

'Gol the Magnificent,' he trembled. 'What power lies inside this not even the Lord Alchemists know.'

But Silas was peering at the globes.

'Fireflies,' he said suddenly. 'It's fireflies making the light.'

'Of course. They're nothing very special, Silas,' said Sulphurius, turning Gol round and round lovingly. 'The Alchemists call them flight bulbs – another little invention of the Order. The glass is tinted with ground lapis lazuli to make it blue. They use them in the Incanting Room.'

'And to study them,' said Sultan, 'will lead towards another valuable field of knowledge and Alchemy: natural history.'

Sulphurius wondered at Gol and Silas examined the flight bulbs, but Rarza was fascinated by a great wicker frame nearby, like a kite, on which were a pair of strange fanning palm leaves made of some peculiar white substance.

'What are those, Sulphurius?' she asked.

'Wings,' answered Sulphurius. 'Waxen wings, on a specially designed wooden frame. I'm not sure I've got their geometry right yet, but one day I shall put them on my back and launch myself from the roof of the Elusive Camel.'

'Why on earth?' asked Rarza.

'To fly away, fly as high as the heavens and the Sun God himself. What greater dream than to fly back to the Gods? Vision, you see, it's everything to the Alchemists.'

Sulphurius grinned but Rarza thought him a little mad and now she was looking up at the wall. Another square of hide was pinned up that said this:

$$♈ \quad ♉ \quad ♐ \quad = \quad △ \quad = \text{Fire} = \text{South}$$

$$♍ \quad ♑ \quad = \quad ▽ \quad = \text{Earth} = \text{North}$$

$$♊ \quad ♎ \quad ♒ \quad = \quad △ \quad = \text{Air} = \text{East}$$

$$♋ \quad ♏ \quad ♓ \quad = \quad ▽ \quad = \text{Water} = \text{West}$$

'The symbols on the back of the History,' whispered Rarza. 'But what does the rest mean?'

'Fire, Earth, Air and Water,' answered Sulphurius, still turning Gol in his hands. 'The Four. Each sign of the Zodiac is ruled by one of the Four. This chart helps me remember the laws too.'

'Man and his symbols,' said Sultan, looking up as well. 'Those markings in their triangles are talismans used to ward off the spirits of chaos. They stand for the Four. In Heleras the Philosophon now even argues that a mix of the Four makes up the entire world, and everything there is in it. There they call them the Four Elements. Another development in the scientific method.'

The Childars were most excited by this bit of information and Ramset was looking wonderingly about the place.

'*With elements four did our Master create,*' whispered Sultan, returning to one of his strange rhymes, '*The earth and all in it, with skill the most great.*'

Sultan was walking around the bubbing vat, inspecting it closely. He raised an eyebrow.

'You've begun to learn about time, Silas, and about things that matter too, like the Turnstones,' he said. 'Now perhaps you will start to master direction too. Which will always help you get somewhere in life.'

Silas remembered what Ramset had said about the Chi Dance.

'In the most ancient earth magic, the holy Four are also signs which have always represented their own directions. Air towards the Sunrise, Water towards the Sunset. Earth towards the Indestructible Ones. Fire away from them.'

A very holy look had entered Ramset's eyes and he was nodding enthusiastically.

'But now those points have been given new names,' said Sultan. 'East, West, North and South.'

Sulphurius had just handed Gol back to Silas but Sultan noticed something lying on the table and picked it up.

'What's this, Sulphurius?' he asked. 'A lock of hair from a red-headed man and petals from a red rose?'

Sulphurius grinned almost guiltily and Sultan now picked up a blue rock too. As he turned it in his hand Rarza saw that it was flecked with gold. She thought it the most beautiful thing she had ever seen.

'Lapis lazuli,' said Sulphurius with smiling, glittering eyes. 'Although in Barbal, they call it bluestone.'

Sultan put it down again and picked up a strange purple stone that looked like glass.

'Crystals. Barbalonians have no idea yet how powerful and mysterious these can be. That will take time indeed.'

'My collection,' said Sulphurius proudly.

Sulphurius beamed and now he took hold of a long, flat stone. It was brown and crumbly, like the rocks that littered the mountainsides in Ederyl. Rarza didn't think it looked like anything special, but Sulphurius held it as if it was as valuable as Gol or a mound of golden Groots.

'What's that, Sulphurius?' asked Silas.

'Something far more valuable than anything from the Street of Gems.'

Sulphurius turned it over carefully and Silas and Rarza suddenly saw a shape. It was like a little animal, flattened, and only in outline, but it was embedded within the stone itself.

'I've collected many of those in my time,' said Sulphurius. 'I believe it was once one of the creatures of the Depthless Sea.'

'The Depthless Sea?' cried Rarza. 'But it can't be. What's it doing in the desert? And inside a stone?'

'That is a very great mystery indeed,' answered Sulphurius.

'Then something turned it to stone?' asked Rarza. 'I

heard a story at our last fire festival that in Heleras there are Gods that can turn things to stone. A fearsome tribe of snake-haired women.'

Sultan took the strange rock from Sulphurius.

'Ah, yes, Rarza,' he said. 'The Gorgolons. And Mazgol the Mighty's Chi brought the Pazgog out of stone too. But it wasn't the Gorgolons or Mardak the Dark that did this, Rarza Stormheart. One sun I hope we may all know the truth of it. Perhaps logic will reveal it, eh?'

'But are not the ways of the Gods hard to conceive?' said Sulphurius, with a rather holy expression. 'And so we must have faith. Faith in their divine revelations. And faith in the Great Work of the Alchemists too.'

Silas and Rarza almost smirked.

'Here, Silas,' said Sultan. 'Keep it. You don't mind, do you, Sulphurius?'

'Not at all, if you don't mind that I keep working,' said Sulphurius, bustling over to the glass vat. 'Perhaps it needs more time for the transformation to take effect, but I'm convinced my recipe is right this time.'

'What are you doing, Sulphurius?' asked Rarza.

'Trying to make gold of course, my dear, so I can grow rich enough to leave the Camel and really get down to my studies.'

Sulphurius turned to the bench and picked up some powder in his hand, which he cast into the flame. But he had clearly miscalculated for the fire blazed so angrily that they all leapt back. There was a terrible splintering, for the glass had just toppled and cracked, and the gloop came spilling onto the floor.

'Dear, oh dear,' muttered Sulphurius. 'That would never have happened with a touch of Demigod.'

'A touch of Demigod?' said Rarza in surprise.

'Powdered Unicorn's horn, for instance, or even better,

essence of Centaur's hoof. That would make the glass virtually indestructible. Capable of withstanding all kinds of reactions.'

'The Entropoth,' said Ramset suddenly. 'That's why the slavers are trading in Demigods.'

Sulphurius had just turned, though, and now his gentle, comic face was transformed into a look of consternation as he saw what was happening to his beloved wings. A trail of the now burning liquid had run across the floor to the base of his winged frame and flames were licking about them furiously. The heat was so intense that they had begun to melt, dropping wax everywhere.

Silas felt like jumping up and down, for he had never seen such wonderful flames, nor an experiment like this, let alone one going so spectacularly wrong. But Sulphurius rushed over to the bench and picked up a bowl of water, which he hurled at the fire. It was too late though. Those wings, with which poor Sulphurius had dreamed of climbing to the Sun and escaping the Camel, had melted into a great heap of white gunge on the floor. Sulphurius looked sadly at the mess, but then his face brightened.

'Well, no matter,' he said. 'There'll be another time.'

'Come, Silas,' whispered Sultan, pushing aside some of the things on the table and spreading out the poster again, 'it's time to translate the poster. Gol, if you please.'

Silas put his hand inside his robe and drew out Gol again and Sulphurius forgot all about his melted hopes. It was glowing brightly.

'What now, Sultan?'

'Just hold the Turnstone and concentrate.'

As the Childar held it up and stared at the poster he felt that strange warmth spreading up his arm, into his neck and then his head. He looked at the poster in utter astonishment.

203

As Silas clasped the Lightbearer those symbols had suddenly changed before the Childar's eyes:

FOR THE CAPTURE
OF SILAS ROOT
MARDAK THE DARK OFFERS THE CHILDAR'S
WEIGHT IN SOLID GOLDEN GROOTS

Let none aid or give him or his best friend Rarza Stormheart succour in the Sacred City or its environs, on pain of imprisonment, Alchemical Torture and death.

'What does it say, Silas?' whispered Rarza nervously.

'Rarza,' answered Silas in horror, remembering that to have power over a thing you have to name it first, 'they do know about us and our names. Mardak has put a reward on our heads.'

Rarza blanched. 'They can't. How could they?'

'By the Seven Stars,' whispered Ramset, 'that is bad.'

'But don't fret,' said Sultan. 'Things seem much worse when inscribed.'

Sultan rolled up the hide again and gave it to Silas.

'Keep it, Silas. One sun it may come in handy too.'

Silas put it into his smock pocket next to Gol and that strange rock from Sulphurius's collection.

'Come now,' said Sultan. 'It's very late, Silas. Poor Rarza can hardly stand on her feet.'

Outside a breeze was beginning to blow sand through the gates of the caravanserai as they put on their shoes again and followed behind the Lesson Master. He led them into a small chamber on the edge of the complex, where Sulphurius had had someone prepare four rough cots woven of raw straw and camel hair. The breeze was strengthening and Sultan hovered for a while, listening to the wind with flickering eyes. It moaned and whistled and for a moment Silas and Rarza wondered if Sandspirits or Pengalisians were trying to get into the chamber with them.

'You know, I love listening to the wind,' whispered the Lesson Master, as he stood there peering up through a little window at the starry night. 'Sometimes it seems to me it is all any of us have to hold on to.'

Rarza saw that Ramset's gaze was fixed on the window too and a little group of stars they could see flickering far, far above them.

'The Indestructible Ones,' said Ramset, as he noticed her, craning his neck and pointing up. 'In my land stone-builders use those stars to position the Faron's great tombs.'

'Tombs?'

'The Pyramidions. Triangulation by the stars is very important to the art of Sacred Geometry and our tombs are gigantic stone triangles that cover the deserts along the banks of Khem's Sacred River.'

Silas thought of their humble little temple in Ederyl and the markers that had been carved for his father's memorial. This sounded much more impressive and he suddenly wanted to see one.

'After Barbal's Waterwheel, the Pyramidion the Mystifier now raises in Khem will be the Second Wonder of the World,' said the Scribe. 'Something at least to withstand the hand that touches all things, be they mortals or animals or stones. The hand of change and of decay. The hand of death and meaninglessness.'

Silas and Rarza shivered. It was getting colder and colder in the Camel.

'But Ramset,' said Silas suddenly, 'I thought the Alchemists believe that change is the law of magic and of life. Why should they want to withstand it, then?'

Sultan turned to look at Silas.

205

'The Alchemists long to transform one thing into another, all right, Silas,' he said, smilingly. 'But they also wrestle to maintain continuity and their own power. And learn perhaps life's greatest secret. What is permanent and indestructible in a world of impermanence. What remains amidst all life's difficult changes. Once we are all dead too. For that comes to us all.'

Outside a camel bellowed somewhere in the darkness and the wind seemed to rise. A strangely passionate note had entered Sultan's voice.

'But the Alchemist seeks a solution to death too,' said Ramset, and the Childars smiled at him hopefully. 'With their magic. In Khem there is nothing more important than the art of Resurrection. The Pyramidions are more than tombs then, they are makinas too, like the Entropoth.'

'Makinas?' said Rarza, wondering how a building could be a machine.

'Yes, Rarza. The Pyramidions are really gigantic Resurrection machines. To keep the Sun God rising every day and to bring the Faron, the Sun's incarnation on earth, back from the dead, again and again.'

'But how?' asked Silas, thinking that this was very impressive Alchemy indeed.

'Deep within Khem's Great Pyramidion, when the Faron's mortal body dies it is embalmed by the priest apprentices,' answered Ramset.

'Embalmed?'

'To preserve his body, Silas Root. An art close to the Alchemists' hearts. It uses kohl,' said Ramset, pointing at the black circles around his eyes, 'which also makes these marks and is used in another substance that can really change your spirit. Alcohol.'

Silas scratched his head.

'Which is another reason I am glad we go to Barbal,' said

the Scribe. 'For a famous embalmer, Tutanamet, was summoned from Khem to the Sacred City and I want to know why.'

The Childars wanted to see Barbal more and more.

'But once the dead Faron is embalmed he is laid in the House of Gold,' said Ramset. 'And surrounded by four great canopic jars containing his own organs, which we call the Sacraments. They will lay his corpse in there, and around it the jars, facing to four holy points.'

'North, South, East and West,' whispered Sultan.

'Yes. While above runs a great passage that points straight up there into the skies.'

Ramset indicated again through the little window at the wonderful heavens.

'Towards the Indestructible Ones. For the Mystifier believes that there lies the home of the Gods themselves.'

A longing had entered the Warrior Priest's voice too, and Rarza trembled as she stared out towards the home of the Gods. Now she wasn't sure if it was the cold or something else that was making her shake. Silas thought mournfully of his father Timon, who had been laid in the humble earth, and nowhere as grand as a house of gold.

'With prayer and Hekka magic,' said Ramset gravely, 'the magic we use so much in Khem, the Mystifiers then begin. Like the Ziggurat, the Pyramidions are really gigantic power-houses to God, and to make them work the Mystifier must lay out the sacraments and open the equivalent of Barbal's Book of Destinies, the Book of the Dead.'

Rarza's eyes glittered.

'But not just the Mystifier, Ramset,' said Sultan. 'All the Alchemists pursue the art of Resurrection. In the Ziggurat, for instance, they seek the Balm of Eternal Life, while in far-off Jesladom they say they search for the secret of

Resurrection too. There they believe not in the Gods but in One True God, who died for all our sins on the Tree of Life.'

The Warrior Priest smiled and shook his head, as if he had never heard such a foolish thing, but Silas found himself thinking of the big tree in the middle of the temple yard.

'And to remember him they drink wine that is changed into his blood by holy Alchemy.'

Silas and Rarza were amazed but Silas suddenly looked angry too.

'What's wrong, Silas?' asked Sultan, sitting down on his cot.

'This journey. All it seems to be leading us towards so far is death. Death or the Underworld.'

'Perhaps it's leading us to something else too, Silas. Transformation.'

'Transformation?'

'Our own transformation, Silas Root. For much as the Alchemists try to change matter, they also work to transform the human spirit.'

Now it was Sultan's turn to point into the skies, through the window, at a little dot of light.

'Look there. It's one of the Seven Wandering Stars.'

'What are they really?' asked Rarza, craning up on tiptoe to look. 'The Seven, I mean. Are they Gods?'

'In Remus, one of the city states in Heleras, they have started to call them the planets, Rarza.'

'Planets?'

'Some Alchemists believe that they are other worlds. Although two of the Wandering Stars are just the Sun God and the Moon Goddess, which rise and set before our very eyes. The others are harder to see yet, but they too have added some of the Gods' names to the Seven Days of the Week. Venus, Mars, Saturn, Mercury and lovely Jupiter.'

Silas and Rarza were looking up in astonishment. Wonder and awe had surrounded them like a warm blanket.

'You know, Ramset my friend,' said Sultan rather wistfully, 'many men will always say that the Gods live up there in the skies. That there is to be found the Garden of the Indestructible Ones, or Olympus, or Valhalla.'

The Warrior Priest nodded gravely.

'Others, though, especially the most advanced Sandworkers, wonder why Gods should live in the skies at all. They say that the heavens just go on and on and on, forever and ever, like a dagger hurled through eternity. That there are no Gods or Demigods at all. That there is nothing but matter and space and time. That's Physica, physics. And Khemia, chemistry.'

Silas blinked.

'But try to think of that,' said Sultan Ash, himself lost in thought. 'Try to think of what lies on the other side of everything.'

As Silas and Rarza thought of the other side of everything their young heads began to spin and Silas remembered the pot. The very effort seemed to hold some impossible paradox.

'You can't, can you?' said Sultan with satisfaction. 'You can't really comprehend infinity. That space or time goes on forever.'

'Then it can't be true,' said Silas almost hopefully.

'Or perhaps there is another very simple answer for that. A problem with reason and logic itself. Perhaps they don't exactly work as well as many say.'

Sultan threw himself down on his cot and the others followed. Both Silas and Rarza were exhausted and Rarza fell asleep quickly enough. But Silas lay there, tossing and turning on his cot, every now and then feeling little painful nips from the camel hair, as he clutched Gol and let his thoughts drift over all that had happened. Silas was neither asleep nor awake but it must have been much later when he opened half an eye and saw Sultan creeping quietly towards the door. Without a sound the Lesson Master opened it and slipped outside.

Silas wondered where he was going, but after a while sleep took him. When he woke he saw that Sultan had returned and was lying on his mattress. He was watching Ramset, who was awake now too, his normally darting eyes staring up fixedly at the dark ceiling.

'What's wrong, Ramset?' Sultan whispered in the darkness. 'You're worried, my friend.'

'Yes, Ashtar,' answered the Scribe, sitting up on his cot. 'So much is happening, but the strangest of all are these Pengalisians. I can't stop thinking about them. I know what you said of time, but how could they really come from a land that doesn't even exist yet? From the future?'

'You believe the Pazgog and the Underworld exist, do you not, Ramset?' said the Lesson Master calmly. 'Aspis too? But you don't normally expect to experience them while you live. Yet, is travelling through time any more remarkable? But *how* exactly seems a problem worthy of the finest Sandworkers, Ramset, or your Mystifier himself. Perhaps the answer lies in Barbal City, like so much else.'

'If we make it in time. The Solstice is close now.'

'Well, try and sleep,' said Sultan Ash. 'Barbal is close too and the secrets are coming together. I think the Gods have answered my prayers and we have survived the journey. But I must plan our next step.'

'Next step?'

'Yes, Ramset,' whispered the Lesson Master gravely. 'One that threatens almost certain death if we are caught. How to get us all inside the Ziggurat.'

THE TEARS OF
ZORASTAR

A Dunetrader peered up at the burning ball of fiery red
and as his wary eyes scoured the Mahara Desert he
grunted and spat the sand from his mouth. Before him the
desert had turned to a vast and depthless sea, a watery morass
that appeared to stretch on forever. The scout was a true
creature of the desert though, in his own element, and he
could not be fooled by the sudden appearance of waves.

Suddenly his eyes narrowed. This was no trick of the light
or phantasm of his imagination. Out of the water bodies were
rising like Sandspirits, thin spindly legs and yellow humps
that seemed to shake the heat from them in droplets of burning air. Line after line appeared, the ships of the desert, camels
that bore other Mahara Dunetraders straight towards him.

The scout swung round immediately and gave a long
piercing whistle towards the dune behind him. He was
answered almost instantly by a throbbing hum. The dune

211

began to shake and move, then fell in on itself and through the little chasm came other Dunetraders, singing the Sandsong as they came. But their voices seemed to quaver and tremble uncertainly and one of their camels stumbled. They exchanged nervous looks and once more their voices climbed in the desert.

The first of the Dunetraders reached the scout and shook his head.

'The power, Faluhan!' he cried. 'It *is* failing fast. As the Pazgog stops throats.'

'Yes, Solomon. But look.'

Faluhan lifted his arm and pointed at the horizon and the approaching camels.

'By Aspis!' whispered Solomon. 'They're from the red dunes. They've a fearsome reputation.'

'I know it. Do we talk?'

Solomon had seen too much death already in the Dunetrader wars to trust to the chance.

'No. Some say it is the caravan from the red dunes that began poisoning the wells.'

'But maybe they have heard of the parley,' said Faluhan. 'There are many caravans on their way to the quarry.'

'But half of them want blood. Each other's blood.'

Solomon was scouring the horizon, searching for something in the approaching figures, and as he gazed at the advancing Dunetraders, rising from the mirage, he shook his head.

'Look at them, Faluhan. They're on the warpath, all right. They'll not be interested in the parley at the quarry. Think how few caravans really are. And if it's they that poisoned the well, we have four of our brothers to avenge.'

Even as Solomon said it they heard a cry from their opponents. A high, ululating shriek like the call of some angry bird. It was an open challenge.

 212

'So then,' growled Solomon, 'the Dunetraders gather at last. But not for commerce and trade, feasting and story-telling, nor simply to race each other to the hungry markets of Barbal City. Now we are here to engage in the ancient art of war.'

Faluhan drew his sword.

'Very well, then. Let them come.'

'Hutt, hutt,' cried Solomon, striking his camel.

Solomon pushed the groaning beast forward, raising his hand as a signal and his men followed. At first both lines of camels slowed, as each Dunetrader began to pick a single opponent and measure one another up, but suddenly Solomon put his hand to his belt and drew his sword.

On both sides there was the clink and hiss of drawing swords, flashing in the angry sunlight, and suddenly the camels started to pick up speed. Their trot turned into a lolloping gallop as the Dunetraders spurred their camels on towards their foe. The air was torn with a terrible bellowing as the charging camels drew nearer and nearer, then struck, like two great waves smashing and crashing into one another.

Men and camels fell in the desert, living bodies opened by metal to the hot air and, in the tempest, trying to keep his bearings in the mayhem, Faluhan swung this way and that with his sword, hacking and jabbing, blinded by sand and anger and blood. The battle swayed and neither side seemed to be winning, although many had already fallen, when a Dunetrader next to Faluhan pointed his sword. Faluhan was afraid to look away, but he saw something that bemused him utterly.

'What in Lol's name is happening?'

On the dunes above stood a line of snorting black horses. On their backs sat helmeted Barbalissaries, golden spears and drawn scimitars in their hands. At their head rode Sergeant Mekmam. There was a cry, an arm was dropped and suddenly the soldiers were racing towards both caravans of Dunetraders.

'An ambush!' cried Faluhan desperately. 'Dunetraders, we're being ambushed.'

The scout's words were useless. The Dunetraders were still fighting each other as the Barbalissaries struck. They came down from the dunes in a wave of devastation. Right and left Faluhan hacked, though he hardly knew who he was fighting now, when he suddenly saw Solomon at his side again.

'Solomon, get to the parley. Tell them what you've seen here. Tell of Barbal's treachery. Perhaps it will sway the Dunetraders.'

'No,' cried the leader. 'My men. I must not leave my men.'

'We're lost already, Solomon,' cried the scout bitterly. 'At least you may save some other caravans. Save the Dunetraders.'

Solomon's eyes flashed and he struck his camel. Faluhan rallied as Solomon fled and his sword had just passed through the stomach of a Barbalissary next to him when he felt a searing pain in his temple. Then he was falling and everything went dark.

'Goodbye, Sulphurius,' called Sultan, waving cheerfully from his camel. 'Thank you for all you've done, my friend. We wouldn't have made it without you.'

'You haven't made it yet, Ashtar. I hope the waterskins help.'

The party had secured an extra camel from the caravanserai and Rarza and Silas were riding it together. The Childars kept looking back, until Sulphurius and the strange caravanserai were nothing but a tiny speck in the heat haze, which suddenly vanished like a puff of wood smoke. The Elusive Camel was gone once more.

In dreams Faluhan the scout lay there in the Mahara Desert, haunted by shadows, gripped by pain, as if drifting across a sea of time and space. Delirium seized him and he began to dream of a delicious, cooling water pipe and the sounds of the Rubaiyats, of camp women tending to him with aloe and kindness and love. But even in his delirium Faluhan knew that he was dying and that in the desert there would be nothing to mark his passing. Nothing to give meaning to his bitter journey.

'Here, friend. Drink this.'

Faluhan heard the strange, floating voice only faintly, as if still in a dream and a pain seared his parched lips, as he mumbled his own bitter imprecation.

'Water, dear God, water.'

Faluhan felt something wet in his mouth and it was as sweet as breathing itself. As he opened his eyes he saw the blaze of sunlight like a halo around the stranger's head.

'Try to be calm,' said Sultan Ash softly, using his hand as a cup to catch the life-giving elixir from the waterskin he was holding. Faluhan lifted his head a little higher and behind the Lesson Master he saw two small figures in hooded robes and a man who made him think vaguely of the distant land of Khem. They had appeared by magic.

'The wars,' murmured Faluhan bitterly.

Silas and Rarza peered about them. Everywhere there were broken and torn bodies, of men and camels, and in the air wheeled the noisy desert vultures that had first drawn Sultan's little party to this desolate spot.

'Oh, Silas,' whispered Rarza. 'It's terrible.'

'My caravan,' said Faluhan faintly. 'Did our leader escape?'

'It seems few made it from this place alive,' answered Sultan gravely. 'Be calm, man.'

Rarza wanted to take Silas's hand.

'Stardust,' said Faluhan painfully. 'It's all because of Stardust. We've begun to notice that our voices are dwindling. Our song cannot move the sand so easily any more.'

The man's cracked lips were bleeding as he spoke.

'Then the tribute,' whispered Ramset, stepping up behind Sultan. 'It does suck magic away. The Mystifier spoke of it. Something grave is happening.'

'There are ancient blood feuds among the Dunetraders too,' said Faluhan faintly, 'over women and camels and wells. The wars grow very bitter. But we were ambushed as we fought.'

'Ambushed?' said Ramset, kneeling down. 'By whom?'

'Zolos's minions. Barbalissaries. He hates the Dunetraders. Though he was once one of us.'

'Try not to talk,' whispered Sultan gently.

'No. We should have asked for a truce,' groaned Faluhan. 'We should have asked them to join us. Zolos sends his men against us, but the Dunetraders are beginning to gather. The call has come for a parley.'

Sultan bent down immediately.

'Parley? What parley?'

His voice had suddenly grown hard. There was something strange and secretive in his eyes too.

'To stop the wars,' answered Faluhan faintly. 'To unite the Dunetraders and turn the forces of Chaos against our real enemy. Barbal. If we can unite the Dunetraders, though such a thing is probably impossible, we shall assault the Ziggurat and destroy Mardak the Dark.'

'But the Order is sacred,' said Sultan. 'You cannot attack the city. This Dunetrader parley. When does it meet, man?'

216

'The sunrise of the Great Solstice,' answered Faluhan so faintly that Silas could hardly hear him any more. 'We had hoped the Barbalonians would be distracted by the festival.'

'In two suns' time, Rarza,' whispered Silas.

'There my caravan would have argued that Barbal itself must be destroyed. That we must no longer fight each other.'

'But where?' asked Sultan, lifting the man by his robe and shaking him hard. 'Tell me where this parley is to take place.'

'In the giant stone quarry, just half a league from Barbal. Near the Towers of Silence. Where they used to hew rocks to build Barbal and vultures flock to feed on Barbal beetles. They say there's even a tunnel there that leads into Barbal. Perhaps we can use it.'

'And who summons them? Tell me quickly.'

Rarza was shocked as Sultan shook the scout again but Faluhan gave an anguished groan and his head dropped back. For a moment Sultan's eyes seemed to be locked on him, searching deeply for something, but if Faluhan had an answer to Sultan's question, he had just given it to eternity. Sultan laid Faluhan in the sand and gently closed his eyes.

'His Chi has evaporated,' he said, sealing up the waterskin. 'His voice will never move the desert sands again, for his spirit has gone to another world.'

Ramset reached into his pocket, and pulled out two golden Groots which he placed very carefully on the dead scout's eyes.

'To pay the boatman,' said the Warrior Priest, as the Childars watched him silently, 'as he journeys to the Underworld and is rowed along the river of blood. World without end, Ammon.'

Ramset stood up and looked about at the Dunetraders.

'In Khem,' he said, 'they would be treated like heroes and returned to their families to be embalmed. But by the Seven Stars, Ashtar, what does this Dunetrader parley mean?'

217

Sultan's eyes were veiled as he walked slowly back to his camel. For a moment he paused.

'It means, Ramset, that Ogog is in even more trouble than the Hooded Master feared. And not just the Lord Alchemist, but ordinary Barbalonians too. If the Dunetraders ever turn their fury against Barbal, there may be no Schism for us to heal at all. No Sacred City either, for that matter. When Dunetraders are roused, they're pitiless. There will be nothing left but ruins.'

Sultan suddenly noticed something in Silas's hand though. A little piece of meat that he had taken from the caravanserai. It had turned almost green, and Rarza caught a very unpleasant scent on the air.

'That's off,' snapped Sultan, snatching it away, 'by the smell of it. Not even the finest spices could hide the smell. If you're hungry, tell me, Silas, or you might find yourself joining these poor Dunetraders. To keep meat out here is a sin for the Dunetraders, one of the earliest heavenly Commandments in fact, for it goes bad all too fast in the heat.'

Sultan threw it away and mounted his camel. They rode for half a day but now the Mahara Desert began to change rapidly. Trees appeared and with them came birdsong. They came through a canyon and on the rocky walls all about them Silas and Rarza started to see strange markings. There were little dots, like stars in the night sky, but around them had been scratched circles and strange ellipses.

'They're very ancient,' cried Sultan as they rode, his voice echoing about the canyon. 'Drawn long ago by mystics who dwelt in caves around here. With Inward Looking, they tried to draw what lies inside matter itself.'

Beyond the canyon they heard a wonderful noise and a sight that put all the violent thoughts of the desert and the Dunetraders clean out of their minds.

They had reached the banks of a thunderous river, crashing over the rough brown rocks below them. The river was called Euphoras, Sultan Ash explained and, like its distant neighbour Tigron beyond Barbal, was sacred to the Barbalonians. The noise was like a wind and among the rocks they saw colours flashing in the sparkling air. An arch of coloured light that spanned the river.

'That sight is said to herald hope,' cried Sultan, 'from the heavens themselves. A rainbow. And the story of water is perhaps truer to Barbal than any they tell at fire festivals.'

'What do you mean?' asked Silas.

'Man cannot live by faith alone,' said Sultan, 'for have you noticed how many cities have grown up near great rivers like this? Water is the key to life.'

Below them, where the river had opened out was a little valley where the grass was so thick and spongy it looked like a lime green carpet that blazed in the sparkling sunlight. It was the Barbalonion plain.

Among its luscious stems grazed curly horned bison and water buffalo, while women drifted hazily amongst the cattle, herding them gently by the river with little sticks.

The land further away from the river was harsher again, though, and thin channels had been cut into the ground from the river, and around them the fields were growing a gentle dusty green. It was still a desert compared to Ederyl, but it was clear this was how the villagers here irrigated the hard ground and grew their food. There were men and women at work in the fields too, ploughing the hard soil.

Beyond this the friends came down into another wide plain and began to notice a strange smell on the air. In the distance Silas and Rarza saw a great column of smoke. Ahead was a kind of lake and then a series of dark pools around it. But these waters – if you could call them waters – were a sticky black that gave off a quite revolting smell. It was the last of these pools that delighted Silas, for it was burning now, sending up gigantic columns of orange flame and thick, blue-grey smoke.

'But how?' asked Rarza, holding her nose tight. 'It's as if the water's on fire.'

'The Tears of Zorastar,' answered Sultan, looking almost fondly into the sludgy black morass. 'Believed to have been formed by the tears of the Sun God himself, Rarza, when he wept for the Fall of the Tower of Barbal.'

Rarza thought of the poor Dunetraders.

'The Alchemists often study its heavenly nature. It's extremely volatile.'

Silas was again gazing wonderingly into the desert flames.

'Since we're so close to the City of Soothsaying, I'll make one prediction,' added Sultan. 'In the distant suns, perhaps after centuries, the Tears of Zorastar shall grow so powerful that whole kingdoms will fight over them and wrestle to draw them from the earth. It shall cause other wars in the desert.'

Suddenly their camels started to bellow furiously. Before them was a long camel train, winding into the distance.

'Look, Rarza!' cried Silas. 'At last.'

The train was making for sacred Barbal. A hazy cloud hovered over it, so that the buildings and towers that reared up behind the walls and scraped at the sky seemed to be on fire too, vanishing and reappearing in the coming sunlight as they advanced on the growing city.

'They're coming for the Solstice,' said Sultan, 'and Mardak's Double Enthronement.'

'The day after tomorrow,' said Silas.

Much closer to Barbal, though, Silas and Rarza were surprised to see figures at work throwing up high mounds of earth and dirt. They were building some kind of barrier around the whole city.

'Can you feel it, Silas?' whispered Rarza.

'Yes, Rarza.'

'Silas. Look at them.'

Although dressed like Barbalissaries, with swords at their belts, and wearing pointed leather helmets, there seemed to be a stange lethargy about the workmen, as though they were wandering about in a dream. Their faces were so pale and drawn they looked like living corpses and, as the little party rode on, an eerie cold had suddenly gripped them.

'Grasht,' whispered Ramset. 'They're Grasht. Zolos's soulless army.'

Barbalissaries were moving amongst the Grasht with whips and spears to direct their work, but they seemed just as frightened as Rarza and Silas. The Grasht's eyes were closed as they worked too, as if they were being directed by some outside force, but although they would occasionally scent the air, at least none of the strange beings turned their attention on the newcomers.

Sultan led them past the Grasht safely enough but just beyond the barrier they saw a deep, wide trench filled with water that encircled the city too.

'The Dunetraders,' said Silas. 'In the Camel that man said Zolos was preparing something for them.'

As they drew closer the Ziggurat loomed up.

'We have to go in there?' shuddered Rarza.

'Yes, Rarza. Remember what Ramset called it?' whispered Silas excitedly. 'A powerhouse to God. But it is certain death to enter it.'

Closer to Barbal's walls they realized that the four gates to the city were heavily guarded with armed Barbalissaries, closely inspecting the wayfarers as they passed within. At the Great Gate stood Sergeant Mekmam. Next to him too was Akadeem, the guard who had taken the signal that night, and a tall Barbalonian who looked like a cross between a soldier and a priest.

'Zolos,' said Sultan, raising his eyebrow.

'They'll be looking for the Childars,' whispered Ramset.

'And Gol,' said Silas, clutching his stone.

Indeed they were – and Dunetraders too, for among them they had stationed Grasht, six of them, three on either side of the Great Gate, and as the travellers approached, the Grasht were sniffing them for the whiff of aloe.

'How will we get in?' asked Rarza.

'A city is a complex thing, Rarza,' answered Sultan, winking. 'A crucible that cooks up many unexpected discoveries. Not even Zolos and the Barbalissaries know all its secrets.'

Sultan led them on and, as they came into the shadow of Barbal's great mudbrick walls, he turned them away from the nearest gate. They dismounted their camels and Sultan slapped them on their haunches.

'Go on with you,' he cried. 'You've done us a great service and we are grateful. But now you are free. There seems plenty of water around Barbal to slake your thirsts.'

The nervous party went on on foot. Sultan was clearly looking for something and at last he spotted a tangled creeper that seemed to run up the entire wall ahead of them. For a moment Rarza wondered if they'd have to climb it, but Sultan pulled the creeper aside to reveal a little wooden door. The Lesson Master pushed it and with a creak the door swung open.

'In we go,' he cried cheerfully, leading them through just in time, for as the secret doorway closed behind them a troop of Barbalissaries came marching along the wall.

Barbal's streets were bustling and almost all of the doorways had been painted with the blood-red talismans to ward off the angel of death. Wanted posters, like the one in the caravanserai, were pinned up everywhere too. There was great urgency in the people's tread, as though they indeed expected great portents from the heavens at the proximity of the Solstice.

'Keep up your hoods, whatever happens,' said Sultan. And Silas, keep a tight hold on Gol. It must never fall into the Black Magician's clutches. Promise me.'

Silas nodded gravely and the Childar suddenly felt a ter-rible weight of responsibility pressing down on him.

'But watch your backs too. If the rumours are true that children are vanishing from Barbal's streets, we must stick together at all costs.'

'Rarza,' whispered Silas, 'keep close.'

Sultan led them along a series of connecting alleyways. At one point, though, the Lesson Master seemed to know where he was. They had come to a house and, telling them to wait, he popped inside.

'I used to stay here,' he explained, when he came out again. 'I just wanted to see the old place again.'

Sultan led them on into one of the main streets of Barbal Bazaar.

'Isn't it wonderful, Rarza?' cried Silas as they walked along. 'All I ever dreamed.'

They were both delighted by all the new sights and sounds and smells, but as the friends pushed through the throng they heard a loud grating and came into a street where there were tables, chairs and stools everywhere.

They noticed that the cobbles were covered in wood shavings and men were at work with hammers and little chisels, or cutting into the wood with strangely serrated metal blades. They had come to the Street of the Carpenters, in the middle of which a wooden cage was being built.

Silas was interested by a pair of green double doors, though, that opened onto a courtyard where he saw the strangest thing yet. He hardly had the words to describe it. It looked like two large upturned tables on wheels, between which was a kind of gigantic wooden spoon, with a thick wind of rope tied around the neck of the spoon, running down to a wooden roller. Silas was wondering if it was one of the Alchemists' inventions when Sultan put a hand firmly on his shoulder.

'It's called a mangonel, Silas, a kind of gigantic catapult and a very dangerous weapon.'

A heated conversation was going on just beside the green doors.

'Well then,' a Barbalonian was saying, addressing a tall man by one of the benches, 'did you get the pig bellies or not, Melbeg?'

'Yes, yes,' grunted Melbeg. 'Fifty anyway. With the Solstice, people will be feasting and sacrificing. Even pigs are harder to come by.'

'Zolos specifically ordered sixty,' scowled the other. 'He always reckons in Barbalonian sixties. We don't want to get on the wrong side of Mardak either.'

'I can't help that. Anywise, at least he'll be pleased with this.'

Melbeg held up a waterskin and pulled out the cork. As the other sniffed it he pulled back in disgust.

'The Tears of Zorastar.'

'Not at all,' said Melbeg. 'Or not any more. With a secret mix of new substances and the right prayers, we've found out how to refine Zorastar's Tears and make them burn far more easily than usual. Watch.'

Melbeg picked up a glass of water and poured it into Zorastar's Tears. The mixture burst into flame.

'There!' he cried delightedly. 'With the Gods' help we've transformed them into a powerful new ally. It changes with water. I'll make a real killing on it. I wanted it to help me in my design for underfloor heating, but all Zolos ever thinks of are his blasted weapons. Zolos will use it against the Dunetraders.'

Ramset looked nervously at Sultan.

224

'The Dunetraders,' he whispered. 'If the parley goes to plan, they will be walking straight into a trap.'

At the end of the street a stall seemed to have been erected temporarily, with flimsy poles and a wide, black awning draped over them to make a tent. The people buying and selling in its shadow looked very furtive, but it was Ramset who took a particular interest in the small clay tablets being passed so surreptitiously back and forth by the merchants.

He was looking very unhappy indeed.

'What's wrong, Ramset?' asked Silas.

'By the Seven Stars,' answered the Scribe angrily. 'They're selling words. Holy words handed out by the Wordmasters to be used freely by all Barbalonians, not meant to be the common currency of ruffians and rogues. This black market is a sacrilege.'

Sultan looked at Ramset rather sceptically though.

'You're high-minded indeed, my friend,' he said. 'But how can you control what people do with the things you give them? That's a problem that has always haunted the Alchemists.'

Ramset looked a little taken aback.

'Besides,' Sultan went on, 'perhaps one shouldn't try to control the traffic in words too much, for, as you would see, Silas, if you crossed from land to land, words change too, like stories and people and things. They've a magic entirely of their own and one as powerful as any spell.'

Rarza thought of the words in the History and Silas nodded, again longing to know what had really been in that Wordbox.

'And yet . . .' continued Sultan.

'Yet?' said Silas.

'And yet the greatest stories, Silas Root, even though they change and grow across the Seven Lands, always seem to be talking about the very same thing. The spirit.'

225

Just up the street they saw two Barbalissaries, barring the way back into the square and talking together. The alley opened at the bottom, but narrowed rapidly at the top and the friends could clearly hear what they were saying.

'The Childars are in the city,' said one. 'They were spotted in the Street of Carpenters.'

Rarza started.

'Then they know we're here and what we look like too,' she whispered to Silas wonderingly.

'Well,' grunted the other soldier, 'if they're really in Barbal they can't possibly escape. Zolos says the Groot reward will do it. Then, when they're in Mardak's clutches – for Mardak is back also, for his enthronement and then to summon the Destroyer.'

'In the meantime, we have our work cut out,' said the first. 'They want some more children.'

The soldiers hurried away and Sultan was about to lead the friends on into Barbal Square when a crowd came bustling down the alley straight towards them.

'Hey!' cried Silas. 'Look out, Rarza.'

Silas found himself being swept backwards though and it was almost more than he could do not to be knocked over. He could just see Rarza ahead of him but she hadn't noticed that Silas was gone.

'Rarza!'

Silas saw an alley to his right and he ducked down it to get out of the way of the mob. The alley was much smaller and dingier than the last, with low-hanging wooden balconies that protruded into the street, casting gloomy shadows everywhere.

There were beggars sitting all about but Silas wandered along, keen not to be caught up in the crowds again and wondering if there was another way back to the alley. Silas heard a strange sound and saw a man sitting in the dust playing a long, wooden flute with a bulbous end and from a basket next to him a hooded snake was rising into the air, twisting and turning at the sound, as though enchanted by the music.

Silas drew closer and saw that there were baskets everywhere and men all about weaving them from straw. Among them others seemed to be weaving sacks too. Dark eyes looked up at Silas as he walked, but just as he was nearing the end of the street he heard another noise behind him and suddenly everything went dark.

'Hey, what's happening?'

Silas began to struggle but it was no good. The sack that had been popped over his head covered him completely and now rough arms grabbed him too.

'Help! Help me!'

'He'll do,' said a voice, 'though he's a small 'un.'

Silas squirmed violently in the sack.

'Do we take him straight to the Barbalissaries?' said another voice.

'Sure. He must be worth at least a Groot. But I wish he'd stop struggling.'

'Then use the club.'

With that Silas Root felt a horrible pain in the back of his head and lost consciousness.

BENEATH THE TEMPLE

Silas Root woke with a start. His head felt as hollow as a metal bell and as he moved his hands he heard the rattle of chains and felt cold metal around his wrists. It was dark about him and all he knew was that someone was sitting right beside him. Silas lifted his hand painfully and another hand moved with him. He was manacled to it.

'Where am I?' Silas whispered faintly, rubbing his aching neck.

'Somewhere deep beneath Barbal City,' said a small voice next to him.

Silas peered round.

'Who are you?'

'My name's Kerbogah. You?'

'Silas. Silas Root.'

Silas's eyes were growing accustomed to the gloom and, as they did so, the Childar stared about him in absolute astonishment. Silas felt as if he had stepped into some terrible nightmare. He was in a chamber – to be precise, a dungeon. All around the walls sat urchins and street children of Barbal City, shivering and filthy from the water and muck that dripped from the ceiling, and each was chained to the wall.

In the middle of the room was a slatted wooden wheel, a smaller version of the Waterwheel, grinding on a single wooden axis. It seemed to be connected to a series of pulleys running up through the ceiling. But what most horrified Silas was that inside the wheel two ragged Barbalonian children were marching on.

As their chained ankles endlessly climbed an invisible mountain that had no summit, the wheel revolved beneath their feet, and the children staggered and fell, picked themselves up and staggered on.

'What is it?' whispered Silas as the wheel turned before them.

'A treadmill, I think,' answered Kerbogah. He was holding four wooden tubes, bound together with twine and trying to blow on them, although they made no sound. Silas looked into his face and liked it immediately. It was bold and open and somehow spoke of courage.

'A treadmill?' whispered Silas. 'But what's it for?'

One of the other children lined up against the wall looked up too.

'It's a makina, of course,' he said wearily. 'You'll have your turn soon enough.'

'My turn?' said Silas. 'But what does it do?'

'Moves the Waterwheel in the square, of course. By a system of ropes and pulleys. The Alchemists love their makinas.'

'Moves the Waterwheel?' said Silas in amazement.

'I know,' whispered Kerbogah bitterly, 'the first Wonder of the World doesn't work by magic at all. That's why they've been stealing children from Barbal's streets, so it wouldn't get out that there is no magic Chi left in the Great Square.'

'They take us off to climb up to the square too,' said another of the children, 'to light the Eternal Flames, while Barbalonians are asleep and dreaming. Though they guard us strictly, of course.'

Silas's head was still throbbing and the pain suddenly began to get much worse.

'But I don't understand.'

'What is there to understand?' said the boy cheerlessly. 'Except that the Alchemists are all a pack of fakes. They can't make gold or isolate the Balm of Eternal Life either. For an age now they've been taking innocent children to run their makina, like pack ponies, claiming all the while that without their magic the rivers would stop flowing and the Sun God rising. They're frauds.'

'So that's the great secret!' said Silas suddenly, remembering what the pot had told him in the lesson house.

'It won't be a secret if I ever get out of here,' hissed the boy angrily. 'When Barbalonians hear about it they'll tear down the Ziggurat with their bare hands.'

'How can this be?' whispered Silas.

'It happened long ago,' answered the boy. 'When the Turnstones were lost, the Alchemists designed a contraption to keep the Waterwheel going, working secretly and deep into the night. They had all the builders slain, but children were the only ones small enough to fit in this secret treadmill and to get up those shafts to keep the flames burning too.'

'But why?' whispered Silas indignantly.

'Without the God-given magic of the Turnstones they had to keep water flowing around Barbal City and into important Barbalonian homes,' said another of the urchins, 'Especially with that prophecy about the Alchemists falling and the temple being rent in twain if the wheel ever stops.

Power's everything to an Alchemist. So they started stealing children, but only ones that have lost their parents or are strangers in the sacred city. Ones who wouldn't be noticed.'

Silas was horrified.

'Mardak and Ogog,' said the boy, 'magic and Turnstones. They're all made up. To keep us all fools and slaves.'

Silas's headache was getting even worse but he suddenly thought of the Pazgog and Gol and all he had seen them do with his own eyes.

'No,' he whispered, 'that's not true.'

'So you're on their side,' the boy said angrily. 'Why don't you go into the Ziggurat and serve Mardak then, like a desert dog? Though anything could happen to you up there. That's what Kalman believed.'

Kerbogah started violently at Silas's side.

'Kalman!' he cried. 'Kalman was here?'

'What's it to you?'

'Kalman's my brother. I've been searching for him.'

'Then you're a Dunetrader?'

'That's right. Tell me what happened to Kalman. Where is he? Who are you?'

'My name's Rathanor, if you must know,' answered the boy. 'And as for Kalman, your guess is as good as mine. I know that they took him upstairs though. Nine days ago. Through that doorway. I pray he's all right. Kalman was always very kind to me. He made me hope again.'

Rathanor was looking over to a door in the corner. It was surrounded by a wooden frame which looked rather flimsy and rotten. In a metal holder on the wall a torch was lodged that sent a dim light into the room.

'It leads along a passage and straight up into the Ziggurat,' whispered Rathanor mournfully. 'They take one of us, every now and then, for their experiments.'

'Experiments?'

All the children's faces grew fearful in the shadows and one started to cry gently to himself.

'On the Balm of Eternal Life.'

'I must find Kalman,' cried Kerbogah angrily, straining against his chains.

'You'll never get out of here,' said Rathanor. 'No one ever has. You'll just have to accept your fate, like the rest of us.'

They sat there in silence and after a while Kerbogah started blowing on his wooden tubes again. They gave only a very faint, reedy noise and he stopped and sighed bitterly.

'Oh, Camel's Blood! I wish Relak hadn't escaped.'

'Escaped?' said Silas, wondering hopefully if Relak was another Dunetrader.

'Under the door. Relak is my pet mouse.'

Silas sighed too and Kerbogah started blowing again.

'What are you doing?' whispered Silas after a while.

'I saved a Centaur in the market,' answered Kerbogah. 'She gave me these.'

'You did?' said Silas, sitting up. 'Mardak has ordered them captured for their hooves.'

'That's what the slaver said,' whispered Kerbogah. 'He talked about a scraping of Centaur's hoof. But why?'

'Mardak needs something supernatural to put in the glass for the Entropoth,' answered Silas, as if it was the most nat-ural thing in the world. 'The magic hourglass he builds. Essence of Centaur's hoof.'

'How do you know?' asked Kerbogah suspiciously.

Silas just shrugged.

'Well, Chiral gave me these,' said Kerbogah. 'They were Chiron's and she told me to blow on them if I was ever in real need.'

A few of the other children looked up.

'The trouble is, I just can't get them to work properly.'

232

The children looked down again but suddenly they heard the sound of keys, and the door to the chamber opened. A huge guard walked in and looked about coldly. He rattled a great bunch of golden keys and went over to the treadmill.

'Time to change the shift, scum,' he grunted.

The Barbalissary ordered the children on the wheel to climb down, which they did most gratefully. Then the guard pointed to Silas and Kerbogah.

'You there. Get up.'

As Silas and Kerbogah stood up they saw now how they were chained together by a long manacle that led to a hoop on the wall. The guard unlocked and shoved them roughly towards the wheel.

'Get off,' growled Silas.

Soon Silas and Kerbogah found themselves marching like the others though, their wrists bound to one another, and the guard slammed the door again.

'What are you doing in Barbal, Silas Root?' said Kerbogah as they walked.

Silas looked around nervously but the others weren't listening. The children were just too exhausted to care.

'I came here with my friends Rarza and Ramset from Ederyl, and my Lesson Master, Sultan Ash. He has lived with Dunetraders – they know him as Ashtar.'

Kerbogah almost tripped on the treadmill.

'Ashtar? It can't be. He was guiding us to Barbal but abandoned us in the desert when news came of Mazgol. But why is he with you?'

Silas had to trust someone.

'Because of the Lightbearer,' he answered in a whisper. 'We've brought it to the city.'

'The Lightbearer?' gasped Kerbogah, his eyes opening wider. 'Gol the magnificent?'

'Keep your voice down, Kerbogah. Gol's in my pocket.

Ashtar brought us together and I suppose we're kind of secret agents. We came to end the Schism and free Ogog. We're on a mission for the Hooded Master.'

'What are you going to do then, Silas?'

'What do you mean, do?'

'I've been trying to think of a way to escape and get into the Ziggurat.'

'Into the Ziggurat?'

'I've got to find out what's happened to my brother. He's up there somewhere. And Ogog is a prisoner in the Ziggurat too.'

'Not for long,' said Silas gloomily. 'The Great Solstice is tomorrow. Time has run out. Mardak will sacrifice him to Zorastar and raise the Uncrowned King of Night. The Destroyer. If Aspis comes, we're all lost. Chaos will consume everything.'

'Then we have to hurry,' said Kerbogah. 'If I can find Kalman, we'll get to my father. The Dunetraders will help us stop Mardak.'

'Dunetraders?' said Silas. 'There's to be a parley tomorrow. In the stone quarry.'

'The stone quarry?' said Kerbogah. 'That's where my mother and our caravan have camped. But why?'

'The Dunetrader caravans are trying to unite. Meanwhile the Grasht are building defences around the city and Zolos makes his secret weapons. They're walking straight into a trap. I think it has something to do with fire and water.'

Kerbogah's face went as white as Gol.

'Then I'll have to warn them somehow.'

'I wish Sultan was here,' whispered Silas. 'He'd know what to do.'

Kerbogah thought bitterly of his friend Ashtar abandoning him in the desert.

'Don't wish,' he grunted. 'Think. Think of a way to escape.'

The two boys seemed to walk for an age, side by side, although it was really only an hour before the guard returned. They slumped wearily against the wall again, but neither of the new friends had a real plan. The guard had hesitated, though.

'You're not finished yet,' he said suddenly. 'Come with me. We have to tend the Eternal Flames.'

The Barbalissary led them straight through that doorway, plucking the burning torch from the brazier and leaving the others in darkness. Silas and Kerbogah found themselves in a low passage that made the children gag as soon as the stale air hit their nostrils. The ground was wet underfoot.

'Where are we, sir?' asked Silas.

'Below the square, of course,' grunted the guard, 'although the system of ancient passageways down here also serves as Barbal's sewers. They go on for miles. You could get lost for a year in here.'

The smell was awful and as they walked, Silas and Kerbogah found themselves going in a circle, for the passage ringed the square above. They passed one opening after another in the walls too, leading off down other dark and grimy passageways.

'Where do they go?' whispered Silas, trying to peer into the darkness.

'All over the place, boy,' answered the guard. 'They were built at the very founding of the city.'

The guard gave them both a shove.

'Keep moving. And don't even think about trying to escape. No one ever gets out of this maze alive.'

They went on and started to notice odd shapes protruding from the passage walls. When the children got closer to them

235

they gasped. There were bones and skulls, shins and ankle joints, held in the very mud walls of the sewer.

'Who are they?' whispered Kerbogah fearfully, in the flaring torchlight. 'Were they murdered?'

'The Alchemists of Barbal,' answered the guard sombrely. 'Barbalonians use the Towers of Silence, but when Lord Alchemists go they're always buried down here in the catacombs. Ogog will be here soon enough himself. Poor fool.'

The children shuddered but Silas could suddenly feel a breath of fresh air on his cheeks. He looked up and saw that in the roof of the passage was a circular shaft that went straight upwards. At its top Silas fancied he saw a faint glow of light. There were wooden rungs leading right up the side of the shaft and a ledge at their base piled with logs and kindling.

'Here we are,' said the guard, stopping and looking up too. 'One of you's got to go up there.'

'Why?' gulped Silas.

'It leads straight up to the square,' answered the Barbalissary, 'through the hollow base of the pilasters to the Eternal Flames. Only children are small enough to get up there. You have to feed the fire.'

'More trickery,' said Silas angrily.

'Get on,' said the guard, but Kerbogah held up his wrist and Silas's with it.

'We can't both go,' he said indignantly, looking up at the narrow shaft. 'There isn't room.'

'No,' said the guard, beginning to unshackle them, 'and since there's no other guard to watch you at the moment, one goes and if he tries to escape, it's curtains for the other.'

Kerbogah had just cast Silas a look. His eyes were flickering strangely, darting back and forth towards a large stick on the ledge, the end of which was dripping with a sticky black substance. Silas suddenly realized what Kerbogah was thinking of.

236

'There,' said the guard as he unlocked their manacles.

As soon as his arm was free, Kerbogah lunged forward, knocking the keys and the torch from the guard's hands. They went flying across the passage floor.

'Hey!' growled the guard, jumping forward to save his keys.

Silas seized the stick. It smelt of Zorastar's Tears and he swung it high, bringing it straight down on the Barbalissary's head. The guard crashed to the ground and lay quite still in the muck.

'I think I've killed him,' whispered Silas fearfully.

The torch was hissing and fizzing on the damp ground and Silas could hardly see a thing, but the guard wasn't moving.

'No,' said Kerbogah. 'But he's going to have a headache when he wakes up, that's for sure, Silas.'

Kerbogah bent down and picked up the torch, which flickered faintly, then began to rummage around. At last Kerbogah found what he was looking for. He pulled the keys from under the guard's body and held them up proudly. One of them had bent in the fall, but Kerbogah put them in his pocket and turned down the passage.

'Come on.'

They stumbled on and the passage grew darker and darker, for the torch was failing. Suddenly it sputtered and went out altogether. Silas and Kerbogah were plunged into darkness.

'We can't manage in this, we'll get lost in the dark,' whispered Kerbogah.

'Wait,' said Silas.

Silas reached into his smock and pulled out the Lucifer Sultan had given him in the desert. It flared as soon as Silas struck it against the wall and in no time at all Silas had lit his own stick, which flamed brightly, sending strange, lurid shadows dancing along the sewer walls.

'Fire,' said Silas. 'Useful for everything.'

Kerbogah wasn't listening. He was looking at Silas's neck. His expression had turned to utter astonishment. In the dancing light he had just seen the little birthmark on Silas's throat.

'You!'

'What's wrong, Kerbogah?'

'You're the Marked One.'

'Marked One? What are you talking about?' said Silas nervously.

'In the desert. A Wordmaster prophesied that I would meet a Marked One, one who would free us all by his sacrifice. One who would bring hope again. You, Silas Root.'

'Sacrifice?' whispered Silas. 'I don't know what you mean, Kerbogah. Stop talking nonsense.'

'But it's true,' hissed Kerbogah, 'the prophecy's all true. The wheel shall stop and the temple be rent in twain. But the Wordmaster said our fates would be bound together. And now they have been. Literally.'

Kerbogah rattled the chains at his wrists and looked very cheerful indeed. But Silas was beginning to feel sick. He didn't like this talk at all of him saving anyone with his sacrifice. Silas put the used Lucifer back in his pocket but as he did so the Childar went cold.

'What is it?' said Kerbogah.

'Gol,' cried Silas. 'It's slipped out again. It was always trying to get away. We'll have to go back, Kerbogah.'

Kerbogah grabbed Silas's arm.

'But, Silas. We'll never find it in the dark. And the guard. We'll just have to keep going for the moment.'

'But, Kerbogah. It's a disaster. If this prophecy has any truth I need the Turnstone to fight Mardak.'

'We can't look now. The guard will be waking up soon. Come on, Silas.'

Even Silas could see the wisdom of this so, desperate as he

238

was, on they went. They seemed to walk for an age but at last they came on some steps and at the top of them was a doorway. Silas had to force it with his shoulder, but it gave way with a terrible creaking. They found themselves in a wide, seven-sided chamber with a mosaic floor, patterned with the same symbols as the Sundial. The Zodiac. All along the walls were ranged shelves and little cubbyholes.

'Where are we now?' asked Kerbogah nervously, looking at the pattern on the floor, sniffing the air like a Grasht. 'And what's that strange smell?'

'Of course!' cried Silas, as the revelation struck him. 'It must be the Room of Changes. In here lies the magical knowledge of centuries.'

Kerbogah blinked in astonishment but Silas was suddenly shaking with excitement. He had realized exactly where he was.

'And the Ziggurat. We're below the Ziggurat, Kerbogah. We've entered it at last.'

Silas went white too in the torchlight.

'And it's certain death for any not of the Order to enter it.'

Silas realized it was too late and Kerbogah hardly heard Silas now. He was looking around at the cubbyholes.

'They're full of clay tablets,' he whispered.

'They're words. Words of Power, Kerbogah. All the Words of Power that have ever been known in Barbal City.'

'But so many!'

'In a way it all started with words, Kerbogah,' whispered Silas thoughtfully, 'when I tried to open a Wordbox in Ederyl. It was a word from the future.'

'The future? What are you talking about now, Silas? What word?'

'That's just the point, Kerbogah. I don't know yet. But it appeared with Pengalisians from the future when Mardak started experimenting on Stardust to build his Entropoth. The makina of time.'

Kerbogah's head was reeling at all this information but he had already begun to pull out some of the tablets, and was wiping them down, for they were all covered in a thick layer of dust.

'Words are so strange, aren't they?' said Silas, as he watched him work. 'You know, sometimes, sometimes it feels to me as if, well, as if I am actually inside them.'

Kerbogah held up one of the tablets in the smoking torch-light and Silas saw that it was as round as a treadmill and from its edges, spiralling inwards, ran strange scrolls and swirls, exactly like they had done on the wanted posters.

'They're in ancient Barbalonian,' said Silas. 'Gol could have translated them.'

Another thought suddenly struck Silas though. He dipped into his pocket again and pulled out the wanted poster that Sultan had rolled up in Sulphurius's laboratory.

'This. It's in ancient Barbalonian too, Kerbogah,' he said, as he held it up, 'but I know what it means.'

'So?' said Kerbogah, looking blankly at the hieroglyphs.

'So I can use the letters to translate these tablets. Logically. Sultan said it might come in handy.'

Silas felt a thrill as he set to, as though he were unpicking the lock of some ancient doorway, but when he had finished deciphering the clay tablets Silas looked almost as bewildered as Kerbogah had done.

'What's wrong now, Silas? What do they say?'

'I don't understand it at all. This one says "Book" and this says one "Scribe". This one says "Taper" and this one "Tablecloth". What heavenly use are they?'

Silas's eyes rested on a larger tablet.

'Now this looks more like it,' he cried hopefully, pulling

it out and turning it over. 'More than just single words, anyway. Only a few ancient sentences perhaps, but bound to hold something truly powerful. There are markings here too. Number markings for Sandwork. A Lord Alchemist himself must have inscribed these.'

As soon as Silas translated, though, he grunted angrily.

'It's still gibberish. "Three drapes, one bolster and five pillowcases from the Lord Alchemist's twelfth bedchamber". What can it all mean?'

'They're laundry lists.'

The voice that had just cried out from the shadows made them jump for their lives.

Silas and Kerbogah swung round to see a man in fine though dirty golden robes, slumped on the floor and chained fast to the wall.

'Who are you?' whispered Silas.

'Ogog,' answered the stranger coldly as the children approached and held the torch closer.

'Ogog? The Lord Alchemist of Barbal?'

'Not if Mardak has his way,' said Ogog sadly. 'But who are you and what are you doing committing sacrilege?'

'I'm Kerbogah.'

'And I'm Silas Root. We've come to free you, sir.'

Kerbogah grinned and nodded.

'That's very kind,' said the Lord Alchemist cheerlessly, 'and how are you going to do that?'

'Quick, Kerbogah,' cried Silas. 'The keys.'

Kerbogah pulled out the bunch of golden keys and tried each in turn on the Alchemist's cruel manacles but, try as he might, none would open them.

'Mardak has it,' said Ogog, 'in the Incanting Room. Along with the Book of Destinies and his blasted Entropoth. He's even stolen my holy throne and my favourite pet chameleon, Seraph. He was always fascinated by it. Damned thief.'

Kerbogah had just noticed two large pieces of broken tablet though, lying on the floor next to the Alchemist.

'They're the Seven Commandments,' whispered Ogog, catching his gaze. 'Mardak stole down here one night, trying to get to the Book of Destinies. The Wordmasters caught him and sent him back upstairs but he had already dropped the tablet and broken it in two.'

Kerbogah picked them up and, as he fitted the halves together again, the shape reminded Silas of the memorial in the temple of Ederyl that his mother Alara had raised for his father Timon. Silas suddenly missed his father more than ever.

Silas took the two tablets and saw that the markings were scored far deeper into the clay than the others had been. From their blackened edges it looked as if they had indeed been burnt there by the Gods, or a firebolt from heaven. Shakily, Silas began to use the alphabet to translate the commandments of heaven, that had guided Barbalonians for so long.

Commandments Against the Seven Deadly Sins

Thou Shalt not be Avaricious – especially after too many golden Groots

Thou Shalt not be Gluttonous – especially over food that turns in the desert heat

Thou Shalt not show Sloth – especially when leaving Ederyl

Thou Shalt not Lust – especially after Barbalonian Perfume Makers

Thou Shalt not Envy – especially the secrets of the Universe

Thou Shalt not be Proud – unless you're an Alchemist
Thou Shalt not show Anger – unless you have to fight a desert war

'Did the Gods really write these?' whispered Silas doubtfully. 'With a firebolt? They're mad.'

'Ah yes,' said Ogog, 'nobody believes in anything any more.'

'Well, that's not surprising,' whispered Kerbogah scornfully, looking angrily around the Room of Changes. 'It's as if everything in Barbal City is a fake, or some kind of bad joke.'

Ogog looked indignant.

'Certainly not.'

'What's that?'

Silas was pointing in the shadows. Kerbogah shuddered too as he saw an archway and, beyond it, a huge dining hall and a long table. All around motionless figures were slumped on the table or lying on the floor, in tattered saffron robes bound with black sashes. It was only now that Silas caught the horrible stench that Kerbogah had first smelt in the chamber. It reminded him of the Pazgog.

There was shattered crockery everywhere and ants and beetles and tiny burrowing creatures were scurrying from their hiding places to taste the food, or continue their labour of picking clean the decaying bodies. In the flickering, flaring light of Silas Root's torch the magical Room of Changes had suddenly become a charnel-house.

'My Wordmasters,' whispered Ogog bitterly. 'Murdered by Zolos with snake venom mixed into their wine, as they gathered to begin the celebrations for the Solstice.'

'Snake venom?' said Kerbogah. 'That's what they were collecting in the Street of Slavers.'

Ogog was nodding sadly and he reached into his pocket and pulled out a little bottle. It was like the one Ramset had found by the oasis, only it was tinted yellow.

'With more of this I might have saved them. Or a few of them at least.'

'What is it?' asked Silas.

'It's a serum. The opposite of venom. An antidote. We've been working on it inside the Ziggurat, for many Lord Alchemists have been poisoned in their time. But never again shall my Wordmasters practise the Word Rite or speak in tongues. This was their last supper. Only one escaped.'

'No, he didn't,' said Kerbogah sadly. 'We buried him in the desert, before Ashtar left us.'

The boys sat down next to Ogog, feeling quite defeated. The sight had terrified them both and now they didn't want to climb higher in the Ziggurat at all. But as they sat there Silas suddenly had another thought.

'The word!' he cried excitedly, lifting his torch and looking round the cubbyholes again. 'The word that went to Ederyl by mistake. Is it in here?'

Ogog pointed to one of the cubbyholes and when Silas went over he found a clay disc with no dust on it at all.

'At last,' cried Silas, thrilling at the very touch of the futuristic icon. 'Now I can find out what started this all.'

'Turn it over then,' said Ogog, 'and read it out to us.'

Silas was trembling furiously as he held the tablet and turned it over to read what was written there from the future. A word so revolutionary, Ramset had said, that it threatened to overthrow the Alchemists themselves.

As the torch swayed, Silas Root looked down. At last he saw the word and the word was:

EVOLUTION

NIMROD

'Evolution,' whispered Silas, shivering strangely and scratching his head. 'But what on earth does it mean? And why should it cause so much fuss?'

'Beats me,' whispered Ogog. 'The Wordmasters were most excited when they inscribed it, though. They said they did not bring it forth in a Word Rite at all, but that it began circulating when Mardak called for the tribute and started experimenting again on Stardust.'

'In the bazaar,' said Kerbogah suddenly, 'when I rescued Chiral and she gave me her dead mate's pipes. A man was talking about Evolutia. He called it the change of all forms.'

'Oh, they didn't get Chiron,' interjected Ogog. 'They only wounded him, but he healed himself and escaped.'

'Whatever,' said Kerbogah. 'But before I freed Chiral a Heleran almost bought her. He said that he'd got the idea in his bath one boring Monday morning. Of Evolutia. How one thing always comes from another. He said he had to tell the Philosophon.'

'Yes. Some of our studies on rocks in the Observing Room,' said Ogog almost fearfully, 'have been leading me to a similar conclusion. Studies on rocks with animals inside them.'

'Animals?' said Silas, dipping into his smock pocket and pulling out the rock Sultan had picked up from Sulphurius's collection.

'That's one,' said Ogog. 'Madark calls them "Fossils".'

'Fossils? But what's it got to do with Evolutia?' asked Silas. 'I mean, Evolution? What does it really mean?'

'If it's true,' answered Ogog, in hushed tones, 'it means rather a lot. It means that animals have been around far longer than we thought. That the law of life is change, for a start, as the Alcemoth says. That everything is changing and that we were not just sent here like a meteor from heaven as our stories tell us. Evolution is really the opposite of Creation.'

Silas nodded slowly.

'The fossil record suggests that the story of Ederyl, of the whole world in fact, is not as the Elders' fables teach. That we were not all placed here in a pretty garden by the Gods in just Seven Suns, but that other things lived there long, long before Childars, or anybody else for that matter.'

Silas and Kerbogah trembled at the thought.

'And it means that man himself comes not from the heavens at all, but from the animals.'

Kerbogah was suddenly thinking of that beautiful woman rising out of the horse's body, but Silas's eyes grew round with wonder and he dropped the rock, which smashed among the word tablets and the broken Commandments.

'But wouldn't that mean . . . ?'

'Exactly, Silas Root. That the Gods don't exist at all.'

Silas gulped. He felt sick again.

'No wonder Mardak wants to suppress it.'

'Yes,' said Ogog, 'because that might mean that there are

no prophecies and that magic doesn't exist either. Just as I was beginning to suspect.'

The Lord Alchemist grinned.

'*Quod erat demonstrandum*. Mardak, with his faith and mysticism and hocus pocus, so wanted to suppress it that he had Zolos send a sergeant of the Barbalissaries to fetch it back from Ederyl.'

'Mekmam,' said Silas, realizing it must have been him that they had first seen in Ederyl.

'But I've seen a God,' cried Kerbogah suddenly, holding up Chiron's pipes. 'A Demigod at least.'

'And what about Gol?' said Silas. 'The Turnstones? I've seen so much magic it would make your head spin.'

'The Dunetraders' voices,' insisted Kerbogah. 'Stardust. All of it.'

'Ah, yes,' sighed the Lord Alchemist, and a strange look came into Ogog's clever eyes. 'I admit it's quite a paradox. The Great Paradox in fact. Why such things exist in our world, when Sandwork and logic and the scientific method, when the theory of Evolution itself, would tell you that they shouldn't do so at all.'

The children looked at each other in wonder.

'Enough now, though. We have talked far too long already,' Ogog added suddenly. 'You must hurry. If you can, get into the Incanting Room and find the key to my chains. Take those stairs over there.'

The boys turned.

'The Book of Destinies is there too. Try to steal it. Ancient custom says that no new Alchemist can be enthroned without it and Mardak will need it for the ceremony. To crown Aspis.'

Silas shivered as he thought of Mardak the Dark. He was so close now.

'And there's supposed to be a charm inside the Book of

247

Destinies,' said Ogog, 'one that could seal the Underworld once more. A magic spell.'

'But I thought you didn't believe in magic,' said Silas sourly. 'Or charms.'

The Lord Alchemst smiled ruefully.

'The Great Paradox, remember.'

'All right,' sighed Silas. 'Come on, Kerbogah.'

Silas and Kerbogah walked towards the stairs and Ogog called out to them, 'Hurry. There is no time. No time at all.'

The stairs pitched steeply upwards, but after only a little while Silas and Kerbogah came to an opening in the wall to the right. There was another chamber here and from its slimy walls hung chains and manacles. As they peered inside the room they heard a voice in the corner.

'At last.'

Silas and Kerbogah crept inside. In the corner two chained figures were hunched against the wall. Next to a boy sat a man whose clothes had become rags. He was turbaned, but in a different way from the Dunetraders. His face was as black as fire charcoal. The lad next to him was trying to give him a cup of water.

They drew closer and the boy looked up fearfully. But as he saw Silas and Kerbogah and not a Barbalissary, he seemed to relax. The turbaned figure held a piece of fire charcoal in his hand and now he started scratching several strange markings on the walls. He crossed them out again and, starting to dribble, suddenly began chewing on the fire charcoal like a dog with a little bone.

'What's wrong with him?' whispered Kerbogah,

'My master's gone quite barmy,' answered his companion sadly, 'working for Mardak the Dark. Poor Al-Jibara.'

'Al-Jibara?' gasped Silas. 'The greatest Number Magician in Moorcaria.'

Kerbogah was looking into the corner of the prison,

though. There lay another man, dressed almost exactly like Ramset, but quite motionless. There was something waxy about his face.

'Who's he?' he asked.

'His name's Tutanamet,' answered the boy. 'An embalmer, from the Land of Khem. He was dying when they put us in here. But he attempted to embalm himself before he went.'

Al-Jibara had suddenly turned to the wall.

'There!' he cried, his huge eyes flickering wildly. 'Now I've got it.'

'Got what, Al-Jibara?' asked his companion, taking his hand.

'It's quite brilliant,' mumbled the mathematician. 'I've been thinking about it all morning. Watch.'

Rapidly Al-Jibara began scribbling on the wall and suddenly there were patterned these strange symbols:

$$L = C + (F x B)$$

'What's that?' asked Kerbogah. 'Another talisman to fight off demons?'

'An equation,' said Silas.

'That's right, boy,' said Al-Jibara, in a patient but deeply excited voice. 'The letters stand for words, you see. And the signs represent addition and multiplication. Sandwork.'

Al-Jibara started pointing out the symbols, one by one.

'Love, Chi, Feeling and Bravery. That's what we have in the mix. According to my calculations anyway, I've just found the perfect equation for Love. It's rather simple, in fact.'

Kerbogah looked at him in amazement, thinking of Chiral's love for her mate and Khayarumi's words in the Great Tent about love being the only real thing there is. Kerbogah suddenly missed his brother Kalman desperately, and Farjay and Relak too.

'Love equals Chi, or the life force,' cried Al-Jibara, 'plus how brave you're feeling at the time.'

Silas shook his head. If the Alchemists were fakes, this crazy mathematician seemed little better. In fact, he seemed quite insane.

'Excuse me,' Silas interrupted irritably. 'Can't you really help us? There's an equation I want to know about.'

Silas grabbed the charcoal from Al-Jibara and scratched on the wall the symbols he'd seen on the paper in the Camel and Kerbogah had seen in the Street of Soothsayers. As soon as Al-Jibara saw it his eyes lit up like flares.

'Ah yes. Mardak wanted to know about that too. For his Entropoth. "$E=MC^2$". That's why he brought me here in fact. Quite a journey. And I think I've cracked it now, so perhaps my life work has not been entirely in vain.'

'Cracked it? What is it?'

Al-Jibara drew himself up portentously.

'It's just what I have been seeking all my life. It appeared suddenly on a wall in the bazaar, as if by magic, and the funny thing is that's exactly what I think it is. The true equation for magic.'

The boys stepped even closer.

'Then what does it mean?' asked Kerbogah.

'Mean?' snorted Al-Jibara scornfully, as if everyone should know exactly what it meant. 'E is for the Entropoth and C is for Chi, of course. I think we all know by now what M is. It means that the Entropoth equals Magic multiplied by the power of Chi, squared. Or, to turn it on its head entirely, Magic equals the Entropoth divided by the Chi ratio. Simple really.'

The man grinned like a child but Kerbogah shook his head.

'What's he talking about, Silas?'

Al-Jibara's companion smiled wearily and nodded at Kerbogah's evident confusion.

'I've begged my Master to stick to what he really knows,' he said sadly. 'But his fear of the coming darkness has driven out his reason and unhinged his mind. And what a mind it was. Once he even worked out how to calculate the diagonal of a square, and the circumference of a circle. Pure genius.'

'Sacred geometry,' burbled Al-Jibara excitedly, 'sacred seven. Use seven to divide up twenty-two. Which, if you really think about it, is double sacred eleven. Divide the second number by the first and the number that comes out goes on forever and ever, never once repeating itself. In Pengalis it's called "pi". It can tell you all sorts of useful things about the real world. Especially about sacred circles.'

Kerbogah remembered that strange busker in the bazaar and his little numbered cube. Once more magical seven had appeared, but with it other numbers too. Al-Jibara looked around and grinned like a naughty child.

'But let me give you a piece of advice,' he said suddenly, clutching the lad's hand again, 'one that may save you from my fate at least.'

The Moorcarian leant closer and almost hissed the warning at the children.

'*In life, be careful who and what you travel with.*'

'What do you mean?' asked Silas.

'I mean, you wouldn't try and cross the Depthless Sea if you hadn't invented a boat yet, would you boy?' answered Al-Jibara angrily. 'Or know what a boat was? That stands to reason. Well, when I went on my journey of discovery I hadn't yet found the means to travel or to fight properly, because they still lay in the future and then all the demons broke loose.'

'Demons?' said Silas nervously, looking about him in the darkness and half expecting the Pazgog to attack.

'Not out there. In here,' said the Moorcarian, rapping his turbaned head furiously with his knuckle, 'in my head.'

Silas remembered what Sultan had said of the Underworld being inside us all and of your Chi Shield protecting you from it.

'And was it worth it?' said Al-Jibara bitterly. 'I could have done so many wonderful things in life. I could have really lived, instead of being haunted by some endless itch I couldn't even scratch, because I don't know enough yet and hadn't the words or the scientific method to understand. Was it all worth the sacrifice? Oh dear.'

Suddenly Al-Jibara's shoulders hunched round and he broke into passionate, shuddering sobs. But Silas only wished that everybody would stop talking about sacrifices.

'There, there,' whispered his companion kindly. 'Don't break your heart, master. Not over Sandwork anyhow.'

'No,' cried the Moorcarian angrily, shrugging him off again. 'You must help me get out of here. I must destroy the Entropoth.'

'Why?' asked Silas.

'Because there is a design flaw. By my calculations it will draw all Chi from the world completely,' answered Al-Jibara coldly, 'suck magic from the universe altogether.'

Silas and Kerbogah looked at each other in absolute horror.

'In the desert,' said Kerbogah, 'the Dunetraders' voices are failing.'

Al-Jibara seemed to have lost interest, though. He had started to write on the wall again.

'Now, let me see. What's next? I know. An equation for hope.'

'Come on, Kerbogah,' cried Silas, 'let's get out of here.'

They left Al-Jibara and his companion to their silly equations and up and up the great stairway they rose, until they came to a long passage. They crept along it and suddenly to the right they came to another room. Another dungeon.

The ground was covered in broken glass, and to their horror they saw that a man was lying tied down to a table. Beside him were the most dreadful-looking instruments, and the figure was dressed in the strangest clothes the children had ever seen. As the boys walked up to him he raised his head wearily and opened his eyes. At first his look was defiant, but as he saw Silas and Kerbogah his face softened again.

'I had to tell him,' he whispered faintly. 'I had to tell Mardak what it means.'

'What?' said Silas, leaning down close to him.

'"Evolution",' answered the man desperately. 'I held out for so long, but they tortured me and I finally cracked. I never told him, though, about the Equation. Jeslas, I'm thirsty!'

There was a pitcher of water and several tumblers on a table nearby. Silas picked the jug up.

'Who are you?' whispered Silas, giving him some drink.

'Nimrod.'

Silas stepped backwards immediately.

'You're a Pengalisian. A spy from the future.'

Kerbogah was looking at Nimrod in astonishment. Although this strange figure was from the future he looked much like any ordinary human being to the Dunetrader.

'That's right. I was in the lab following up my ideas on Chaos Theory when it happened,' whispered Nimrod. 'I was suddenly translated back here and materialized in the bazaar. In the Street of Soothsayers.'

Silas began to nod. It was all fitting together.

'I hadn't any Groots, so I earned some writing the Equation on a wall. But I didn't tell them what it means, I promise. Then Mardak captured me and brought me into the temple. At first we talked like friends, and he seemed so interested in who I was and my work that I gave him some new words – words from Pengalis. We talked like fellow scientists.'

Silas was nodding.

'But then I realized that I was breaking the Alcemothic Oath. So I wouldn't tell Mardak any more. That's when he clapped me in irons and started to torture me. But he couldn't get it out of me. You aren't ready to understand yet. It's too soon.'

'It's all right,' whispered Silas, but he shivered as he noticed the horrible marks on the poor man's throat.

'I'd hoped to be gone before this,' said Nimrod wearily. 'The transfer here only lasts for a certain time, you see. It is all very unstable. I could be sucked back to Pengalis at any moment.'

'There are others here,' said Silas suddenly, 'from Pengalis.'

'Others?'

'They're coming to rescue you, Nimrod. We heard about them in the Elusive Camel. Mandrax and three others.'

Nimrod went white.

'You've got to help me get out of here.'

'Why, Nimrod?'

'Mandrax isn't coming to rescue me. They're furious with me for all my doubts about whether the scientific method is so scientific. If they get their hands on me they'll take me back to be punished.'

'Help me, Kerbogah,' said Silas, starting to unmanacle Nimrod.

They sat him up and gave him the water pitcher, which he drank from gratefully.

'But how did you really get here?' asked Silas.

'It's to do with time,' whispered the Pengalisian, 'and

254

everything being relative, as the Equation tells us. It'd be hard for a Barbalonian to understand it yet.'

Silas scowled.

'I'm not from Barbal, I'm a Childar. Just tell me.'

'It's because of String Theory really,' answered Nimrod, 'which challenges even the truth of the Equation. You see, in Pengalis we no longer believe in the ordinary reality of matter. If you know how, it's possible to weave through space and time, into other worlds and different dimensions. It's to do with the vibrations of matter and the echoes they leave across space-time.'

In Kerbogah's head it was suddenly as if the Dunetrader's shaking Sandsong was shifting the desert, and he touched Chiral's pipes.

'Though what has happened here is even more extra-ord-inary than time travel. Because this isn't only the past, it's . . .'

Nimrod stopped and seemed to change his mind about something.

'Anyway, I was doing some experiments with SIP,' he said instead. 'Stellar Imaginarium Periforate.'

The children looked at him blankly.

'Stardust. You call it Stardust. It pulled me back to another place where someone had been working with Stardust.'

'The Camel,' said Silas. 'Sulphurius was working on Stardust in the Camel too. But the Equation, it's the Equation for Magic, isn't it, Nimrod? The Entropoth equals Magic times . . .'

'Don't talk nonsense,' snapped Nimrod, 'it's nothing of the sort.'

'But Al-Jibara,' said Silas, looking rather offended, 'he just said . . .'

'Oh, that old fool,' whispered Nimrod. 'He's driven him-self quite mad trying to understand it. Mardak brought him

255

here from Moorcaria when I refused to comply. But that simpleton couldn't possibly crack it. It does have something to do with Chi, though, as Al-Jibara thinks, although in Pengalis we call Chi by another name.'

'What name?'

'Energy.'

'Energy,' whispered Silas, rather liking the word.

'Yes, boy. Energy − E − equals Mass − M − times the Speed of Light − C − squared. We know in Pengalis that Energy is the force that animates all things,' said Nimrod, 'and if you need a real rule to work by, try this for size: *Energy cannot be created or destroyed but only transformed from one form into another.*'

Silas was shaking his head in utter bewilderment as Kerbogah stepped forward.

'What's it like in Pengalis?' asked the young Dunetrader.

'We've discovered so many wonderful things about the world,' answered Nimrod wistfully. 'About the revolution of the Earth about the Sun. About how to split light and atoms and harness your Chi. So much has been revealed by the insights of mathematics and algebra, geometry and physics, chemistry, natural history and geology. By the mind of man. Like neutrinos that stream through us all the time and black holes. And yet . . . it lacks a certain magic, I suppose. Indeed, magic has been abolished forever.'

'Forever?' said Silas.

'In Pengalis we're told that the only way to understand the world is using the scientific method. So we have pulled down our priests and Gods to unravel the great detective story of life, through the Evolution of mankind.'

'Evolution,' said Silas. 'The Lord Alchemist says it proves there are no Gods. That everything is changing and evolving.'

'I'm not so sure. That's why I was experimenting with Stellar Imaginarium Periforate. Stardust.'

'Oh,' said Silas.

'Not that I don't believe in Evolution,' continued Nimrod. 'We've the proof in the fossil record. But in Pengalis we treat Evolution almost as a holy thing, just as our scientists have become the High Priests of our world. Although we quite forget where the story of Evolution came from, and how long the idea has been around in the mind of man. In the very idea of Gods themselves and the patterns of man's stories. And there's something wrong with Pengalis. Despite all our knowledge, and all our methodolgies, in Pengalis we still cannot really solve the big questions.'

'Big questions?' whispered Kerbogah.

'Where it all really came from,' said Nimrod wearily, 'and where it is all going. Above all, what it all means. In our arrogance Pengalisians think that because we've discovered so many clever things, like magnetism and sparks of electricity, like molecular weights and radiation, like conductivity and uranium, we actually invented them ourselves. But we did nothing of the sort, of course. We only invented the language to categorize and describe things that have always existed. All we have done is to harness their miracles, you see, as your animal slavers harness their living slaves, as the Alchemists have harnessed children to turn your Waterwheel.'

Silas nodded slowly. Light was beginning to dawn.

'And despite all our talk of reality,' said Nimrod sadly, 'in our rush to embrace science we forget that science is really just a language too, and forget how to use another language as well, a language that is so desperately important to man. Without which he is nothing at all. Lost in a desert.'

'What language, Nimrod?'

'The poetry of meaning and wonder,' said Nimrod gravely. 'The language of the soul. Think of a world without priests and temples, without Gods and Alchemists and Ziggurats. Think of a world stripped of belief or faith or Warrior Priests or Centaurs.

Would that not rob life itself of wonder and make it as barren as a desert? Can you really call that progress? We've made so many advances in Pengalis, it's true. But in doing so we have forgotten so much.'

'What?'

'The power of ancient wisdom and understanding,' answered Nimrod. 'Of prayer and of dreams too, free from the daily language of pettiness and judgement and greed that chains us all. For do not your Gods visit you in dreams and tell you truths that you know before you even discover them?'

'I suppose so,' said Silas, remembering his own strange dreams.

'And your prayers lead to revelation,' said Nimrod. 'What do you call it? The breath of Inspiru. Many claim they can see clearly with nothing but logic and experimentation. But most are in fact rather stupid and science has never advanced just bit by bit, like clay bricks in a city wall. Like Evolution, it takes time and then sudden leaps, leaps of inspiration and strange connections to see the truth. Revelations.'

Nimrod started to cough.

'Water. May I have more water?'

'All we've proved,' said Nimrod, 'is so amazingly strange. Just as strange as Gods or Centaurs. Like space and time, or particles seeming to be in different places at the same moment. Or gravity and String Theory. So I for one don't believe in any simple reality, or that we Pengalisians are near the end of knowledge, as some smug Pengalisians claim. In fact I think we are only at the very beginning of a quite staggering journey.'

'And the Gods?' whispered Silas.

Nimrod seemed to grow very animated.

'Neither the Equation nor Evolution actually prove there is no Creator, no higher spirit and no meaning or purpose to the universe.'

'Then you,' said Silas, 'you're searching too, for the Final Alchemical Proof.'

'In my way,' said Nimrod modestly. 'May I drink now though?'

Silas turned to see if the jug was full.

'Tell me, Nimrod,' he asked as he did so. 'How close is Mardak the Dark? To the Proof?'

'He . . .'

Suddenly there was a clattering and Silas swung back. On the bench where Nimrod had been lying were little bits of broken crockery. The Pengalisian had vanished into thin air. Where he had been lying there was just a thin sprinkle of glittering sand, and that vanished soon too.

'The transfer, Kerbogah,' cried Silas. 'He's gone home.'

'Well, we must find the Incanting Room, Silas,' said Kerbogah, putting down the pitcher, 'and my brother.'

Silas nodded and they left the room and went back into the passageway. At the far end of it they could see a strange blue light, coming through a doorway.

'Flight bulbs,' said Silas. 'Sulphurius said they light the Incanting Room.'

'Mardak,' whispered Kerbogah, as they reached the end of the passage. 'Do you think Mardak is . . . ?'

'I don't know, Kerbogah,' gulped the Childar. 'Come on.'

They were shaking furiously but Silas stepped straight inside. They were standing at one end of a long hall now with a wooden ceiling and at the other end stood a solid gold throne, backed by sunlit windows, casting bands of light and dark into the huge chamber. All around were the strange flight bulbs, flickering with their living blue light.

'The Seat of the Alchemist,' whispered Silas, looking at the chair, 'stolen from Ogog.'

It was what was standing just beyond the chair in the

259

haunting blue light, though, that made the boys gasp in utter astonishment.

The giant hourglass was the most beautiful thing Silas and Kerbogah had ever seen in their lives. It rose to twice the height of the children, and its two giant spheres, perfectly proportioned and transparent, were contained within the finest ebony and sandalwood frame. The sliver of glass between the Entropoth's globes was as delicate as a water reed and all around the frame were symbols, inlaid in the most wonderfully wrought golden filigree.

At each corner of the frame were marks of the Sign of Four and along each of the edges ran the twelve signs of the Zodiac, patterned in hammered gold. Amongst them too were scrolls and whorls in curling Barbalonian script and at the top of the frame were those familiar hieroglyphs.

'The Equation again,' said Silas. '*Energy equals Mass times the Speed of Light squared.*'

In one of two carefully scooped grooves, either side of that strange equation at the base of the Entropoth, sat something that made Silas Root tremble.

Mazgol was the same size as Gol, but it was perfectly black. The Turnstone was glowing, or not exactly glowing, for the light within it seemed to be moving inwards rather than outwards, as Gol had done when the Pazgog had first attacked, so that, moving towards its core the stone seemed to get blacker and blacker, until it reached a point that was so black it seemed to swallow all the light around it entirely. Silas felt a strange sense of hopelessness.

'Mazgol the Mighty,' he sighed, 'whose power is night.'

The children were trembling but Kerbogah's eyes were fixed not on Mazgol but the upper globe. It was two-thirds full of sand, only the sand was glowing too and sparking and flashing with little bursts of incandescent golden light.

'Stardust!' cried the young Dunetrader. 'The tribute.'

Silas looked at it wonderingly but Kerbogah was shaking furiously.

'Mardak,' he whispered. 'He's started the Entropoth already.'

Kerbogah pointed at the lower globe. Silas could see it now. He hadn't noticed it before, because of the fineness of the Stardust, but it was trickling steadily through the glass stem into the lower bulb.

There was a great deal of Stardust in the upper globe and almost nothing in the lower and Kerbogah immediately wondered how long it would all take to run down. But Kerbogah suddenly realized that as it did so and hit the bottom of the glass, something strange happened to the magical Stardust. As soon as it settled it turned jet-black.

'We must smash it,' said Kerbogah suddenly. 'Or the power of the Dunetraders' voices will be sucked away forever.'

'Or worse,' said Silas, thinking of an entire universe without magic, 'if Al-Jibara tells the truth.'

Silas was strangely reluctant at the idea of damaging the beautiful thing, though, even if it might really rob the world of magic, but then he had another thought.

'I don't think we can smash it, Kerbogah. The glass was blown with essence of Demigod in it. Centaur's hoof. Sulphurius said it makes it almost unbreakable.'

'We must try, Silas. I bet if I was a grown-up I could shatter it with my voice alone.'

Kerbogah was looking about the Incanting Room and he suddenly noticed that leaning against the Seat of the Alchemist was a heavy wooden staff, the bulb of which was wrought with two carved snakes winding all around it. It was the staff of the Caduceus.

Kerbogah picked it up but he saw something lying on the ground too. It was a little medallion necklace, in the shape of a new-born camel. He picked it up too and held it in his palm.

'Kalman!' he gasped. 'Kalman was in here. What's happened?'

Kerbogah turned back to the Entropoth and, very solemnly, raised the heavy Caduceus high above his head.

Silas felt confused as Kerbogah prepared to bring it down on the magical hourglass. For a moment he almost reached out to stop him, but as Kerbogah swung and brought it down as hard as he could, the Caduceus simply bounced off the glass.

'Powdered Centaur's hoof,' said Silas.

Kerbogah lifted the staff again but, before he could strike, something so extraordinary happened that it made Kerbogah drop the staff and Silas rock back on his heels. Inside the Entropoth's upper globe the Stardust had begun to swirl and churn. Images began to appear out of the storm like Sandspirits. They were struggling forwards, like Dunetraders lost in a gale.

'But it can't be!' cried Kerbogah, pressing his face to the glass.

Inside the upper globe was a great white tent and three figures pulling themselves towards it through the blizzard. It was Karleg and Ashtar and the last of the Wordmasters.

'It's us,' whispered Kerbogah, 'on the night of the storm.'

'The past,' said Silas. 'My Lesson Master said that the Chi of Mazgol could reveal a dark and dangerous past.'

As Silas and Kerbogah watched, the image began to change. There was the treadmill and a boy was marching on it next to Rathanor, his eyes tired and lost.

'Kalman!' cried Kerbogah delightedly. 'It's my brother Kalman!'

But the scene changed again. They could see the Incanting Room now and there was Kalman, seated in a chair, watched by priest apprentices fingering their worry beads. A figure suddenly stepped towards him.

'Zolos,' hissed Silas.

As Kerbogah's brother took the bowl gratefully and drank, the watching apprentices strained forward. He drained it and put it down and smiled. But to the boy's horror, from inside the folds of his robe Zolos suddenly pulled out a gold-handled knife. There was no time for a scream. In a single stroke Zolos tugged back Kalman's head and passed the blade across his throat.

Kalman's eyes glittered with surprise and confusion and he held a startled hand to his neck as the skin parted and deep red blood began to gush down his chest. The talisman around his neck dropped to the floor. None of the priest apprentices watching him in the Entropoth did anything at all. They simply stared, wondering if the Balm of Eternal Life would work. They had seen the rite before and it did not take long. Kalman slumped in the seat and his head fell forward.

Kerbogah put his hands to the glass and gave a terrible cry of pain.

'Murdered! That's what became of my brother. He's dead.'

Tears were streaming down his face.

'But why?' he sobbed. 'Why?'

Silas put his hand gently on his friend's shoulder.

'For the Balm, Kerbogah,' he whispered angrily. 'The Balm of Eternal Life.'

Already the sand had begun to swirl once more and now they were looking at a figure with jet-black hair, flecked with grey, who was bent over a desk and kept putting his hands to his head and hunching his shoulders. Then, as his arm began to move rapidly, he seemed to be scratching something on the desk. But that picture faded too and suddenly there was a ravishing woman. She was being led into the desert by a group of Wordmasters under an angry red sun.

'Tapputi,' whispered Silas. 'Mardak's bride. The Wordmasters left her to die out there in the desert.'

'Yes, boy,' said an angry voice behind them. 'And so I took my revenge on them all.'

The children swung round.

He was tall, as he stood in the doorway to the Incanting Room, and dressed in a long black robe with a high, stiff collar worked with gold filigree. He wore a rough leather apron over his robes but the children could not see his face, for the magician was wearing a terrible golden mask. The Mask of Tulon. A pair of eyes glittered through slits and where the mouth should have been was an O. The gold was worked into the shape of a face, but one without any lines or wrinkles to give it character and so the Black Magician looked like he was wearing the face of a haunted child.

Kerbogah flinched as, at his back, Zolos stepped into view too, flanked by seven Barbalissaries.

Kerbogah was suddenly looking at the magician's shoulder, though. There sat a little lizard, staring out impudently into the Incanting Room. One of its legs was lifted almost questioningly and as it held it there it looked a little like a hand. It was a chameleon. Seraph, thought Kerbogah, and he missed Relak desperately.

Despite his sorrow and anger at seeing Zolos, Kerbogah was fascinated by the lizard's eyes. They protruded like the tips of pine cones from the chameleon's head and, as they swivelled this way and that, they seemed able to look in different directions at the same time. A fly buzzed past and the creatures tongue suddenly shot out and pulled it into his mouth.

'So, Silas Root,' hissed Mardak the Dark. 'We meet at long last.'

MARDAK THE DARK

Silas and Kerbogah were trembling terribly as they stared at the Black Magician.

'How do you know me?' whispered Silas. 'My name?'

Those eyes seemed to smile behind the mask.

'The Entropoth, of course, Silas Root,' answered Mardak, stepping fully into the Incanting Room. His voice was muffled behind the gold. 'With Mazgol's power it can look backwards. And I've been watching you for a long while, boy. While you brought it safely to Barbal for me.'

'Gol,' said Silas. 'You sent the Demon to try to steal it too.'

'Yes. For only when Gol and Mazgol sit side by side in the Entropoth,' said Mardak, 'will my makina be truly ready to show to the people. For then its full power shall begin to work. And with the Turnstones' Chi woven together it will reveal to me not only past and future, but the heavenly dream that brought forth everything. It shall truly open the seven seals.'

'Seven seals?' said Kerbogah.

'Behind which Truth lies!' cried Mardak, glaring scornfully at Kerbogah. 'The first seal is childhood and the second is matter, the nature of the four elements. The third seal is space and direction and the fourth is time. The fifth seal is love and hate, emotion that binds us to things, while the sixth seal is almost as powerful as all the rest put together: language.'

'Language?' whispered Silas.

'Which allows us to read the nature of the world but in doing so can wrap us in chains so tight our spirits might never escape, for words are never the things themselves, only ciphers for the things that really are, icons created by our minds.'

'And the Seventh Seal?' whispered Silas Root.

'Death,' answered Mardak. 'The Last Frontier. When I set it to work at the Solstice and give up my sacrifice to the heavens, then the Entropoth shall show me at last.'

'Show you what?'

'The face of God,' cried Mardak the Dark hungrily. 'The image of the Creator. Inside my hourglass. The ultimate proof.'

Silas gulped.

'But only when Aspis himself is crowned,' whispered Mardak. 'The Destroyer.'

'But why would you wish to raise the Lord of the Underworld. To crown the Uncrowned King of Night?'

'The power of true Alchemy has always drawn on all the secret forces of the universe,' answered Mardak coldly. 'Darkness as well as light. As above, so below, as it says in the Alcemoth. But how else to summon *Him*? How else to look God in the face at last than to bring forth his opposite? Aspis woke with the black Turnstone and the Doorway began to open. If the Creator does not show himself when Aspis comes, then I shall give up my beliefs indeed.'

'But what if he does come?'

'I shall ask him, of course, for the greatest secret of holy Alchemy,' cried Mardak the Dark, 'the secret of Resurrection and the true recipe for that which we in the Halls of the Rising Sun have sought for so long. The Balm of Eternal Life.'

'So you can live forever,' said Silas scornfully.

'So I can *love* forever,' hissed Mardak.

The Black Magician turned and pointed to a stone table in the far corner of the Incanting Room. A body was lying there, wrapped in bandages and covered in muslin, and to the right and left of it, and at the head and feet, there sat four earthenware jars. The canopic jars. Even under the wrappings Silas and Kerbogah could see that it was a woman.

'Tapputi,' whispered Silas. 'Tutanamet embalmed her too.'

'My beloved,' said Mardak bitterly. 'Perhaps now you begin to understand, Silas Root. When I confront the Creator and ask him the secret of life I shall resurrect my beloved bride.'

'And if he doesn't come?' said Silas.

Those eyes grew dark and angry behind the gold.

'Then I shall rule with Aspis the Destroyer at my side,' said Mardak bitterly, 'and take revenge on life itself.'

'You are evil,' flashed Silas.

Those eyes glittered.

'What do you know of evil, foolish boy?'

'You broke the Seven Commandments, Mardak.'

'Thou Shalt Not?' said Mardak coldly. 'About as useful as laundry lists. About as useful as all the silly rules that have haunted Barbal or Ederyl for so long. So, Silas Root, why don't you join me?'

267

'Join you?' said Silas in astonishment.

Kerbogah turned and looked fearfully at his friend.

'Of course,' cried Mardak. 'Become my apprentice. Have you not entered the temple? It is sacrilege for any but one of the Order to do so. And you show great promise. There is so much we can learn and do together. So much I can show you.'

On Mardak's shoulder Seraph's tongue was flicking in and out, testing the air. Silas suddenly felt as if he were facing one of the Seven Deadly Temptations, but Mardak walked over to a high table near the Entropoth and placed his hand on a green book with a heavy gold buckle. The Zodiac was patterned on the front, just as it had been on the back of Sultan Ash's History.

'This, for instance,' said Mardak, stroking the cover. 'Wouldn't you like to read it, Silas Root? Wouldn't you like to know its true secrets?'

'The Book of Destinies,' whispered Kerbogah, with a pang of longing in his voice.

Seraph suddenly jumped down onto the book and his cantilevered eyes swivelled about the Incanting Room.

'That's right, boy. The oldest book in existence.'

Kerbogah blinked. Seraph had just changed colour. The chamelon's body had turned from the colour of the desert to a livid green as it sat on the book. Mardak saw his look.

'Chameleons,' he whispered, stroking its head. 'Wonderful at camouflage and one of the greatest exemplars of the magic of Evolution. Seraph has been naughty, though. After all, it was through his eyes that the Mystifier used astral journeying to spy on Ogog.'

The chameleon's tail flicked on the book.

'The book,' said Silas. 'That's how you summoned Gol and Mazgol?'

Mardak took Seraph and put him back on his shoulder. Then he opened the Book of Destinies.

'I never summoned the Stones of Deep Power,' he answered softly. 'The ancient calendars in here, generated by centuries of stargazing and Barbalonian astrologizing, told me the date when they would reappear, that's all. So I got ready, and here we are.'

Mardak slammed the book shut again.

'And why?' whispered Mardak. 'Why do you suppose that the Turnstones appeared together, Silas Root?'

Silas dropped his eyes.

'Because there can never be one without the other,' cried Mardak, 'black without white, no more than there can be day without night, light without dark, power without slavery. Only a true Alchemist knows that. Just as he knows that to rule in the Upper Kingdom you must first rule in the Lower Kingdom. That to make a serum you must drain the snake and master the nature of poison. That to heal, you must also know how to kill.'

'But you broke the rules,' insisted Silas, 'you broke the sacred Alcemoth. It says you should never do any wrong or harm.'

'Rules!' scoffed Mardak the Dark. 'Like the rules your blessed Elders laid down before they banished you, Silas Root, for nothing more serious than wanting to read a word? Would you too live in slavery, like the animals in the Street of Slavers or those children working the wheel? Beasts of burden, like most ignorant, bewildered men.'

Silas thought angrily of the poor children.

'The true Alchemical Torture is to be born into this mysterious world with no rhyme nor reason and never to find a real answer. But I, Mardak the Dark, I would free mankind forever. I would abolish fear and sin, and think anything I can. I would know all things too.'

'But all along,' said Silas, 'you tried to suppress the word yourself and killed the Wordmasters.'

'And you banned Sandwork and reason in the streets,' said Kerbogah.

'And why do you think Alchemists keep so many secrets, hiding their wisdom in strange symbols?' said the Black Magician calmly. 'Because knowledge is power, and some are meant to know, while others are meant to follow. Just as some are meant to remain safe at home and others to roam the wide world, to search the very universe itself. The Elect. You, for instance, Silas Root.'

'Me?' said Silas. He had begun to sweat.

'*When I was a child I thought as a child, I spake as a child*,' whispered Mardak, '*but when I became a man, I put away childish things*. You've been banished, Silas Root, thrown out of Paradise. And the things you are learning you may never unlearn. You cannot go back. None of us can. But you can go forward, if you have the courage for it, that is. To glories and truths none has ever known or seen before.'

'To darkness,' whispered Silas bitterly.

'Not at all,' said Mardak. 'They think I hate Sandwork and reason. They think I hate knowledge. But it is not true. Why else would I use its power, the insights of the Equation and Pengalis, to build the greatest makina of all time? I am the High Priest, but I would also be the Lord Alchemist.'

Silas and Kerbogah stared at him.

'The Entropoth is more than a makina, though,' whispered Mardak. 'It draws not just on logic and invention but the secret insights of heaven, given to us in dreams and inspiration and stories. That is why what it can show is affected by thoughts themselves. Just as I believe that the universe itself sends us messages if we listen carefully to it. And although when I heard of Evolution I knew it was true, yet I knew it was not enough.'

'Not enough?'

'I knew that if we are all changing and evolving, as

270

language changes and evolves, perhaps the reason there seem so many paradoxes and mysteries in life is that our own minds have not evolved enough yet to see the whole picture. A picture that we ourselves are part of.'

Silas shivered.

'A picture that one day will be revealed to us like the face of God himself,' said Mardak, 'or herself. As Alchemists, first we must seek the truths, but then we must travel to the borders of those truths. Then perhaps man will begin to wake from the dream of life. Until then we are all children struggling out of the dark. As Mankind is like a child, struggling out of the fable of history.'

Within his fear and anger Silas found himself listening intently to Mardak, and wanting to travel too, on and on, to greater and greater discoveries.

'It is within us that I think the real secrets dwell, Silas Root,' said Mardak. 'You know in Pengalis they even believe that our very bodies are like a sentence, made up of four letters, that weave together in an endlessly spiralling pattern. Perhaps we are all part of some secret pattern then, some secret coded language, written into the very fabric of the universe.'

Silas thought of what Sultan had said in the desert about the real key to Chaos Theory being to see the pattern, and Kerbogah thought of that strange lad he had met in Bolor's tavern who could see numbers without even trying.

'And although Evolution and science challenge the existence of the Gods,' said Mardak gravely, 'science can never quite touch what is always vanishing from our sight. What is always elusive. Until tomorrow. Until the Great Solstice. So give it to me, Silas Root. Give me the Lightbearer.'

Silas stepped backwards.

'I can't. I haven't got it any more.'

'Liar!' screeched the Black Magician, stamping his foot. 'It's in your pocket.'

'No,' said Silas defiantly, knowing now that at all cost he must protect the whereabouts of Gol. 'I hid it before the Barbalissaries snatched me. In the bazaar.'

'Search him,' said Mardak angrily.

The Barbalissaries and Captain Zolos rushed over and caught hold of Silas roughly, but they soon turned to their master and shook their heads.

'Nothing, my lord,' snarled Zolos, 'just a used match.'

'Then tell me where it is,' cried Mardak furiously. 'I will send Zolos to fetch it.'

'Never,' said Silas, through gritted teeth. 'You'll never find it.'

In that moment Silas was wondering bitterly if he himself would ever find the Lightbearer again.

'Really,' whispered Mardak and his eyes began to glitter coldly behind that horrible golden mask. 'And what of your friends, Silas Root? Don't you care about them?'

'My friends?'

'We captured them near the Sacred Square.'

'No,' cried Silas, 'you're just trying to trick me.'

Again Mardak's eyes glittered.

'If you don't believe me, look there. My makina gives you proof.'

Mardak was pointing at the Entropoth and as the children turned they saw that the Stardust had started to swirl again. There was the street outside Bolor's tavern and to Silas's horror he saw Rarza, Ramset and Sultan pressed up against a wall, four Barbalissaries' golden spears at their throats.

'No!'

'I've promised the people a sacrifice,' said Mardak coldly, 'for Aspis cannot rise unless blood washes the Sundial, and darkness cloaks the Sacred City. Very well then, Silas Root. If you do not tell me where Gol is by . . . by the time the hand of Zorastar strokes the mid point of the Sundial in the square tomorrow, your friends shall be sacrificed with Ogog.'

'No,' cried Silas bitterly. 'You can't sacrifice my Lesson Master. He serves the Hooded Master himself.'

'Indeed,' said Mardak scornfully, 'which is why I do not need to sacrifice him, Silas Root. For Sultan Ash is dead already.'

Silas stepped back in horror.

'Dead?'

'Your friends came to Barbal openly,' said the Black Magician, 'but there is only one fate for spies like that filthy Lesson Master. Sultan Ash is dead.'

'No.'

'See.'

Again Mardak pointed to the Entropoth and there stood Sultan, facing Mardak now. But inside the glass the Black Magician raised the Caduceus in ths hands and struck Sultan brutally to the ground.

Silas was trembling from head to toe and he suddenly remembered what Sultan had said of their being old adversaries. He wanted to kill the Black Magician with his bare hands.

'Take them back to their friends,' shouted Mardak. 'Below the Ziggurat. Let them think on it.'

Zolos and the Barballisaries grabbed hold of Silas and Kerbogah. As the Captain Lord's hand fell on Kerbogah's arm he felt a hatred and fury burn in him that could have shattered his body and in that moment he knew that he must avenge his brother Kalman.

They were hauled from the Incanting Room as Mardak stroked his lizard and down through the Ziggurat they plunged into the darkness of the city's sewers. As they entered the passageways Silas's eyes began scanning the ground, searching for the Lightbearer, and as they passed one of the twenty-four tunnels to the Eternal Flames they saw that the guard had gone.

'This way,' grunted Zolos, pushing Silas down a particularly slimy passage. 'Your friends are in our deepest dungeons.'

Zolos gave Kerbogah a shove too but Kerbogah rounded on him.

'Don't touch me,' he snarled. 'When my caravan finds out what you did to my brother . . .'

Zolos smiled in the shadows.

'Dunetraders,' he grunted. 'They're nothing to me, boy. We know of the parley. If they attack I will finally destroy them.'

'You murdered him,' said Kerbogah furiously. 'My brother, Kalman.'

'Indeed,' said the Captain Lord. 'For the foolish balm.'

'Foolish?' whispered Kerbogah. 'You call it foolish? Then why?'

'To sate the superstitions of the priest apprentices, of course,' answered Zolos coldly, 'and to gain myself acceptance in the Ziggurat.'

'Then you don't believe,' whispered Silas. 'But why do you follow Mardak?'

'I am a soldier, boy,' said Zolos, 'not a priest. I believe in power and might and wealth. Who would seek eternal life when he can have dominion in this world? It serves my purposes to join with Mardak.'

Zolos smiled again and shook his head.

'I have learned much from him, and Ogog too. How to isolate venom for a start and poison the Dunetraders' wells.'

'You!' cried Kerbogah. 'It isn't Gods or the Underworld that are evil. It's man. You!'

Zolos smiled.

'You're such innocents.'

They had reached two cells in the side of the passage. Silas's heart leapt. Rarza and Ramset were sitting on a stone bench in one of the cells, shackled together. They jumped up in the shadows as soon as they saw him.

'Silas!' cried Rarza. 'You're alive!'

Zolos looked at them scornfully and, opening the door to the second cell, thrust Silas and Kerbogah roughly inside.

'Think well, boy,' he cried, slamming the cell shut again, 'and ponder your friends' destiny very carefully.'

Zolos laughed as he turned in the shadows and strode away with his Barbalissaries. Rarza ran over to the bars.

'Silas. Thank Lol you're safe. But how did you get here and what does he mean, our destiny?'

Silas took Rarza's hand through the bars. Ramset was standing quietly behind her.

'I was kidnapped, Rarza. They've been trading in children to turn the wheel and light the Eternal Flames.'

'Children?' said Rarza.

'Like Kerbogah here and his brother, Kalman. He's a Dunetrader, Rarza. But so much of what the Alchemists have been doing in Barbal is just trickery.'

Ramset stepped even closer.

'How do you know, Silas?'

'We've been inside the Ziggurat, Ramset,' answered Silas. 'We've met him at last. Mardak. And Ogog too. But Mardak is mad, Rarza. Somehow we must stop him. And we've an ally.'

Silas turned to his friend.

'Sultan was guiding Kerbogah's caravan through the desert. They're outside the city now.'

Kerbogah smiled and so did Rarza. The camp boy thought how very pretty Rarza was.

'Sultan,' whispered Rarza. 'The Barbalissaries took him

off when they captured us outside the tavern. I don't know where he is.'

Silas went pale and he hung his head bitterly.

'Sultan is dead, Rarza,' he whispered, though he could hardly speak. 'Murdered by Mardak. I saw it in the Entropoth.'

Ramset dropped his head too and clasped the jewels at his throat.

'Then may Rahr himself bless his immortal soul. For he was a good friend to me. World without end. Ammon.'

The cells were filled with sorrow as they stood silently, thinking about the man who had taught them so much. It was Rarza who finally broke the silence.

'So what does Mardak want now?'

'He wants Gol, Rarza. And unless I give it to him he will . . .'

Silas paused and looked at his friends. He couldn't bring himself to tell them. Kerbogah stood up though.

'He'll sacrifice you both, with Ogog,' said Kerbogah, staring at Rarza boldly. 'Tomorrow at mid-sun.'

The blood drained from Rarza's face.

'But if I do give it to him,' said Silas, 'then Aspis will come. The Uncrowned King of Night. Mardak hopes he will look on the face of the Creator in the Entropoth and ask him the secret of eternal life. He will bring his beloved Tapputi back from the dead.'

Rarza was trembling, but suddenly her bold eyes flashed.

'You mustn't give it to him then, Silas. Whatever happens.'

'But you and Ramset . . .'

'We'll find a way,' whispered the brave Childar. 'Together.'

'I can't give it to him anyway, Rarza,' Silas sighed, sitting down heavily. 'Gol dropped out of my pocket, somewhere between the treadmill that works the Waterwheel and the Ziggurat. It's hopeless. We're lost.'

Kerbogah sat down beside him too.

'Don't give up hope, Silas Root. The prophecy, remember. The pattern. You've come to free us all. It is written.'

Ramset and Rarza looked at Silas in astonishment.

'What is he talking about, Silas?' asked the Warrior Priest. 'What pattern?'

'It's to do with this birthmark,' answered Silas glumly, pulling down his smock to reveal the strange pink shape on his neck. 'The prophecy says that not only would Gol and Mazgol appear again together, but that a Marked One would come. Kerbogah insists it's me.'

Rarza looked through the bars and remembered how the other Childar children had sometimes laughed at Silas for it in the lesson house.

'I always knew you were special,' she whispered fondly.

'It's the Yaharl,' said Ramset suddenly, stepping forwards too. 'Which the Yaharlars draw in the sands as they seek enlightenment.'

The little birthmark, though faint on Silas's skin, was indeed almost exactly like the circle with two lines interweaving through its centre, like the snakes around the Caduceus. The Warrior Priest was clutching the jewels around his neck once more and Kerbogah shivered as he remembered what Mardak had said of our very bodies being made up of four strange letters.

'Maybe I am marked,' said Silas sullenly. 'But I haven't got Gol any more.'

'It doesn't matter,' said Kerbogah suddenly, 'because we can't just sit here. There must be a way out. Among those passages. To the Dunetraders.'

'But which?' said Silas. 'The guard said no one could get

through that maze alive. Besides, we'd just be bringing them straight into a trap.'

'Not if we warn them, Silas.'

Silas shook his head. It seemed hopeless indeed and they sat there in the gloom. A terrible darkness had surrounded them and as Rarza thought of poor Sultan Ash a tear rolled down her cheek. But just then she heard a sound.

'What's that?'

The others could hear nothing but Rarza was sure now.

'There. Listen.'

Silas thought his ears were playing tricks on him but suddenly he heard it too. A tiny squeaking.

'Relak!' cried Kerbogah, jumping to his feet. The little desert mouse had just appeared beneath the bars of their cell. It scurried straight towards Kerbogah and ran up the arm he had just bent down to offer his little pet.

'Oh, Relak. Dear Relak. Where have you been? I've been worried sick about you. Relak, what's that you've got?'

The little mouse seemed not only well but perfectly happy and it had something in its mouth that it was chewing on. It was a little blue beetle.

'It's a scarab,' said Ramset.

Silas had already jumped up and his eyes were glittering brilliantly in the dark.

'Kerbogah!' he cried. 'Your mouse. It's been outside the city.'

'What do you mean, Silas?'

'That scarab. It's a desert beetle. And you remember, Rarza, what that poor scout said about the place where scarab beetles lived near Barbal?'

'The stone quarry,' they both cried together.

Even as the revelation came Silas's eyes clouded over again.

 278

'He's small enough to get out,' he sighed, 'but we haven't a chance. We can't cut those bars.'

'No,' cried Kerbogah, jumping up too, 'but we can unlock them.'

Silas, Rarza and Ramset heard a rattling.

'The keys,' cried Silas delightedly.

Hope surged through the friends like a Chi jolt as Kerbogah rushed to the gate. He began to try the keys in the lock. The friends heard a sharp snap and the door swung open. In an instant Silas, Kerbogah and Relak were in the passage, and Silas took the bunch of keys from Kerbogah, and tried them on Rarza and Ramset's prison. One after the other they went in and one after the other the keys failed. At last there were only two left, including the one that had bent when they had attacked the guard. With his heart in his mouth, Silas tried the last good key in the lock. It stuck fast.

'Oh, bother,' grunted Silas, and looked up guiltily at Rarza. 'Rarza. What can I do?'

'Silas,' said Rarza suddenly. 'Go with Kerbogah. Find the tunnel and get out of the Sacred City. Bring the Dunetraders.'

'No, Rarza. I . . .'

'Please, Silas. Do as I say. It's our only hope now.'

The Warrior Priest put a hand on her shoulder.

'Rarza's right, Silas, it's the only way.'

Silas was going to argue but they heard a noise in the passage beyond. Voices were coming straight towards them. Barbalissaries.

'Go, Silas.'

Silas's eyes flickered as he looked into Rarza's pretty face, but Kerbogah was pulling him away. As the voices rose in the passage Silas and Kerbogah turned and ran. The soldiers were getting nearer and nearer, but Rarza sighed gratefully.

'Thank the heavens, Ramset. At least he'll be safely out of the city.'

279

'Yes,' said the Warrior Priest softly, 'the prophecy talks of Silas's sacrifice. It must not be, Rarza Stormheart.'

Silas and Kerbogah were hurrying along the main sewer, in a circle, passing passage after passage but Kerbogah suddenly stopped and put down his mouse.

'Now, Relak,' he whispered desperately, 'I know you can't understand me. But you're our only hope. The fate of all of us depends on you now, little mouse.'

Relak had finished his beetle snack but he was already feeling hungry again and, quite by instinct, he began to run back the way he had already come.

'Don't lose sight of him,' cried Silas, as they ran after him, 'or we're lost.'

After only a short while Relak stopped. He was sniffing the air and squeaking violently. The boys felt felt something on their faces too, like Chi. It was the faintest breath of wind, coming down the dark passage. Relak's powerful nose knew that it had the scent of the desert on it and of fresh scarab beetle.

'Come on, Silas,' cried Kerbogah, scooping up Relak and putting him in his pocket. 'This way. What's wrong now?'

'I can't, Kerbogah,' said Silas, standing there still. 'I can't just leave them. Not now. I swore an oath in the desert and Ramset saved my life. Once from the Pazgog and once from poison. You go. Summon the Dunetraders. But I must find the Lightbearer and if you don't come, I must find a way to save my friends.'

Kerbogah looked admiringly at Silas.

'Will you give Gol to Mardak?'

'I don't know, Kerbogah,' answered Silas, 'if I can even find it. I've got to think of a plan. To use logic and reason. To use my mind. Poor Sultan said it was very powerful. Besides, those children, perhaps they'll help. Get to the Dunetraders,

Kerbogah. Bring them tomorrow if you can, but warn them too of the trap.'

Kerbogah nodded but his eyes suddenly lit up with a memory.

'What's wrong, Kerbogah?'

'When the Wordmaster told me that I would meet you, Silas, he told me to warn you too. He said that you'd be betrayed, by one very close to you. I've been worrying about it since we arrived.'

'Betrayed?' said Silas nervously

'He said that you would know the tree by its fruit.'

Silas stood there trembling, thinking of all that had happened, searching though his own memory. Suddenly an image flashed into his frightened brain that made him feel sick. It was of Rarza sitting in the desert when Sultan had made them swear, eating an apple.

'But it can't be,' said Silas, looking back down the passage. 'Not Rarza.'

'He told me to tell you too,' said Kerbogah, 'to stick to the centre, and to follow above all what the Alcemoth teaches. The search for Truth.'

'Truth,' said Silas bitterly. 'What's that, Kerbogah? But go now. Quickly.'

Kerbogah began to run down that dark passage and freedom, but he suddenly stopped and looked back.

'Don't worry, Silas Root,' he called. 'We shall come tomorrow. Our destinies are bound together.'

Kerbogah turned and the brave young Dunetrader was running away into the darkness, as fast as his legs could carry him. Silas could hear loud voices now from Rarza and Ramset's cell and, thinking that he might find Gol in the chamber where the treadmill was, he began to creep towards it in the darkness. But Silas soon stopped again. He could see the door ahead but outside it was the guard he had struck with the torch, his head now wrapped in bloody muslin bandages. He was with another Barbalissary.

'If I catch the little runt,' the guard was saying, 'I'll throttle him. He stole my master keys.'

'Keep your eyes on the chamber, Sentinor,' said the other. 'A brand-new makina for the sacrifice is being assembled in the square and Zolos says there must be no mishaps tomorrow. Keep the children at work.'

The noise behind Silas grew louder and suddenly he realized voices were coming from behind. They had already passed the passage Kerbogah had taken and the way ahead was barred by the guards. There was nowhere to hide. Silas looked up.

The three Barbalissaries, who had just discovered Silas and Kerbogah's escape, were in a frenzy as they ran towards the chamber and too furious to see the shape ahead of them or the pair of feet suddenly disappearing up the shaft in the ceiling. The guards at the chamber came running towards them and they all collided right below Silas.

'What's going on?'

'Silas Root.'

'Where is the little brat?' said Sentinor dangerously.

'He's gone again. When Mardak hears, he'll tear down the Ziggurat. Dawn steals towards Barbal.'

'Order out the guard,' cried another Barbalissary. 'Search the sewers. Search the whole damned city.'

Two of the soldiers set off at a run to raise the guard but the one who had just given the order grunted again.

'You, Sentinor. Stay here. Keep an eye on the prisoners and the chamber. Let no one near either.'

'What if he's in the streets already?' asked Sentinor. 'Most of our men are too busy preparing for the Dunetraders, if they attack.'

'Mardak has other servants. And it's still night. Up there the Pazgog holds sway.'

The sergeant turned towards the Ziggurat, leaving Sentinor standing below Silas. He didn't move, but thankfully he didn't look up either.

Silas's heart was in his mouth and he didn't know what to do at all. The very mention of the Pazgog had clamped a cold hand about his throat but he was thinking too of what the Barbalissary had said of things being ready in the square and he suddenly had an idea. Silas looked up and thought of the Pazgog, but one by one he moved his hands on the wooden rungs and began to climb.

It seemed to take an age to reach the top of the shaft. As he did so he saw how the Eternal Flames were suspended on their plinths. The golden fire bowls rested on slatted wooden boards, with a hand-hold on the under side that allowed you to slide them back and swivel them round without tipping the bowls over. Silas drew it back and bright moonlight shone down onto his face.

Silas lifted himself and found his head emerging from the hollow plinth itself into the Great Square of Barbal. His hunch was right. There was no one around but Silas gasped, for it was the first time he had seen Barbal Square. Along either side of the square the flames flickered on their stands and in the centre, the giant gold Sundial stood waiting. Nearby was the large pillar, its top empty, and to the southern side of the square the pond and the gigantic Waterwheel, still turning its golden buckets to feed the city with water. But no longer by magic. By theft and pain and cruelty.

There was something else in the square though that hadn't been there when Kerbogah and the Dunetraders had arrived. It stood near the Sundial, backed by the huge studded doorway to the barracks. It was the wooden cage from the Street of the Carpenters.

Silas pulled himself out of the shaft and as he dropped down into the dust of the square he suddenly heard a snarl. Something inside the cage had just got up. Silas drew closer. There were two creatures in one side of the cage, which was partitioned by a slatted grille. Their hungry yellow eyes glittered in the moonlight as they saw Silas Root. They were lions from the Street of Slavers.

Silas gulped and stepped up to see how the cage worked. The top of the grille was attached to a rope that ran out across the square towards the Waterwheel. The rope ran through a hoop on top of a pole that had been erected nearby and then to the edge of the Great Wheel itself.

Silas noticed that to the edge of the wheel, which steadily revolved through the water, a giant hook had been attached. He realized how the strange makina worked. The rope operated the grille in the cage and if it was attached to the hook on the wheel it would be drawn in gradually and lift the grille, releasing the lions into the neighbouring compartment. A channel ran from a bowl in front of that compartment straight towards the Golden Sundial. The click-click of the wheel echoed in the silent square.

'Rarza,' whispered Silas, marvelling at the makina's ingenuity, but horrified at his discovery. 'Ramset.'

Silas felt sick at the thought of what this ghastly invention meant, but it was nothing to the feeling that suddenly seized him. It wasn't the snarling lions. It came from high over Barbal.

The shadow of the Pazgog's wings was on him again, like a ghastly cloak. That terror and hopelessness seized him and Silas wished more than ever that he had Gol to protect him. But Silas made a dash for it. He raced towards another plinth and pulled back the trapdoor that bore its flaming bowl. Silas was just in time, for as he pulled it shut over his head again, the Demon gave a blood-curdling cry and swooped towards him.

The Pazgog's beak met nothing but flame and embers though, which rose in a shower of burning sparks to add to its fury. It beat its great leathery wings in frustration at having missed its prey again, but Silas was safe and climbing down again into Barbal's sewers. Suddenly the Pazgog rose once more and, winging its way to its pillar, settled there. The demon statue had just scented morning on the air.

Down the shaft Silas climbed and at its bottom he dropped back down into the sewers. He suddenly realized that he was beyond Sentinor now. The doorway to the tread-mill chamber was only just up ahead. Even as he walked towards it he heard another voice.

'Come, Sentinor. Change of plan. We need you to take the Childar and the Scribe to the Room of Changes and pre-pare them and Ogog for the sacrifice.'

The guards left and in that moment Silas knew only two things. That if he was to fight Mardak the Dark this day he had to find Gol the Lightbearer. And that somehow he had to stop that cage from working too. Silas took out the bunch of keys and turned one in the chamber lock.

The children looked up in amazement as Silas stepped inside. Two of them were working the treadmill as Silas began to unlock the others' manacles. It didn't take long but they just sat there, looking about fearfully. Their time in the chamber had robbed them of all will or courage and they were too used to taking orders to think for themselves.

'Come on,' said Silas angrily. 'You've got to help me.'

'Help you?' whispered Rathanor from the shadows. 'Tell us what to do.'

'I've – I've come back to free you all,' cried Silas.

The children had long since lost hope, caught as they were in Barbal's terrible makina.

'Leave us be,' said another child, as if brainwashed into submission. 'We're perfectly safe down here. At least they feed us.'

'Safe? You're nothing but slaves,' grunted Silas angrily, 'and what are you going to do? Wait here until they take you to the Incanting Room and slit your throats? Like poor Kalman?'

Rathanor lifted his head.

'Kalman?'

'He's dead, Rathanor. Murdered. They cut his throat in the Incanting Room. And the same fate awaits you all.'

The children looked horrified and Rathanor stood up.

'What shall I do?'

'There, Rathanor' answered Silas. 'The doorframe. Pull it away from the wall. We need some kind of wedge to start with, and next . . .'

Rathanor dragged another boy to his feet and together they started to pull at the frame, which came away with a great splintering, as Silas started to look around furiously. But Gol was nowhere to be seen.

'Oh, Lol. Where is it?'

'What are you looking for, Silas?' asked Rathanor.

'A stone. A white stone.'

'He's got it, Silas,' said a voice. A boy was pointing at a frightened little urchin in the corner. 'He found it rattling around the treadmill.'

'Give it to me,' said Silas, towering above the child, who was cupping something in his hand.

'No. It's mine.'

'Look,' said Silas, more kindly. 'There isn't time to explain. But I need it. We all do. It's our only hope.'

Very sheepishly the urchin raised his arm and opened his hand. Silas took Gol with a sigh of gratitude and as soon as he did the stone began to glow.

'What is it?' whispered Rathanor in amazement as the frightened children all gathered round.

'A Turnstone,' answered Silas, clutching it tightly and feeling the warmth of hope surge up his arm again, 'Gol the Magnificent. The Lightbearer.'

In the terrible chamber the light of Gol played on their startled faces and made them look human again.

'It's here to help us,' said Silas, 'the Light of the World.'

THE TICKING
OF THE SUN

'Hail mighty Zorastar, to thee we pray as we welcome
in your Solstice. And offer up our sacrifice in
blood.'

Mardak the Dark still wore his apron and that mask of
pure yellow gold. On his shoulder sat Seraph. As he spoke
beside the wooden cage, and the lions prowled, his voice
echoed behind the glinting metal and sang around the great,
dusty square of Barbal city. The sun, splintering into ribbons
of fiery pink, was climbing above the baked earth walls, making the Barbalonians standing in the square blink and turn
away their faces in the drifting smoke, rising from the Eternal
Flames. The Great Solstice had come at last.

The Barbalonians were gathered, awaiting signs and great
portents from the Gods. A great hush lay over them now as
they crowded nervously together to witness Mardak's
sacrifice and enthronement. They had heard rumours of

many Dunetraders close in the desert too and there was a terrible fear in the city. All along the tops of Barbal's walls stood armed Barbalissaries and, beside them, not one but twenty of those great wooden machines; the mangonels.

Barbal Square was full to bursting. There were soldiers along the edge of the square and near the Great Waterwheel and the ancient Sundial, where there also stood rows of priest apprentices, fingering their worry beads. The hungry spectators were pointing and whispering, especially at the statue of the Pazgog with its open wings and the lions in the cage.

A column of priest apprentices suddenly came towards them from the direction of the Ziggurat. Four of them bore the Seat of the Alchemist, and laid in its middle was the Book of Destinies and another book with it – Sultan Ash's History. Another four bore the Entropoth forwards. It sparkled in the early light and a gasp went up among the crowd. They placed the Entropoth on one side of the Sundial, to the right, and the Seat of the Alchemist on the other. At the base of the magic hourglass sat Mazgol the Mighty.

'Barbalonians,' cried Mardak, his voice cold and commanding as the priest apprentices stood back respectfully. 'I have returned to give the Gods their ancient tribute. Human blood.'

Mardak turned to Zolos and nodded. The Captain Lord of the Barbalissaries lifted his arm and the line of apprentices parted. Through the throng, herded by Barbalissaries, came the Lord Alchemist himself and behind Ogog were Ramset and Rarza Stormheart. All three were now dressed in sacrificial robes of pure white and they looked exhausted and terrified as they blinked in the morning sunlight.

The lions roared and snarled and clawed at the wooden bars with their huge claws as they smelt the scent of Childar and Scribe and Lord Alchemist. There was an approving

289

murmur all around the square, as the second compartment was opened and the three victims were thrust inside.

'Mighty Zorastar!' cried Mardak, peering up at the Sun God. 'These I offer you, in tribute and sacrifice. But by the laws of ancient Alchemy though, it must be you yourself that accepts the sacrifice. Just as my Tapputi was offered up to you in the desert. A trial by ordeal.'

Mardak raised another hand and now priest apprentices ran forward and attached the end of the rope to the Waterwheel. As the wheel went on turning, the long coil of rope began slowly to wind in. It took an entire revolution to move an inch. The spectators all seemed mesmerized with this strange device and Mardak pointed to the golden Sundial and the shadow already stretching out from the metal arm at its centre, touching the first of the signs of the Zodiac. It was beginning to shine like Mardak's golden face.

'When the shadow of the Fire God brushes the mid-point of the Sundial,' he cried, 'then the rope shall finally be pulled taut, for it has been measured to absolute perfection by our finest Sandworkers. Then the grille will rise and these mortals shall be consumed. It will prove that holy Zorastar is willing. Their blood shall flow down the channel across the dial and then you shall behold portents indeed, as I am enthroned.'

Mardak raised his hand again and from the corner of the square came more priest apprentices. They were bearing something carefully on their shoulders and as they reached the Entropoth they laid the gauzy form gently on the ground. The Barbalonians pointed and whispered. It was Tapputi's embalmed body.

Captain Zolos was looking rather nervously at Mardak though.

'But my Lord,' he whispered. 'Gol. We still haven't found Gol. Nor that brat.'

 290

Mardak's eyes smiled cunningly.

'Watch, Zolos,' he whispered, 'and learn.'

With that Mardak stepped up to address the Barbalonians once more.

'Even now they have hope of salvation,' he cried and Rarza's heart nearly stopped. 'As all in time shall taste my mercy. A salvation that was never granted to my bride Tapputi.'

Ogog looked up sadly in the cage, but the Barbalonian spectators began to mutter disapprovingly, for they loved a spectacle and the scent of a sacrifice was in their nostrils. They were suddenly as hungry for blood as the lions.

'Their lives may be spared,' cried the Black Magician, 'if one in the city gives himself up for sacrifice instead. The Childar, Silas Root. He was in my clutches, but last night he vanished. He alone may take their place. I swear it now, that if he does so and gives himself up for sacrifice, not one hair on his friends' heads shall be harmed.'

In one of the shafts below Barbal Square Silas Root heard Mardak's offer. He touched the mark on his neck nervously. It was all coming true. If this was the pattern, then the only way Silas could save his friends was to give himself up. To sacrifice himself. Silas suddenly remembered what Sultan had told him in the desert of the God's fondness for sacrifice. His heart felt like lead.

'Silas,' whispered a voice just below him. 'Are you ready, Silas?'

Silas looked down the shaft and shook his head at Rathanor.

'Not yet, Rathanor. Wait. The Alchemists seem to achieve half their effects with tricks, so why shouldn't we? Besides, we must pray that Kerbogah succeeds and the Dunetraders come.'

*

'Give voice. For the caravans are assembled at last. Any who would give voice at the parley may speak now.'

In the giant stone quarry, just a half league from Barbal, a Dunetrader let his strong voice echo around the stones. Vultures wheeled above, scouring the ground for beetles. Around him now peered eyes as harsh and furious as the sun, but none among the myriad of assembled caravans stirred. Behind them all around the great stone quarry stood their camels, their women and their camp boys, but they had come reluctantly to the parley and the ranks of men were set against each other, for there was no faith between the Dunetraders and blood was on their hands, and hatred in their hearts.

Yet one of them did stride forward. It was Solomon, the Dunetrader who had escaped the ambush in the desert.

'Today, my friends,' he cried, 'today we must turn our anger and our voices on Barbal. For when they attacked my caravan in the desert they raised a sword against us all that we must—'

Suddenly another man stepped forward. He was huge and his face was as dark as pitch. A livid scar ran from the side of his mouth, down to his Adam's apple. As he walked the other Dunetraders stirred, for he carried anger in his bearing like a cloak.

'No,' he cried coldly, his voice hardly reaching to the back of the serried ranks of Dunetraders who had come to parley. 'Do not listen to Solomon. Have you become sheep that you gather here in the sands without drawing your swords? Have you no hearts and no honour? The caravans are at war and too much blood has been spilt for a parley. Souls must be avenged.'

'No, Balthazeen,' cried Solomon. 'The fighting between us must cease. The Dunetraders are not enemies. We must unite and turn our anger and our voices on our real enemy. Mardak the Dark.'

 292

'Two of my brothers lie dead, Solomon,' cried Balthazeen scornfully, 'slain by Dunetraders, and you dare to say we are not enemies? Even the wells have been poisoned. I claim the right of blood feud. It is the Sandlaw. The ancient right of vengence, a blood feud that shall echo across eternity.'

'It is true that there has been much death and much sorrow,' said Solomon calmly, 'but think of the cause of it. Stardust. Did we not begin to fight again because of the tribute? But we turned our anger on each other, when all along it should have been directed against Barbal. Against Mardak the Dark. Now Zolos attacks the caravans too.'

Another Dunetrader stepped forward. He was older than the others and beginning to stoop.

'So we come to it,' he said wearily. 'But who are we to attack the Sacred City? Have you gone mad, Solomon? It is the holy Alchemists and the priest apprentices who keep the world turning and the forces of chaos at bay. If you do this thing, I warn you, there shall be no end to it.'

'Dunetraders have no need of the Alchemists, old man,' cried Solomon, 'or priest apprentices. And now Mardak steals our magic, the power of the desert itself. The power of the ancient Songtrails. The Sandsong must not fail. We have had our quarrels, it is true. We shall no doubt have them again. But are we not united by a power they will never understand in the city? The ancient power of Song? A power which, if it does fail, will leave us nothing but broken nomads to root among the ruins of life. You must believe.'

'Yes!' came a shout. 'Let us turn on Barbal, let us sow salt in its ruins.'

Some of the Dunetraders shouted approvingly and put their hands to their swords, but Balthazeen spat scornfully in the dirt.

'I'll not fight side by side with my kin's murderer,' he cried.

293

There was an equal murmur of agreement among the Dunetraders.

'They will not fight beside us, husband,' whispered a sad voice in the crowd. 'We'll never get our children back now.'

Selera stood next to Karleg and around them were Khayarumi, Imlay and Farjay.

'They must,' said Karleg angrily. 'We must find Kalman and Kerbogah.'

Balthazeen was already turning and walking away though, and as he did so he cried out.

'I will return with my caravan. And then we shall resume the wars. This time there shall be no quarter.'

Solomon spoke again, pleadingly now.

'Stay, Balthazeen. All the caravans must be with us,' he cried. 'The rampart the Grasht have built will be hard to cross and, besides, in suns to come let it not be said that any stood apart. For although the Dunetraders compete freely and fairly, caravan to caravan, to trade along the Songtrails and to bring the cargoes first to the bazaars, at heart we are one. Born of the desert. Knowing the ways of the Four, of Water and Firelight, of the Sandlaw and the Free air.'

Some Dunetraders began to nod in agreement again but Balthazeen spoke for a final time.

'And if we do, do we not risk everything, Solomon? Zolos's Barbalissaries are no strangers to fighting. As for the Grasht, what can defeat those demons? And the Pazgog, if night comes during the attack, what can we do against that?'

'That's enough for me,' grunted the old man who had spoken.

Balthazeen was already on his camel and had begun to turn his caravan. Half the Dunetraders were leaving too.

'It's hopeless,' said Karleg bitterly.

But suddenly a young voice rang out boldly across the quarry.

 294

'Wait. Hear me, Dunetraders.'

A small figure had just emerged from the shadows of a rock wall. The boy was covered in dust and sweating terribly and he blinked as he ran into the sunlight. A little desert mouse was peeking from his robes.

'Kerbogah!' cried Selera, clutching her husband's arm. 'You're safe, my darling.'

Kerbogah didn't run towards his parents though.

'Listen to me,' he shouted instead, jumping on a rock. His voice was piping and quavering with emotion and someone among the watching Dunetraders laughed.

'Why should we hear a boy? Your voice could not move a single grain of sand in the desert. Only adults may address the parley.'

Kerbogah held his ground and drew himself up to his full height.

'A boy I may be,' he cried defiantly, and his voice seemed deeper, 'but a boy who has been inside the Ziggurat.'

Farjay started and looked wonderingly at his friend. The Dunetraders were regarding him with a sudden interest too.

'And a boy who has met Mardak the Dark.'

Karleg looked at his son in utter astonishment.

'A boy too who knows what will happen today if we do not have the courage to fight for what we believe in. Who knows that Mardak has built the Entropoth to commit the ultimate sacrilege, to look upon the face of God. And who, when he has murdered the Lord Alchemst, will raise Aspis, the Destroyer. The Uncrowned King of Night.'

Many of the Dunetraders gasped fearfully and another voice sang out.

'Then we must get away from here. We must all hide in the desert.'

'But a boy who also knows,' cried Kerbogah, holding the Dunetraders with his anger and his courage, 'how the

Alchemists blend truth with lies. How many of their secrets are there to trick and deceive us. The Great Waterwheel, it has no magic Chi at all.'

'What do you mean, foolish lad? It has worked on its own for centuries.'

'No. It works by the sweat of children, stolen from the streets to run a treadmill below the square and taken up into the Incanting Room too, to be murdered. Murdered to test their Balms of Eternal Life. Like my poor brother, Kalman.'

Selera screamed and slumped into Karleg's arms and the Dunetraders had begun to mutter angrily.

'Is this true?' cried one.

'Zolos hates us all,' answered Kerbogah. 'It was he who poisoned the wells, not Dunetraders.'

The Dunetraders were all murmuring angrily now.

'And this day he prepares a fire trap if we attack. But attack we must.'

'Why, boy?'

The mood of the Dunetraders was perfectly balanced now.

'To help one who comes to fulfil the ancient prophecy,' cried Kerbogah, 'and with it brings Gol the Magnificent and hope to us all. The Marked One. Silas Root.'

The eye of Zorastar rose in the brightening East and it began to grow hotter and hotter in the Great Square of Barbal city. The lions in the cage felt it and they lay down, panting and looking hungrily at their meal beyond the wooden grille.

Ramset and Rarza Stormheart were watching the Sundial, for, as Zorastar rose, the shadow of the sun on the dial crept slowly round the arc. All about came the steady click, click, clicking of the Great Waterwheel of Barbal, tightening the fatal rope and echoing through their frightened minds.

 296

'Time,' whispered Ramset sadly. 'There is no time.'

It was as if the very work of the holy Alchemists in the Ziggurat had indeed been to set time itself in motion though, for, as the sand trickled through the magic hourglass and the wheel clicked the rope tighter and tighter, to the friends in the cage it suddenly seemed as if the mighty Sun itself, like some heavenly clock, high in the heavens above them, was ticking.

'Do you think they've got to the Dunetraders?' whispered Rarza in their prison.

'Now we can only wait,' answered Ramset, 'and pray.'

The Warrior Priest put a hand on Rarza's shoulder.

'I'm sorry, child.'

A great hush fell on all assembled. Many were wondering if the rope would work, while others grinned and grimaced as they thought of the cage door lifting and the lions springing and tearing into the prisoners' flesh. With the thought of this sacrifice to the Gods and mighty Zorastar it was if, for a while at least, the great daylight hunger of Barbal was being appeased.

The shadow on the Sundial crept on towards the crest that marked midday, the very zenith of the Great Solstice. The rope had been well measured, for it was tauter now, and soon, as the grille rose, the wild beasts would be released on Rarza and Ramset and Ogog.

But suddenly there was a murmuring in the crowd and a strange sound. Rarza and Ramset turned expectantly, but as the Barbalonians parted like a river, through their ranks came an extraordinary sight. It was the Yaharlars Kerbogah had seen outside Barbal. They were walking in a line with their flattened palms held to their foreheads, chanting their strange chant.

'Aaaaaaaa-om.'

As they saw the Childar and Ramset and Ogog in the cage

297

their eyes flickered sadly, but rather than doing anything at all they went on walking and chanting, turning away on the far side of the square and disappearing again into the maze of the city.

'It is nearly time, Barbalonians,' thundered Mardak. 'Time to anoint the Sundial with blood. Don't you care, Silas Root?'

As if conscious of what was being said the lions began to roar furiously and one lifted its tail and padded towards the grille.

'Look,' cried Ramset desperately.

The movement of the sun edged the shadow on the golden disc even closer to midday. The prisoners span round and saw the rope was almost taut and the grille begin to move.

'We're finished,' cried Rarza. 'It's over.'

But suddenly a shout went up from the city wall. On the top of it Sergeant Akadeem was standing there, pointing out beyond Barbal.

'Listen!' he growled.

As the soldiers looked out towards the distant rampart they began to hear it too, faintly at first, like water heard far away, the sound of voices. The Barbalonians started to mutter fearfully, for at first there was nothing to be seen beyond the rampart as those strange voices rose, like a coming storm, more sensed at first than felt, and as the sound got clearer and clearer, a rising, chanting hum even older than the Ziggurat, the Barbalonians began to point and murmer too. Around the sacred city the top of the earth ring was starting to crumble, to crumble under the force of those angry voices.

> *Born of Desert, work of clay*
> *Sing the songs that make our way.*
> *Camel riders, tribe of tunes,*
> *Chant the path and clear the dunes*

Suddenly they started to appear, climbing above the flimsy rampart, camels bearing turbaned figures from the desert, one after the other, until there were hundreds of them sitting facing the holy city, throwing out their voices angrily across the distance. The Mahara Dunetraders had come.

'They're here,' cried Rarza, clutching the cage bars.

'The Gods be praised,' whispered Ramset, seizing the jewels at his throat.

Mardak was standing by the Entropoth and he could suddenly feel fear moving like flame through the crowd, as those bellowing camels came on, carrying chanting Dunetraders over the rampart towards the water trench that ringed the city in front of them. They were riding towards Barbal's four great walls, hundreds of them, singing as they came, casting their voices angrily towards the city and the Ziggurat. As though the force of their indignation alone at the impertinence of the Alchemists could ensure that a true magic would live forever on earth.

Zolos seemed strangely calm though.

'Excellent,' the Captain Lord cried. 'They've come at last, Mardak, as we knew they would. And when the Babalonians see what we have prepared for them, it will truly seal your power. My trap is sprung.'

Mardak nodded coldly and turned to raise his hands to the Barbalonians.

'Fear not,' he cried, 'for although the Lord Alchemist may have abandoned magic and prayer, I and my captain have the Gods themselves at our backs. The Sacred City has never been in danger from the likes of mere Dunetraders. Behold.'

Zolos lifted his hand too and Akadeem, Mekmam and several Barbalissaries on top of the walls nodded back at him. The soldiers bent down and as they raised their arms the prisoners saw that they held bladders in their hands, like balloons, black and sticky and dripping with liquid. They were pig's bladders and the air was suddenly thick with the smell of Zorastar's Tears. The Barbalissaries began to load the filled bladders into those huge wooden spoons on the mangonels. The rollers were turned and the ropes tautened, stretching back the spoons until it seemed they would break.

Akadeem drew his scimitar high into the air and as he dropped his arm the Barbalissaries cut the ropes with their own swords and the spoons were hurled forward from the tops of Barbal's walls, catapulting the pig bellies through the air towards the advancing Dunetraders. Some landed well short and burst open on the ground, but most dropped straight into the moat. As they did so, Rarza Stormheart gasped in utter astonishment in the cage.

'Look, Ramset.'

Right around the sacred city, a huge ring of fire, burning and blazing before the Dunetraders, had suddenly sprung up in the moat. Their voices fought with the flames, but the Dunetraders were lifting their arms to shield themselves from the furious heat and turning away their faces. They could not pass the circle of flame that had suddenly surrounded Barbal.

'Barbalonian Fire!' cried Mardak triumphantly, as the flames danced around the Sacred City. 'Zorastar is among us indeed. Even the Fire God serves Mardak the Dark.'

The look of triumph in Mardak's eyes was transfiguring and he raised his hands to the heavens as though he would take the sun in them. Ramset, Rarza and Ogog sagged in the cage and although he still did not have Gol, Mardak began to smile behind the mask. The lions roared and the shadow of the sun moved, in that exact moment, onto the point that marked midday. The friends' hopes, raised and dashed so suddenly, were finally gone. The grille lurched and the lions' paws were scraping beneath it. Even Ramset cowered.

But deep below him a voice cried out in the sewers.

'They're here,' shouted Silas. 'The Dunetraders are here. We must stop the sacrifice. Now.'

Rathanor turned and the word was passed back like a Barbalonian whisper along a line of frightened, defiant children. In the chamber two of the children lifted the doorframe they had wrenched from the wall.

'Jump,' one cried.

The two children working the treadmill leapt clear of the machine and the others lunged forward with the doorframe, jamming it with all their might into the contraption.

In the square there was a great splashing and juddering from the Waterwheel. First the wheel jolted forward, almost pulling the rope taut and lifting the grille. Then, with a terrible noise, it span backwards on itself, letting the gate that held the lions drop back down again.

To the consternation of the Barbalonians, the first Wonder of the World, the great Waterwheel of Barbal City, which had turned by magic for as long as anyone could remember, stopped moving altogether. With it everything came to a sighing halt and the strange solar ticking ceased. A fearful moan went up among the superstitious crowd and one or two of the sacred peacocks even took to the air with a screech.

'The Wheel has broken,' cried a Barbalonian fearfully. 'Zorastar refuses Mardak's sacrifice.'

'What's happening?' whispered Rarza in the cage.

'It must be Silas,' cried Ramset. 'Silas has stopped the wheel.'

Some Barbalonians were trying to get out of the square now and the frightened crowd were pushing back and forth. The Barbalissaries around the square lifted their spears, worried that panic would break out, and began herding them together like animal slavers. Suddenly another arm went up. It was pointing this time not towards the Dunetraders but at one of the plinths around the square. The throng could not believe their eyes.

From the plinths, emerging through the very bowels of the earth and knocking over those golden fire bowls, clambered children. The ragged urchins popped up like startled moles, bolting everywhere, darting between the legs of priest apprentices and spectators and Barbalissaries.

Mardak looked appalled and suddenly he grabbed Zolos's dagger and rushed towards the cage. He opened the door and grabbed hold of Rarza, slamming it shut again, and dragged her out straight towards the Sundial. Mardak the Dark held the knife angrily to her throat.

'Very clever, Silas Root,' he cried, looking about him frantically for his invisible adversary, 'but there are many ways to skin a cat.'

Mardak pressed the blade closer.

'So give yourself up, Silas Root. *Now*. Or I'll kill Rarza Stormheart myself.'

'But Zorastar denies the sacrifice,' cried a Barbalonian.

'Zorastar denies nothing, you fool,' hissed Mardak angrily. 'Zorastar doesn't exist. He's just the sun. But the real face of God awaits. He awaits your sacrifice, Silas Root.'

'No, Silas,' cried Rarza, trying to shake Mardak off. 'If you can hear me, don't. He must not have the Lightbearer.'

Rarza Stormheart suddenly gasped. Silas, covered in dust and dirt, was climbing from one of the shafts himself. The brave Childar bowed his head as he walked straight towards Mardak. The square was hushed again by the spectacle, for in his hands Silas held up the white Turnstone.

'Gol,' gasped Mardak. 'Give it to me, boy. Then I shall show you all the true face of God.'

'Don't, Silas,' cried Rarza.

Silas looked calmly at his friend as he drew closer.

'I must, Rarza,' he said softly, 'for this was always meant

to be. It was prophesied and none can escape their destiny. Whatever happens now, at least we know that magic does exist.'

Zolos had run forward and two of his Barbalissaries grabbed Silas's arms. Mardak let go of Rarza and striding up to Silas, snatched hold of Gol.

'At last,' cried the Black Magician triumphantly, 'they are united once more. The Black and the White. Soon you shall truly see miracles.'

Mardak walked calmly to the Entropoth and placed Gol carefully at its base next to Mazgol. As soon as he did so the Stardust in the upper globe began to churn more violently than it had ever done before. It filled the entire globe, like a sandstorm.

'We must wait,' said Mardak, 'to summon Aspis. He shall only come with the sacrifice and darkness.'

Mardak walked round the Sundial and sat down in the carved seat of the Alchemist. Ogog clutched the cage bars angrily as he saw the High Priest sitting in his chair.

'While we wait,' said Mardak, picking up the Book of Destinies, 'until Silas Root and Ogog give their blood for *his* coming, we shall be entertained. Zolos will lead the Grasht from my barracks to deal with the Dunetraders.'

Silas suddenly thought of Sultan lying dead somewhere in the Ziggurat and felt such a fury rising inside him that he might have torn the temple apart with his bare hands. He ripped himself from the soldiers' grip and ran straight at Mardak the Dark. Silas's fist came up under Mardak's chin, as he sat there, and as he struck the Black Magician the book dropped from his hands and the golden mask was knocked clean from Mardak's face.

As he saw the mask fall, Silas Root steeled himself for the shock of gazing on those horrible, disfigured features. But as he looked at Mardak seated there he was suddenly drained of all courage or power or understanding. He felt a sense of utter betrayal wash through him and Silas's legs went weak as a lamb.

'Sultan Ash,' he whispered feebly. 'It's you.'

SEVEN HEADS

'**W**hat's wrong, Silas?' said Sultan, in a voice altogether different from how Mardak's had sounded, muffled behind the gold. 'I said this journey was leading us to transformation. For all is change.'

The Barbalonians were looking on in utter bewilderment, for they too had heard of the ugliness of Mardak, yet his face seemed perfectly normal and he was smiling mischievously under that mop of blond hair.

In the distance the cries of the struggling Dunetraders came to the city, but Silas had no thought for them.

'But you're dead,' he whispered in horror.

'Am I now?' said Sultan. 'Haven't you learnt yet to distinguish truth from lies?'

'But I saw it in the Entropoth.'

'You saw what I wanted you to see. What the Entropoth shows can be influenced by thoughts, remember. My thoughts.'

'But why?' said Silas with a shudder. 'Why all this trickery?'

'What better way to make sure that Gol reached the city safely than to shadow it myself? I had to disguise my voice of course, but I was always a master of disguise and for years it has let me move where I wanted, spying and learning all the while. Collecting Stardust too.'

'But then you didn't really need the tribute . . .'

'To unsettle the caravans and, yes, to set them against each other. While I also wanted to find out how the Mystifier had been watching me for so long. That Ramset revealed.'

'And how the Barbalissaries knew my name. That night at the caravanserai. You betrayed us then.'

'Twice I went to speak to Mekmam,' said Sultan, nodding, 'to tell him to put up that poster, to keep the pressure on, and to advise him when I would return. But I told one of the guards too, as soon as we entered the city.'

Silas remembered bitterly how Sultan had slipped into that house.

'But apart from Gol,' said Sultan, 'I still had not found out the secret of the Equation. That's why I was still wandering, as Zolos tortured Nimrod. It was only in the caravanserai that I finally understood it.'

Sultan slipped a hand into his pocket and pulled out the piece of paper from the Camel.

'Then you don't serve the Hooded Master at all?' said Rarza angrily, running up beside Silas.

'Mardak serves no master,' answered Sultan Ash, casting away the paper and clasping the arms of the Seat, 'but Truth and Revelation.'

'But you were our friend,' said Silas bitterly. 'You were on our side.'

'Sides?' said Sultan mockingly as he sat there. 'There are no sides, Silas Root. Not to a true seeker anyway. Don't you

306

understand yet? I've been teaching you all along too. I always wanted an apprentice worthy of my own talents and in you I found one. For as much as changing physical things, it is the Alchemy of the Spirit that I would master. Your spirit.'

'No,' said Silas desperately.

'Soon now, Silas,' whispered Sultan calmly, 'soon we shall truly sit above the secrets and look upon the face of God. Then I shall learn of the Balm and my beloved Tapputi shall . . .'

Silas and Rarza were backing away, astounded and horrified with the change that had come over Sultan, or Mardak, or Ashtar, or whoever he really was.

'But to do that you must raise Aspis. The Destroyer. You can't.'

'Can't?' said Sultan scornfully. 'Thou Shalt Not?'

'The Dunetraders will stop you.'

'Dunetraders!' snorted Sultan, looking out towards the flames. 'They've fallen into my trap, just as you did. They will never pass the flames that protect us. I told you I would teach you the nature of the Four. And is not Fire your favourite?'

Silas shivered. He felt as if he had nothing left to cling on to. The bitterness in his stomach towards Sultan Ash was like a physical pain and he thought in that moment that there is nothing more terrible in life than lies.

But suddenly Rarza cried out.

'Look, Silas. The Dunetraders.'

Silas's heart leapt too.

Through the ring of fire about Barbal Dunetraders and camels were emerging like mirages out of the flames and riding towards the walls of Barbal. One by one they began to draw their swords.

'Then Kerbogah did reach them,' cried Silas, pointing towards the ring of fire. 'He warned them of your trap.'

'But how?' whispered Rarza. 'It's Magic.'

307

It wasn't magic at all, for the Dunetraders and their camels were swaddled from head to foot in cloth, which they had soaked in water from their waterskins to protect them from the heat, after Kerbogah's warning. They tore off the sodden swaddling now and started to chant again. Riding the leading camel, Silas saw a face that made him proud.

'Kerbogah!' he cried, punching the air with his fist. 'Good for you, Kerbogah!'

Farjay was next to Kerbogah with his father Karleg. Imlay and the poet Khayarumi too. Sultan Ash sprang up from the Seat of the Alchemist as the army of Dunetraders advanced.

'Zolos, you fool!' he cried. 'Can you do nothing right?'

Captain Zolos was already bellowing orders again, though, and as the Dunetraders reached the encircled city, the Barbalissaries went flooding to defend their positions around the walls.

'It is no matter,' cried Sultan, though a doubt had entered his voice. 'They will never breach the walls.'

Even as the High Priest said it a cry went up so loud and powerful that it seemed to shake the clouds. The Dunetraders' voices were rising again. The noise of so many caravans was furious, like a great wind. And around the Great Gate ahead of them the walls of Barbal began to shake.

Louder came the voices and louder, a mighty vibration and suddenly a part of the wall was falling, splitting and crumbling, tumbling down. In one go the arch above the Great Gate of Barbal City broke and, pushing the doors aside on their hinges, the Dunetraders came streaming through.

'No,' cried Sultan Ash.

'To the streets,' bellowed Zolos.

Barbalonians were running everywhere in panic. Priest apprentices were knocked over in the crush and some Barbalonians began to fight with the Barbalissaries. It was as though the very rule of the Alchemists was crumbling before their eyes. Rarza didn't lose any time in the confusion. She rushed back to the cage and, flinging open the door, released Ramset and Ogog.

'The Darkness,' hissed Sultan Ash. 'They must be held until then. When the sacrifice is made and Aspis comes.'

Sultan rounded on Zolos.

'The Grasht,' he said. 'Unleash the Grasht.'

'But, master,' said Zolos, 'the sunset. It is hours off.'

'Such little faith,' said Sultan coldly. 'Do you think that I chose this day lightly? I have read the Book of Destinies. I have read the ancient calculations of the Alchemists. And this day brings not only the Solstice but a very special heavenly event. In just an hour. Until then let the Grasht fight.'

Zolos gave the order and while some Barbalissaries ran to surround Sultan and protect him, others pulled open the doors of those strange barracks and the Grasht emerged into the sunlight. Many of the Barbalonians recognized their loved ones among them but the pale white army returned no recognition. Their eyes were closed as they scented. There must have been two hundred of them marching from the barracks.

'Grasht,' cried Zolos, 'you know the quarry. Dunetraders. Reeking of aloe and anger. Smell them out.'

The Grasht seemed to nod as one.

'Grasht,' commanded Zolos again, 'my soulless horde. Your hour has come. Go, go to meet your enemy and wipe their voices from the earth forever.'

The Grasht drew their swords and began to march out past the statue of the Pazgog to meet the Dunetraders, as the Barbalonians left in the square parted in terror. The Dunetraders were coming up the alleyways of Barbal now, up the hill to the square, fighting the Barbalissaries as they came. But as they saw the Grasht, many of the Dunetraders started to falter. But the Grasht had scented them and suddenly they began to open their eyes. Those terrible black orbs shone like Mazgol.

'Silas,' cried Rarza, 'what can we do? We must help them.'

On the far side of the Sundial Ramset, Rarza and Ogog had joined their friend.

'Gol,' whispered Silas.

Silas turned and dashed towards the Entropoth. He snatched up Gol from its base, but Sultan had seen him.

'You are welcome to it, Root,' he cried, across the Sundial. 'It does not matter any more. The Entropoth is truly set in motion. The reaction is unstoppable now.'

The Stardust was indeed still swirling in the top globe and trickling down too to form a black powder in the bottom.

'But what of your sacrifice?' cried Ogog scornfully across the square.

Before Sultan could answer Silas saw two figures running into the square. The boys both had swords in their hands as they darted this way and that among the Grasht. It was Farjay and Kerbogah.

'Well, done, Kerbogah,' cried Silas, as they reached him.

Kerbogah was looking across the Sundial, though, in horror at Ashtar, dressed in black and gold.

'Mardak,' whispered Silas. 'Mardak is Ashtar. We have all been deceived. And I fear the Dunetraders won't be enough to save us. The Grasht are too strong. Too many.'

As the friends watched the fight they realized that the Grasht were indeed too strong for the Dunetraders, for they fought without any fear at all. Kerbogah suddenly unslung the pipes at his back and lifted them to his lips. He began to blow. At first nothing happened. Again only a windy, reedy noise came out.

Perhaps it was Kerbogah's anger that helped him, but suddenly they heard a strange music surrouding them.

Almost instantly, Silas and Ramset and Rarza saw a sight that amazed them as much as the Grasht. From one corner of the square came a rearing figure, hooves stamping, her magic bow in her hands.

'Chiral,' cried Kerbogah delightedly.

The Demigod looked magnificent in the smoky sunlight. One after the other her Arrows of Desire were drawn from her quiver and loosed from her bow, and one after the other the Grasht fell before the Centaur. The Demigod reared up and struck some down with her hooves, then galloped towards the children.

'Chiral, you came!' cried Kerbogah, as she reached them. 'You were still in the city.'

'I swore I would repay you, child,' said the Centaur. 'Gods do not break their promises. I was waiting for your call. In the Street of Straw Workers.'

Rarza noticed that the beautiful creature's back was covered in bits of hay.

'Now Chiron is dead,' cried the Centaur angrily, pulling out another arrow, 'I care not for my own life.'

'No, Chiral,' said Kerbogah, handing her the pipes. 'Chiron is not dead. Ogog told us. He was only wounded – that is all.'

Faster than ever before her arrows flew from her golden bow and now Chiral was not just aiming at the Grasht but at the Barbalissaries on the top of the walls. Suddenly one struck Sergeant Akadeem right in the heart and with a terrible cry he fell. Another took Mekmam in the throat.

Sultan Ash was looking in astonishment at what was happening as he stood beyond the Sundial, for the sight of a Demigod had surprised even him. But he had been calculating too and suddenly he pointed.

'There.'

They all looked up and a hiss of horror and amazement

spread through the square. Across the face of the sun itself, across the eye of Zorastar, a shadow was beginning to move.

'An eclipse!' cried Sultan. 'Calculated centuries ago. Now!'

Suddenly Sultan himself ran towards the Entropoth and snatching up Mazgol from its base, he set himself below the statue of the Pazgog. For a moment he looked down at Tapputi and then up at Zorastar.

'Mazgol shall help you,' he cried, 'help you Alchemize day into night.'

Sultan raised the Black Turnstone towards the darkening sun and began.

'By all the powers of the Lower Kingdom, hear my prayers. By the forces of darkness and by the Chi of Mazgol the Mighty.'

Mazgol began to glow again, as it had done on the Entropoth. But now, rather than falling inwards, the darkness seemed to seep out of it, spreading across Barbal like a fog, to add to the terrible eclipse. The dark mist rose in the square and it was as though an ancient night was falling over the Sacred City. The Grasht, wailing and moaning as they beheld Chiral, seemed to gain strength again from the darkness and many Dunetraders fell before them.

'Aspis,' cried Sultan Ash, 'come to my aid. Demons and Sandspirits, rise from the ground to do my bidding.'

As the friends looked on they gasped in horror. From the ground where the children had come, from the shafts where the Eternal Flames had once burnt by trickery, shapes were rising with the darkness. The Barbalonians began to scream as those swirling forms came swooping towards them and whirled among the fighting Grasht and the Dunetraders.

'The true Army of the Underworld,' cried Sultan triumphantly.

The spirits were attacking the Dunetraders and as they fell

on them many of the desert traders seemed to lose their reason, swirling round in a terrified fury.

'Their Chi Shields,' cried Ramset. 'They're attacking the Dunetraders' Chi Shields.'

The friends were back to back, for some of the spirits had begun to swoop towards them too. But Chiral began stamping in the dust.

'Our spirits,' cried the Demigod, 'we must protect our spirits. Quickly. Form a circle.'

Silas looked back at her.

'Yes,' cried Kerbogah. 'That's what the Wordmaster said, Silas.'

'And the Chi Dance,' said Ramset.

The friends drew tightly together and suddenly Chiral was galloping round them, making a circle in the dust with the end of her bow. Ogog and Kerbogah and Farjay, Silas and Rarza, stood side by side next to Ramset and in front of them was the beautiful Centaur.

'How many of us are there?' cried Chiral.

'Seven,' answered Silas, making the calculation.

'Magnificent!' cried the Centaur.

Yet the magic circle did not quite work, for though a few spirits were held back, others were still swooping amongst them.

'Hurry,' cried the Demigod. 'We need talismans too. The Sign of Four. Mark them in the dust, inside the circle, to protect us. North, South, East and West.'

Ramset began to scratch those strange triangles in four places around the circle. Exactly as he closed the last triangle they all felt a strange sensation and suddenly the spirits were gone from around their heads. They could still see them beyond the circle, but as they swooped they seemed to glance off an invisible wall.

'It's magic,' said Ramset, 'a magical Chi Shield.'

They stood together looking out at the battle, protected by the signs for Fire, Earth, Air and Water. The Sacraments. But in the square the darkness was everywhere and the Dunetraders were being consumed by the spirits, or struck down by the Grasht.

'We must help them,' cried Kerbogah.

'The Lightbearer,' shouted Ramset. 'You must use the Lightbearer, Silas. The Light of the World.'

Silas thrust his hand into his smock and pulled out the Turnstone. Gol blazed with that brilliant light, which seemed to cut through the darkness like a knife. Again it burst like a star, pushing back the dark of Mazgol in an ever-expanding circle itself and suddenly the Dunetraders could see dimly once more, although in the skies the sun was extinguished completely. It was just an eerie black disc now. Among the demons Kerbogah suddenly caught sight of a figure, hacking and jabbing with his sword.

'Father,' he cried.

Karleg turned to look up and to his horror Kerbogah saw a Grasht strike at him. It knocked his sword from his hand but Khayarumi was beside him and the poet struck down the Grasht with a single blow. Karleg was still being assailed, though, not by a Grasht or a Barbalissary but one of the spirits. He saw it swoop like a giant bat. Karleg had nothing to defend himself with, but as he stood there and thought of his son Kalman, as he saw his comrades fall at his side, Karleg suddenly felt a fury bubbling up in his throat.

'No,' he cried. 'I am a Dunetrader.'

Something was forming in the depths of Karleg's very being.

'Aaaaaaaa-om.'

The sound shot out with such force the spirit was blown into shards of glittering dark light. The other Dunetraders had seen Karleg and now their voices rose too, fighting the spirits, not with words but pure sound. But as Karleg fought with his voice a real figure came running at him: Captain Zolos.

'No, Father!' cried Kerbogah, seeing him in the mêlée. Kerbogah jumped from the circle, and lifting his sword ran straight at Zolos. He felt such anger in him as he thought of dear Kalman it might have carried him there on wings. Just in time he reached his father and as Zolos lifted his scimitar, Kerbogah lunged. His sword went deep into the Captain Barbalissary's side.

'For my brother,' spat Kerbogah, 'and the children of Barbal.'

Sultan turned and his eyes were sparkling. There stood Silas Root holding up his Turnstone in the circle and, across the Sundial, Sultan Ash, holding up his beneath the solar eclipse, as Zolos sank to the ground.

'Come back, Kerbogah!' cried Silas. 'Quickly!'

Karleg had been caught up in the fighting again and Kerbogah dashed back to safety.

'You're a worthy opponent, Silas Root,' cried Sultan, smiling coldly. 'You and your allies. As I knew you would be. But even you have much to learn. Come, Aspis. Lord of the Lower Realm. The Uncrowned King of Night. Come forth and take your rightful place once more on earth.'

'He can't,' whispered Ogog as Gol glowed and burned in Silas's hand. 'He cannot summon him without the sacrifice.'

'But look!' cried Ramset.

The comrades shuddered as they realized that there were dead Dunetraders and Barbalissaries everywhere and that their blood had seeped across the square and turned the Sundial bright red. The sacrifice was already made.

'Rise, Aspis,' Sultan intoned. 'Come to my aid. I will give you dominion in the world of men. Your servants await too. I and the Pazgog.'

On its pillar the Pazgog, seeming to awaken from stone, moved its head slowly, though it had not been fully released by Mazgol or the eclipse.

'No,' said Silas desperately. 'I don't believe it. It isn't true.'

Rarza was pointing now. A huge shape was already rising from the pool in front of the Waterwheel, much larger than the Pazgog, or the spirits around the square, and as it did so the light of Gol began to dwindle again. The terrible being lifted like a column of sand in a desert storm, although it was not gold but black and it towered over Barbal City.

'Aspis,' cried Rarza, looking up in terror. 'The Destroyer has come.'

Ramset dropped to his knees in the circle and clutched the amulets at his throat.

'By the Seven Stars,' he exclaimed. 'He has unleashed Aspis. The Uncrowned King of Night.'

The shape of the God was a gigantic snake and as the Barbalonians left in the square began to scream and wail, even Sultan Ash looked horrified, for where at first they thought it had one head now they saw that it had seven.

The enormous seven-headed hydra rose higher above the city and then, flicking its ethereal black tongues, those heads began to strike left and right at the Dunetraders. The darkness had come again and now the light of Gol was contained in the circle alone, lighting up the seven friends as the terrible serpent struck. One after the other the Dunetraders felt its sting and as soon as they did so they fell to their knees, seized in agony, and their skin began to turn black.

'We're lost,' whispered Ramset.

'No,' said Silas in the ghastly light. 'We must use our minds, our reason. Think, Ramset.'

It was Chiral who acted next, though. She had dropped her bow and taken up the pipes from Kerbogah. They heard an ever stranger music surround them and suddenly Rarza pointed in astonishment. Aspis had stopped striking at her victims and instead was beginning to sway, rhythmically, back and forth above them.

'The snake, Kerbogah,' whispered Farjay. 'She's charming the snake.'

'But she can't hold it for long,' cried Sultan, laughing at them. 'She's only a Demigod, while Aspis is the Lord of the Underworld. The Destroyer.'

Sultan pointed at the Entropoth.

'Now,' he cried, 'show yourself at last. If you exist, that is. The Creator of All.'

As they watched from the circle and Chiral charmed the snake it seemed at though an image was trying to form in the Stardust storm in the top of the Entropoth. A face.

'At last!' cried Sultan. 'The Final Alchemical Proof. Then I will ask you how I may raise my bride once more.'

But no face really appeared in the makina.

'Show yourself, coward,' cried Sultan furiously, 'or have you abandoned mankind?'

Suddenly Rarza was trembling furiously and pointing again.

'Look, Silas.'

The child was looking not at the Entropoth but at the body that all the while had lain quite motionless in front of the hourglass. Tapputi had just moved her hand and suddenly she lifted under the gauzy bandages and sat upright.

'My Tapputi!' cried Sultan joyfully. 'You've come back to me! Then the power, the power of Resurrection lies in the shadows. Oh, my darling. You are more valuable than power or knowledge or God.'

Tapputi rose to her feet and the veil dropped from her. For a moment, as the friends looked, they all saw how lovely she was. But only for a moment. For as they looked they saw the tautness and the yellowness of her embalmed skin. Tapputi had not come back to life at all. Her spirit was gone, and like the Grasht she walked towards her lover with closed eyes and held out her waxy hands. The Barbalissaries surrounding Sultan began to back away in horror, and Sultan too, as he held up Mazgol, seemed filled with doubt.

'Tapputi. My beloved.'

Tapputi opened her mouth to speak, but no words came. Suddenly she opened her eyes. They were as black as fire charcoal. Tapputi had almost reached Sultan and she lunged at his neck and tried to kiss him.

'No!' cried Sultan in horror. 'No!'

He hurled Tapputi away from him into the dust at the base of the Entropoth.

'Cheated,' he cried bitterly. 'Are we not always cheated? We try to touch heaven and it vanishes. We try to love and it is taken from us. We try to live and all we are given is death.'

But something was happening in the circle. A spirit had breached it and gone swirling around their heads.

'Why?' whispered Silas.

'There,' said Kerbogah.

At the edge of the circle, to the East, they saw the chameleon. Seraph had jumped down from Sultan's shoulder and come scurrying towards the magic circle. Now the lizard's tail was flicking back and forth in the dust and it had almost expunged the talisman.

Suddenly there was a squeak. Relak had jumped from Kerbogah's robes. The mouse ran straight at the chameleon and bit it in the tail. The lizard looked startled and scuttled away. In an instant Ramset had made the mark again and the spirit vanished.

Sultan swirled round in his black robes and peered up at mighty Aspis, still being held by the Centaur's haunting melody. A strange look came into his eyes.

'Aspis,' he cried, 'Destroyer. Lord of the Underworld. Take your dominion once more over the world of men. Side by side we shall rule, you and I, careless of any Creator, and both shall have an eternal revenge.'

The word 'Revenge' itself seemed to rouse the snake and suddenly one of its heads broke free. It darted straight towards the circle and breaching the invisible shield, its fangs struck. There was a cry of agony and Ogog fell to the ground.

'No,' gasped Silas. 'The Lord Alchemist.'

As he crouched down, Ogog was reaching a blackening hand into his pocket. He pulled something out and held it to his trembling lips.

'The antidote,' whispered Silas, seeing the little bottle. 'Snake serum. He must take it.'

As they poured it into his lips and Ogog felt the serum coursing through his veins his skin lightened again. The Alchemist may have been saved, but Chiral was wheeling left and right as she wrestled with Aspis.

'We must do something,' cried Rarza. 'She cannot hold it much longer.'

'The book, Silas,' whispered Ogog faintly. 'The charm in the Book of Destinies.'

Silas swung round and saw the book lying in the dust near the Seat of the Alchemist.

'Rarza,' he cried. 'Take Gol.'

'No, Silas. Don't breach the circle again.'

But Silas thrust the Lightbearer into Rarza's hand and leapt from the magic circle too. The spirits were on him again and he felt as if he were losing himself in a labyrinth of shadows. But as he ran something strange came on him. Almost instinctively, Silas began to whirl around as he had seen Ramset do in the desert.

'The Chi Dance,' cried Ramset proudly. 'Silas is using the Chi Dance to fight the spirits.'

Silas had no weapons but he cut left and right with his hands and knocked the spectres aside. But as he reached the Entropoth his foot caught on something on the ground and he went flying. The screeching spirits swooped but when Silas lay there something else came to him.

'In us,' he whispered. 'They are only in us. That's what they believe in Heleras.'

Silas remembered something else too. The Alcemoth.

'No, you are not real,' he cried furiously. '*I swear to tell the truth, and to keep my mind pure and to abstain from any law . . .*'

The spirits glanced off him and Silas got up and dashed towards the golden chair. He snatched up the Book of Destinies and saw that Sultan's History had fallen in the dust. Aspis turned one of her heads with a terrible hissing, but before it could strike, Silas was with his friends once more. The darkness of Mazgol in the square had become so thick it was like a fog. Gol's power seemed to be fading and Aspis struck at the Dunetraders again and again. Tapputi had got up and was walking towards Sultan once more too.

'Keep her off me!' he wailed to the Barbalissaries.

Silas laid the Book of Destinies carefully on the ground in the centre of the circle and unclasped the buckle in the faint light of Gol. But as he opened it, Silas's heart sank immediately.

> *Burble, barble, bibble, babble,*
> *Words play games with lord and rabble.*
> *Stones and rivers, Gods and men,*
> *No Creation, but what then?*

'Oh, not more nonsense,' cried Silas angrily.

There were so many pages wrought with script that Silas knew he would never find the charm. Silas slammed the book shut. On the front he saw the Zodiac in shimmering golden lettering.

'The symbols!' cried Rarza. 'It's like the History, Silas. It needs a prayer. The breath of Inspiru. Inspiration.'

Silas placed a hand on the front of the book but as he tried to pray nothing came to him. Not one thing. After all that had happened Silas Root wasn't sure what he believed in any more.

'I can't . . .'

'Search inside yourself, Silas,' said Kerbogah, kneeling beside him. 'That's what the Yaharlars teach. Inward Looking.'

'And your feelings,' said Rarza, putting her hand on his shoulder. 'They're as important as your thoughts.'

Silas took a deep breath and suddenly a voice came to the Childar, a voice from deep within that contained both love and pain, and with that his heart offered up its own prayer. He was thinking of his father Timon and he realized how much his loss had hurt him.

'*My father*,' he whispered, '*who art in the heavens, blessed be your name.*'

The Zodiac glittered and the Book of Destinies fell open again. There it was.

A TIMELY CHARM
FOR SEALING THE UNDERWORLD
Anithisisor
Hermeticum in Diabolis
Et Barbalem Archaeologis
Alchemicum et transiat Interpretor

Silas stood up with the Book of Destinies and began to intone the strange words before him. As soon as he heard him, Sultan Ash wheeled round.

'No, Silas Root!' he cried furiously. 'Don't.'

'. . . *et transiat Interpretor.*'

Suddenly a stream of light shot out of Gol like Chiral launching her magic arrows. Not one ray of light but seven and they were not white, but red and purple, green and orange, and other colours too. There was a terrible hissing, for the rays had struck Aspis in her seven throats and as soon as the seven shafts hit, the snake's horrible heads were thrown backwards. The Destroyer's horrifying throats were shaking uncontrollably in the light and one by one the spectres around the square began to vanish. For a moment the beams hovered there and the square was filled with hope, for before them they saw that they had formed a great arch right over the square, a rainbow.

The Grasht too seemed to have lost all will and motion and suddenly the Dunetraders where cutting them down, while in the heavens above the sun was passing out of its eclipse.

'It's working,' cried Silas triumphantly.

'Hooray,' cried Rarza Stormheart, hugging Silas.

The seven colours were blending again and the light of Gol, white once more, was spreading, while the darkness of Mazgol was fading steadily. The light of Gol grew and pushed it back, turning it in on itself. It was as if a new dawn had come.

Farjay was literally hopping up and down with excitement and Ramset was giving thanks to Rahr on bended knees. But as the last of those terrible heads dissolved and the entire body of Aspis evaporated, the final head flicked forward for the last time and there was a piercing cry.

'Rarza,' gasped Silas. 'No.'

In her excitement Rarza had stepped outside the line of the circle and Aspis had caught the Childar before it

322

evaporated. Rarza dropped to the ground and her blood began to flow. Silas leapt to Rarza's aid and scooped her up in his arms.

'Silas,' gasped Rarza, 'I . . .'

'Rarza, sweet Rarza, I am sorry.'

'You have saved us, Silas,' whispered his friend faintly. Her lovely skin was already turning black with the poison and tears were streaming down Silas's cheeks. He knew how deeply he missed his father and how much he would miss Rarza too.

'Death,' he whispered. 'It's all around us. Always.'

'Oh, Silas, I see it.'

'No, Rarza,' cried Silas.

Silas swung round angrily and snatched the little bottle from Ogog. But as he held it to Rarza's lips and tipped it up, only a few drops of the Alchemical serum dripped out. For a moment her lips seemed to glow again, like crimson petals, but only for a moment.

'Empty,' cried Silas bitterly.

Rarza slumped in his arms and closed her eyes. She was gone.

Silas laid her pretty head gently on the ground and turned furiously to see Sultan watching him. The Dunetraders were rallying in the square and suddenly one of them gave a cry and rushed from their ranks towards Sultan. Karleg seized hold of Sultan and held his dagger to his throat. None of the Barbalissaries wanted to aid him now.

'You!' cried Karleg as he looked into Ashtar's clever face.

Sultan Ash just smiled back defiantly.

'So we meet in another storm, my friend.'

'Traitor,' spat Karleg angrily. 'But at least the storm has passed.'

The battle had turned and the light of Mazgol had dwindled to nothing in Sultan Ash's hand. As Karleg held him, he slipped the Turnstone into the folds of his apron. As he did so Gol seemed to fade too and once more Barbal was lit by the Sun God Zorastar alone.

Around them the battle was over, and Dunetraders were streaming into Barbal. Most of the Barbalissaries had thrown down their weapons and Barbalonians ringed the square, whispering and pointing in astonishment. But all Silas could do was stare down hopelessly at Rarza. Silas got up slowly and wheeled round on the Lesson Master.

'You murdered the Wordmasters,' he cried, 'and now you've murdered Rarza.'

Something strange came into Sultan's eyes as Karleg held him, almost a sadness. He was looking not at Rarza but at Tapputi, who lay quite motionless in the dust again.

'It comes for us all in the end, Silas,' he whispered. 'It will come for both of us one sun, unless we find the secret. The true secret you have stopped me finding this day. The Alchemy of the Soul. The Balm of Eternal Life.'

Yet around them they heard the most wonderful sound. It thrilled through their bodies. There, above Rarza Stormheart, knelt the Centaur on her folded front legs, her tail waving behind her. Chiral was holding up Chiron's pipes and as the Demigod's beautiful lips played on them a different music surrounded them. It was so lovely that it seemed to heal the air itself. Chiral was holding Rarza's hand too and her clear blue eyes were looking deep inside her.

'Her Chi is weak but alive, Silas,' whispered the Centaur, 'and there is just time. But there is another ingredient, Silas Root. Apart from Chiron's healing music. The greatest serum of all and the most powerful Alchemy. Love.'

Silas blushed.

'Take your friend's hand, Silas Root.'

Again the music came, as ancient as the Dunetraders' voices, as Silas knelt and took Rarza's hand. In that moment he felt his heart might burst. His own hand was hot and it was as if he could feel a Chi flowing down his arm, into the girl. Suddenly Rarza twitched and opened her eyes. Her skin was losing its terrible hue, just as Ogog's had done.

'What's happened to me?' Rarza whispered faintly, as if stepping from a dream. 'I've been in such a strange place. There was a dark red river and I was being rowed in a golden . . .'

'It's all right,' said the Centaur gently, 'you're with friends now.'

'Rarza,' cried Silas delightedly. 'You're alive, Rarza.'

They helped Rarza to her feet and now the leaders of the Dunetraders were gathering around the Entropoth and the Seat of the Alchemist. But suddenly, there was a great *crack*.

As they all looked up at the temple, towering over the square, they gasped. The Ziggurat, the ancient temple of the Alchemists, weakened by the Dunetraders' voices, had broken. A giant fissure had run through the middle of the Ziggurat, literally splitting the Halls of the Rising and Sinking Suns in two.

'The ancient curse,' came a groan from a Barbalonian. 'When the wheel stops the temple shall be rent in twain. It is the prophecy.'

'The prophecy,' whispered Kerbogah next to Silas. 'It is fulfilled.'

'And you have freed us all, Silas,' whispered Rarza, taking his hand again.

'But we've failed in our mission,' said Silas quietly, 'to heal the Great Schism.'

'Fool,' hissed a voice. Sultan Ash's voice.

They turned coldly to confront the Lesson Master.

'How could you ever heal it, Silas Root? The great battle between the Rising and Sinking Sun? Between East and West? Between thought and feeling, mind and spirit? Not even the Hooded Master will ever do that, for man's nature will always be split in two.'

Sultan was still straining against Karleg's grip, but the Dunetrader held him fast.

'And now,' said Sultan, smiling and looking up at the temple, 'the word is made flesh.'

'But at least sacred Barbal is free,' said Silas proudly, 'and Ogog shall be restored as the Lord Alchemist.'

Ogog nodded gratefully.

'We have freed the children too. Now you are the prisoner.'

'Yes, Silas,' said Sultan Ash calmly, 'but so are you. For we are all prisoners. Spirits imprisoned within these feeble bodies. And what will you do? You think you can go back now into Ederyl and forget all you have seen?'

Silas had a hankering to go home. To see his mother Alara again, and to lay flowers at the foot of that memorial in Ederyl. And yet something else was working in the Childar. A deep longing. To travel on. To cross the Depthless Sea and journey into the land of Khem. To see Heleras and Jesladom and Moorcaria with his own eyes.

'Why did you do it?' whispered Silas in confusion. 'Why did you steal us away from lovely Ederyl?'

'Lovely Ederyl?' said Sultan scornfully. 'You yourself were banished and have you learnt nothing on your journey? You talk of Ederyl as if it was a story that would go on forever. But didn't you learn what Evolution proves? Grow up, Silas Root.'

Silas was shaking angrily.

'Such wonders we could have beheld together, Silas,' said the Lesson Master almost sadly. 'But you and Barbal were not ready. Not ready for my vision. Not ready for my Entropoth.'

Silas looked questioningly at the strange hourglass.

'The Stardust,' he whispered. 'When it falls to the bottom it turns black. What is it?'

Sultan's eyes sparkled.

'Dark Matter,' he growled in reply. 'In Pengalis they believe it makes up most of the universe.'

'The Entropoth,' said Kerbogah suddenly. 'It's destroying the power of the Songtrails. We must smash it.'

Karleg and Imlay, Farjay and Khayarumi were all nodding. Again Silas felt that strange reluctance, but as he looked at the Grasht and the dead Dunetraders all around the square, he nodded too.

'Yes.'

'You can't, Silas,' cried Sultan immediately. 'It's impossible. The glass was blown with . . .'

Silas rounded on Sultan again. He looked hard at that hooked nose and that flaring golden hair. At those clever eyes.

'The Book of Destinies,' Silas whispered angrily. 'You said it yourself, sir. It teaches us that *nothing* is impossible.'

'Why don't you listen to your studies, Silas?' said Sultan Ash, and now he sounded just like the Lesson Master again. '*No sense is nonsense.* Of course some things are impossible. Reason tells us that, and logic. What we know now, like the Mappa Mysticum, such things may contain understanding of great value, but they also contain errors and mistakes. It is distinguishing the two that counts in life. Only that brings discernment.'

Silas was silent.

'There are laws, Silas Root. Scientific laws that even you cannot break. What is impossible is impossible.'

But suddenly Chiral reared furiously on her hooves.

'My brother,' she cried bitterly. 'He was worth more than this . . . this thing.'

They jumped back as the Centaur brought her hooves crashing down against the bottom globe of the Entropoth.

As she struck the beautiful object, it made a shattering sound and glass and Dark Matter went flying everywhere.

327

Kerbogah blinked, for a little speck had gone flecking into his eye. But suddenly the air was filled with the most extraordinary sound, like a great sighing.

The Stardust was trickling out and vanishing in the air and for a moment Silas fancied he saw shapes like Sandspirits, but then they were gone too, dissolved by the sunlight. Yet something in the mood of Barbal had changed and as they looked around at the Grasht and the dead Dunetraders, lying on the ground, they realized that their faces were changing. A calm and a peace had come upon them all. Tapputi too looked lovely as she lay there.

'Souls,' murmured Ramset. 'Their souls were being trapped inside the glass. But they are free.'

'What have you done?' asked Sultan in a furious whisper. 'I thought you wanted to be an Alchemist, Silas Root.'

Karleg pulled back Sultan's head and pressed the knife closer.

'Silence.'

'What shall we do with him?' said old Imlay.

'Sacrifice him,' said Farjay, 'to the Sun God.'

'The Dunetraders will demand blood vengeance for all that has happened,' said Imlay in agreement.

The friends were looking round nervously.

'No,' said Silas. 'There has been enough sacrifice. Hold him in the cage and we'll decide his fate later. In the meantime we must attend to the dead and the wounded.'

Sultan was placed in the wooden cage as the Dunetraders gathered their dead and took them beyond the City to be laid with honour on the Towers of Silence. Silas and Rarza and the others went about the square helping the sick and wounded and all around some of the Barbalonians had begun to pick up the overturned bowls and replace them on the twenty-four plinths. They were lighting the Eternal Flames themselves.

For hours they worked, so many had fallen, but as they worked four characters came creeping down the Street of Fables.

'Phew,' whispered Mandrax, 'I'm glad we didn't get caught up in that. Special Ops wasn't needed after all. Now Nimrod has gone and the week is up, our mission is over too.'

'And what a week,' said Tellor. 'I wouldn't have missed it for the world.'

'I know this is Barbal,' said Habulan. 'But you said we are in a place that no one has ever been before.'

'That's right,' grunted Mandrax.

'Tell us where then, for Jeslas' sake. We've come back to the past, haven't we? So now we know that time travel is real.'

'The past,' said Mandrax, and he smiled. 'Yes, Habulan. But it's even more remarkable than that.'

'Then *where* are we?' they all cried at once.

'Where?' said the Pengalisian. 'We are inside a book of course. A very ancient book.'

'A book?'

'Yes, the transfer has translated us inside a book, even as it was being written. One of the first of the Incunabula.'

'Not the Bible,' said Tellor wearily.

'Of course not,' said Mandrax. 'Far, far older than that, Tellor, although it has certain influences, and probably even more mistakes. We are inside the most ancient of Barbalonian texts. The Book of Destinies.'

With that, as suddenly as they had first appeared in the desert, the strange Pengalisians all vanished. None of the busy Barbalonians noticed them or anything but their own labours, except a boy, one of the lads who had been freed from the treadmill. The same boy who had held Gol.

He had been looking down the street and, turning away, then back again, had been surprised to see that the men he thought were there had disappeared and in the air was the faintest shimmer of glittering gold.

In Barbal Square the sun was beginning to fall as Silas and the others approached the wooden cage once more.

'Let him out,' said Ogog, who had been giving orders again right around the city. 'We shall take him inside the Ziggurat.'

'Let him rot forever in his own dungeons,' agreed Karleg.

'Have you forgotten what I did for you, Karleg?' said Sultan, as two Barbalissaries hauled him out. 'I saved your life in that storm. And Silas, would you have seen any of this without me? Not to mention all I have taught you. I gave you the very tools with which to fight me too. Is this how you reward me?'

'Reward you?' said Rarza in amazement. 'You betrayed us.'

'Betrayal,' snorted Sultan. 'Then have I not taught you another valuable lesson about life? That everything has its opposite. May I not be one too? A true anti-hero?'

'Stop it,' said Silas, covering his ears with his hands.

'Take him,' said Ogog suddenly.

Sultan's eyes twinkled, though. In the cage he had been calculating again, and now in the heavens he saw Zorastar blaze for a final time and at last its light was extinguished in the West. Even as it faded, Sultan tore himself from Karleg's grip and as he ran, the Pazgog on the plinth flapped its great stone wings. The night had released it.

'Look out!' cried Chiral.

The Pazgog rose and came sailing straight towards Sultan Ash. They all felt the grip of despair around them and, seizing Sultan by the shoulders with its talons, the Winged Servant lifted him up with a triumphant screech. Karleg struck out with his sword and Chiral reached for an arrow, only to find that her quiver was empty. High into the air the

Lesson Master sailed, in the clutches of the Servant, and his black robes flapped behind him like a great kite.

'Look for me in Khem, Silas Root,' cried Sultan Ash, as he rose higher and higher into the skies holding up Mazgol, 'My star is rising.'

Silas and his friends stood looking up at the skies in disbelief.

'But thank me, Silas. For I have been giving you something else too,' cried the Lesson Master faintly, 'that may help you to face life's iron reality. Words. Use them well.'

The Lesson Master looked down from on high.

'I tell you this, Silas Root. You will either change the world or be changed by it.'

With that Mardak the Dark and the Pazgog sailed off towards the glistening moon. The friends stood there helplessly, blinking in astonishment.

'Silas,' said Rarza, still unsteady on her legs. 'What are we going to do?'

'I don't know,' answered Silas, and he reached inside his robe and took Gol from his smock pocket.

'The Barbalonians,' whispered Karleg. 'They won't like it now the wheel has stopped. How will they get water into their homes?'

'Perhaps they themselves will turn to children,' said Kerbogah, thinking of his brother sadly, 'to do their dirty work for them.'

'Perhaps,' said Karleg, 'but perhaps this will change the way they see the world, as that man said in the Street of Soothsayers. Perhaps they will not rely on their priests so much and look to reason to help them.'

'Look, Silas.'

It was Kerbogah who was pointing at the Turnstone which had begun to glow again. As Silas held it up in his palm they heard a great creaking, and to their amazement the wheel began to turn once more, all on its own. The water was bubbling along the channels around Barbal. Then, from beyond those tumbled city walls, in the darkness they began to hear another sound too, a little like Chiral's pipes. They turned and saw that the Dunetrader caravans were already beginning to wind off again into the desert, in every direction, away from the Sacred City. Their camels tilted like little boats on the sand, among their Songtrails.

'At least the Dunetraders know now that the tribute of Stardust shall not continue,' whispered Karleg, 'and that the voice of ancient song is safe in the world. Thanks to you all. They may return to their own trade routes, as they have done since time began, and sing their way through the sands in peace.'

The Childars were grinning and suddenly Karleg saw Selera walking towards them.

'We failed in our mission to heal the Schism though,' said Silas. 'Look at the temple.'

But there came another voice behind Silas.

'The temple is all around us, child,' it whispered smilingly. 'Always. You only have to see it.'

It was the Yaharlar who had spoken to Kerbogah in the desert, and he was holding up his hands to his forehead. His companions did the same and they bowed low to Silas and Rarza, Kerbogah and Farjay. With that the Yaharlars turned and began to walk towards the Great Gate.

'Aaaaaaaaa-om.'

Old Imlay was standing next to Khayarumi the poet, looking down at the shattered Entropoth in the dust.

'So, Khayarumi,' he whispered. 'Do you believe in the power of the Alchemist's magic now?'

The poet paused and looked at him slyly.

'Magic? I don't know, old man,' he answered. 'But I never realized I was such a dab hand with a sword.'

Imlay grunted but he smiled.

'And I know this,' said Khayarumi. 'Art is a poet's only true master and all real art comes straight from heaven, like a shooting star. Inspiration, that's what counts. But I believe something else too,' added the poet.

'What now, Khayarumi?'

'I believe I need a drink, Imlay,' he said, slapping the old man on the back. 'Let's try Bolor's place.'

Night was deepening as the friends, led by the trotting Centaur, set off for Bolor's place too. The Barbalonians had returned to their homes, but as they slammed their doors, most of them were wiping away those strange symbols.

'Ogog,' said Silas as they went, 'you are the Lord Alchemist once more.'

'And one who shall try to use wisdom to rule,' said Ogog softly, 'one who shall restore Sandwork and reason. But one too who shall always leave a space for magic.'

'But now Sultan . . . now Mardak is gone. You have no High Priest in the temple.'

'But I have one in mind,' said Ogog and he bent down. When he stood up again Seraph was sitting on his palm, his eyes swivelling about.

'Who?'

'His name is Al-Jibara.'

Silas and Kerbogah smiled under the glistening moon of Barbal Square.

EPILOGUE

Bolor's place was packed to the rafters. They had all sat down to eat at the table with the candlestick on it, and Chiral was making quite an impression. Khayarumi ordered them all the Special, which they were tucking into delightedly. There was much singing and drinking, whirling and dancing.

But as Silas sat next to Rarza he noticed that she was holding something. A book.

'The History,' whispered Silas, 'Sultan's History.'

'I picked it up in the square,' said Rarza.

Silas was looking once again at the spine.

'Rarza,' he said. 'It says it contains a new and unofficial version of the Alcemoth.'

'I know,' said Rarza. She was already placing her hand on the symbols and mumbling to herself. Rarza put it on the table. It fell open at the Alcemoth and as Silas read it his eyes widened.

'The last part,' he said. 'The last part is different.'

This is what the Alcemoth now said:

Through magic, study and invention I shall
pass these secrets on to the people, for all
the people are changing too and so are
Alchemists themselves, and I shall never
knowingly do any wrong or harm. In the
name of Lol and Enlis and the greatest
laws. Change: change and love.

'Love,' said Silas. 'Change and love.'

Rarza blushed but Silas grinned hugely.

'One thing we never found out though, Rarza.'

'What's that?'

'The solution to one last riddle. We never found out who
was stealing the sacred peacocks.'

Khayarumi had heard them

'Oh didn't we?' cried the poet, sitting up. 'I'm not sure
old Bolor would agree with you there. Or his cook Mishtar.'

Bolor was passing the table and he suddenly stopped dead.

'What are you talking about?'

'I'm talking about your secret,' said Khayarumi.

'Secret?' scowled Bolor. 'What secret? I don't 'ave any . . .'

Khayarumi rose impressively.

'The secret of such a roaring trade in your little tavern, of
course, Bolor. The secret of vanishings in the Great Square
too. The secret of the Special. Bellberry sauce, if my senses
don't lie, over a pan-fried bed of sacred peacock.'

Imlay almost choked on his food and the little tavern
keeper blanched, so deep with cold fear he looked like one of
the collywobble flowers in the market. In the kitchen the
hunchback Mishtar had just drawn a long carving knife.

'It's not my fault,' stammered Bolor, and great beads of
sweat came rolling down his face, which he wiped away with

his filthy apron. 'With wars in the desert and all that chaos, the trade routes were disrupted something terrible. Prices in Barbal went through the roof. Enough to bankrupt any honest man. I couldn't work the margins, so my cook and I turned to stealing those stupid birds in our sacks. But how did you . . . ?'

'The taste,' answered Khayarumi. 'Not to mention the shape of these bones.'

'Please,' said Bolor, 'you mustn't tell them. You musn't . . .'

But Ogog had risen to his feet. The Lord Alchemist had overheard everything.

'It's all right, Bolor,' he whispered kindly. 'There's been enough judgement already. Serve us some more. It's quite delicious. But this time it's on the house. And no more bird-napping from now on.'

Bolor beamed and Mishtar put down the knife, while the whole party burst out laughing. They drank again, and toasted, and soon the place was filled with laughter and dancing and the party was spinning wildly about the room like Dancing Derwishers. Imlay's beard flashed like a white snake, but Karleg and Selera held each other close, for they were still mourning their son. Silas was tired, though, and he sat down again, his head in a total spin. He held Gol lightly in the palm of his hand.

'Well, Silas Root,' said a piping little voice suddenly. 'You've done well. In fact, you've done wonders.'

Silas swung round and the voice spoke a second time.

'Didn't I promise I would come again?'

Silas blinked. The voice had come from the middle of the table. There on the candlestick the metal lizard had just opened its eyes.

'Hermet,' gasped Silas.

'That's right, Silas,' said the lizard cheerfully. 'I was a pot last time. And now I'm a chameleon. Though not a real one. Well, Silas, how are you feeling?'

Silas leant closer as the revellers danced about him.

'I'm not sure. It's all been very strange.'

'Things changing shape, you mean?' said the lizard. 'Well, that's what the Alchemists are so keen on. You know in Pengalis they've even worked out how to change the elements themselves, and to make gold.'

'But. It's like . . . it's like some silly story.'

'Silly story,' said the chameleon, looking rather offended. 'Well, I wouldn't say that in front of the Tellweaver of Barbarag, if I was you. That Alchemist holds stories as more important than anything. Especially because the best ones seem to share a pattern.'

Silas remembered what Sultan had said near the Black Market.

'Are you really a God?' asked Silas suddenly.

The chameleon's eyes seemed to smile.

'Are *you*? I certainly come like the Gods, suddenly and without warning. But think of me as inspiration. One day you may ask yourself where that, like language itself, really comes from. But now I have a message for you.'

'A message?'

'Yes,' said the chameleon, 'from the Creator.'

'The Creator?' said Silas in astonishment. 'Then he does exist.'

'Of course he exists. Who do you think designed you? You even saw him in the Entropoth. He says you mustn't worry too much about Gods, or the one true God, or no God at all though. That Mardak's Alchemical Proof is already in your hands.'

'In my hands?' whispered Silas. 'How?'

'What is God?' asked the chameleon, 'and what is the spirit?'

Silas shook his head.

'*Of what we cannot speak, thereof should we remain silent,*' whispered the lizard strangely. 'But the Creator suggests that you look on God as the border between knowledge and belief. A border that is always shifting and changing in the Seven Lands, as what we intuit about the universe comes up against what we really know, or can speak of about the real world, with the language we have at the time.'

Silas's head was trobbing again.

'That's the truth,' said the lizard.

'The truth?' said Silas. 'What is truth?'

'Ah, jesting Silas,' said the lizard, 'truth is very simple. Truth is that which is not a lie.'

'Oh,' said Silas.

'But ask yourself this, Silas Root. Will it really be possible to know everything there is in the universe one day? And if you suspect not, think of God as what lies outside that and what we still believe to be possible and wonderful too. Then you might not be half so scared too, like everyone else.'

'Scared?' said Silas.

'Of what man calls death,' whispered the chameleon, 'and reality. If energy cannot be created or destroyed, then perhaps neither can the spirit.'

'Thank you,' whispered Silas.

'Not at all,' said the candlestick, 'it's been quite an adventure. And there are many, many more to come. Goodbye, Silas Root.'

The candlestick closed its eyes and Silas looked up to see Rarza Stormheart standing next to him.

'What's wrong, Silas?'

'Nothing, Rarza. Come on. Let's dance.'

ALCHEMY The common misunderstanding about Alchemy is that it was only concerned with the practice of trying to turn base matter into gold. In fact, proper Alchemy had a far wider remit. It was at once a pseudo-scientific and a spiritual practice, concerned with the transmutation of all things – which is rather difficult if you don't know what they are yet . . .

BABYLON This ancient city, lying between the Tigris and the Euphrates rivers on the Mesopotamian plain, was the centre of an ancient civilization where the wheel is said to have been invented, as well as the earliest forms of writing and calculation. The Babylonians calculated in units of 60. The city of Babylon is associated both with an ancient spirituality and also with great sin.

BARBAL From the Tower of Babel, the Biblical tower thrown down by God.

THE CADUCEUS The emblem of a staff twined about with snakes is associated with Aesculapius, the Greek god of healing, and modern medicine in the West still uses the Caduceus as its symbol. Homeopathy works on the principle that all things have their opposites.

CHI Element of Taoist philosophy, a kind of marvellous energy that moves through all things.

DICE It was Albert Einstein who devised the General Theory of Relativity, defined by the equation '$E = MC^2$'. He famously commented that 'God does not play games of dice'. Chaos Theory, Heisenberg's Uncertainty Principle, Dark Matter and String Theory are all concepts in modern Theoretical Physics.

ENTROPOTH From the modern word 'entropy'.

EVOLUTIA Though, of course, we associate Evolution with Charles Darwin, the idea of one thing emerging out of another is essential to the way we perceive the world, and is as old as time.

GILGAMAR The earliest known epic poem is called the Epic of Gilgamesh. It contains many things that are echoed in the Bible, including the Great Flood and the story Imlay tells about Gilgamar in Bolor's tavern.

KHEM A real name for Ancient Egypt, or the Land of the Black Soil, where the practice of Alchemy did indeed develop. The Two Kingdoms of Egypt were the Upper and Lower Nile.

LINEAR A One of the most famous forms of tablet inscription was in fact Linear B, discovered not in the Middle East, but on the Greek Island of Minos (modern-day Crete). After much scholarly effort, it was discovered to be a royal inventory of laundry.

MARDAK THE DARK 'Marduk' is the name of Babylon's God-Hero, an ambivalent character who shows both great wisdom and great foolishness as he tries to grow.

OF WHAT WE CANNOT SPEAK . . . The mathematician and philosopher Ludwig Wittgenstein said, 'Of what we cannot speak, thereof should we remain silent.' Much of his thought was concerned with theories of language and how language is not really a thing in itself (as you might imagine when you learn it) but a tool, like a spoon or a knife, with which we can see, understand and manipulate the world about us. He believed that if we cannot be as precise as a mathematician in our use of language, then we simply cannot talk about a thing – and therefore should not worry about it. Very few people seem to have taken his advice.

OUROBOROS The image of the snake, eating its own tail, is an ancient image of eternity, but also signifies the concept of nothing, or Zero. The snake, of course, is a powerful symbol across all cultures and faiths. In the Bible it is the serpent that tempts Adam and Eve in the Garden, and it is therefore associated with evil and the devil. In other cultures, however, it is also a symbol of great power and wisdom – especially in the form of the Dragon.

SANDWORK In India, mathematics was named 'sandwork' after the method Ashtar demonstrates in the Great Tent with the board and pebbles.

TAPPUTI The name of a real Egyptian perfume maker. Alchemy must have developed out of practices like perfume making, embalming, the manufacture of dyes and so on. And out of Alchemy came modern-day science. Isaac Newton, who discovered gravity, himself practised as an Alchemist.

DAVID CLEMENT-DAVIES

THE
SIGHT

It is an icy night in the country that long ago was known as Transylvania. The wintry ground crackles as a hunter's paw breaks the hard earth. The wolf pauses, her breath like smoke in the cold air, then a howl pierces the night. But it is her eyes, not her howl, that speak of danger.

Beware of the Sight.

In the shadow of the Carpathian Mountains, a pack of wolves seeks shelter from the vicious winter. A legend clings to them – a story of man and wolf, of power and death. The Sight has come into their world. They will never be the same again . . .

DAVID CLEMENT-DAVIES

FIRE
BRINGER

There is a prophecy among the deer. One day, a fawn will be born with the mark of an oak leaf upon his forehead. His courage will lead the deer to freedom; his strength will defeat their greatest enemy.

Rannoch was born on the night his father was murdered. In a herd where hunger for power has destroyed all that is good, he must escape to survive. Hunted by stags with antlers sharpened for the kill, Rannoch begins his treacherous journey. But he will return – to face the destiny that he was born for; to conquer the force that drove him away . . .

In a dark, troubled time, the prophecy is about to come true.

A selected list of titles available from Macmillan Children's Books

The prices shown below are correct at the time of going to press.
However, Macmillan Publishers reserves the right to show new retail
prices on covers which may differ from those previously advertised.

David Clement-Davies

Fire Bringer	0 330 39010 4	£6.99
The Sight	0 330 48385 4	£6.99

Julie Bertagna

Exodus	0 330 39908 X	£5.99

Peter Dickinson

Blue Hawk	0 330 41546 8	£4.99
Eva	0 330 48384 6	£5.99
The Ropemaker	0 330 39713 3	£6.99
The Tears of the Salamander	0 330 41540 9	£5.99

All Pan Macmillan titles can be ordered from our website,
www.panmacmillan.com, or from your local bookshop
and are also available by post from:

Bookpost, PO Box 29, Douglas, Isle of Man IM99 1BQ
Credit cards accepted. For details:
Telephone: 01624 677237
Fax: 01624 670923
Email: bookshop@enterprise.net
www.bookpost.co.uk

Free postage and packing in the United Kingdom